'I don't think I have ever read a book more appropriate to its title than this. It is indeed a hopelessly romantic tale with ... g.co.uk

'A delicious romcom.' *Marie Claire*

'An endearing tale of broken and rescued hearts.' *In Style*

'Indulge in the escapist world of *A Hopeless Romantic* . . . candyfloss that's hard to resist.' *Elle*

'A superior romcom with heart and soul.' *Bella*

Praise for *Going Home*:

'Where's all the passion, romance and comedy we love gone? Enter Harriet Evans and not before time.' *Heat*

'Few debut novels are set to make such an impact as this.' *Daily Mirror*

'Harriet Evans' debut novel is a great romcom, packed with intrigue and suspense.' *New Woman*

'A lovely, funny heartwarmer . . . Evans' comic style and loveable characters make it effortlessly readable.' *Marie Claire*

'A joy from start to finish – sharp, funny and modern as well as warm, cosy and nostalgic.' Fiona Walker

'Fabulous . . . I loved it' Sophie Kinsella

By the same author

Going Home

HARRIET EVANS

A Hopeless Romantic

HARPER

This novel is entirely a work of fiction.
The names, characters and incidents portrayed in it are
the work of the author's imagination. Any resemblance to
actual persons, living or dead, events or localities is
entirely coincidental.

Harper
An imprint of HarperCollins*Publishers*
77–85 Fulham Palace Road,
Hammersmith, London W6 8JB

www.harpercollins.co.uk

This paperback edition 2007
1

First published in Great Britain by
HarperCollins*Publishers* 2006

A catalogue record for this book is
available from the British Library

ISBN-13: 978-0-00-719846-7
ISBN-10: 0-00-719846-9

Set in Sabon by Palimpsest Book Production Limited,
Grangemouth, Stirlingshire

Printed and bound in Great Britain by
Clays Ltd, St Ives plc

For the magnificent specimen, my mother Linda.
With all my love.

How to understand it all! How to understand the deceptions she had been thus practising on herself, and living under! – The blunders, the blindness of her own head and heart! – she sat still, she walked about, she tried her own room, she tried the shrubbery – in every place, every posture, she perceived that she had acted most weakly.

Jane Austen, *Emma*

Maria: I don't remember any more.
Brigitta: Your face is all red.
Maria: Is it? I don't suppose I'm used to dancing.

The Sound of Music, screenplay by Ernest Lehman

PART ONE

CHAPTER ONE

Laura Foster was a hopeless romantic. Her best friend Jo said it was her greatest flaw, and at the same time her most endearing trait, because it was the thing that most frequently got her into trouble, and yet falling in love was like a drug to her. Having a crush, daydreaming about someone, feeling her heart race faster when she saw a certain man walk towards her – she thrived on all of it, and was disastrously, helplessly, hopelessly incapable of seeing when it was wrong. Everyone has a blind spot. With Laura, it was as if she had a blind heart.

Anyone with a less romantic upbringing would be hard to find. She wasn't a runaway nun, or the daughter of an Italian count, or a mysterious orphan. She was the daughter of George and Angela Foster, of Harrow, in the suburbs of London. She had one younger brother, Simon, who was perfectly normal, not a secret duke, nor a spy, nor a soldier. George was a computer engineer, and Angela was a part-time translator. As Jo once said to her, about a year after they met at university, 'Laura, why do you go around pretending to be Julie Andrews, when you're actually Hyacinth Bucket?'

But Laura never stopped reality getting in the way of fantasy. By the time she was eighteen she had fallen for: a runny-nosed, milk-bottle-glasses-wearing primary-school outcast called Kevin

3

(in her mind Indiana Jones, with specs); her oboe teacher Mr Wallace, a thin, spotty youth, over whom she developed a raging obsession and calluses on her oboe-playing fingers, so ferociously did she practise (she would stand outside his flat in Camden in the hope she might see him; she wore a locket which contained a bus ticket he'd dropped around her neck); and about fifteen different boys at the boys' school around the corner from hers in Harrow.

When she went to university, the scope was even greater, the potential for romance limitless. She wasn't interested in a random pull at a club. No, Laura wanted someone to stand underneath her window and recite poetry to her. She was almost always disappointed. There was Gideon, the budding theatre director who hadn't quite come out of the closet. Juan, the Colombian student who spoke no English. Or the rowing captain who was much more obsessed with the tracking machine at the gym than her. Her dentist, who charged her far too much and then made her pay for dinner. And the lecturer in her humanities seminar who she never spoke to, and who didn't know her name, who she wasted two terms staring at in a heartfelt manner.

For all of these Laura followed the same pattern. She went off her food; she mooned around; she was acutely conscious of where they were in any room, thought she saw them around every corner – was that the back of his curly head going into the newsagent's? She became a big, dumb idiot whenever any of them spoke to her, so fairly often they walked away, bemused that this nice girl with dark blonde hair, a sweet smile and a dirty laugh who seemed to like them was suddenly behaving like a nun in a shopping centre, eyes downcast, mute. Or they'd ask her out – and then Laura, for her part, usually came tumbling down to earth with a bang when she realised they weren't perfect, weren't this demigod she'd turned them into in her mind. It wasn't that she was particularly picky – she was just a really *bad* picker.

She believed in The One. And every man she met, for the

first five minutes, two weeks, four months, had the potential in her eyes to be The One – until she reluctantly realised they were gay (Gideon from the Drama Society), psychopathic (Adam, her boyfriend for several months, who eventually jacked in his MA on the Romantic Poets and joined the SAS to become a killing machine), against the law (Juan, the illegal immigrant from Colombia), or Josh (her most recent boyfriend, whom she'd met at a volunteer reading programme seminar at work, decided was The One after five minutes, dated for over a year, before realising, really, all they had in common was a love of local council literacy initiatives).

It's fine for girls to grow up believing in something like The One, but the generally received wisdom by the time Laura was out of university, as she moved into her mid-twenties, as her friends started to settle down, was that he didn't really exist – well, he did, but with variations. Not for Laura. She was going to wait till she found him. To her other best friend Paddy's complaints that he was sick of sharing their flat with a lovesick teenager all the time, as well as a succession of totally disparate, odd men, Laura said firmly that he was being mean and judgemental. James Patrick – Paddy to his friends – was a dating disaster, what would he know? To Jo's pragmatic suggestions that she should join a dating agency, or simply ask out that bloke over there, Laura said no. It would happen the way she wanted it to happen, she would say. You couldn't force it. And that would be it, until five minutes later when a waiter in a restaurant would smile at her, and Laura would gaze happily up at him, imagining herself and him moving back to Italy, opening a small café in a market square, having lots of beautiful babies called Francesca and Giacomo. Jo could only shake her head at this, as Laura laughed with her, aware of how hopeless she was compared to her level-headed, realistic best friend.

Until one evening, about eighteen months ago, Jo came round to supper at Paddy and Laura's flat. She was very quiet; Laura often worried Jo worked too hard. As Laura was attempting

5

to digest a mouthful of chickpeas that Paddy had marvellously undercooked, and as she was trying not to choke on them, Jo wiped her mouth with a piece of paper towel and looked up.

'Um . . . Hey.'

Laura looked at her suspiciously. Jo's eyes were sparkling, her heart-shaped little face was flushed, and she leant across the table and said,

'I've met someone.'

'Where?' Paddy had asked stupidly. But Laura understood what that statement meant, of course she did, and she said,

'Who is he?'

'He's called Chris,' Jo replied, and she smiled, rather girlishly, which was even more unusual for her. 'I met him at work.' Jo was a conveyancing solicitor. 'He was buying a house. He yelled at me.'

And then – and this was when Laura realised it was serious – Jo twisted a tendril of her hair and put it in her mouth. Since this was a breach of social behaviour in Jo's eyes tantamount to not sending a thank-you card after a dinner party, Laura put her hand out across the table and said,

'Wow! How exciting.'

'I know,' said Jo, unable to stop herself smiling. 'I know!'

Laura knew, as she looked at Jo, she just knew, she didn't know why. Here was someone in love, who had found The One, and that was all there was to it.

Chris and Jo moved into the house she'd helped him buy after six months; four months after that, he proposed. They started planning a December wedding, a couple of weeks before Christmas, in a London hotel. Jo eschewed grown-up bridesmaids, saying they were deeply, humiliatingly naff, much to Laura's disappointment – she was rather looking forward to donning a nice dress and sharing with her best friend on this, the happiest day of her life. Instead, she was going to be best woman, and Paddy was an usher.

6

It seemed as if Jo and Chris had been together forever, and Laura could barely remember when he hadn't been on the scene. He slotted right in, with his North London pub ways, his personality so laidback and friendly, compared to Jo's sometimes controlled outlook on life. He had friends who lived nearby – some lovely friends. They were all a gang now, him and Jo, his friends, Paddy and Laura, sometimes Laura's brother Simon, when he wasn't off somewhere being worthy and making girls swoon (where Laura was always falling in love, Simon was usually falling into bed with a complete stranger, usually by dint of lulling them into a false sense of security by telling them he worked for a charity). And there was Hilary too, also from university and christened Scary Hilary – because she was – and her brother Hamish, their other friends from work or university, and so on. And so Laura's easy, uncomplicated life went on its way. She had a brief, intense affair with a playwright she thought was very possibly the new John Osborne, until Paddy pointed out he was, in fact, just a prat who liked shouting a lot. Paddy grew a moustache for the autumn. Laura got a pay rise at work. They bought a Playstation to celebrate – games for him, karaoke for her. Yes, everything was well within its usual frame, except Laura began to feel, more and more, as she looked at Jo and Chris so in love, and as she looked at the landscape of her own dull life, that she was taking the path of least resistance, that her world was small and pathetic compared to Jo's. That she was missing out on what she most wanted.

Under these circumstances, it's hardly surprising that the next time Laura fell, she fell badly. Because one day, quite without meaning to, she woke up, got dressed and went to work, and everything was normal, and by the next day she had fallen in love again. But this time she knew it was for real. And that's when everything started to go wrong.

CHAPTER TWO

Chris the groom coughed and stood up, looking rather nervous. Laura smiled at him, pretending to listen. She should have been paying attention but she was daydreaming, in a reverie of her own. She was thinking about her grandmother, Mary Fielding. Laura's grandmother was the person Laura loved most in the world (apart from whoever it was she was in love with at that moment), even more so perhaps than her parents, than her brother.

Mary was a widow. She had lost her husband, Guy, eight years before, and she lived on her own in a small but perfectly formed flat in Marylebone. There were various reasons why Laura idolised Mary, wanted to be just like her, found her much more seductive than her own parents. Mary was stylish – even at eighty-four she was always the best-dressed person in a room. Mary was funny – her face lit up when she was telling a joke, and she could make anyone roar with laughter, young or old. But the main reason Laura adored her grandmother was that Mary had found true love. Her husband, Guy, was the love of her life, to an extent Laura had never seen with anyone else. They had met when each was widowed, in Cairo after the Second World War. Mary already had a daughter, Angela, Laura's mother. Guy also had a daughter, Annabel, whom Laura and Simon called aunt, even though she wasn't really related to them.

Because of her mother's natural reserve, it was Mary whom Laura told about her love life, her latest disasters, the person she was currently in love with. Because she lived in central London, and so not that far from Laura's work, it was Mary whom Laura called in to see, to talk to, to listen to. And it was Mary that Laura learnt from, when it came to true love, in large part. She did not learn it from her own unemotional parents. No, she learnt that true love was epic stuff.

One of Laura's favourite stories was how Mary and Guy had realised they were in love on a trip out to the pyramids to see the sun rise. It had been pitch black as they rode out, crammed in a Jeep with the other members of their club in Cairo. And as the sun rose, Guy had turned to Mary, and said, 'You know I can't live without you, don't you?' And Mary had replied, 'I know.'

And that was that. They were married six months later.

George and Angela, by contrast, had met at a choral society function off the Tottenham Court Road, when they were both at university. Somehow, Laura felt this wasn't quite the same.

'You are the love of my life,' she heard a voice say. 'The woman I want to grow old with. I love you.'

He was staring at her intensely, his eyes boring into hers. Laura raised her hand to his chest, and said, breathlessly, 'I love you too.'

Beyond them the sun was rising, flooding the vast desert landscape with pink and orange colour. Sand whipped in her face, the silk of her headscarf caught in the breeze. She could feel the cold smoothness of the material of his dinner jacket against her skin, as he caught her and pulled her towards him.

'Tell me again,' Laura whispered in his ear. 'Tell me again that you love me.'

And then, suddenly, a microphone crackled loudly, jerking Laura back to reality, as someone cleared their throat and said,

'To my beautiful wife, Jo!'

9

'Aah,' the wedding guests murmured in approval, as Laura came back down to earth with a bump. There was some sniffing, especially from Jo's mother up on the top table, as Chris raised a glass to his new bride, kissed her, and then sat down to a welter of applause and chair-shuffling.

'Aah,' Laura whispered to herself, leaving her daydream behind with a sigh. She looked at Jo, her best friend, so beautiful and happy-looking, and found tears were brimming in her eyes. She turned to her flatmate Paddy, sitting next to her, and sniffed loudly.

'Look at her,' she said. 'Can you believe it?'

'No,' said Paddy, raising an eye at Chris's cousin Mia. Paddy had recently begun to teach himself how to raise one eyebrow, in a 'come to me, pretty laydee' way. This involved several hours of grimacing into Laura's hand-mirror in the sitting room of their flat, whilst Laura was trying to watch TV. She got very irritated with her flatmate when he did this, and was frequently telling him that being able to raise one eyebrow was not the key to scoring big with the ladies. Wearing matching socks was. As was having a tidy room. And not acting like a crazy stalker when some girl said no after you asked her out. These were the things that Laura frequently told Paddy he should be concentrating on, and yet, much to her deep chagrin, he ignored her every time. For Paddy's retort would always be that what Laura knew about dating was worthless.

What a perfect, happy day, Laura thought, as she gazed around the room, clapping now the speeches were over. She was gripping her glass, searching for someone. Suddenly her eye fell on Jo and she watched her for a moment, truly radiant, happy and serene in an antique lace silk dress, her hand resting lightly on her new husband's as they sat at the top table. Laura couldn't help but feel a tiny pang of something sad. It wasn't just any bride sitting there in the white dress, with the flowers and the black suits around her. It was Jo – Jo whom she had danced with all night in various Greek nightclubs, with whom she had spent hours in Topshop changing rooms, whom she had stayed up all night with whilst she sobbed her heart out after her last boyfriend Vic dumped her. It was her best friend, and it was weird.

She blinked and caught Jo's eye, suddenly overcome with emotion. Jo smiled at her, winked, and mouthed something. Laura couldn't tell what it was, but by the jerking of her head towards the best man, Chris's newly single brother Jason, Laura thought she could guess what Jo was on about. Laura followed her gaze, shaking herself out of her mood. Jason was nice, yes. Definitely. But he wasn't . . . dammit, where *was* he?

'Who are you looking for?' said Paddy suspiciously, as Laura cast her eyes around the room.

'Me?'

'Yes, you. Who is it? You keep looking round like you're expecting to see someone.'

'No one,' said Laura, rather huffily. 'Just looking, that's all.'

'There's Dan,' said Paddy.

'Who?' asked Laura.

'Dan. Dan Floyd. He's raising his glass. He's talking to Chris.'

'Right,' said Laura calmly. 'Ah, there's Hilary. And her mum. I should go and say –'

'Laura!' said Jo, coming up behind her, dragging someone by the hand. 'Don't go! Here's Jason! Jason, you remember Laura?'

'Hey. Of course,' said Jason, who was an elongated, blonder version of Chris. 'Hi, Laura.'

'Er,' said Laura. 'Hi, Jason, how are you?'

There is nothing more likely to induce embarrassment in a single girl than the obvious set-up at the wedding in front of friends. Laura smiled at Jason, and once more cast a fleeting glance around the room. Where was he?

'Good, thanks, good,' said Jason, as Jo nudged Paddy and grinned, much to Laura's annoyance.

'See the match on Wednesday?' Paddy asked Jason, in an attempt at blokeish comradeship.

'What match?' said Jason.

'Oh . . .' Paddy said vaguely. 'You know. The match. The big game.'

'What, mate?' Jason repeated, scratching his head.

'Anyway, great to see you, mate,' said Paddy, changing tack and banging Jason hard on the shoulder, so that he nearly doubled up. 'So, Laura was just saying – Laura? Help me out here.'

Jason gazed at Paddy, perplexed. Laura looked wildly around her, searching for an escape, and then someone over Jason's shoulder caught her eye.

'Jason split up from Cath two months ago,' Jo hissed in her ear, in a totally unconvincing stage whisper, as Laura gazed into the distance. It was him, of course it was him, she would know him anywhere. 'You know, he's living in Highbury now? Laura, you should –'

But Laura was no longer standing next to her, she had turned around to say hello to their friend Dan, who had appeared by her side. Vaguely she heard Jo's tutting, vaguely she was aware that she should be making an effort.

For Jo hadn't seen the look on Laura's face after she was tapped on the shoulder by Dan. In fact, Jo and Paddy hadn't been seeing quite a lot of things lately, and if they had, they would have been worried. Especially knowing Laura like they did.

'You had a good evening, then?' Dan was saying to Laura, smiling wickedly at her.

'Yes, thanks,' she replied, looking up at him, into his eyes. 'Good speeches.'

'Great,' he said, shifting his weight so that he was fully facing her. It was a tiny movement, almost imperceptible to Jo, Paddy, or any of the other hundred and fifty people in that room, but it enclosed the two of them in together as tightly as if they were in a phone box.

Dan smiled at her again, as Laura pulled her shawl over her shoulder and she smiled back helplessly, feeling her stomach turn over at his sheer perfectness. His dark blond hair, the boyish curling crop which curled over his collar. His tanned, strong face, wide cheekbones, blue eyes, lazy smile. He reminded her of a cowboy, a farmhand from the Wild West. He was so relaxed, so easy to be with, so easy to be happy with, and Laura glowed as she gazed up at him, simply exhilarated at the prospect of a whole evening in his company – a whole evening, where anything could happen. Suddenly she could barely remember whose wedding it was.

He was here. She was here with Dan, and he was hers for the rest of the evening, and for those hours only she could indulge herself with the secret fantasy that they were a couple who'd been going out for years. Perhaps they were married already. Perhaps Jo and Chris had been the only witnesses at their beach wedding in Barbados two years ago. Dan in a sarong – he would suit a sarong, unlike most men. Her in a silk sundress, raspberry pink, her dark blonde hair falling loose behind her back. Some spontaneous locals and other couples gathered at the seashore, crying with joy at how perfect, how in love they obviously were, totally pole-axed by the strength of emotion, the purity of their love. Laura and Dan, Dan and Laura. Perhaps . . .

'Laura!' a voice said sharply. 'Listen!'

Laura realised she was being prodded in the ribs. The lovely bubble of daydream in her head burst, and she tore herself away from Dan, and looked around to see Paddy glaring at her.

'I was talking to you!' he said, affronted. 'I asked you a question four times!'

'I'll see you later,' Dan murmured, shifting away from her. 'Come and find me, yeah?' and he very lightly ran his hand

13

over her bare arm, a tiny gesture, but Laura shuddered, looked up at him fleetingly, even more sure than ever, then turned back to Paddy. As Dan moved off, he raised his glass to her, and smiled a regretful smile. Laura screamed inwardly, and turned away from him towards Paddy.

'Sorry,' she said. 'What was it?'

'Is this fob watch too much?' said Paddy, fingering the watch hanging from his waistcoat. 'I think it is. I'm not sure, but perhaps it overloads the outfit. What do you think?'

'Ladies 'n' gennlemen,' came a bored-sounding voice from the back of the room. 'Please make your way back into the Ballroom. Mr and Mrs Johnson are about to perform their first dance. Ah-thann yew, verrimuch.'

Laura looked wildly around her, as if trying to prioritise the many tasks on her mind. She glared at Paddy, who was still obviously waiting for an answer.

'Yes, it is,' said Laura wildly. 'Far too much. I totally agree. In fact, it's *hideous*,' she said crossly. 'You'd better take it off and throw it away. I'm going to the loo – see you in a minute,' she finished, and hurried away.

Dan, Dan, Dan. Dan Floyd. Even saying his name made her feel funny. She muttered it on her way to the loo, feeling sick with nerves, but totally exhilarated. Laura had got it bad. She *knew* it was bad, and she knew if any of her friends found out they'd tell her it was futile, she should get over it, but she couldn't help it. It was meant to be. She was powerless in the face of it, much as she'd tried not to be. Dan Floyd, looking like a ranger or an extra from *Oklahoma!*, calm, funny, and so sexy she couldn't imagine ever finding any other man remotely attractive. Laura wanted him, plain and simple.

She had constructed a whole imaginary life for them, based around (because of the *Oklahoma!* theme) a small house in the Wild West with a porch, a rocking chair – for Laura's granny Mary – corn growing as high as an elephant's eye in the fields, and a golden-pink sunset every night. Mary would drink gins on the porch and dispense wise advice, and would sit there looking elegant. Dan would farm, obviously, but he would also do the sports PR job thing that he did. Perhaps by computer. Laura would – well, she hadn't thought that far. How could she do her job in the prairie? Perhaps there were some dyslexic farmhands who'd never learnt to read properly. Yes.

Her friend Hilary was in the loos when she got there, washing her hands. 'Oi,' she said. 'Hi.'

Laura jumped. 'Oh. Hi!' she said brightly. 'Hey. Great speech, wasn't it?'

'Not bad,' said Hilary, who didn't much like public displays of affection, verbal or physical. She ran her hands through her hair. 'That idiot Jason's there, did you see?'

'Yeah,' said Laura. 'He's quite nice, isn't he?'

'Well,' said Hilary, in a flat tone. 'He's OK. If you like that kind of thing.'

'He's split up from Cath,' Laura said encouragingly.

'Yeah, I know,' Hilary replied coolly. 'Hm. I might go and find him.'

'OK. See you later,' said Laura, and shut the door of the cubicle. She rested her pounding head against the cool of the white tiles. She was stressing out, and she couldn't help it. It was the first time she'd seen Dan since they'd kissed, so fair enough. But she didn't know what to do. Dan had got to her. The worst bit of all was, she didn't just fancy him something rotten. She really *liked* him, too.

She liked the way he was always first to buy a round, that the corners of his blue eyes crinkled when he laughed, the rangy, almost bowlegged way he walked, his strong hands. She liked the way he rolled his eyes with gentle amusement when Paddy said something particularly Paddy-ish. She liked him. She couldn't help it, she did. And she knew he liked her, that was the funny thing. She just knew, in the way you know. She had also come to know, in the last couple of months, that there was something going on between her and Dan. She just didn't know what it was. But somehow, she knew tonight was the night.

Dan was a friend of Chris's from university. He'd moved about five minutes away from Laura about six months ago, round the corner from Jo and Chris towards Highbury – and she'd known of him vaguely since Jo and Chris had got together. In July, Dan had started a new job, and more often than not Laura found herself on the tube platform with him in the morning. The first couple of times it was mere coincidence. Now, at the end of summer, it was almost a routine. They would buy a coffee from the stall on the platform and sit together in the second-to-last carriage, deserted in the dusty dog days of August, and go down the Northern line together until they got to Bank. And they would read *Metro* together and chat, and it was all perfectly innocent.

'Dan? Oh yeah, we're tube buddies,' Laura would say nonchalantly, her heart thumping in her chest.

'They're transport pals,' Chris and Jo would joke at lunch on Sundays. 'Like an old married couple on the seafront at Clacton.'

'Ha, ha, ha,' Laura would mutter, and then she would blush furiously, biting her lip and shaking her hair forward over her face, burying herself in a newspaper. Not that they ever noticed – it's extraordinary what people don't notice right under their noses.

But to Laura it was obvious, straightforward. From the first time she'd recognised him on the tube platform, that sunny July day, and he had smiled at her, his face genuinely lighting up with pleasure – 'Laura!' he'd said, warmth in his voice. 'What a nice surprise. Come and sit next to me.' Through the sun and rain of August, September and October she would run down the steps to the tube platform, hoping he'd be there, not knowing what was going on between them. They had built up a whole lexicon of information. Just little things that you tell the people you see each day. She knew when his watch was being mended, what big meeting he had that day; and he knew when Rachel, her boss, was being annoying, and asked how her grandmother had been the previous day. Out of these little things, woven over each other, grew a web of knowledge, of intimacy, and one day Laura had woken up and known, known with a clarity that was shocking, that this was *not* just another one of her crushes, or another failed relationship that she couldn't understand. She and Dan had something. And she was in love with him.

Oh, the level of denial about the whole thing *was* extraordinary, because you could explain it away in a heartbeat if you had to. 'We go to work together, because we live round the corner from each other. It's great – nice start to the day, you know.' Whereas the truth was a little more complicated. The truth was both of them had started getting to the station earlier and earlier, so they could sit on the bench together with their coffees and chat for ten minutes before they got on the tube. And that was weird. Laura knew that. Yes, she was in denial about the whole thing. She knew that, too. It had got to the stage where something had to give – and she couldn't wait.

Laura collected herself, breathed deeply, smoothed the material of her dress down, and came out of the loo to put on more lip gloss. She realised as she looked in the mirror that she was already wearing enough lip gloss to cause an oil slick – it was a nervous reflex of hers, to apply more and more when in doubt. She blotted some on the back of her hand, and strolled out of the door nonchalantly, looking for Paddy or Hilary, someone to chat to. It was strange, wasn't it, she mused, that at her best friend's wedding, knowing virtually everyone in the room, she could feel so exposed, so alone. That on such a happy day she could feel so sad. She shook her head, feeling silly. Look over there, she told herself, as Jo and Chris walked through the tables of the big ballroom, hand in hand, smiling at each other, at their friends and family. It was lovely. It was a privilege to see. Out of the corner of her eye she saw Hilary pinning Jason against a wall, yelling at him about something, her long, elegant hands waving in the air. Jason looked scared, but transfixed. Another man scared into snogging Hil, she thought. Well done, girl.

Someone handed her a glass of champagne. She accepted it gratefully and turned to see who it was.

'Sorry,' whispered Dan casually, though he didn't bend towards her. He said it softly, intimately, and clinked his glass with hers. 'I thought I'd better leave you to deal with Paddy's sartorial crisis by yourself. Where did you go?'

'Loo,' said Laura, trying to stay calm, but it came out, much to her and Dan's surprise, as a low, oddly pitched growl. He smiled. Laura smiled back, and ran her hand through her hair in a casual, groomed manner, but forgot the lipstick mark of gloss still adhering to the back of her hand. Her hair stuck to the gloss, and her hand became caught up in her hair as she flailed wildly around with her hand in the air, covered in hair.

'Arrgh,' said Laura, despair washing over her as she stood in front of Dan. Her hand was stuck. Dan took the champagne out of her other hand, put it on a table, held her wrist and slid her fingers slowly out of her hair. He smoothed it down, swiftly dropped a kiss on the crown of her head in a sweet, intimate gesture, and put his palm on the small of her back as he guided her through the room onto the terrace.

'Thanks,' whispered Laura, trying to walk upright and not cower with embarrassment. 'I should go back out, to see the first dance, look . . .'

'No problem,' said Dan calmly. 'In a minute. I just want to do this.' And he slid his hand round her waist, drew him towards her, and kissed her. No one else was watching, they were all turned towards the dance floor where Mr and Mrs Johnson were dancing. They were alone on the terrace, just the two of them.

Dan pulled her towards him, his hands pressing on her spine, his lips gentle but firm on hers. He made a strange, sad sound in his throat, somewhere between a cry of something and a moan. Laura slid one arm around his neck and drew him further towards her. The other arm was by her side, she was still holding the champagne glass. It tilted, the champagne spilt, and neither of them noticed.

After a short while, they broke apart slowly, and said nothing. There was nothing to say, really. Laura drained the meagre contents of her glass and leant into Dan. They stood there together as the music died away and applause rippled out towards them, aware of nothing else but themselves, alone in their bubble.

'Well,' Dan said eventually. 'I didn't know *that* was going to happen tonight,' and he put his arm around her.

Laura twisted round, looked up at him. 'Oh yes you did,' she said, smiling into his eyes. 'Of course you did.'

That was Laura's second glass of champagne, and she found Paddy and Hilary on another terrace having a cigarette so she joined them. After her third glass, thirty minutes later, she was a bit tired. After her fourth, she felt better again – and she'd eaten from the buffet as well. After her fifth and sixth, she danced for an hour with Jo and Chris and their other friends. And after her seventh glass, she didn't know how it happened, but she found herself in one of the free taxis going home with Dan Floyd, and they were kissing so hard that her lips were bruised the next day. And that's when it really started, and Laura went from knowing lots of things about Dan and how she felt about him and her place in the world in general to knowing nothing. At all.

At one point during the night, she propped herself up on her elbow and leant over him, and kissed him again, and he kissed her back and they rolled over together, and Laura pulled back and said, 'So . . . what does this mean, then?' It just came out.

And Dan's face clouded over and he said, 'Oh gorgeous, let's not do this now, not when I want you so much,' and he carried on kissing her. Something should have made Laura pull away and say, No, actually, what does this mean? Are you going to tell your girlfriend? When will you leave your girlfriend? Do you like me? Are we together? But *of course* she didn't . . .

CHAPTER THREE

Yes, Dan had a girlfriend, Amy. Just a tiny detail, nothing much. They were as good as living together, too – although she still had her own place. Another detail Laura tried to forget about. She had *almost* managed to convince herself that if she didn't tell anyone about her – well, what was it? A 'thing'? A 'fling'? A fully formed relationship just waiting to move into the sunlight of acceptance? – her liaison with Dan, then perhaps the outside world didn't matter so much. And it didn't, when she was with him. Because he was The One, she was sure of it. So it became surprisingly easy for Laura, who was basically a good girl, who never ever thought she could do something like this, to turn into a person who was sleeping with someone else's boyfriend.

She had tried, after Jo and Chris's wedding. She told herself – and Dan – that it wasn't going to happen again. She bit her nails to the quick about it because, much as Laura might be clueless about some things, she was clear about other things, and one of those was: don't sleep with someone who has a girlfriend. She'd already tried going cold turkey from him, as autumn gave way to winter, and as she realised she was falling for him, badly. She tried avoiding him at the tube station – but she couldn't. She tried to forget him – but she couldn't. When she thought about him, it was as if he was talking to her, pleading with her, communicating with her directly. Laura, it's you I want, not Amy. Laura, please let me see you, his eyes and his voice would say in her head, until the noise got so loud it was all she could hear. Every time was the last time. Every time was the first time.

Laura knew it was wrong to be thinking like this. But she assuaged that secret guilt in her head with the knowledge that Dan and Amy weren't getting on well. Dan himself had told her it wasn't working out. Well, he had in so many words, with a sigh and a shake of the head, in the early days of their coffee mornings together on the tube platform. And she knew from Jo that Dan was going out with Chris and his other mates more, playing more football, watching more football, in the pub more, working harder. Added to which, no one in their group ever really saw Amy. They were together, but they were never actually together. She was completely offstage, like a mystery character in a soap opera whom people refer to but who never appears. You know when a couple are happy together – mainly because you don't see either of them as much, and when you do they're either together, or they talk about each other. Or they're just happy. You know. Laura knew – as did everyone else – Dan wasn't happy with Amy. Dan wanted out, he just didn't know how to get out.

And, actually, Amy wasn't really her friend. They occasionally all went out for drinks, Jo and Chris, Dan and Amy, Hilary, Paddy and Laura and so on, especially now Chris and Dan had moved nearby. But Amy rarely came along, and in any case, Laura had long ago realised she couldn't stand her. Never had been able to, in fact. Because not only was Amy a quasi-friend of hers, they had also been at school together, many moons ago, and there is no more mutually suspicious relationship than that of two ex-schoolmates who are thrown together several years later. Added to which, Amy had been one of the mean girls who had teased Laura relentlessly about her love for Mr Wallace the oboe teacher, and had spread the subsequent rumours surrounding Laura giving up the oboe.

She'd even told Laura's mother Angela about it, at a school concert, all wide-eyed concern. Angela Foster had got the wrong end of the stick, and assumed Laura was being pestered by Mr Wallace. She'd complained. He'd nearly been fired. The whole thing was deeply embarrassing. So Laura's dislike of Amy was genuinely historical, rather than based upon the fact that Amy was with the man Laura felt quite sure she loved. This made her feel better, in some obscure way.

Amy ate nothing, exercised obsessively, talked about shoes and handbags the entire time (like, the *entire time*) and she played with her beautiful red hair. Non-stop. It was her thing. She always had, even when she and Laura had been eight-year-olds in plaits and virgin socks at school. Twenty years later, the same white hand would smooth down the crown of its owner's hair as Amy softened her voice to tell a sad story – about a friend's mother's death, or something bad in the news. Or said something deeply meaningful at the pub, which made Laura want to gag childishly on her drink.

The thing was, Laura knew Amy was the kind of girl men fell for, even though she led them a merry dance. Laura wasn't. She was nice, she was funny, but she knew she was ordinary, nothing special. Why would anyone, especially Dan, choose her when they could be with Amy? Why was it he got her so well, laughed at her jokes? What amazing thing had led him to think of her as this perfect person for him, just as she knew that he was her Mr Right? It perplexed her, as much as it exhilarated her. It was extraordinary, it was magical, and so even though it was underhand and stressful, she carried on doing it.

'So, then she said I should know why she was pissed off. And I'm thinking, well god, woman, you're pissed off the entire time, how the hell am I supposed to tell the difference between you being annoyed because I was late back from football or annoyed because I didn't notice your new haircut? Is that for me? Hey, thanks so much. Toast, too. Wow.'

23

Laura set down the tray on her bed. She peered out of the window. It was two months after Jo and Chris's wedding, a cold, grey Saturday morning in February. Dan shifted up in bed, crossed his legs, and pulled the tray towards him.

'This is great,' he said, pouring some tea. 'Come on, get back into bed.'

Laura hopped in beside him. He handed her a cup of tea and kissed her. 'Mm. Thank you,' she said.

Dan and Amy had had another huge row the night before and Amy had stormed back to her own flat. Laura cleared her throat.

'So, what did she say next?' she asked, desperate for more details, but not wanting them too, fearing what he might say or not say.

Dan frowned momentarily, as if thinking something through. He put his mug back down on the tray and took her hand, looking serious. 'Forget about it,' he said. 'I'm sorry.' He looked down. 'It's crap of me. I'm so crap, boring you with all this stuff. It's . . . I've got to sort it out.'

'Yes,' said Laura, her heart beating fast.

'Not just for me,' said Dan, looking intently at her. 'For . . . for Amy as well, you know?'

'Yes, of course,' Laura said, less urgently. 'Amy.' She picked up a slice of toast and bit into it. 'Mm.'

Dan smiled, and picked up another piece. 'So, I'm pretty much free today now. Do you want to . . . you know. Spend the day together? I know it's last-minute, but we might as well make the most of it.' He leant forward and kissed her.

'Er . . .' Laura said, swallowing fast. She had lunch with Paddy and Simon, but she supposed she could cancel. And instead she and Dan could go to Kenwood House. Muffled up in scarves and hats. Drink hot chocolate and walk through the grounds hand in hand. Kiss in the lanes of yew trees that led away to the Heath. Her eyes sparkled. She'd cancel Paddy and Simon – they were boys, they didn't mind about that sort of thing. Although – gah. Simon, more a graduate of the love 'em and leave 'em school, was *always* taking the piss out of her about her love life. Saying she was a romance addict, that she'd ditch her own brother at the last minute if there was a chance of a red rose heading her way. And she'd done it a couple of weeks ago to him as well . . . the cinema, shit. She bit her lip. He was going away soon. She was a bad sister.

'Don't cancel anything special for me,' Dan said, as if reading her mind. 'It was just a suggestion.' He stroked her knee. 'God, it's so nice to be here, sweetheart.'

'I think I was supposed to be having lunch, but it's quite a vague thing,' said Laura, trying not to choke on her toast. 'I'd . . . of course I'd prefer it if . . .' His hand was lying on the duvet. She hooked her little finger around his, and said, 'Yes, I'd love to spend the day with you. We should talk, anyway.'

Laura was always trying to do this, stage moments where she and Dan 'talked'. But it never seemed to work. She desperately wanted there to be some kind of agenda to their relationship, instead of Dan turning up when he could, secretive texting or emailing, hurried, passionate, mind-blowing sex at one in the morning when he would drop by unannounced on the way back from the pub, wake her up, shag her senseless and then go back home – to what, Laura didn't know. Every time they tried to talk, something else would get in the way. Dan would tell her a funny story, or kiss her neck, or have to leave because Amy was calling. They'd tried not seeing each other, but the truth was it was so easy to have this relationship, it was so full of pleasure and excitement that, two months after they'd first got together, nothing had really changed. Dan was still with Amy, trying to sort it out or break it off gently. And Laura – Laura was so wildly happy with the whole thing she would no more have irrevocably ended it than she would have moved south of the river.

When she looked at the facts of the relationship, the bare facts, only then did she get depressed. He was still with his girlfriend. And whilst he and Laura got on really well, she also had to admit that what they spent most of their time doing was not having a laugh and enjoying each other's company but – having sex. And god, the sex was great, that was part of the problem – it had obscured the actual facts of the relationship, or whatever it was, for some time now.

On New Year's Eve, Laura and Paddy had gone round to the newly married couple's house for a party, along with lots of other people, but Dan wasn't there. He was on holiday with Amy, in Prague. Laura had stood on Jo and Chris's balcony along with Paddy and watched the fireworks over London. It was a clear night, sharp and cold, and for once the fireworks from the Thames were visible. They fizzed in the distance, tiny and indistinct, and around them, across the rest of London, streets and parks and houses were lit up by similar flashes and bangs, stretching as far as they could see. Simon had been there next to her, and as he hugged her tightly, he asked,

'So, sis. What's your New Year's resolution, then? Tell me.'

'Ha,' said Laura despairingly. She gave him a squeeze back. 'You wouldn't believe me if I told you.'

'Oh, really,' said Simon, not actually listening as his eye had fallen upon an attractive brunette in the corner of the room. 'Love life?'

'Yes,' said Laura honestly.

Simon looked at her briefly. 'Who is it this time, then?' he asked.

Laura resented the tone in his voice. 'It's – not like that.'

'Oh,' said Simon, not believing her for a second. 'Right,' he added vaguely. 'You should do something about it.'

'Thanks,' said Laura. 'I am.'

Simon smiled, 'Really?'

She nodded.

'Well, good luck then,' he said. 'Who is it this time? Someone at work? Ken Livingstone?'

'Go away,' said Laura. 'You're no help.'

26

'Well, don't just stand there,' Simon said. 'I mean it. Do something about it,' and he shrugged his shoulders apologetically, as if admitting this wasn't helpful, and moved across the room in search of his prey.

Laura watched him go. He was right, though, wasn't he? She'd been searching for true love for as long as she could remember. This year, it was going to happen. She just had to make it happen.

So, shivering on that cold balcony on New Year's Eve, as Jo and Chris kissed each other, and Paddy danced crazily and inappropriately with a scared-looking cousin of Chris's, and Simon charmed the pants – literally – off the brunette, Laura clenched her fist, and went to bed that night with a new iron resolve. Three weeks after her 'thing' with Dan had begun, but months after she had realised that he was the one for her, she had to do something about it. Even now, nearly two months later, she remembered it clearly. It kept coming back into her head like a drumbeat.

She had to know, she had to sort this thing out, because somewhere in her lovesick, crazy brain was a small voice telling her that this wasn't how normal people behaved, fell in love and that small voice had been getting louder and louder since before Christmas until now, two months afterwards, it was like a foghorn in her ear. She and Dan had to take the next step. Well, Dan had to take the next step and finish with Amy, then Laura and Dan had to take the step after that, which was to work out if they could be together.

So they would go to Kenwood House on this cold February Saturday, with the hot chocolate/gloves/yew trees, and during that time they would talk, and Laura would explain, calmly and clearly, that Dan had to sort his situation out, otherwise they couldn't be together any more.

'Talk,' Dan said. 'Yes, talk.' He looked at her, their fingers still entwined. Laura smiled at him, took the toast out of his mouth, put the tray down on the floor, reached for him, and they crawled back under the duvet, muffling their laughter, and then, a while later, their moans as they came together again and any further discussion was put aside for the moment.

An hour later, Laura emerged from her room, carrying the teapot, and padded into the kitchen in her bare feet. Paddy was sitting at the little table by the French window, gazing out at the view. Their flat was in a slightly cramped, dodgy Victorian mansion block, and had interesting design features – the French window, for example, opened not onto a charming balcony with pots of geraniums and basil, but a sheer drop down four floors. The boiler was in Paddy's bedroom, and the sitting room had three electricity sockets, but all right next to each other, by the door, nowhere helpful like underneath the bay window where the television was. It was Paddy's flat, bought for him with some help from his elderly parents, since he was a teacher at a school nearby and earned in a year what most bankers earn in a month. He and Laura were very happy there, though the water frequently turned itself off, the windows rattled, and the lino was curling because they had laid it themselves. Added to which Paddy had a mania for collecting interesting things from around the world, and so the flat was stuffed with a) painted gypsy floral watering cans, buckets, etc., b) elephants made of wicker he'd picked up travelling through Africa, and c) comic books.

Paddy didn't look up as Laura came into the kitchen, humming to herself. 'Morning,' she said brightly. 'How are you today, love?'

'Fine,' muttered Paddy bitterly. 'Oh, just fine.'

'Oh, right,' said Laura, nonplussed. 'Er, are you, though?'

'Oh, don't worry about me,' Paddy told her. 'I'll survive,' he spluttered into his tea. He stared moodily out of the window. Since he spent quite a lot of his leisure time doing this, Laura ignored him and put the mugs down on the counter.

'What are you eating?' she asked curiously.

'I made scrambled eggs with tomatoes,' said Paddy shortly. He gestured to the plate, which looked like pink brains. Paddy was an enthusiastic but disconcerting chef.

'Oh,' Laura lied. 'It looks nice.'

She ran the mugs under the tap.

'It's not enough that Mia hasn't answered any of my texts,' Paddy said, picking up the thread after a few moments' silence. Laura obediently swivelled round to listen. 'I've texted her four times, why hasn't she replied? Oh no. I have to sit in solitary silence, with *CD:UK* my only companion, and listen to my flatmate – who I've known since she was five – screaming with pleasure as some git rogers her senseless at eleven a.m. for about the fifteenth time that morning.'

Laura bit her lip to stop herself grinning. 'Sorry.' She went over and patted him on the shoulder. 'I'll make you some tea. Why don't we all go into the sitting room and have some tea?'

'No, thanks a bundle,' said Paddy, pulling his tattered paisley dressing gown about him with an attempt at dignity. 'I prefer to watch *Saturday Kitchen* on my own, thanks very much, not squashed up on the sofa with you and Mr Playaway whilst he tries to molest you under my very nose.'

'OK, OK,' said Laura. This was going to be tricky. Of course, no one knew about her and Dan – not yet anyway. She hadn't even told Jo. But she'd had to tell Paddy because Dan always came to her place. She hated making him party to it and thereby making him lie. It wasn't for long, and so far he'd been great, but . . . She filled the kettle and affected a tone of nonchalance. 'Er . . . any plans for today?'

Paddy looked up suspiciously. 'Yes,' he said. 'You know I have. We're going out to lunch with Simon.'

'Simon?' Laura said in a tone of blankness. She pulled a mug off one of the hooks above the sink and examined it. 'Urgh, this is dirty.'

'Your brother Simon, who's about to go to Peru for four months.'

Laura winced. Simon worked for a charity. He was taking time off from work to travel to Peru, volunteering for another charity.

Paddy went on, 'And then you know perfectly well we're going round to Jo's because Chris is away and she wants a hand with painting the kitchen.' He glared at her. 'Oh my god, you're piking. I can't believe it.'

'What?' said Laura. 'I don't know what you're talking about.'

'You lying bitch,' said Paddy. 'Go back in that bedroom, ease those chafed thighs onto the bed and tell Dan you're not spending the day with him or whatever it is he's suggested you do. You're coming out to lunch.'

'Honestly, Paddy, I had no idea,' Laura pleaded with him, aware how weak she sounded. 'Sure, Jo mentioned going round, but it was ages ago – I didn't think it was a proper plan . . . no one emailed me about it this week – I thought it was a casual arrangement.'

'Casual arrangement?' Paddy repeated.

'Yep,' Laura said. 'And lunch – hey, you'll have a much better time without me there. You never see Simon on his own, you can really catch up. And stuff.'

Paddy looked at her, and Laura realised the atmosphere in the kitchen was no longer one of grumpy, amused sniping.

'No, Laura,' he said quietly. 'That – that thing you've got next door with Dan. *That's* a casual arrangement.'

'No it's not,' said Laura in a small voice.

'Oh god, you stupid girl,' Paddy slapped his hand to his cheek. 'I don't care. Just don't try and lie to me. It's not a big deal, Laura, honestly. But –' he held up his hand as Laura made to speak '– don't lie to me. You know it was arranged ages ago. You, of all people.'

'What do you mean?' said Laura, feeling her chest tighten.

'I mean, I've always thought you were a good person, someone I could trust, someone I could rely on. Thick and thin, and all that.'

'Oh for god's sake, Paddy,' Laura said, her face reddening, feeling cross all of a sudden. 'That's such crap. It's only lunch, get over it! I am – I am a good person. Dan – I – you *know* how I feel about him, don't do this.' The kitchen tap was encrusted with limescale and she wrenched it round to turn it on, running her finger around one of the mugs as she thought of what to say next.

Paddy turned his back on her and looked out of the window, as if he was counting to five. Then he turned around again.

'Hey, love,' he said in a gentle voice. 'I know how you feel about him. But it's never going to happen. He's never going to leave Amy. Can't you see that? He's a wanker, and he's using you.'

'How dare you say that,' Laura retorted, her voice rising. She turned the tap off. 'How dare you! That's bullshit. He's not like that, it's not like that. It's just . . . complicated. He can't just dump her, I don't want him to do that. We have to wait before we can be together . . . we . . . oh.'

She slumped down into a chair, tears in her eyes. The lino squeaked under her feet. 'It sounds so fucking clichéd,' she whispered. 'I'm so stupid.'

'You're really not, darling,' Paddy said, patting her hand across the table. 'You're just mad about him, and what's wrong with that, eh? You've got to . . . you've got to sort it out, that's all. You know what you're like.'

Laura stood up again and went over to make the tea. 'I have to, I know,' she said. 'It's just. It's just – I can't think of anyone I'm ever going to like more than I like him.' Hot tears ran down her cheeks and she rubbed her eyes, feeling like a little girl in the playground.

It was true, that was the awful thing. She knew all this, she thought she was a sensible girl. But some kind of love had taken hold of her and refused to let her go, and it wasn't a happy, easy, joyful thing, it had her in a vice-like grip.

She looked up at Paddy and smiled, trying to be brave. His

face contorted with sympathy, and he walked over to where she stood and gave her a big hug. 'Do something about it, darling,' he said, his voice muffled against Laura's shoulder. 'Give him an ultimatum. Or give yourself an ultimatum. Get pregnant. No –' He stood back and shook her. 'Forget I said that. Really, don't get pregnant.'

'I won't,' Laura said, touched, for Paddy really did look alarmed. 'Don't be stupid.' She picked up the mugs. 'I'll do something about it, honestly.'

'Deadline. You need a deadline,' Paddy said, sitting back down and picking up the newspaper, which was lying on the table. 'Ooh, travel. Book a holiday,' he said casually, throwing the travel section at her. It flapped through the air and Laura caught it, scrunching it in her hand, and wedging it under her arm. 'Book a holiday to somewhere fantastic and then you have to go,' Paddy suggested. 'You know, in a few months' time, when everything's sorted out. God, I'm brilliant. As you once were, young woman. Go off and shag that worthless young man in there. I'll make your excuses to Jo, but she's not going to be happy. You know she's not, you blew her out last week.'

It was true. Laura had arranged to go to Borough Market with Jo, but something else had come up, a Dan-shaped something else.

'It's her birthday in a couple of weeks. I'll make it up to her then,' Laura said gratefully.

'Honestly. The things I do,' Paddy murmured.

'Thanks, Paddy,' Laura said. She paused, as if she might say something else, gazing at the back of his head as Paddy picked up his tea and turned a page of the newspaper. 'Thanks a lot. I . . . well.'

A watery ray of pale sunshine was shining weakly in through the window. Laura turned and left, her head bowed in thought.

'I've cancelled lunch,' she announced as she came back into her room.

Dan sat up in bed and spread his arms wide. 'Great, great news, my gorgeous darling girl,' he said. His hands slid inside her ratty old dressing gown, slipped open the tie, and he pulled her towards him. Laura laughed.

'Let me put the pot down,' she said, as he started kissing her. She crouched down, put the paper and the teapot on the floor, stood up again, and said, as Dan flung the duvet to one side, 'So, what do you want to do today?'

'You,' Dan said, jumping on her with the kind of alacrity usually reserved for sailors on shore-leave. 'God, I could be with you all day, you are so fucking gorgeous. Mm.'

'No,' Laura said, laughing, as he pulled off her dressing gown. 'I mean later. I've cancelled lunch. We could go out, you know. Maybe . . . er, Kenwood House for . . . er, hot chocolate.'

Dan didn't answer, but carried on doing what he was doing. Laura sighed, and pushed him away. 'Dan, listen.'

'Yes, yes,' Dan said. 'Hot chocolate.'

'No,' she said. 'I mean we go out to get hot chocolate, at Kenwood.'

'What are you talking about?' Dan asked, looking down at her. 'Why do you want to go and get hot chocolate at Kenwood? Is there a festival there or something?'

'No,' Laura explained. 'I mean – what shall we do today, then? We should do something. Go out, you know, make the most of it. The sun's just come out.'

Dan cupped her breast in his hand and bent over to kiss her again. 'I can't, darling,' he said. 'We can't. Someone might see us. Imagine if they did.' He looked up, his expression anguished. 'I'm sorry. This is crap.'

'But,' Laura said, trying to be patient, 'who are we going to bump into amongst the yew trees at Kenwood?'

'The what?' Dan asked. Laura watched him intently. 'No, we just can't. We should . . . we have to stay here. Not for much longer, I promise. But things might be tricky for the next couple of months.'

'Why?' said Laura, not understanding, and reluctantly waving goodbye to her winter wonderland dream of laughing and joking in a Missoni print cape as she and Dan carelessly drank hot chocolate and held hands amidst the frosty trees.

'I mean,' said Dan, 'if I'm going to split up with Amy, you and I won't be able to see each other whilst it's going on. I mean on our own, not the usual in the pub with everyone else there. Right?'

'Oh right,' said Laura, not daring to hope he was saying what he was saying. 'So . . .'

'So,' said Dan, bending over her nipple and kissing it gently, 'this might be the last time we get to do this for a long time. So – we should – make the most of it . . .'

'Yes,' gasped Laura suddenly, understanding him, and pulling him down. 'Yes . . . I see . . .'

As Dan moved down her body, Laura closed her eyes, and the last thing she saw was the crumpled cover of the *Guardian*'s travel section. 'Road Trip: Florida's Hidden Treasures', the front page declaimed. A road trip, she thought, and abandoned herself to something more immediate.

CHAPTER FOUR

Laura worked for an inner-city London council, as a schools and business co-ordinator. She loved her job, contacting local businesses, trying to get them to support their nearby schools, arranging volunteer reading programmes or school sponsorships – where companies or individuals could sponsor a school, donate money, and feel good about themselves. She loved it because she could see how it made a tangible difference, how much disillusioned company secretaries enjoyed reading with a six-year-old once a week, or how much it benefited a school to have a thousand pounds for new computers that some corporation or anonymous donor could easily spare. She had been there for nearly four years now, and the previous year had been put in charge of their new fundraising scheme, and the reading volunteer programme, which meant a lot more work, but she loved it. At least, she used to love it. Like everything these days, it seemed to have lost a little of its allure.

If Laura had stepped back from her situation, chances are she would have seen that she was behaving badly. The trouble was, her lack of perspective meant she couldn't see the main reason why she was in thrall to Dan: he made her feel gorgeous. He made her feel devastatingly attractive, that she was so powerful to him he had to have her, he couldn't control it. It made her feel just marvellous, and a little bit dirty too. It was dangerous, because Dan was like all the others, in that Laura had fallen for him hook, line and sinker, without really stopping to think about it. Only this time it was harder and deeper than ever before – and with no control over the situation she'd got herself in, and no endgame in sight. Having always thought of herself in the bottom half of the class in terms of looks, attractiveness and intelligence – not to mention sporting prowess – Laura couldn't quite believe the effect she had on Dan.

Laura knew she wasn't working as hard as she should; she knew her boss Rachel was on her case about things. She knew she hadn't been a good friend, or daughter, or sister, since Dan came along. She forgot birthdays, she was late for work, her mind wandered. But she consoled herself with the knowledge this was a temporary situation, and in a few short months – by the summer – they would have sorted it out and could be together. And then she would make everything all right.

Dan just needed a push, that was all. Just a little something to let him know she wasn't going to wait around forever, that she had deadlines of her own, too. She had another life apart from him and she was neglecting it, he had to see that.

The following Wednesday afternoon, Laura was in the office when the phone rang. It was pelting with rain, which rattled on the windows of the shabby, draughty Victorian building in Holborn. It was an old school, and hadn't been redecorated since the pupils had been moved into the big glass comprehensive south of the river, close to London Bridge, in 1972. In summer Laura would wander up to Lamb's Conduit Street and around the Inns of Court. On days like today she and her four other colleagues stayed inside, reheated soup in the ancient, sticky microwave and huddled around the fan heater which guzzled electricity and dispensed minimal heat.

Laura looked up wearily from her emails and glanced

suspiciously at the caller display panel. A teacher from St Catherine's primary school nearby had said she would be calling to discuss a problem with the latest batch of teaching volunteers, who'd just started at the school once a week, helping individual children with their reading. This was a pretty big firm of financial advisers called Linley Munroe, and it was something of a coup to have them onboard – perhaps they might be induced to get involved in other ways. Laura didn't particularly like Mrs McGregor, though she could see how devoted she was to the school and the children. She knew from experience that Mrs McGregor was the kind of person who had her own world view and couldn't be persuaded that anyone else's was admissible. In her own way, she was pretty hard-line, especially since her arrest during the demo she'd organised the previous spring at the NUT conference. This had renewed her zeal in a way that made her even harder to deal with, and Laura knew why she was ringing – she made the same complaint, along different lines, every year. Laura picked up the phone with a heavy heart.

'Hello?' she said tentatively.

'Laura? Laura Foster?' came a slightly husky voice down the phone.

'Yes,' said Laura, resigned.

'Oh Laura, I really must talk to you. I'm afraid this is a very bad situation, very bad indeed. Something's going to have to be done, it's a disaster. A catastrophe.'

'Yes, hello, Mrs McGregor,' said Laura.

'Well, Laura,' the voice was saying five minutes later. 'I've told him. You may think you can come here and believe you're doing something marvellous, helping these kids, so you can sleep easy at night in your big banker's flat. Well, you can't behave like that and get away with it. I'm not putting up with it any more, really I'm not.'

'I explained the guidelines to him and all his colleagues, back

37

in October,' Laura repeated. 'I'm sure this Marcus bloke's just got his wires crossed. As I said, you know we've never had any problems with Linley Munroe so far, Mrs McGregor.'

She gazed at her in-box and looked flatly round the office. In Rachel's absence, Shana was on another call, Tim was out on a visit and Nasrin was clearly reading *Pick Me Up* and not doing any work at all.

'I don't care,' Mrs McGregor said quickly. 'Laura, I'm afraid who they *are* isn't relevant here, not for my kids, anyway. That Marcus – he's a big thug. I know those kids aren't perfect, but . . .'

'Look,' Laura cut in, wanting to avoid another ten minutes of Mrs McGregor. 'I'll talk to Clare at Linley Munroe, tell her to have a gentle word with Marcus. But I really don't think he should be banned, Mrs McGregor. He's obviously enjoying it, and – well, let's face it – all he did was tell this boy to shut it – it could have been worse, couldn't it? They call each other the most horrific things in the playground, don't they?'

Her email beeped and her eyes flicked instantly to the screen. She opened the message and read, her heart pounding.

'Do they?' Mrs McGregor said. 'Not in my experience, Laura. Sure, there are rude words, but . . .'

Laura wanted to reread and reply to the email. She said shortly, 'Oh come on, Mrs McGregor. You know what I mean. Fuck, bum, willy, vag— And . . .' she paused, realising what she'd just said, 'er. Well, we used to, anyway. That sort of thing.'

Mrs McGregor was silent. Then she said, 'Well, I must say. Honestly, Laura.'

'It's an illustration,' said Laura briskly, marshalling all her inner resources and kicking herself ferociously on the ankle, whilst Nasrin and Shana gaped open-mouthed at her and started laughing. Laura flapped her arms at them to shut them up, and said, with what she hoped was an air of finality in her voice, 'I'm sure if Marcus Sussman used inappropriate language he was doing so to try and communicate with them. But I totally understand what you mean and I'll make sure it doesn't happen again.'

Mrs McGregor droned on in the background, but Laura didn't listen, only vaguely registering that she had to get rid of her in order to reply to this email.

'. . . have to speak to Rachel about this, Laura, yes, I will. Nasty man. Smooth young prat with cufflinks who thinks he can treat these kids like dirt because he went to university and they didn't. It's vile. And I'm surprised at you for not seeing it.'

'They're ten, Mrs McGregor,' Laura said, finally losing her patience. 'Of course they haven't been to university, don't be stupid. Fine. Talk to Rachel, but I'm surprised you're being so blinkered. I always knew you were an inverted snob but I didn't think you'd let it derail the volunteer programme like this.'

'Oh!' Mrs McGregor inhaled sharply. 'Laura Foster. You'll regret this, I promise you. Yes you will,' and she slammed the phone down.

'Laura!' said Shana, her eyes sparkling with the unexpected office excitement. 'Fuck, bum, willy, vag? What the hell . . .?'

Laura put her head in her hands and moaned softly to herself.

'It was brilliant,' said Shana joyfully. 'Best thing I've heard in ages.'

'Oh dear,' said Laura, finally looking up at Nasrin, who put the magazine down and gazed at her. 'St Catherine's again. Mrs McGregor. Stupid old bitch, I hate her,' she said defiantly. 'I'm going to get in trouble, aren't I?'

'She always makes a fuss, every year,' Nasrin said placidly, picking up *Pick Me Up* again. 'Rachel knows that, don't worry. She's just a sad old rebel without a cause.'

Laura turned back to her email again. Now she was free to read it properly, she didn't want to. Mrs McGregor had spoilt her afternoon.

A holiday is a great idea. You and me, nothing else. Imagine what we could do all week. Why don't you start thinking

about where to go. July is best for me, by then everything'll be sorted. We can celebrate properly. I want you.
  Dxx

Laura blushed with pleasure. The email, the email she'd been waiting on for over two days since she'd tentatively emailed him on Monday to ask if he thought they should go away. And here it was. He wanted to go away with her, everything would be sorted by then – so when was he going to talk to Amy? And then they'd be together. He was serious about her, she knew he was. Going on holiday, that was a big step, but they were ready for it. They'd spent so much time together they knew each other better than most other couples, and they certainly got on better than most other couples – look at Dan and Amy, she thought, and then realised they weren't the best couple to compare Dan and herself to. Laura rolled her eyes at her own stupidity, but her heart was singing, and the rest of the day passed more pleasantly than she'd expected.

The next day it was still raining, and Mrs McGregor wrote a letter of complaint to the local education authority about Laura. She faxed it to Laura's boss Rachel, who gave Laura a formal warning. She had no choice, she said, looking firmly at Laura as she twiddled a pencil between her fingers. Laura watched the pencil, sliding in and out and around, and wondered what all the fuss was about. Mrs McGregor was wrong, she was a horrible woman and she was wrong. Marcus Sussman was a bit hearty but he seemed to be a nice man: all he'd done was to tell a kid who called him 'a fucking cunt' to shut the fuck up – well, was that so bad? No, not in her book. Who cares, she thought, mentally shutting down and blocking out the memory of Mrs McGregor's droning voice.

  'I won't say I'm not disappointed,' said Rachel, leaning over her desk towards Laura. 'I thought that was one of your strengths, people management. You've always been so good at it, Laura. They love you at St Catherine's, too. What happened?'

Laura looked at her and felt tears start in her eyes. She was being stupid, she knew it, behaving so irresponsibly, but she didn't know how to start to explain. So she just said, 'Oh, you know. I just – she really was so vile. I just couldn't take it any more. I'm really sorry, Rachel. You know it won't happen again. Can I ring Mrs McGregor and apologise?'

Rachel smiled at her, slightly more warmly than before. 'Of course. Thanks a lot. You know how it is, Laura. We have to follow procedures. You know that. Just don't let it happen again. And watch that Marcus Sussman. You're sure he's OK?'

'Absolutely,' Laura said. 'I promise she's making it into something from nothing. This is the last time, I won't let you down.'

'So, darling,' said Angela Foster that evening, smoothing the sofa cushion over with her hand. 'How's work?'

She glanced around the sitting room, as if she expected a troupe of tiny tap-dancing mice to can-can out from a hole in the skirting board and pirouette off with her handbag.

'Fine, fine,' Laura said hastily. 'Today was . . . er, fine. Thanks so much for these, they'll look great.' She gestured to the pastel-spotted blinds her mother had bought her from John Lewis as a belated birthday present. 'It's so nice of you to bring them round, Mum, you shouldn't have.'

'Not at all, darling,' said Angela. 'And I wanted to see my girl. We haven't seen you for such a long time, you know. You're so busy these days.'

Laura changed the subject hastily. 'So, Mum. Have you got time for a cup of tea or do you have to go?'

Angela looked at her. 'I can see you're longing for me to stay,' she said dryly.

'No, of course I am,' Laura replied hastily. 'Of course. Do stay. I've got some biscuits, too. Sit down, Mum. I'll put the kettle on. Sit down, make yourself at home.'

41

'I'll try,' said Angela, lowering herself gingerly onto the blue sofa with its tea-stained arms and cigarette holes in the cushions. She moved aside Paddy's copy of *Maxim* with her heel and sat with her ankles neatly crossed. She smiled up at Laura.

Laura sighed and hurried into the kitchen, glancing anxiously at her watch. Dan had said he'd come round later, and she didn't want the two to collide. Not that it was likely they would – he only ever turned up after the pubs shut, whereas her mum was usually in bed and fast asleep by that time. She hunted desperately in the cupboards as she waited for the kettle to boil, searching for biscuits of some description, but of course could find none, and then one of the kitchen unit doors finally gave up the ghost and pitched itself sideways, the MDF cracking and ripping as the door fell flat on the floor. 'Shit,' Laura said, picking it up and wedging it back into place again. She had heard similar sounds the previous night, very late, after Paddy had got back from a marathon drinking session, and suspected he might have done exactly the same thing himself, leaving it as a nasty surprise for her the next day. No biscuits, then. Laura grabbed some slightly soggy Carr's water biscuits and took them back into the sitting room with the tea instead.

'How nice,' said Angela, taking one. 'Hm.'

'I couldn't find any biccies,' said Laura. 'So sshh, just enjoy them.'

'The flat's looking nice,' Angela said, obediently changing the subject. Laura gritted her teeth. Her mother was a Grand Master of the art of faking it. Laura knew she didn't do it on purpose, but her superbly repressed nature meant that whenever an unkind or negative thought crossed her mother's mind, she obviously felt she had to atone for it by saying the opposite of what she thought. It was quite a good barometer, actually. 'What a lovely short skirt, darling!' meant 'I am embarrassed to go with you dressed like that to the Hunts' wedding anniversary party, you look like a common prostitute.' Or 'Your friend Hilary is very lively, isn't she? Dad loved talking to her,' meant

'Your friend Hilary drinks more than is socially acceptable at a barbecue buffet lunch in Harrow and is nothing more than a jail-bait husband-stealer.'

'Thanks, Mum. It's a bit of a tip at the moment. Paddy's been on half-term and he just lazes round reading newspapers all day in his dressing gown.'

'Ahh,' said Angela fondly. She had more than a soft spot for Paddy. 'How is James?'

It was strange, Laura thought, musing over this, that James Patrick could read mothers – and his female friends – like open books, and yet be so disastrously out of sync with the opposite sex for the rest of the time. Half-term had been notable for Paddy's attempts to catch the attention of the girl in the flat downstairs, which involved hanging around the stairwell and by the pigeonholes for half the day, and smiling mysteriously, raising the eyebrow he'd now learnt to raise, and generally looking like an unemployed spy. The girl in the flat downstairs – whom Laura had met, she was called Becky and seemed really nice – simply cast him looks of something amounting to concern for his mental state every time she saw him. He was despondent about it, because he really liked her. And before he'd decided he fancied her, and had started acting like a lunatic, they'd actually got on quite well, during the few times they'd chatted. Added to which, Mr Kenzo from the flat opposite now thought Paddy was clearly a delinquent or else some kind of dodgy sex practitioner, and spent a lot of time watching him watching Becky, which all contributed to the atmosphere of light comedy pervading the stairwell of the block of flats.

'He's fine. Bit gloomy at the moment.'

'Any girls on the horizon?' said Angela hopefully.

Laura didn't want to get into Paddy's love life with her mother. She cast around for something else to say about him. 'He's giving me a hard time –' Laura stopped, cursed herself and then went on, '– for not tidying up more,' she finished, inwardly hugging herself for her own ingenuity.

'Well, I'm sure he's right,' said Angela. 'You are a bit messy. Still, it's nice to live with someone who is too, isn't it? You're only young once, it does no one any harm to leave the Sunday papers strewn about once in a while.'

'True, very true, Mum,' Laura agreed with a grin. Angela sipped her tea and smiled back at her over her mug, a lovely smile with her eyes, and Laura thought how pretty her mum would be if she'd only do that more.

'How's Aunt Annabel?' Laura said after a pause. Annabel had a beefy-faced husband and was the mother of the dreaded Lulu and Fran. A long time had passed since Laura and Simon happily played with Lulu and Fran on the beach in Norfolk as children. Now they were all grown-up, Lulu was a trust-fund skeleton who hung around with posh Eurotrash, and Fran was a porky, demented sports physio, with a loud, bellowing voice. Simon and Laura spent every family gathering trying to avoid them.

Angela swallowed her tea daintily and said brightly, 'Oh, she's fine, I hear. Granny saw her a couple of weeks ago. Lulu's got a wonderful new job reviewing restaurants and cafés for some magazine in Notting Hill. Isn't that great?'

Angela said this rather mechanically. Laura said incredulously, 'How can Lulu have a job reviewing restaurants? She hasn't eaten anything since 1991.'

'Darling,' said Angela. 'Don't be mean.'

'Oh come on, Mum,' Laura said. 'She's anorexic. It's not right to be that thin.'

'I know.'

'Why doesn't Aunt Annabel do something about it? She could run the UN if she wanted to.'

'They look at things in a different way from us, dear,' Angela said vaguely. 'They're different. Thank god.'

Laura was taken aback. Any criticism of their relatives coming from the mouth of her usually perfectly correct mother spoke volumes. But she said nothing, and instead pushed the IKEA catalogue on the coffee table towards her mother. 'So, Mum,' she said. 'Show me the new sofa you like? And look – here's the lamp I thought looked nice.'

Angela grabbed the catalogue almost gratefully, and opened it. 'The lamp with the blue shade, that's the one you want?'

Laura nodded. Angela looked genuinely excited, as she always did when a conversation about reasonably priced furnishings was in the offing. 'And once you've put these blinds up – ooh, it'll look really lovely, especially with spring coming,' she said, drinking her cup of tea. 'I should be on my way soon, you know. Dad's back from Norway tonight and I ought to have something ready for him, poor thing.'

Since Laura's father George was an engineer, something slightly strange in IT development systems, neither Laura nor her brother ever fully understood what it was that he did. It seemed to involve lots of flying about on business, anyway. He was a manically overenthusiastic cook when at home, though, who loved everything from barbecuing to casseroling, and was more than happy to do the lion's share of the catering in the Foster household. It had become borne in upon Laura over the years, however, that it was her mother who had always got stuck with the really mundane tasks, like the packed-lunch preparation or the spag bol on a Wednesday evening after work.

'Ooh, what are you making?' Laura asked.

'Lasagne,' said Angela firmly. 'You know your father. He'll be full of the joys of rollmops and herrings and smorgasbords. Well, I'm not having it, I'm really not. He can wait till summer's here for that kind of thing.' She drained the last of her tea and stood up. 'Right, darling, I'll be off.'

'Oh, OK,' said Laura. 'Thanks so much for the blinds, Mum. They're great. I love them.'

'I'm glad, darling,' said Angela, kissing her on the cheek. 'Your Granny picked them out with me. She said they were very You. And – oh my goodness, that reminds me. I nearly forgot. Honestly, where am I these days?'

'What?' said Laura, handing her mother her coat.

'Granny. You know it's her eighty-fifth birthday in July? Well, we want to have a little party for her at Seavale then.' Seavale was Mary's house by the sea in Norfolk. 'With Aunt Annabel and Robert, and Lulu and Fran.' Laura groaned, but Angela ignored her and carried on. 'I think Simon will still be away travelling, so it's even more important you're there. I just wanted to check – you're around in July, aren't you, darling? No holiday plans or anything?'

'Well . . .' Laura said. 'Er.'

Angela looked at her. 'Er?'

'I'm not sure,' said Laura.

'The whole of July? You're *not sure?*' said Angela disbelievingly.

'Well,' said Laura, collecting herself. Good god, she was being stupid. 'Any time's good. I was thinking . . . thinking I might be on holiday in July sometime, but I'll wait till you tell me a date and then plan it round that. Of course I'll be there. And do tell Granny thanks for the blinds, too. I love them.'

'You could ring her up and tell her, she'd be over the moon. She'd love to hear from you. Maybe you could meet for lunch, she was saying she hadn't seen you for a while.' Angela wrapped her scarf carefully around her neck.

It was true. Mary was not usually offstage. She was normally someone Laura saw once every other week, even if it was just to pop in for a drink after work, or to meet for a coffee. But Laura hadn't seen her for a while. She pushed the thought from her head, and the associated guilt, and said,

'Yes, I must call her. I must. Just been quite busy. Now, safe journey,' she added. 'Paddy will be disappointed he missed you, you know how much he loves you.'

Angela blushed. 'Go on,' she said. 'Thanks for the tea, darling. And call Granny. I'll let you know when we decide for the party.'

'Yep,' said Laura, standing at the doorway. She waved as

her mother disappeared down the curving staircase, and wandered back into the flat, kicking a stray football out of the way. As she stood in the hallway she realised it had been Christmas when she'd last seen her grandmother. That was ridiculous. It wasn't as if she could say she lived in the middle of nowhere, either. Mary lived behind Baker Street – 'within walking distance of Selfridges, good for the soul, my dear' – in Crecy Court, a Thirties apartment block that Laura absolutely loved. It was like a step back in time, a veritable Who's Who. She shared the block with Cedric Forsythe, an old Rank actor from the Fifties, who'd starred opposite Margaret Leighton and Celia Johnson; Jasper Davidson, a painter who'd lived in St Ives until he'd broken his hip three years ago; and Dilys Darcy, a long-forgotten Fifties crooner who'd been best mates with Alma Cogan and whose memory was sharper than a tack.

She went to pick up her mobile, to get her grandmother's number off it. There was a text from Dan.

Can I come over? Have told Amy I'll be late tonight. I really need to see you and I want you. I miss you so much, beautiful girl. Please say yes. D

As Laura stood holding the phone, the doorbell rang. She started, dropped the phone, and went over to the intercom.

'Hello?' she said.

'Did you get my text?' said the voice. 'Is Paddy there? Can I come up?'

'Dan?' Laura said shakily.

'Yes, it's Dan,' the voice said, amused. 'Who else sends you text messages saying they want to come over and give you a good seeing-to? Am I one in a long line, should I join a queue?'

'Aaagh,' said Laura. 'I was just confused. I was about to call someone and I was just conf— oh, come up, sorry, I'm just being thick.'

'Are you sure?' said Dan. He lowered his voice. 'I can't stay long, I just wanted to see you.'

Laura's legs wobbled a bit and she smiled into the intercom.

47

And then, out of nowhere, she found herself saying, 'I'd love you to come up. But not if you can't stay. Oh Dan, I'm sorry.'

'What?' said Dan.

'I mean,' said Laura, 'you're not just coming up for a quick fuck and then scooting off again. Not that that wouldn't be nice. It would –' and she almost wavered, then checked herself. 'Hm. I want you too, but no, that's not going to happen. I'm really sorry. Night, darling.'

'OK,' said Dan. He paused. 'I'm sorry,' he went on. 'You're right. Shit, oh well. I deserve it. Soon, soon, you know? Can you do me a favour?'

'Depends,' Laura said cautiously, dreading him asking her to come outside and do it on the porch.

'Can you look out of the window and wave, just so I can see you tonight? Right, I'm off then. Bye my darling. I wish . . .'

'Bye Dan,' Laura said softly. 'I love you.'

The line went dead as she stuffed her fist into her mouth. I love you? Why? Why had she said that? Damn. She ran over to the window, and gazed out across the quiet suburban North London street. The rain had stopped and the night was clear, and on the street below she could see a tall figure staring up at her. She opened the window and looked down, and there he was, a small figure below her, his gorgeous face turned up towards her.

'I love you too,' he shouted, and his voice echoed in the silence of the street. 'I love you.'

Laura stood there, her eyes filled with tears. And then she blew him a kiss and shut the window.

CHAPTER FIVE

Laura's parents still lived in the house she and Simon had grown up in, on the nicer edges of Harrow – Eastcote, really. In the late Seventies George and Angela had stretched themselves to the limit to buy the semi-detached, mock-Tudor villa with off-road parking at the front, three (and a half) bedrooms, a downstairs lavatory and a separate dining room. The garden was large enough for a climbing frame, a barbecue, a shed and a vegetable garden, as well as a conservatory-cum-patio where the Fosters would entertain in the summer months. There was an excellent primary school a ten-minute drive away, and the neighbours were all very nice. It was a good area. Respectable. Quiet. Theirs was the sort of road no one drove down to get to anywhere else, and the sort of neighbourhood where the nearest corner shop was a drive away, through quiet tree-lined streets with identical Thirties houses, and the only break in the monotony of the houses was the occasional car dealership on the corner. Cars – make and model – maps, routes and the price of petrol were all very important in Eastcote. And the garden centre at Syon was a nice drive away, too.

When Guy died eight years before, the family-minded George had hoped that Mary would want to move in with them. He thought she might be lonely, since Guy and Mary had been such a twosome. They had never really sat easily within the extended family as a whole – especially as Angela and Annabel were not naturally close. They were almost better grandparents than they had been parents, fond and funny, interested, interesting, wildly exotic to Simon and Laura. And they complemented each other perfectly: where Mary was amusing, a fund of endless stories and pearls of wisdom, Guy was kind, reliable. He could make things out of bits of string, could tell stories about places on the Silk Route, of emperors thousands of years old. His affection was boundless – for animals, strangers, loved ones – but most of all, for Mary. Always Mary; and she, in turn, only had eyes for Guy.

So when Guy had had a heart attack, unexpectedly (because he was the kind of person whom you expected would live forever), George and Angela drove over to Oxford to help Mary pack up, and as they were putting Indian carvings and strange Egyptian rugs into boxes, Angela asked her mother breezily if she'd like to come and live with them in Harrow. Simon and Laura had both moved out by then. Besides, no matter what you thought of Mary (and her daughter and son-in-law both thought her a little unconventional), you had to agree she was fun to have around.

But Mary said no. She sold the Arts and Crafts-style house in North Oxford where she and Guy had lived happily together for twenty years – when they were in the country, or not by the seaside, that is – packed up all her possessions (of which there were an exotic few – she had lived in Cairo, India and Jerusalem, as well as all over England), and moved into the tiny flat in Marylebone, where she proceeded to have a whale of a time, much to the consternation of her daughter, but to the great amusement and delight of her grandchildren.

For the teenage Laura, her overactive imagination permanently on the go, it was the very idea of sophistication, and going back to dreary, dank Harrow afterwards, with its identical houses, its small-town morals and ideas, was always horribly depressing.

To this day, her grandmother's flat was still a magical place for her, stuffed with silk kimonos, old sequinned evening capes, oil paintings and blurred black-and-white photos showing the bygone days of a Colonial age. And Harrow was . . . well, boring street after boring street, where the neighbours knew all the latest details of your job and your flat, and secretly hoped you weren't doing as well as their own daughter of the same age.

Laura had never loved Harrow much, especially compared to Mary and Guy's house in Oxford, or Seavale in Norfolk, but she'd never really thought about it. Now, it came to represent everything that was hollow and dreary in her life. When Easter came and went with no change in her own situation, and she found herself spending an especially miserable bank holiday at home with her parents, watching her father's new DVD of Morecambe and Wise, she found herself loathing Harrow, loathing pretty much everything, even Morecambe and Wise. Normally Laura loved Morecambe and Wise, they made her snort with laughter, but sitting on the sofa in between her mum and dad, whilst they chuckled along merrily to the 'There is Nothing Like a Dame' sketch and tried to identify the Seventies TV presenters – 'Oh look, Angela, is that old Reggie Bosanquet?' – was almost painful.

Also painful was her brother's absence. Simon had been in Peru for a few weeks now, and Laura found her thoughts drifting to him, resentment at his freedom mingling with missing him. He should be on the sofa in suburbia, enjoying salmon en croute and the bank holiday crossword in *The Times*, not her. She should be in Tuscany, walking hand in hand with Dan through an ancient piazza, stopping for an espresso at a café in the shade of a cathedral, laughing at each other in the bright spring sunlight. Laura in big shades and a headscarf, a stone lighter, dressed in Missoni, or a cheap version of Missoni; Dan handsome and tall in chinos and a polo shirt. But no.

Her father dropped her at the station on bank holiday Monday, since it was on his way to the garage to get some replacement wiper blades. As Laura waved him off he said, 'Great to see you, Laura love. Thanks for coming over. It's been really good, hasn't it?'

No, Laura wanted to say, it has been wrong. It has been very wrong. You have made me listen to your Seekers albums three times. You and Mum spent Sunday afternoon rearranging the pot plants on the patio in height-ascending order, and laughing about it like it was actually funny. Parents. She would never understand them for as long as she lived. She leant into the car and smiled at her dad. George coughed, and said, 'We've loved having you over, Laura, you know. You know, love, you can always come and stay, it's not that far, is it.'

Laura was taken aback; she raised her hand to her cheek, suddenly moved, despite herself, and felt awful for having had such impure thoughts.

'Ta Dad,' she said, slinging her bag over her shoulder. 'See you soon.'

'See you soon, my love. Have a great week. Call your grandmother!'

Paddy was out when Laura got back. Dan was away for the weekend, she knew it. She thought he was with Amy – she hadn't asked, she didn't want to seem clingy, she loathed girls like that. Ho hum. She went into the kitchen to make herself a cup of tea, feeling rather low after a weekend with people, and realised that the evening stretched ahead of her, nothing to do. She tried her grandmother, but the crisp message on Mary's phone said clearly yet elliptically, 'I am not here, please try later,' and in the background could clearly be heard the sound of Jasper or Cedric – one of the old roués who lived in her block of flats – saying loudly, 'Come on, Mary, we'll miss the train, old girl!' and another voice, also either Jasper or Cedric, saying, 'Have you got the cocktail shaker?' Since Mary had apparently told George and Angela the reason she was unable to spend the Easter weekend with them was that she was staying with a sick old friend in a nursing home near Oxford, Laura heard this message with something amounting to rage, and not a little admiration, too.

Jo, she thought with a start. I'll ring Jo, of course, haven't seen her for ages and ages – perhaps I could pop over there tonight and have a catch-up. She still hadn't seen the final photos from the wedding – gosh. That was a big deal with Jo, whose desire to record every moment of her life on film was only matched by Chris's. Paddy had predicted their first child would be called Pixel.

Laura sat down on the sofa with a cup of tea and dialled Jo's mobile.

It rang for a while, the ringtone rather strange, and then Jo's voice answered, muffled.

'Hello?'

'Jo?' said Laura, discomfited.

'Hello?'

'Jo, it's me,' said Laura. 'Hello?'

Jo's voice said brightly, 'Laura! Hello. What's up?'

'Well –' said Laura. 'I was just ringing to say hi.'

'Hi! Look, I can't talk for long, Laura. We're just on our way into the souk.'

'The what?' Laura asked, confused. She stood up and looked out of the window.

'The souk!' said Jo. She raised her voice suddenly. 'Chris, wait for me! Don't go in without me! And don't give that man money!' Her voice lowered again. 'We're in Marrakesh, aren't we.'

'You're *where*?' Laura said.

'Marrakesh! For ten days! Oh, it's so cool here, Laura, you'd love it.'

'I didn't know you were going to Morocco,' said Laura.

'No,' said Jo. 'I haven't seen you for ages, have I? You've been invisible lately, Laura. I emailed you last week but you didn't reply.'

Laura vaguely remembered some email from Jo, but she paid

little attention to emails these days, unless they were marked URGENT or were from 'Floyd, Dan'. The crackle on the line meant it was hard to work out whether Jo was pissed off or not, but Laura couldn't help feeling *she* was the one who should be cross, not Jo. Jo should have told her. She should have been in touch more. It wasn't Laura's fault Jo was out of circulation now, with her husband and her nice house. Lucky Jo, with her beautiful brown eyes, her pale heart-shaped face, her tiny frame, her sensible, neat ways, with a great job and an adoring husband. It wasn't fair.

Even thinking 'it wasn't fair' made Laura feel pathetically childish, but a small voice inside her was saying she had a right to be. It *wasn't* fair. But then, she thought, it was no more than she deserved.

She sighed, and leant against the window. 'Look, I'd better let you go,' she said, keeping her voice light and chatty. 'I'm sorry, I had no idea. You lucky things! Have a great time!'

'We are,' said Jo. 'Thanks, love. How are you, then? How's things?'

'Fine, fine,' said Laura hurriedly. 'All good. Let's do something when you get back, OK?'

'That'd be great,' said Jo warmly. 'We're back in five days – are you around on Saturday?'

'Not sure,' said Laura, hedging her bets, then hating herself for it. She cleared her throat. 'Yes. Yes I am. Let's do something then. Give my love to Chris, won't you? And don't spend loads of money on leather purses you don't need.'

'Hardly,' said Jo firmly. 'I don't fall for cheap sales tricks. You know me.'

Laura put the phone down, vaguely dissatisfied, and thinking she was right in feeling Jo had been a bit crap not to let her know. She checked her mobile in case Dan had texted whilst she'd been on the phone. Nothing. Nothing all weekend.

She told herself it was just a matter of time. Dan had told her he was biding his time, waiting for the moment when he could pick the big fight that would wrap things up. Laura was partly horrified by this tack, since there is not a woman alive who understands why men do that, and not a man alive who will voluntarily sit down and say, 'Look, we need to have a long talk about our relationship, touching on all points in order, including why I'm not more sensitive to your needs or aware of what I've done wrong.' No, Dan was waiting for Amy to crack – it was a kind of Who Will Blink First situation.

Laura still didn't know a) how often they were seeing each other, b) if they were sleeping together, and c) what the timescale was. In her happy, optimistic moments, when Dan was next to her in bed, his arms wrapped around her, she would answer a) hardly ever, b) of course not, they couldn't be, and c) any day now. In the bleak moments of reality, when a combination of she and Paddy, Jo and Chris, Hilary, Dan and assorted others (but mercifully rarely Amy, who preferred the company of her girl-gang in the flashier West End bars) were in the pub, she would gaze desperately at Dan as best she might without giving anything away, torturing herself and crying long into the night as she remembered how he hadn't looked at her, or had made a joke to someone else that he'd made to her the day before, then she would answer those questions differently. a) probably more than she realised, b) well, they might be, and c) she had no idea.

CHAPTER SIX

In May, Amy suddenly came out fighting. She started making plans for her thirtieth birthday in September. She let it be known that she wanted to hire a villa in Spain for two weeks, she and Dan, and have various friends fly out at different times, all gathering together on the middle Saturday for a huge party in the garden of the villa, which Dan was going to organise. She was back in the game. She even made an appearance at the pub.

Laura hadn't seen Amy for about six months. She had become, in her mind, this vast, beauteous Amazonian woman, with tiny stick-thin wrists and a huge expensive handbag and matching shoes. She was dazzlingly beautiful, terrifyingly confident, and she knew something was up with Laura and Dan. In Laura's nightmares, Amy walked up to Laura and dragged her by the hair out of the pub, pulled all her hair out, then kicked her into the road.

The trouble was, in these nightmares Laura kind of sided with Amy, not with herself. If she'd heard just the facts without knowing the details of it, she *would* side with Amy. But, she kept telling herself, just a little longer, and then it'd be over. And when she and Dan had been together for twenty-five years and were as happy as ever, no one would remember the slightly murky beginnings of their relationship. It would be lost in the mists of time, and Amy would be off married to a billionaire banker – it wasn't even as if she and Dan were happy, after all. She was doing her a favour, in the long run.

So when Laura walked into the Cavendish and saw Amy, as tall and beautiful and stick-thin as ever, sitting on the sofa laughing girlishly with Jo, and realised that she *was* the terrifying Amazonian beauty of her nightmares, and that she, Laura, was still – well, normal, normal height, normal hair, normal *everything*, it was all she could do not to walk out. Amy gave her a lizard-like, thin-lipped smile, which meant nothing, as Amy pretty much hated all girls, except her own, incredibly similar friends, who were kind of like the Pussycat Dolls mixed with the clique in *Mean Girls*.

'Hey,' said Chris as Laura came over to the bar. 'There's your tube buddy, Dan!'

'Hey, tube buddy,' said Dan, bending over to kiss Laura. How could he be so nonchalant, Laura wondered, as his hand squeezed her shoulder fleetingly and he kissed her on the cheek. 'Can I get you a drink?'

'Oh, a beer thanks, tube buddy!' said Laura. 'Hi, Jason. Hey, Chris. How was Morocco?'

'Haven't seen you since then, have we? Can't believe it. It was great,' said Chris, hugging her. 'Got some fantastic photos to show you! The girls are over there, go and say hi.'

The girls. Laura went over to where Amy and Jo were sitting. Jo jumped up immediately. 'Laura, hi!' she said, her eyes sparkling. 'God, it's so good to see you, babe! How long's it been? How long? This is crap, we mustn't leave it that long next time.'

'Hi, Laura!' said Amy. She looked down at Laura, both actually and metaphorically, thought Laura, and all three sat down again. Woah, what an evening of direness lies ahead of me, she thought. Dan put her beer down on the table and smiled at her. Amy leant back and caught his hand. He smiled mechanically at her, and released himself, walking back over to the bar to rejoin Chris. Laura didn't know whether to laugh or cry.

'I know we've had our problems over the past year,' Amy confided to Jo and Laura, an hour and a couple of drinks later. 'But lately, he's been . . . so different, I think he's realised.'

'Realised what?' said Jo.

'Oh, I really hope he's realised . . . Gosh, it's awful saying it out loud, isn't it?'

'Oh honey,' said Jo. She patted her hand. 'I know . . .'

Jo was no fan of Amy's either, but she was a far more tolerant person than Laura. Laura looked at her best friend, the blister of resentment that bubbled inside her building ever more. She was still cross with Jo, who had got back from Morocco and hadn't rung her – Laura had given in, after a few days' silence. In the old days, before this started, they knew everything about each other. Of course, Jo had no idea about her and Dan. But Jo hadn't even *tried* to have any idea. In Laura's addled mind, Jo was somehow to *blame* for not having supernaturally guessed her best friend's deepest, darkest secret, which she was going to endless lengths to conceal. But Laura thought she should have worked it out, should have known this huge, all-consuming thing that had happened to her. Laura was dying of love, hopelessly entangled, obsessed – couldn't Jo *see* that? Was she blind? Or just not the friend Laura thought she was?

'Well,' Amy blinked slowly, her huge eyes gazing at Jo with intensity. 'That, you know, he'll lose me. I'm going to finish with him if he doesn't shape up, and I've told him that.'

Laura looked round to see if Dan could hear any of this conversation. Chris and his brother were at the bar, talking to Hilary, but she couldn't see Dan anywhere. She turned back and looked at Amy, and suddenly felt the old hot flush of guilt wash over her. Oh god, this is awful, she thought, through the waves of agony this conversation was inflicting on her, not least of which was a huge dose of shame and mortification at her own behaviour over the last few months.

'Well, that's great, Amy,' said Jo kindly. 'I hope it works out, if that's what you want.'

Laura flashed her a look as if to say, We hate Amy, what are you doing? But Jo only glanced at her briefly in return.

'I really think it will,' said Amy, smoothing down her hair and smiling. 'I hope by then . . . well, I'm going to drop some gentle hints about what I'd like more than anything else for my thirtieth. If you know what I mean!'

'Great,' said Jo, taking a sip of her drink. 'Well, we'll just have to wait and see!'

'What?' Laura asked stupidly, thinking, What does she want? Some new shoes, probably, knowing Amy.

'Oh Laura . . .!' Amy looked at Laura as if she was a little alien, or a Mexican peasant unfamiliar with her ways, and Laura thought again to herself that girls who had been at school together many years ago and weren't friends should not be allowed to mix socially. It disrupted the natural order of things. She and Amy should be people who blanked each other in the street, not people who had to pretend to be pally and share bowls of olives in a gastropub. *This*, she told herself, was why she hated Amy, of course. It was *nothing* to do with the fact she was going out with Dan.

Amy delicately ate an olive, and licked one of her fingers. She smiled at Laura pityingly. 'An engagement ring, of course.'

A pip from the lemon slice in Laura's gin and tonic wedged itself in her throat and she nearly choked. 'Right,' she gasped, determined not to lose control. 'Right. Aaah. Aaaaah. Loo. Excuse me,' and she got up and stumbled outside, to the clear fresh air of the May night. She stood there taking big gulps of air, one hand clutching her throat, the other rubbing her stomach, a habit she had had since she was little. Right indeed. She looked in through the big glass windows of the Cavendish, over to the squashy leather sofas where her friends sat, and wondered how things had come so far, got so out of control, so ridiculous. She looked at Jo, methodically folding up her cardigan, neatly stowing it in her bag, and felt helpless. She felt a million miles away from her best friend, from those she thought she knew.

As if by magic, Dan appeared around the corner. He had been to get some cigarettes. He jumped when he saw Laura standing outside, and she nearly screamed.

'What the . . . what are you doing out here?' Dan said testily.

'Having a breather,' Laura replied, suddenly furious at him, especially at his tone. 'Listening to your girlfriend talking about her thirtieth birthday in September, how she wants us all to fly out to Valencia and watch whilst you *propose* to her in front of all of us – oh Dan, *Dan* . . .'

She started sobbing, great racking, heaving sobs that shook her, and Dan pushed her away from the window and against the shop next door. He put his arms around her, holding her so tightly she thought she might not be able to breathe.

'Now, listen,' Dan said, putting a thumb up to her cheek to wipe away a tear. 'I have been such a shit to you. And to her, but this is about you. I promise you, that is not going to happen. I promise you I'm going to talk to her in the next couple of weeks. This has to end. I can't be with her any more, I just can't stand it. And I want to be with you.' He held her tighter and kissed her. She could feel him growing hard against her leg. 'I want to be with you, do you understand me?'

'Yes,' Laura whispered. 'So . . . it's over with her, then?'

'Yes,' Dan said solemnly. 'Shit. I'm going to have to do something about it now, aren't I?'

'Yes, you are,' Laura said, hiccupping.

'Good. Now,' Dan bent down and kissed her again. 'I'm so sorry I've been so useless. It's not fair on her, or me, and especially not on you. We will be together, I promise.'

'You really promise?' Laura said, wanting a final reassurance.

Dan gripped her wrists and pressed himself against her. 'Shit,

Laura, I don't know what else I can say . . .' He looked around, shaking his head. 'I want you to believe it, I really do, but until I've talked to her I can't . . . if only there was some way.'

Laura said slowly, 'How about that holiday? In July? That one we talked about. Florida road trip? Ending up in Miami. Two weeks, just us.'

She looked into his eyes, and could see the glimmer of uncertainty – of something else, what was it? – there. He looked back at her, trying to breach that final gap between them. Laura started to turn away and Dan grabbed her again and said, 'No, fuck it. Book it. I'm just scared. But I'm being weak and crap. Book it.'

'Seriously?' Laura said, trying to stay calm, though a big smile broke out across her face. Dan laughed.

'Seriously.' He kissed her again. 'I mean it.'

He stepped back and the release of his weight on her made Laura feel light-headed. It reminded her of something she and Simon used to do when they were little, stand in a doorframe and press their hands out against the wood for a minute at a time, and then, when they stepped forward their arms would float above their heads, as if of their own accord, weightless, drifting, like feathers in the sky . . .

He walked back into the pub without looking behind him once, and Laura hung back for a few seconds. This was their usual routine. If someone she knew appeared, she'd just get out her phone and pretend to be texting. She turned towards the door, but as she was pushing it open, someone caught her elbow. She spun round, half with shock, and saw Jo behind her, standing on the pavement. Her face was pinched, her pupils huge.

'Laura . . .?' she said. 'Laura?'

'What?' Laura replied, completely calm. Nearly six months of this had made her a professional. She was certain Jo hadn't seen anything. She held up her phone. 'I was just texting someone, reception's terrible in there.' She gestured inside.

'What's going on?' Jo said, not reacting.

'Nothing, what do you mean?' Laura replied, slightly on edge. There was something about Jo's usually cheery, open expression that made her nervous.

'You're screwing Dan, aren't you?'

'What?' Laura said. '*What?*' she repeated. 'I wish. Come on, let's get back inside.'

'I saw you,' said Jo, advancing slowly towards her. 'I saw him kiss you, I saw you both just now. Laura, *Laura!*' The words were tumbling out of her, she looked distraught. 'What the . . . what the fuck are you doing? How long has this been going on? Does Amy know?'

'It's nothing,' said Laura, her self-preservation gene kicking in. 'Completely the wrong end of the stick. You know how matey we've become.'

Part of her wanted more than anything else to tell Jo, to confess all, to ask her best friend's advice. But she couldn't. She'd chosen it this way, and soon it would all be sorted out. Just a little while longer . . . if she could just hold her off for a little while longer. Jo would be pleased, she would.

But Jo wasn't showing much sign of being pleased for her now.

'I know what I saw,' she said. 'Oh Jesus. All this crap about you two being friends on the tube platform, that's how it started, isn't it? I *knew* you were up to something. But . . . Dan! Laura, I know you're a screw-up when it comes to relationships, but . . . not again! What the fuck are you doing?'

'Whatever I'm doing,' Laura said, feeling really angry, 'it's none of your business, so why don't you just butt out, OK?'

'Oho, no,' Jo said, coming right up to her, her brown eyes enormous in her pale face. 'It *is* my business, love. It's my business when my supposed best friend starts shagging our best man behind everyone's back, and then sits there in the pub pretending to be all matey-matey with his *girlfriend*. It's my business when my best friend lies to me all the time, and I never know where she is, and it turns out that's because she's having an affair with one of our best friends. It's my business when I send you an email saying I'm taking Chris to Morocco for a surprise to cheer him up because of his granddad and you send a long reply going on about how *fat* you think you are! And you never even call, you don't remember I've even gone!'

'I didn't –' Laura said, putting out her hands.

'You're not interested,' Jo retorted, her eyes filling with tears. Laura was horrified. 'You're just not interested in anything but yourself. And normally I wouldn't care, because you've done it before, but like I say – it's started being my business.' She took a deep breath. 'One more thing, Laura. It's my *business* when my *best friend* forgets my fucking birthday and Dan Floyd fucking drops a birthday card round from her that she's obviously bought at some *corner shop* when the two of you took a break from shagging each other senseless! You selfish cow! I can't believe it. Well, that's the awful thing. Actually, I can.' She stepped back again, collecting herself. 'I'm sorry,' she said. Screeching, Italian-style emotion was not Jo's normal mode of behaviour. She coughed. 'Yes. I'm sorry.'

'That's OK,' Laura said, shaking her head. 'Look, Jo –'

'No, let me finish,' Jo said politely. 'Look, Laura. I hate this. I'm sorry, but I always end up having this conversation with you! You're always doing this. Some guy, you think he's totally right for you, and you can't see what everyone else can see, because you're off in Laura Land making up some fantasy about it.'

'Shut up,' said Laura. She was furious. 'It's not how you think. You don't understand. It's complicated.'

'Listen to yourself,' Jo said. She pulled her handbag over her shoulder and folded her arms. 'You sound like every cliché ever. You're *not* Julie Andrews, Laura! And Dan's not fucking Captain von Trapp! Don't you ever learn? Don't, *don't* treat me like I'm stupid! God, Laura, what – what's going to happen?'

'Don't worry,' Laura said urgently. 'Look, Jo, I know it looks bad, but it's really not. We're in love. He loves me and I love him. He's leaving Amy, in about two weeks, he's just got to sort some stuff out. We're going on holiday. To Miami.'

There was nothing she could say to convince Jo, and she didn't even want to try that much. She didn't know what was going to happen or even what to do. So she just said, 'Look, let's go inside. Don't tell anyone, will you?'

Jo stared at her. 'Of course I won't,' she said eventually.

'Not even Chris,' Laura said anxiously. 'He really mustn't know, no one can know, Dan's really paranoid about it.'

'I'm sure he is,' said Jo. She opened the door. 'Fine, then. We won't talk about it.'

'Fine,' Laura echoed.

Amy was standing at the wide bar next to Dan, flinging her hair over her shoulder. She looked up as Jo and Laura walked in, both silent.

'Danny's getting some more drinks, girlies,' she called. 'Laura, Jo, what do you want?'

Jo didn't answer, she went over to Chris, bent over and whispered in his ear. Chris immediately got up.

'Actually,' Jo said, 'Chris and I have to go, got to shoot off. Really sorry. See you all soon,' she finished.

'Yeah, bye,' Chris called out.

No one else seemed to notice this remarkably smart exit except Laura, who stood at the bar feeling sick.

'OK?' Dan said, nudging her absent-mindedly, his arm still round Amy's waist. 'Do you want another drink?'

'I'm fine,' said Laura. 'I'm fine.'

Laura didn't talk to Jo about their conversation outside the Cavendish. In fact, they didn't really talk at all after that night. Over the next few weeks they met with the others, sat next to each other, had funny conversations, but the intimacy of their friendship vanished overnight. Laura didn't worry about it – well, she did, but she knew she could put it right at some point.

She kept telling herself she shouldn't feel guilty. Jo had totally overreacted, and, in fact, had been completely horrible, when she should have at least tried to understand. No, Jo was making the whole thing into some great big bitchy slanging match because Laura had forgotten her birthday, for Christ's sake! It was pathetic, that's what it was, and with things the way they were she didn't need anyone else being negative or unhelpful. So what if she missed her, if her hand went to the phone several times to call her or text her. So what if one night on the sofa with Paddy, *Dirty Dancing* came on and Laura was ashamed to find herself almost crying, because it was her and Jo's favourite film, and they usually had to talk to each other the whole way through, saying the lines together in unison. Sure, Jo was her 'best friend', but what did that really mean these days? Especially now she was shacked up with Chris, and hardly had time for Laura anyway, going off to Morocco and places without even telling her. It was fine, Laura told herself. She'd been a grown-up when Jo had got together with Chris. Jo just needed to calm down about her and Dan, and see what it was, that she loved him with all her heart. And then she'd be OK. There would be loads of time to patch things up afterwards, when she and Dan were properly together.

So when she should have been writing her yearly review for Rachel, Laura was booking the Miami holiday online. She extended her credit-card limit, then she took out a loan, not wanting to ask Dan for money. She spent the day sorting out cars and flights and hotels, emailing Dan to get his opinion, waiting in desperation for his replies, soothed and cheered when he would sign off '*I can't wait, I can't wait*', miserable when he didn't reply. And so it continued, the ringing, the texting, the secrecy, the desperate late-night arrangements that left her exhilarated, terrified, confused, happy, addicted. The holiday became their secret focus, and as the days lengthened and as May shifted into June, Laura didn't ask what was happening with Amy. They were going in July; she had put the – hefty – deposit down, that was all she needed to know. The itinerary was in her desk, along with the file of emails from Florida hotels and car-hire firms.

And then one day, without warning, the axe fell.

CHAPTER SEVEN

'Laura, can you come in here for a second?' came Rachel's voice from the office.

Laura finished the email she was typing, stood up and smoothed her skirt down. It was nearly the end of the day and she was starving. Paddy's birthday dinner was that evening and a whole bunch of them were going to an amazing steakhouse in Stoke Newington called Jean Michel's. Laura loved it there, it was food heaven, and in preparation she had eaten only a yoghurt and a banana for lunch.

She was in a good mood, too, though a little hung over. The previous night she had been out with Hilary, who had been ranting about Jo, because she thought Jo had been rude about Hilary's new boyfriend Richard, whom Hilary herself was pretty rude about too, but that didn't seem to matter. This ranting had been fuelled by Laura's incipient issues with Jo and a lot of cheap white wine, which was taking the whole day to wear off. Never mind, she told herself. In two weeks' time she and Dan would be on holiday, and everything would be sorted out.

Laura poked her head around Rachel's door. 'Hi,' she said.

'Hi, Laura,' Rachel said. 'Come in. Shut the door a moment, will you?'

Laura froze at this request, knowing from long experience

that the shut-the-door request either meant a promotion or something really bad. Usually something bad. She racked her brains, running through a list of options about what this could be as she pushed the door slowly shut. She'd done something wrong. Again. Someone had complained. She turned around, genuinely mystified, and then she saw a pile of letters on the desk in front of Rachel. Of course! It was pay-review time. They'd had an email about it yesterday. Laura sat down gratefully, sweating slightly, and promised God that when she got back to her desk she'd work extra hard, finish that report for Rachel she should have done two weeks ago instead of finding a hotel near the NASA Kennedy Space Center for her and Dan (Dan was obsessed with space, and wanted to spend at least a whole day there), which had been her original plan for the rest of the day.

'Laura,' Rachel said, smiling kindly at her. 'You OK?'

'Yes, sorry,' Laura said, slightly breathlessly. 'Just thinking about something. How can I help you?'

That sounded good, she thought. Polite, responsive, involved. They were big on being 'involved' where Laura worked.

'I need to talk to you,' Rachel said. She fiddled with one of the buttons on her cardigan. She was normally very much in control; this was odd. 'I've – I've been worried about you.'

'Oh?' said Laura. She crossed her legs and shifted forward in her seat, leaning attentively towards Rachel. 'What do you mean?'

'Is everything OK, Laura? At home?'

Laura felt as if she were in an episode of *Grange Hill*. 'Eh? You mean – with my mum and dad? Yes, of course it is.'

'No, I mean with you,' Rachel said, her smile remaining fixed. 'In your life. Is everything OK? No . . . problems?'

'No, of course not,' said Laura automatically. 'What do you mean?'

'Your behaviour . . .' Rachel trailed off, and then gathered

68

herself for the full attack. 'I'm afraid we are all rather concerned about your behaviour and the deterioration of your performance in the last few months. Laura, I have to ask you: Are you using drugs or alcohol in any way that might affect your work or home life?'

Laura's jaw dropped. The first thing that flitted through her mind, unbidden, was, How can you say that to me! I'm George and Angela Foster's daughter! I'm from Harrow!

She looked at Rachel, whom up until this point she had always thought of as a reasonably sane person, and blinked.

'No, of course I'm not,' she said. 'Of course I'm not.'

She assumed Rachel meant using alcohol in a *seriously* bad way, not the four white-wine spritzers she'd had the previous night with Hilary.

'This . . . this isn't about the pay reviews, is it?' she said weakly.

Rachel looked bewildered. 'No, of course not,' she said. 'This is what I mean about you, Laura. It's absolutely not about the pay review. Oh god. How do I say this?'

'What?' Laura said, feeling something, a cold clamminess seize hold of her. 'It's about the fundraising project, isn't it?' she said wildly, trying to throw some obstacle in the way, something that would stop the conversation going any further, something that would mean she had control over where this was going. 'I've nearly finished, honestly. I've got to speak to a couple more people, but since Easter was early I haven't been able to pin them down and —'

'Laura,' Rachel said quietly, putting her hand out towards her over the desk. 'We're suspending you.'

There was a silence, broken only by the sound of the printer whirring outside the door. Someone coughed, far away.

'Laura?' Rachel said.

'What?' said Laura. 'Are you serious? I mean – are you . . . What?'

'Laura,' Rachel said. 'I'm so sorry. I don't know what else to do. I think you're a great person to have on the team, and I've loved working with you – well, at least, I used to. But I'm afraid you – your – well, over the past six months or so, your performance has deteriorated so much that I'd – I'd –' She looked down at her notes. There was a pause.

'Just say it,' said Laura, sitting bolt upright in her chair.

'I'd call you a liability.' Rachel looked up at her again, and that's when Laura knew this was for real. She was composed. Cold, even.

'You're late. And I don't mean ten minutes late now and then. You're consistently late, and you never explain why, even though I warned you formally about it three months ago.'

'Rachel, but you were always being late when you were seeing Boyd!' said Laura.

'I was late once a week, on Mondays, because he lived in Nottingham and I spent the weekends with him,' said Rachel, and her voice quavered. 'But I made the time up, more than made it up. Laura, can't you see the difference?'

'But –' Laura said. It was true, she'd been getting in a bit later this year, but that was because Dan was working on a project at the moment that was nearer than before so he was getting a later train and she'd wait on the platform to go with him . . .

'It's not acceptable, Laura. You're getting in at ten every day when most of us have been in since well before nine. You take long lunches every day. You leave at five on the dot. Your absence report is staggering – do you realise you've been off sick for twenty-five days over the past year?'

'I was sick!' Laura gasped.

'No you weren't, Laura,' Rachel said. 'You just couldn't be bothered to come in. They were all on Fridays or Mondays. What were you doing?'

Laura remembered the Friday morning in January when she and Dan had been on the train platform, and Amy had rung

70

him to say her father wasn't well and she was taking the day off and going down to Dorset for the weekend. They'd looked at each other, there on the bench in the winter gloom, and Dan had grabbed Laura's hand, walked briskly out of the train station with her, taken her back to her flat and basically ravished her all day, all night, and for the rest of the weekend.

She smiled at the memory. She could feel her cheeks flushing. Dan went out of the flat once, on Saturday afternoon, to get some milk, and he brought back the papers and some roses for her. OK, they were nasty petrol-shop roses, but roses are roses.

'Things . . .' she said carefully, trying not to smile again. 'I know, I know,' she continued suddenly. 'I know I've been a bit crap. But – it's all going to be fine. When I get back from holiday – you know – oh, I wish I could say more than that, but I can't. I'm sorry, Rachel. I know I've been useless.'

'That's exactly it,' Rachel said, looking grave. 'Laura, look, the problem is you *don't* know you've been useless. You've had two formal warnings – this is your third.' She leant forward, her dark brown eyes huge, full of concern. 'That's why I have to suspend you. You're lucky you're getting that, you know. I should just be firing you, but oh, Laura, I think you're so good. I just – I just don't understand it!'

A tear rolled down Rachel's cheek. Laura watched it as it splashed onto her personnel file. Rachel went on, 'You're rude to the volunteers, you're hopelessly disorganised, nothing ever seems to get done. Four schools didn't have any reading programmes in place for the New Year just because you hadn't got the forms and police checks sorted out. And you know how desperate those schools were for help.'

'They –'

'And the fundraising,' Rachel said. 'You know we're looking for a big cash injection. You know how crap funding this year is. You were in charge of it, and you've done nothing about it, have you?'

'Well –' said Laura. 'Linley Munroe – Marcus Sussman – I was going to contact them for the . . . but then he . . .'

'Oh Laura,' said Rachel softly. She swallowed. 'It's just – I just don't understand why you, of all people . . . why you've lost interest, why you don't even seem to care.'

'I do care!' Laura said. 'I do. It's just . . . I've been crap.'

As she said it, she realised how inadequate the words were. How she was someone who'd always prided herself on getting the job done, not letting people down, how she'd scorned others for their blinkered approach, their inability to get off their arses and do something to make a difference to their lives, other people's lives. Over a hundred children, the ones who most needed some individual attention, some special reading time, had been let down by her. Money that people could use, that could really make a positive difference in someone's life, perhaps permanently – not there. Just because she never got round to it. Because she was thinking about herself. About her and Dan. And Amy. She was the blinkered one. She heard Jo's voice clearly in her head. *Don't you ever learn?*

'And the holiday,' Rachel was saying. 'You've never cleared it with me, never asked for time off. You know we have to clear it with each other. Everyone else in the office is away, I couldn't have let you go then in any case.'

'Well, I'm going,' Laura said stubbornly.

'I know you are, love,' Rachel said. She smiled sadly. 'It doesn't matter what you do any more. I'm suspending you, effective immediately, you'll be on thirty per cent of your pay and we're getting someone in from Lambeth to cover your job. Our school programmes finish next week. I want you to take two weeks to think about things. A fortnight from Monday, OK? And then we'll call you back in after the school terms are over and see where we are.'

'See where we are?'

Rachel shuffled the papers on her desk. 'Well. Where we

are with a view to reinstating you again. Or whether we have to . . . make this permanent.'

Surely this couldn't really happen, surely they were just threatening her? It was a bad dream and she'd wake up in a minute. She was a responsible person, a working girl, like all her friends. How would she explain it to them? To her parents? To her grandmother? She didn't get – suspended, it was ridiculous!

'But what will I tell – everyone?' Laura said angrily. 'You can't do this to me. You really can't, seriously. This is fucking ridiculous.'

'No, it's not,' Rachel said. Her voice was distant, unfamiliar, suddenly. 'I just don't get it, honestly I don't, Laura. I'd always thought you were one of the best, the brightest of all of us. I hoped one day you'd run the programme, or become an adviser, a consultant, perhaps even working with the Government . . . I honestly thought you could do whatever you wanted. Be someone who made a real difference . . .'

She left the sentence unfinished. Laura stood up and held the handle of the door in tears. She shook her head at Rachel, wordlessly. Rachel sighed, and looked at her.

'There's a boy somewhere at the bottom of all this, isn't there?' Laura heard her saying to herself as she ran out. 'God, there always is . . .'

CHAPTER EIGHT

Laura picked up her bag and fled, ignoring the pop-eyed looks of her co-workers. She rattled down the stairs and went outside, into the grimy, sweaty, traffic-laden street. It was a hot, muggy afternoon. She wiped her eyes on the back of her hand, and rummaged around in her bag for a cigarette – she'd put Hilary's cigarettes in her bag by mistake the previous night and though she hadn't smoked for a while, she wanted one now.

She stood there in the busy street, smoking, and looked around her, feeling totally alone. Whom could she call to explain this shameful and awful news, someone she could wail at, who would be genuinely surprised that this had happened? She'd been treated outrageously, that was for sure, she was bound to get sympathy.

And then, unbidden, came into her head the thought that she didn't know quite who to call. All her friends seemed so down on her lately. Jo and Chris – well, she was barely speaking to Jo, and she hadn't seen her on her own since their argument at the pub. Laura wasn't going to get into that at the moment. Paddy – well, Paddy had made it quite clear what he thought lately – he was always on her case about various things. Be on time. Clear up your room. Don't have sex with Dan in the shower and break the curtain rail. It was like living with a parent. Of course, she could call Dan . . . but she didn't really want him to know. Not just yet. She'd see them all that night, she'd have to tell them then anyway.

Laura leant against a signpost as the traffic roared past and the streets filled up with people leaving work. A tear slid out of one eye. She must be a pretty terrible person for it all to have come this far.

Well, she told herself, trying to perk herself up. She wasn't going back there, no matter what happened. How dare they treat her like that? How dare Rachel? When Laura had worked hard for her for three years, never complaining, staying late. Was it really a crime to screw things up and be late sometimes? Rachel was just a bitter old spinster, that was her problem. She didn't want anyone below her getting above their station. That was the answer. She . . .

And then, without warning, an image flashed into her mind, of Rachel turning up at her flat two years ago, the day Laura had sprained her ankle, really quite badly. She had got back from the doctor's with some crutches and was lying on the sofa feeling miserable and in a lot of pain. She'd called Rachel to tell her what had happened. Rachel had left work, gone to Marks and Spencer and bought the kind of things you can eat without moving from the sofa. Picnic eggs, crisps, freshly squeezed orange juice, raspberries, gin and tonic in little cans. She'd also bought her *The Castle* on video, which is the funniest film ever made, and they'd sat there watching it and laughing uproariously, until Laura felt much better again. And when Rachel had been dumped by Boyd from Nottingham just before Christmas, she'd never complained, never made a big deal about it, even though she was obviously devastated. And what had Laura done about it, to be a friend? Nothing.

Laura bit her lip and shook her head, willing the memory away. She felt tired and hungry, having eaten virtually nothing all day. She stood up firmly, swung her bag over her shoulder and marched towards the tube station with purpose. But the truth was she had no idea what she was doing or where she was going.

She didn't tell Paddy the truth. She lied and said she'd been sick and had come home from work early. She looked so forlorn and pale, in the heat, that Paddy obviously believed her as he stood there fiddling with his keys, looking down on Laura as she lay on the sofa.

'Are you sure you're going to be all right on your own?' he said anxiously.

Bile flooded Laura's stomach at her deception. She clutched her stomach and winced with real pain, and Paddy looked at her with compassion.

'Oh babe,' he said. 'Poor thing. Look, call me any time and I'll come home early if you want.'

'It's your birthday,' Laura said grimly, clenching her teeth. Bring the guilt on, she thought. I deserve it. 'Go away. Have a great evening. Give the others my love. I'll see you later.'

'OK,' said Paddy. 'Really sorry, babe.' He tightened the thin, patterned tie he was wearing and shook his head from side to side. 'Well, I'm off. Ladies, watch out. The birthday boy's a-comin'!'

He yelped and tried to moonwalk out of the sitting room. Laura heard him yelp again as he crashed into the hall table, and then the door closed behind him and the flat was silent again. She lay staring up at the ceiling, quite still, for a long time, and then she reached onto the floor and picked up the phone.

'Dan . . .' she said. 'Yes, I know. Yes, I know. Listen! Can we meet tomorrow? I know . . . yes, me too. No, not for that. Paddy's in. No, he's in tomorrow, we can't. No, I want to talk to you. About the holiday. And things. Where . . .? Where? Oh, OK then. Is it on Rathbone Street? Yep. OK, see you – yes, see you there. Me – me too. No Dan. OK.'

*   *   *

Laura was still on the sofa when Paddy got back. The flat was stifling hot, it was a humid, sticky evening. The TV was on, there was a nearly empty bottle of Sauvignon Blanc rolling around on the floor, and an empty packet of pistachio nuts. Most of the shells were also on the floor, although a few had made it into the bowl. She was fast asleep, left arm over her stomach, her right arm dangling over the sofa. Two nut shells were glued to her breastbone. Paddy stared at her for a minute, then crouched down and threw a pistachio nut at her face.

'Wha—?' Laura said thickly, blinking rapidly. 'Paddy? What – where am I?'

Paddy rocked back on his heels, then stood up. He turned away from her. 'Get up, old girl,' he said softly, and pulled the blinds down. 'Time for bed. Go on.'

He followed her as Laura shuffled into the corridor, clutching the empty wine bottle.

'Did you have a good time?' she asked blearily. 'How was it?'

'Good, good,' said Paddy, and even half-asleep she could tell he was quite drunk. 'Good, good, good. Missed you though, everyone did. How're you feeling? Any better?'

Laura looked down at the wine bottle in her hand, then up at Paddy. 'Er . . . much better, thanks.'

'Did Dan come round?' Paddy said blankly.

'What?' said Laura, still clutching the bottle. 'Dan?'

'Did he come round?' Paddy repeated, and he blinked.

'No!' said Laura. 'I wasn't feeling well.'

'Right,' said Paddy. 'I know.'

Laura said, 'I didn't miss your birthday so I could stay in and get Dan round, you know.'

He said nothing, but nodded at her.

'I didn't,' Laura said obstinately, but she almost didn't believe herself.

'Sure,' said Paddy.

'I promise. Hey, Paddy.' She put her hand on his. 'Seriously, man. I wouldn't lie about that.'

'I know,' said Paddy, but it wasn't convincing. He raised his hand in greeting, turned and went into his room, and Laura was left standing on her own in the corridor.

Her brain was juddering into gear. How has it come to this? she thought, curling her fingers tightly round the neck of the bottle. How can things have got to this? She thought about her date with Dan tomorrow, about what she was going to do, and her resolve strengthened. Right, she said to herself, going into the kitchen. That was the last time. The last time I lie about something, the last time I hurt the people who really love me. She threw the bottle into the recycling box in the kitchen, and stretched, yawning. Her eye caught sight of a curling photo on the fridge. It was of her, Simon and Paddy at Simon's fourth birthday party. Mary crouched down beside them, holding a cake alive with four candles. Simon's cheeks were puffed out, and beside him sat a smaller but identical Paddy and Laura, aged five and six respectively, their faces agog with the action. It always made her smile.

It made Laura smile then, comforting in its familiarity, and she turned out the kitchen light and went into her room. She didn't clean her teeth or wash her face, she simply fell into bed and pulled the cool sheets up and around her. She was going to take action tomorrow, she was going to do something to pierce the bubble that she'd been living in, to face up to the truth and let the real world in again. So she could get on. So she could get over it. Her last thought before she fell asleep again was, If I can get through tomorrow, I'll be fine.

CHAPTER NINE

Early evening, and the heat of the day hung over the city. It was inescapable, both in Laura's flat, which was airless and oppressive, and out on the street where it was dirty and bad-tempered. The city smelt, not of the delicious smells of summer in London, mown grass and barbecues and cigarette smoke and petrol, heat rising from the ground. No, tonight, on this unbearably hot Friday night, it smelt of sweat, stale beer, a whiff of dustbins and people. Too many people.

Laura stood against the upholstered pad by the stairs of the bus as it lurched its way from the cooler, leafier roads of North London down into the heart of the city. The bus was sweltering, crowded, uncomfortable, and she grew angrier and crosser as it jolted down Oxford Street.

She was late to meet Dan. Even though she'd had nothing to do all day, even though no one knew she wasn't in work, not even Paddy. No one had called, no one had noticed her absence from email or the phone. She had sat in the flat all day, talking to no one, eating nothing, smoking a lot and thinking about this evening with an increasing sense of dread. There was no one she could talk to, anyway. No one who knew how badly she'd fucked up, and she wanted it to stay that way. And no one who knew about her and Dan – apart from Paddy.

Throughout the day Laura's mind swam back to the scene in the sitting room late the previous night. She had to make it up to Paddy somehow. And Jo. Yes, Jo too. She had enough on her plate at the moment, though. No, she'd sort this situation out first, and if it worked out – a big if, but she knew it would, it had to this time – then at least, no matter what else happened, she and Dan Floyd would finally be able to tell everyone they were in love, they were a couple, and Amy was history. If she could only get off this horrible bus. Laura ran her hand over the back of her neck. Her hair was twisted up in a clip, but her neck still felt sweaty. She leant against the wall, and the bus lurched forward, jolting her into a hot flush again.

'Why the hell do they heat these things in summer?' she muttered, then realised the perfectly normal nice girl next to her had moved away, clearly thinking she was one of those crazy bus people who feel the need to carry on conversations with themselves. The heat of the walls seemed to burn the backs of her legs, and the prickly synthetic upholstery she leant against made her want to itch all over. All the windows were open – tiny, mean slivers one had to pull down with a bang. But no fresh air came in and there was no breeze to cool her down.

Laura sighed. She shut her eyes and tried to pretend. It was two weeks' time. She was in Florida somewhere, on a beach with Dan, wearing a kaftan and her cool new pink jewelled flip-flops. The heat was unbearable, but it was OK, she could go inside to the air-conditioned terrace bar and get a drink with lots of straws and sparklers in it. And lie on the cool linen cushions, feeling the material crisp and crunchy beneath her back. She and Dan were walking along the beach hand in hand. It was night, and the sound of music and chatter could be heard in the near distance. Dan stopped, pulled her to him, and said, 'Darling, I love you – will you –'

'Get out of my fucking way!' someone behind her finished, and Laura turned, alarmed, and realised she was standing in front of the exit. A woman pushed past her, shoving Laura out of the way, and a steady stream of people followed her, all tutting at Laura.

Thankfully, the next stop was hers. She swung her bag over her shoulder, avoiding the eyes of her fellow passengers, and hopped off the bus. 'That idiot girl there,' someone said as she left.

Laura walked briskly down the street, her heart racing, and turned off into Rathbone Place. Halfway down she slowed and leant briefly against some railings. This was all wrong, she thought to herself. She was supposed to get there calm and collected, she was going to be strong and cool (but yet devastatingly attractive), not some dishevelled sweaty heap, who arrived late for a summit meeting with her quasi-boyfriend having been suspended from her job the previous day. No, she was not that person. Not any more. She clenched her fists, stood up, and marched on her way, down the dark, grey street, pleasantly cool, away from the heat in the evening shade.

The Newman Pie Rooms was above a pub, the Newman Arms, tucked away off Oxford Street. It was one room, decked out in old-man's-pub traditional style, with a few tables and a board on the wall announcing what pies were on offer that particular day. It was one of Laura's favourite places – Dan had taken her there on one of their first evenings out together. It was a great hidden secret, and, more to the point, certainly not the kind of place you'd ever catch Amy in.

Laura's legs shook slightly as she climbed the rickety twisted stairs, but she reminded herself once again that this choice of location for their summit meeting must be a good thing. Dan was reading the paper, but as he caught sight of her he leapt to his feet, folded it up and shoved it into his back pocket. He smiled at her, his eyes huge, drew her into his arms, kissed her and hugged her, tightly, for a long time.

'Hello babe,' he said, resting his forehead against hers. 'How are you?' He smoothed the hair away from her face, and tucked it behind her ear.

'I'm fine,' Laura replied, smiling back at him. She wound her arms round his neck. 'I'm OK. Yeah, fine.'

'Good,' said Dan, looking over her shoulder. 'Sorry . . . no, it's fine. So you're really OK? I missed you, baby. I really missed you.' He pulled her down onto the bench next to him, and casually put her hand over his crotch.

Laura smiled at his cheek, still the same Dan as ever, and looked at the menu board. 'Yep, I'm really OK,' she said, pretending to ignore him, but moving a little closer.

The couple at the next table looked at her distastefully.

'Perhaps I should move there,' said Laura, pointing at the chair opposite.

'No,' Dan said, and kissed her ear gently. He whispered, 'Please, I want you near me. Who knows when it might be next?'

'Well,' said Laura weakly, 'that's what we need to talk about, kind of, isn't it?'

Dan was looking at the menu board this time and didn't answer. He snaked his arm around Laura, and gently cupped one of her breasts. Laura wriggled with pleasure and nerves. This wasn't going the way she'd anticipated. She leant into him, gave into it.

'I missed you too.'

'Hm?' Dan said. 'I'm having the lamb and mint pie, what about you?'

Food. A day spent at home mulling over her problems and failing to come up with solutions had not calmed Laura down one jot. It was twenty-eight degrees outside, more inside, and she was feeling fairly emotionally fraught. She had eaten very little that day, and had actually been sick before she came out. A lamb and mint pie was not really what she was in the mood for.

'Um,' she began, knotting and unknotting her hands in her lap. 'I'm not that hungry, you know. I feel a bit funny. I might just have a salad.'

82

'Really?' Dan looked at her as if she was insane. 'You're OK, aren't you?'

'Yes . . .' Laura said, beginning to be slightly irritated that the question kept being asked yet not followed through. She steeled herself and put her hand on Dan's wrist. 'Look at me.'

He turned to face her.

'I am fine,' she said. 'I'm really fine, in fact. But we need to talk. There's . . . things we need to discuss. Tonight.'

Dan looked slightly alarmed.

'Right. Why aren't you hungry?' he said after a pause.

Bemused, Laura attempted to stick to the point she was trying to muddle her way through to, without actually saying, '*I was sick earlier today because I've been suspended from work, and this is driving me up the wall.*'

'I'm not . . . it's just . . .' She stumbled a bit, and Dan looked even more apprehensive.

'What?' he said. 'Laura, what's wrong?'

'Nothing. Well, I was a bit sick today, but that's normal . . . nothing. Look . . .'

Dan's reaction to this news was unexpected. His jaw dropped and he gaped at her, then gasped several times as if short of breath.

'You were sick?' he said. 'Why?'

Laura wanted to be touched by his concern, but he was looking genuinely horrified. She found it a little off-putting. How could she explain everything to him? Why couldn't he understand?

'I . . . well. I haven't been feeling too good. Lately.'

'Are you . . . ill?' Dan said, his jaw muscles clenching. 'Have you been off work?'

'Well . . . actually, I have,' Laura said. 'Something's happened. That's what . . .' she swallowed. 'Things are going to be difficult over the next couple of months, Dan,' she said softly. 'That's why I have to know what's going on with us. I have to know, I can't do it any more.'

She sat back in her seat, shaking with adrenalin, and reached out to take his hand, but Dan put his head in his hands and was silent. Laura watched him, a growing sense of unease welling within her.

'Fuck . . .' Dan said eventually. 'Oh fuck.' He looked up again, and ran his eyes up and down her body. 'Just tell me. Tell me the truth. You're . . . fuck, you're *pregnant*, aren't you?'

A waitress had materialised beside them during this sentence. She let out an involuntary gasp.

'Shall I come back?' she said, glancing from one to the other and looking ultra-curious.

'No,' said Laura, slightly maliciously, though it was only afterwards she recognised the emotion for what it was. Dan was sitting stock still, staring into space. 'Fuck,' he repeated.

'I think we're ready to go here,' Laura said calmly. 'Can I just have the Greek salad, please? And Dan – you want the lamb and mint pie, don't you?' No response was forthcoming, so she nodded to the waitress. 'Yes, he'll have that, and some broccoli, too, please.'

'Another beer?' said the waitress, gesturing to Dan's pint.

'I think so,' said Laura briskly, 'and can I have a bottle of house white, too, please?'

'One bottle?' said the waitress incredulously. 'For you?'

'Yes, please,' said Laura airily. 'I've got a bit of a wine head on, you see. When you need a drink, you just need a drink, don't you!'

'Hm,' said the waitress, looking appalled, and she strode off towards the bar, beckoning the barman over towards her and instantly engaging him in whispered conversation, which involved staring blatantly at the happy couple and the rolling of eyes.

Dan awoke from his semi-coma with a start. He stared at Laura, and rubbed his chin. Laura stared back at him, and her heart melted again. He was so gorgeous, with the day or two's growth of beard, the tanned, chiselled face. Their children would be beautiful, if they took after their father, there was no doubting that. However . . .

'How . . . when?' said Dan hoarsely. 'Not you . . . Fuck, this is . . . Laura, you swore you were on the pill. Have you told . . . How? When? Why did you . . .'

Laura looked at his face again. The questions, the accusations, the problems ahead. And she was glad, glad it wasn't true, glad she wasn't giving Dan this news.

She put her finger on his lips. 'Why the fuck would you think that?' she said, half-laughing.

Dan didn't smile. He looked even worse, if anything.

'You stupid man,' she said, laughing a little as the waitress returned with the drinks. 'I'm not pregnant, did I ever say I was?'

'*She's . . . not . . .*' the waitress hissed over their heads, gesturing towards the barman at both of them, her finger waving wildly and shaking her head.

'You're not?' Dan said. 'Really?'

'Really,' said Laura dryly.

Dan licked his upper lip, which was dewy with sweat, and said hoarsely, 'Thank god for that.' He slumped back into his seat and took his drink, almost sullenly. 'Thank god. Sorry, Laura love, but you had me there for a moment. The timing . . . not good.'

'I didn't say . . .' Laura began, then broke off. She patted his arm. 'Calm down, Dan. I wouldn't do that, I'm not stupid.'

Dan took a huge swig of his drink. 'No, you're not,' he said simply. 'That's one of the things I've always loved best about you, you know.'

'Me?' Laura said, taken aback. 'Really?'

'Yeah,' Dan said, fiddling with a beer mat. 'You know. You're so . . . just smart. You know? You make things better. You're organised. You do that job, you know. Help all those kids, give them a better start and shit. And the way you organise things, remember everyone's birthdays, all that stuff. It's . . . it's . . .'

85

He put his pint down and turned to her, and Laura was astounded to see he had tears in his eyes.

'It's . . . it's just always better when you're in the room.'

Laura had often wondered, since the fifth day of bumping into each other at the station and chatting away till they missed two trains, when Dan had said, 'This is ridiculous. Tomorrow let's meet fifteen minutes earlier. We can have a coffee. Yes?' and she had trotted down onto the tube platform to find him waiting for her, a smile of welcome on his face, holding a coffee he'd bought from the stall in his hand for her, what exactly it was about her that he apparently liked so much – so much that he was willing to risk such a lot for her, for himself. And now she knew. She was dependable, she was nice. She was organised. She got the job done. A set of more prosaic, no, *boring*, qualities, she thought, it would be difficult to find, and had she been displaying any of those qualities lately? No, absolutely not.

She swallowed, trying to look on the bright side, and immediately an image flashed into her head of Amy, stunning, slim Amy, reclining at home, flicking through a magazine, gingerly blowing nail varnish dry on one tiny fingernail. Wearing some exquisite lace and silk nightgown, specifically for lounging around in, probably.

She looked at him, swallowed again, and gripped the side of the table. She knew the moment was coming, inexorably she could feel it creeping towards the conversation, like a marching beat.

'Thank you,' she said.

'I mean it,' Dan replied. 'When you're around . . . I just feel better. You look after me. The way you . . . you make breakfast, for instance, you remember I like to put the Marmite on myself.' He ran his hands through his hair. 'That sounds crap, but you know what I mean. You listen to me if I've had a bad day.'

And how many times have you ever asked me about my day? Laura suddenly thought. It was a straightforward question, but suddenly she couldn't think why she hadn't thought it before, six, seven months before. How many times? She wanted him to see her as the unattainable, the alluring woman of mystery, who drove him to the edge of distraction, not . . . not this. Pleasant. Kind. Ugh.

'. . . And you . . . I don't know. You care about me, I can tell you stuff. And Amy – she never . . . well, to be honest, I just think that's why we don't . . .' He stopped suddenly.

'She never what?' Laura said sharply.

'Well, she's never that interested,' Dan said, almost in a rush. 'She's just completely self-obsessed. You know what she's like. This bag. That dress. How expensive is this or that because I can only buy it if it's ridiculously overpriced.'

His tone was angry, almost vicious. He rubbed his hands over his eyes, like a little child.

'Sorry,' he said, and turned to her. 'I'm just really tired, that's all.'

He stared at her, almost hungrily. 'Oh, Laura. I know we need to talk, but . . . can't we just leave? Go back to yours? You know . . .'

'No!' said Laura, much more loudly than she'd meant to, and Dan jumped, as did the middle-aged American couple at the table next to them.

'Right, then,' Dan said, smiling at the couple, who obviously thought Dan and Laura were mad. He handed them a bar towel to mop up the beer that the husband had spilt, and gave them a charming smile. Laura did too, and found herself thinking, What a great couple we make. 'No!' she said again, more to herself, and the wife jumped again.

Dan stared at her and said, slightly impatiently, 'Laura, what's going on with you? You're behaving like a schoolgirl who's afraid she'll be caught for bunking off or something, darling. What's up?'

Laura took a deep breath. 'What's going on?' she said, holding her nerve. 'With us. I want . . . er . . . I want some answers.'

'Well,' Dan said. He ran his hands through his hair again. 'Darling, I've told you. Well . . . god, you know how I feel about you . . .'

'It's not enough,' Laura said gently. 'It's not enough any more. Dan, we're going on holiday in two weeks' time, for god's sake! And you're supposed to be leaving Amy before that. You – you know how I feel about you. This has been going on for – how long is it now, seven months? – and we're nowhere nearer being together than we were at the beginning of it. It's not enough. We have to sort out – sort it out. I'm – I'm in love with you. It's killing me, this is. We have to sort it out. Otherwise . . .'

Laura trailed off. She didn't know what the otherwise was, or at least it was too terrifying for her to come out with. She looked around the room slowly, and let her eyes come back to Dan, to see how he was taking this, but her nerve failed her.

'Otherwise . . .' she said softly, and lowered her head again.

Dan held her head in his hands, lifted it up and looked at her. He looked serious, more serious than she'd ever seen him.

'Laura . . .' he said. 'There's something I have to tell you. I didn't want to, but you're going to know sooner or later. God . . . I can't believe I'm doing this to you.'

'Wait a minute,' Laura said.

'No, let me finish,' Dan cut in. His hands were clammy against her cheeks. 'I didn't want to tell you tonight, I just wanted to see you, for us to have a nice evening, one last night.'

Laura's stomach clenched and she felt sick again.

'What?' she said quietly. 'Dan, what is it?'

'Amy's pregnant, Laura.'

Dan released his hands, and Laura could feel the sweat on the sides of her face. He was quite sweaty in general, she thought, as if watching this scene idly from another room, another life.

'Laura, are you listening?' Dan said sharply.

'Yes . . .' Laura cleared her throat. 'You . . .'

Her eyes filled with tears, and one ran down her cheek. She

gave a tiny cough, almost a gasp, and sat up straight. No, she wouldn't cry. She would *not* cry.

'Laura . . . I wanted to tell you, I've been trying to . . .'

'How pregnant?' Laura said calmly. 'When's it due? It's yours, I presume?'

'Yes, of course,' Dan said. 'Of course it's mine.' He wiped his hair off his forehead. 'It's . . . it's due in January.'

'Three months,' Laura said after a moment, calmer still. 'She's three months' pregnant. How long have you known?'

'About a month. Laura, I've been trying to find a way of telling you. I couldn't . . .' Dan punched his fist into his thigh, quietly. 'I – fuck. Look, it's a mistake, she did it on purpose, I – I don't know what to do, but I've got to – we're going to make a go of it, I have to. Of course I have to.'

Amy. Of course it wasn't a mistake, Laura thought. Amy was as likely to accidentally get pregnant as hippogriffs and unicorns were to be found wandering in Hyde Park. She had planned this down to the last letter and Dan, Dan – oh god, Dan was the sacrificial lamb, and she, Laura . . . she had to leave. She had to leave, or else break down completely.

Dan was wringing his hands, quite literally clutching them in an agony of inaction. He touched her arm. 'Laura,' he said. 'I know you must hate me. But believe me, I hate myself more. I can't – I've completely screwed this up, my whole life up, and hers. And yours, and that's – that's worst of all, because – oh god . . .'

He broke off, and buried his head in his elbow.

'I'm going to go,' Laura said, and again she had the sensation of watching herself from another room, from afar, and that other person was cheering her on, saying, Well done, girl, you're doing well.

Dan grabbed her arm as she reached for her bag. 'Listen, Laura. Listen to me, just one thing before you go. Please.'

Laura turned to face him, and looking at him nearly broke her composure, but she steeled herself.

89

'Look, Laura,' Dan said. 'I realise . . . it's over now, you and me.'

'Well, I kind of assume so now,' Laura said, repressing all emotion and taking refuge in heavy sarcasm. She removed his hand from her arm, shaking slightly. 'It's one of my rules. Practically the last one left that I haven't broken, actually.' She laughed bitterly, feeling the breath catch painfully in her throat as she did. 'Don't carry on shagging someone who tells you he's in love with you and that he's going to leave his girlfriend, then gets his girlfriend who he was supposed to be dumping six months ago pregnant, and makes you realise the whole fucking thing was a pack of fucking lies.'

She stood up, and pulled her bag slowly up onto her shoulder. 'Bye, Dan,' she said. 'Bye.'

'It wasn't a pack of lies,' Dan said, as she turned to go. 'If you want to punish me, you've got your punishment. I love you. I always will. I never lied to you, Laura.'

He put his hands flat down on the table. The left one had a scar across the back, where he'd sliced it in a powerboat when he was six. Laura looked at it, and thought, I knew that. I know he got that scar in a boating accident when he was six. I don't know anything else. Nothing at all.

She tried to think of something to say back to him, something grand, something great, something worthy of Carrie Bradshaw or Barbra Streisand in *The Way We Were*. But there was nothing to say, and the moment wasn't about that any more. There was nothing for her to do but leave, and as she stood in the frame of the doorway, she half-waved at him, and turned and quietly walked down the stairs again.

CHAPTER TEN

Laura's other granny, who had died ten years previously, was very much like her son George. Deidre Foster was a paragon of respectability, her home a shrine to suburban living. When the neighbours put their house on the market in 1980, the potential crisis of unruly or undesirable new people next door almost sent her into a decline. Hers was the only home in which Laura had ever seen a knitted toilet-roll holder. She had vases screwed into the walls with dried flowers in, a tasteful landscape photograph printed on canvas and framed in gold above the (fake) fireplace, and two tea services: one for everyday, and one for Sundays and special occasions.

Deidre had a saying for every occasion, it was her stock-in-trade. This one predictable trait offset the others, made her more likeable, more human sometimes. It was an instinctive emotion in an otherwise reserved woman, this desire to soothe, to mend, to make things better. 'Hold your head up high, and don't let them see you cry.' 'It'll all come out in the wash.' 'Better safe than sorry.' 'A stitch in time saves nine.' 'More haste less speed.' (That one, in particular, had never made any sense to Laura.) 'Too many cooks' and so on. As Laura and Simon grew older, they had become squirmingly predictable, a sign for each of them to avoid the other's eye and stuff their fists in their mouths so as not to laugh. They had never seen the point of them, never listened between each of those lines to what lay beneath – their grandmother's desire to help, to give advice, to rationalise a world she sometimes found baffling and could not talk about for fear of breaking down and betraying herself and everything she had built up to be important.

As Laura marched briskly out of the pub, she paused for a split second at the door, clutching the old brass handle, her hand smearing the metal with perspiration. Her vision blurred as her eyes filled with heavy, painful tears. She knew he would be watching out of the window as she left. She had to hold her head up high. She couldn't let him see how hurt she was. This wasn't Mary and Guy, and their early morning moment in the pyramids, this wasn't it at all. It was all a lie. She was Granny Deidre's granddaughter; she would repress all her natural urges, bite down her feelings and walk calmly under the window where Dan would be watching, away from the moonlight glow of the lamppost on the corner, up Rathbone Street till she could safely turn the corner. And then she could collapse, and scream. *Hold your head up high, and don't let them see you cry.* Granny Deidre had said that to Laura when Laura was being bullied by a particularly vicious girl at junior school. It was good advice then, and it was good advice now.

Legs shaking, eyes still filled with tears, Laura walked along the street, up Conville Place, past the cafés where people were sitting and enjoying the evening's warmth. A man at a table on the corner raised his espresso cup to her and nodded as she turned left and headed down into Mortimer Street. He raised his eyebrows as Laura stopped, put the ball of her hand flat against her lips and cheek, and breathed deeply, expecting the tears to flow.

But they didn't. She couldn't cry. It was as if she were in a shock so sudden she didn't know how to react. The clarity of her mind startled her. It was over with Dan, there was no question that it wasn't. There could be no reconciliation, no

92

'I've changed my mind', no 'I'm leaving her'. Amy was *pregnant*, and whatever happened between them, Laura had to be out of it. She was surprised, she noted with detached interest, that she could see it with such clarity, that it wasn't mired for her in a welter of excuses and what-might-have-beens. No. It was over.

Laura strode down Mortimer Street, welcoming the cool breeze that played around her shoulders and the back of her neck after the unbearable heat of the restaurant. Ahead of her stretched the city, unfurling into relaxation, gently welcoming, quiet and warm and beautiful. She passed the wide, dark driveway of the ornate Royal Marsden Hospital, and carried on walking.

She probed her feelings delicately, like a child touching the cavity of a newly lost tooth, to see how it hurt, where it hurt, how much. It was strange, foreign to her, she didn't know how to deal with it, and so she kept on walking into the night, along the wide street, the branches of the trees that lined it gracefully dipping and framing her in the quiet breeze.

She had lost her job. She had lost her best friend. She had lost – she winced suddenly as she thought of it – nearly all the money she had in the world on a holiday she now wouldn't be going on. For what? For a golden dream, a sweet, stupid boy with a beautiful smile. For that. For someone who had never even given her any definite idea of his commitment to her. He loved her, she knew that. He was going to leave his girlfriend, she knew that. But how and when and what would happen after that – she had never had any idea.

Laura had reached Regent Street. She looked about her, bewildered at the purr of sudden, slow-moving traffic. Down to her left lay the lights of Oxford Circus, the permanent chaos and snaking crowds of people visible to her even now. To her right loomed the ascetic outline of All Souls Church and Broadcasting House behind it. Ahead lay the white-faced formal squares behind Oxford Street. Where was she going? She didn't know. She couldn't face Paddy or being at home just yet. She just wanted to walk.

So she did. She crossed the road and carried on, through the impersonal grandness of Cavendish Square, past Coutts, past the Wigmore Hall, along the jumble of shops and mansion blocks on Wigmore Street. She kept a steady pace, not swerving or stopping, just walking, looking ahead, pounding the streets, trying to walk herself back into sanity. She had to keep on going; it was rather like being very drunk and trying not to throw up in the back of a cab or a bus that was speeding you safely home, wishing with all your heart you could be outside.

She walked until she could see the vast space of Portman Square and the back of Selfridges looming up ahead of her. She didn't know what to do then – didn't want to go towards the roaring hustle of a main road. She could go and see Mary, she thought suddenly, and then her heart sank. No, of course she couldn't. This wasn't the kind of situation her grandmother had ever found herself in. Better to keep on walking. So she ducked right, up the Georgian Duke Street to gracious, leafy Manchester Square, past the Wallace Collection, its windows black and unblinking. She turned into Manchester Street, and crossed the road.

Suddenly a car swerved around the corner and nearly smashed into her. It missed her by a hair's breadth, and the driver swore at her and sped on, not even pausing. Laura fell against a car, and ricocheted slowly off it so she was sitting on the edge of the kerb in between two parked cars.

Then she cried; consumed with the shock, the loneliness, the feeling of terror that had flashed through her. She cried silent great heaving sobs, fat tears spilling out of her, dropping between her legs into the gutter. She felt totally alone; powerless, with nowhere to turn. She was bone-weary, flattened. And, most of all, she felt stupid.

Amy was *pregnant*. She and Dan were going to have a baby, an actual live baby. *This* was reality, not the dream world she, Laura, had invented for herself about it all. How could she have been so naïve, so stupid? What was she doing?

Laura ran her hands through her hair, riding out the jerking sobs that racked through her. As they subsided, she breathed out, and a juddering, blubbery sound escaped her that even she, in her darkest hour, found strangely funny. It made her smile to herself, a wobbly smile. She chewed her lip, still sitting on the edge of the kerb, and sat motionless for a moment. When was the last time she'd actually had a relationship based on reality, instead of some completely invented fantasy she'd written in her head? In her stupid, silly, romantic head.

The calm after her crying was cathartic. Laura stood up slowly, her legs shaking, and took a deep breath, feeling as if she was breathing properly for the first time that night. She exhaled again and closed her eyes. So far so good. It was deathly quiet on the street, and nothing broke the silence. She started walking again, more slowly.

But emotional exhaustion is a curious thing; it can be as debilitating as physical exhaustion. Suddenly she was tired, dog-tired, and when a black cab swung into view a few seconds later she hailed it gratefully, and sat huddled in the back, staring blankly out of the window for the journey home. She crawled up the steps to the flat, vaguely stabbing at the front-door lock with her key more in hope than in expectation of being allowed in. She was back at home, in her flat, and beyond thinking about anything else she knew she was safe again. She wanted to sleep, that was all she could think about. For once in her life she didn't know what she was going to do now, and she was too tired to let the thought surprise her. It was over, and she was going to sleep, and beyond that Laura didn't care about anything any more.

CHAPTER ELEVEN

Laura couldn't remember going to bed. She didn't remember much, and when she woke up it was early Saturday afternoon. Which meant that she had slept for around twelve hours. She had no job to go to on Monday, no friends, no money, no Dan . . . She rolled over and closed her eyes again. Her pyjamas were sweaty, and so was she. She tried to think about the previous night, reached for her phone to check for messages, and then swallowed and gripped her hands into fists. She wasn't going to. She felt nothing, nothing at all, and she closed her eyes again, and sank back into an exhausted, defeated sleep.

When Laura woke up again, it was later in the afternoon and she realised she was starving. She pulled on her jeans and, zombie-like, went downstairs to go to the shops round the corner. She was stumbling back, clutching in her arms a paper, some crisps, some wine and some chocolate, when she felt dizzy and thought she was going to collapse. When she reached home, she leant against the wall of the communal hallway, unsure how she was going to get up the stairs again, feeling so totally alone and sad she didn't even know how to respond to her own feelings. Should she cry? Scream? Yell? Smile bravely? She didn't know, she was simply sick of the treadmill in her head going round with the same old thoughts over and over again. What was she going to do now?

What she really wanted to do, Laura realised, was curl up under the pigeonholes and go to sleep for a year. Would anyone notice, would they care? No. And she deserved it. More than anything, she realised helplessly, she wanted a shoulder to cry on, and the reason she had no one was entirely her own fault.

Laura gritted her teeth. She would go upstairs. She would.

Back on the fifth floor at last, she fumbled for her keys, and the door behind her opened. It was Mr Kenzo, who lived in the flat opposite.

'Laura!' he cried at her back, as Laura held her haul from the shops in one scooping motion and tried to turn the key in the lock. The paper and can of coke slid out of her hand, and the sections of newspaper feathered across the floor.

Laura stared at them, and tried not to cry. She bent down, as Mr Kenzo also bent down, tut-tutting, and folded them deftly up.

'My dear, my dear,' he said, handing them and the can back to her. 'Are you OK? You look not well, let me tell you.'

'Thanks,' said Laura blankly. 'I'm going in now,' and she turned away and tried to unlock the door.

'Do you need some help?' said Mr Kenzo, unfazed by her rudeness. He stepped forward, and took the key from her. As he turned it in the lock, it was pulled open from inside, and Mr Kenzo half-fell forward into Paddy's arms. Paddy had opened the door and was watching them both with bemusement, his hands in the pockets of his dressing gown. Laura just stood there, numbly holding her things, not wanting to go in or stay out, not really caring. Paddy looked at her and gave a grimace of concern. He pulled his hands out of his dressing gown and scratched his long, thin nose, then set Mr Kenzo back down on the ground and said heartily,

'Sorry, Mr Kenzo! How are you? Helping Laura out there, are you?'

'Yes, yes,' said Mr Kenzo, clasping his hands rather nervously – he found Paddy rather hard to read, clearly being from the school of thought that said men should work with their hands and sit around in cafés waving those hands and yelling at their friends, rather than opening the door in the early evening in a dressing gown and jeans, unshaven, with long, messy hair.

Mr Kenzo gave Paddy a packet of crisps. 'She dropped these, take them please.'

A voice on the stairs said cautiously, 'Er – James? Laura?'

Not really caring who it was, Laura turned for the door again, but the expression on Paddy's face stopped her. He was smiling in a dazed, stupid fashion, and running his hands through his hair.

'Becky!' he said. 'Hi! Hi-ya!'

Becky-from-downstairs, who was still very much the object of Paddy's affections, appeared on the landing. 'Hello, Mr Kenzo,' she said, not at all ruffled by the strangeness of the scene in front of her. She shifted her bag on her shoulder. 'Hi, James – er, someone's signed for this recorded delivery, and they pushed it through my door, and I think it's for you.' She held out an envelope bearing the legend 'Ticketmaster' on it.

'Oh, yeah!' said Paddy, leaping forward and taking the tickets from Becky. Laura watched as he gave her a super-enthusiastic smile. 'Thanks. Thanks Becky! Yeah, that's great. Just my . . . er . . . it's my, er, Snow Patrol tickets. Yeah!'

'It's your tickets for *We Will Rock You*, isn't it?' said Laura, with an interested expression.

'Queen?' said Mr Kenzo. 'Ah, fabulous.'

Paddy kicked her in the shin, and Laura took this as her cue to leave. 'Thanks again, Mr Kenzo. Bye, Becky.'

'Er, bye Laura,' said Becky.

She pushed past Paddy into her own corridor, turned and said again, 'Sorry, Mr Kenzo.'

Mr Kenzo's creased face smiled kindly at her. 'Why you saying sorry? You are having bad day. Go in. And look after her,' he said confidentially to Paddy, as Laura stared blankly at him, wondering if perhaps he were the Angel of Death.

'Thanks again,' Paddy said to Becky. He swivelled from her to Laura, standing in their hallway. 'Er . . .' he said.

Becky smiled at him expectantly. Laura cleared her throat.

'I'll – see you around, Becky,' said Paddy. 'I'd better go in. That's really kind of you. Great, thanks again.'

As the door slammed behind him, Paddy turned to his flatmate in the corridor with an exasperated expression. 'You're awake. At last! I didn't know where you'd gone. You've been asleep all day, you know?'

'Yes,' said Laura, walking towards her room. She stood in the doorway. 'I'm going back to bed. I don't know when I'm coming out again. Go after Becky, Pads. Ask her out. And when you get back, if anyone calls, tell them I'm not here.'

'Laura –' Paddy was looking after her, a plaintive expression on his face.

'Sorry, Pads,' she said.

'But –'

'Leave me alone,' said Laura, a sob rising in her throat, batting her hand at Paddy, who was standing incredulously in the corridor watching her as she walked away. 'I'm so tired.' She said it almost to herself. 'I just want to sleep. Just leave me alone.'

Laura went back to bed. She ate the food she could eat without leaving the bed. The wine she left – it wasn't a screw-top and she couldn't face getting the corkscrew from the kitchen. She ate a Crunchie bar in two mouthfuls. She was too tired to read the paper. She picked it up, scanned it, but the story about a school of orphans in Zimbabwe made her cry again, so she threw the paper on the floor and turned over, facing the wall, tears rolling across her face. The salty, MSG flavour of the crisps was around her mouth, and she licked her lips, sniffing. She closed her eyes.

About an hour later there was a knock at the door.

'Laura?' came a voice tentatively.

Laura opened her eyes, but said nothing.

'It's me,' said Paddy. 'Look. Are you OK?'

Laura chewed her lip, praying he wouldn't come in, banking on a bloke's natural aversion to crying women. This was particularly strong in Paddy, sweet though he was in other ways.

'What's wrong, Laura? I'm . . . I'm worried about you!'

Laura pulled the duvet over her head as tears filled her eyes again.

'Look,' said the voice again. 'I'm going out now. I don't want to bother you. I'm not going to come in. Will you just say "Yes" now to let me know you're alive and you haven't been attacked or anything?'

It was a good tactic. Laura patted the duvet away feebly with her hands, and said quietly, 'Yes.'

'Right,' came Paddy's voice, sounding relieved. 'Look, darling. I'm sorry about whatever's happened. Is it Dan?'

'Yes,' Laura said. 'Don't. Don't worry.'

She didn't know why she said it, except she really didn't want Paddy thinking she was actually dying or something. It was her problem, not his, poor man.

Paddy said cheerily, 'Oh. Well, you'll sort it out, I'm sure. I know you, Laura! You know what you want, don't you?'

There came no answer, so he said, 'Well, bye then,' and seconds later Laura heard the front door slam. She lay there quietly for a moment, then put a pillow over her head and screamed, as hoarsely and loudly as she could, till the urge to shout had gone out of her and she was crying quietly again until she fell asleep.

All through Sunday, Laura slept or lay in bed feeling sorry for herself, not moving. She didn't have anything to do, and she had absolutely no one to answer to, and all she wanted to do was hate herself a little bit more, and the solution to that seemed to be to lie festering in a hot, sweaty bed, with greasy hair and greasy fingernails and skin, feeling achy and uncomfortable. White saliva remains crusted in the corners of her mouth. Her breath smelt rank. That day she ate only a packet of crisps and another chocolate bar. Her stomach rumbled, she felt alternately sick and hopelessly weak, with head-rushes every time she sat up or turned over. Her pyjamas were bunched up around her, uncomfortable, twisted in the baggy sheets. She left her room twice, to go to the loo, scuttling each way like a crazy person so she didn't see Paddy. She heard sounds of him moving about, a television on in the sitting room at the other end of the flat, but he didn't come near her and for that she was grateful. She just wanted to be alone, to feel as totally rotten as it was possible to feel, to push herself as far away from the hopeful, deluded girl who ran out to see Dan every week with smooth silky tanned legs and clean, shiny hair.

She slept fitfully, and she kept dreaming. She dreamt she was running to tell Dan something, but she couldn't get to him; though her legs were long and she was running as fast as she could, she never seemed to make it any further. She dreamt Dan was lying next to her, his arms wrapped around her, and that he was kissing her neck, her shoulders. She dreamt he had texted her to tell her it was all a mistake, but each time she woke up and checked her phone there was nothing. She dreamt she was on holiday with Dan and Amy and her friends, in a huge villa somewhere, and she could hear them laughing but didn't know where they were, where any of her friends were.

Early on Monday morning she was awake, gazing around the room, looking at the detritus of her self-incarceration through the grey haze cast by the curtains. By this time Laura had been in her room for over two days, and she was starting to freak herself out. But the thing about self-loathing is it stops you from taking the smallest of steps to make yourself feel better – even tying your hair back in a ponytail, or opening the window for some fresh air. She desperately wanted to get up, get out of bed, have a shower, but she couldn't. It was easier to lie there and not do anything. She couldn't go in and talk to Paddy. He'd told her all along she was stupid for seeing Dan! She couldn't tell her parents; the shock of the whole sorry mess would kill them. She couldn't call Jo, though she desperately wanted her wise, sanguine best friend's advice. Of course she couldn't call her – imagine what she'd say! Imagine how she'd enjoy it. And then there was the job, the money too . . . Laura closed her eyes again, and realised that perhaps of all the lows over the past couple of days, this was probably her lowest moment. She didn't even have the energy to cry, and somehow that made it much worse.

She thought about what she had to do now, and the enormity of it overwhelmed her. Fix things, fix things left, right and centre. And then, in the middle of it all, get over this man. Straight away. Laura knew she'd been stupid, but three days on, she still knew Amy's pregnancy drew a line under their affair once and for all. There was no way they could carry on. She wouldn't even have wanted to, even if Dan had left Amy for her. No, it was over. Apart from the baby, being with Dan had effectively ruined her life. She *had* to understand the consequences of a bad relationship.

When she looked across the months to come, long Dan-less months of not sharing things with him, telling him things, being with him, her stomach clenched in sharp pain and her heart beat so loudly in her chest she felt it might burst. It was over. And so was that part of herself. When she thought about how she'd misjudged it, how she'd run ahead and fallen in love with him without stopping to look at whether he was the person she thought he was – well, she wanted to kick herself. Except this wasn't the first time and she knew enough to recognise she'd done it before. One thing was for sure, though: it was the last time.

Yes, the last time she'd fall like that. Absolutely the last time. A clean slate. A smooth, glowing feeling washed through Laura, stopping the cramps in her stomach. A clean slate, a project, someone to be, a new her. She looked past the grey-blue curtains at the crack that let the sunlight in. Yes, the good feeling persisted. She would be someone new. That was the only way to be. She was going to change.

Laura's problem was that she kept casting men in roles they weren't suited for. Just as, aged sixteen, she had cast Mr Wallace in the role of a Pre-Raphaelite-esque musician when in fact he was a rather weedy, nervous, weak man unable to withstand the breathless attention of a budding, pubescent girl. Just the same as she had been with lovely Josh, for a year before Dan, casting him in the role of decent, kind house-husband, the perfect partner, the modern male, when – what was it that she had actually loved about him, really? Laura tried to think, and couldn't come up with the answer. He was a great man – kind, funny, clever, hard working – but there was no way he was the man for her, she realised now. Why hadn't she seen it? And why hadn't she seen it with Dan? Why had she learnt so little from her time on earth and not bloody seen it at all with Dan? The man she'd cast in the role of ultimate love of her life, Mr Dependable, ride-off-into-the-sunset-with soul mate. Well. Hah.

The sun was growing brighter. Laura swallowed, tasting a bitter, mouldy fur on her tongue. She sat up, her hands on her knees, and was considering what to do with this newfound zeal – whether to convert it into something by taking the first of a thousand small steps and jumping in the shower, or whether to lie back and think about it some more. What should she do? The energy of the question fazed her, and she would have probably lain back down and closed her eyes again, a fatal tine of the fork to take, when, thank god, fate intervened.

Laura didn't know what happened first, the sight of it or the sound, but as she was sliding back down under the duvet again there was a sickening *thump* noise, and the window flew into a million pieces, hitting the curtains and flying past, hurling fragments onto the bed. A pigeon landed at Laura's feet. Dead. Or dying.

It took a few seconds before Laura realised the person screaming loudly was her, and it was involuntary, her first involuntary action of the last two days. She couldn't move. She sat staring and screaming at this twitching, bloodied pigeon, its feathers scraggy and ugly, its red-pink worm-like claws convulsing on her duvet, as Paddy burst into the room.

'Stop!' shouted Laura. 'Don't come any further! There's glass on the floor – STOP!!!'

Paddy slid to a halt, inches from a huge dagger-shaped shard of glass.

'Fuck! Fuck me!' he yelled. 'What the fuck! Laura! What have you done!'

The pigeon twitched again. Laura suddenly heard her mother's voice saying (every time she wanted to feed pigeons in Trafalgar Square or Piccadilly Circus), 'They're flying rats, dear. Vermin. Crawling with fleas and god knows what else.'

'Get away from me!' she said incoherently to the pigeon. 'Fuck! Off!'

Paddy calmed down before she did. He looked from the broken window, where the curtains were fluttering plaintively in the summer breeze, across the path of devastation wrought by the flying glass, now in a shower across the floor, to the bed where the pigeon lay a couple of feet from Laura, who was surrounded by feathers, blood and glass, as well as crisp packets, cans, chocolate wrappers and bits of paper. He said, slowly, 'I think you should get out of there. Where are your slippers?'

'Don't know,' said Laura helplessly. She added, 'I don't wear them in summer. They're too hot.'

'Oh good grief,' said Paddy. 'Flip-flops?'

'I don't know,' said Laura. 'Oh – there.' She pointed at her chest of drawers, below the window, which was covered in glass, and below it a collection of glass-strewn flip-flops.

'Wait there,' said Paddy, and he trotted lightly down the

corridor, returning with a pair of wellington boots which he used for fishing trips (last year's Paddy craze).

'I'm going to throw them gingerly at you,' he said.

Laura looked at him. 'What does "throw them gingerly at you" mean?' she said crossly. 'Just throw them. Don't knock me out. And don't – urgh! Oh Paddy – urgh. Don't throw them at the pigeon. Urgh!'

Paddy had prided himself on his spin bowling at school, and indeed was reckoned to be rather good at it. He tossed each welly in the air, and miraculously each landed, in a slow, spinning arc, in Laura's outstretched hands. She pulled them on and climbed out of bed. Stepping around the glass and rubbish by her bed, she leapt across the mound of it by the door, and landed next to Paddy.

'Er . . .' she said, not knowing how to ask. 'Paddy . . .?'

Paddy stepped forward and gently picked up the dead pigeon. He dropped it into Laura's wastepaper basket, and picked the receptacle up.

'Cup of tea?' he said.

'Yes,' said Laura. She pulled her hair back and tied it into a ponytail. 'Yes, yes please.'

'Going to buy a new duvet and bin?' said Paddy, as he pulled the bedroom door firmly shut behind them.

'Oh, you bet.'

It was Paddy's last week of term, so he left for work a while later, by which time they had had several cups of tea, called a glazier (Laura), deposited the pigeon in some newspaper and a bag in the rubbish bins outside (Paddy), and donned rubber gloves and begun the work of – once again gingerly – collecting each piece of glass that had managed to spray itself remarkably widely around Laura's room (Laura). By the time the glazier showed up after lunch, Laura had showered and dressed and had stripped and washed her sheets. She threw away the duvet – she knew it was wrong and a waste of the world's resources, but it was almost fetid AND covered in dead pigeon. There was no way she'd ever sleep with it again, she knew, and no amount of boil washes could clean it for her.

The glazier was a short, squat man, who looked as if he had been born in blue dungarees. He was called Jan Kowolczyk.

'Well, well,' he said when Laura came to check on him after a little while. 'Nearly finished here, young lady, then all will be good as new again.'

Laura nodded. She agreed. It was all part of it, she knew. Her feeling of having been evangelically cleansed. She had had her time in the wilderness, and A Sign had come to her to show her The Way. Sure, it was a disease-ridden pigeon, and it had almost given her a heart attack, but she had felt and interpreted its symbolism as keenly as if she were an A-level student reading Emily Brontë for the first time. And she knew what she was going to do next.

'Thank you,' said Laura, smoothing her long, black linen skirt down with her hands and then clasping them lightly in front of her. Her hair was clean and soft, tied up in a neat ponytail which brushed the back of her neck. The breeze through the window blew gently across her face and chest. She felt so in control now. She glanced around the room, her eye falling on the bookshelf, piled high with her own books and videos, the self-indulgent ones she daren't have out in the sitting room. It was an unspoken agreement between her and Paddy. *The Godfather* and *Spinal Tap* were out in the sitting room, along with various thrillers and classics and the usual clutter of shared possessions. But each flatmate kept their own personal tastes to their bedroom. So Paddy's room had all his weird sci-fi and fantasy novels, his *Buffy* and *Angel* boxed sets, whilst Laura kept all her Georgette Heyers and her romantic comedy videos in her room.

She looked at them affectionately, the rows of pink and purple plastic video-box covers and the lines of paperback books, their spines cracked with repeated rereading. An idea came into her head, one so terrible she shrank from putting it into action, but she realised that to make a fresh start she would have to. She gazed unseeingly at these architects of her doom. Really, she could blame them for a lot of what had happened. Putting ideas in her head. She needed a different role model now. Perhaps she didn't need them any more. Perhaps – no, that was a bit too extreme, wasn't it?

Her eye fell upon an old hardback of *Rebecca*, at the end of the shelf, and she picked it up, idly leafing through the pages. Maybe it was time to read it again. She needed cheering up.

Laura adored *Rebecca*, it was one of her favourite books. She loved the poor, unnamed Mrs de Winter with a passion, wanted to be her, and desperately loathed evil Rebecca, whom she saw in her mind's eye as looking very much like Amy. And Maxim . . . well, he was the embodiment of everything a romantic hero should be . . . in every way. Brooding, dark, passionate, brusque – just perfect, and she . . .

Laura brought herself up short. The breeze through the window picked up and she suddenly felt her blood run cold, as Mr Kowolczyk the glazier whistled quietly in the corner.

That's it. You see? she said to herself. *This* is why you're in so much trouble. Get a grip! Mrs de Winter was a complete idiot! She should have married some nice banker from Cheam and lived a nondescript life with him instead of falling head over heels in love with Max de Winter, driving around Monte Carlo, weeping hopelessly over people and fleeing burning buildings. There, right there, was a symbol of what she was doing wrong. She, Laura Foster, would not behave like that any more. She would emulate someone else instead. Mrs Danvers, in fact. The good old reliable housekeeper.

At this idea Laura felt her heart beat faster. Yes, Mrs Danvers. OK, she was a bit mad. In fact, you could call her a homicidal maniac with an obsession with a dead person, namely Rebecca, and an unpleasant penchant for appearing silently in doorways. And she was a pyromaniac. But – but, Laura thought, as this idea took root – at least she wasn't a fool. She was neatly dressed, ran the house beautifully, moved silently, and was always in control of her emotions. It was so true, Laura couldn't believe she hadn't seen it before. Mrs Danvers was the kind of person one would do best to follow (well, up to a certain point), not useless Mrs de Winter, who bleated and cried and kept saying things like, 'Oh Max, what shall we do? Oh Max, I do love you so much! Oh Max, I have just fallen over as I have no spine to support me.' No, Mrs Danvers knew keeping the house in order was best. Keeping yourself busy. Putting aside bad things. Having respect for one's friends and family. OK, perhaps sometimes in a rather extreme way. But it was as good a place to start as any. As Laura ran through the list of broken fences she had to mend, she felt slightly sick, and then suddenly she realised what she had to do, whom she had to see. Not just because she ought to, because she actually wanted to.

Laura straightened herself up. She smoothed down her skirt and pursed her lips.

'May I get you a drink, Mr Kowolczyk?' she asked politely. 'A cup of tea, maybe? Or can I offer you some coffee?'

She gave a thin smile, and raised one eyebrow, as Mrs Danvers would. Mr Kowolczyk looked at her, somewhat bemused.

'What?' he said.

Laura came to. 'Er, sorry, sorry,' she said, collecting herself hurriedly. 'Just – er. Coffee? Tea?'

'Yes, coffee please,' said Mr Kowolczyk. 'Three sugars. Look –' he waved vaguely towards the window with his chisel, and smiled kindly at her. 'Fresh air, yes? Nice to get fresh air into your room.'

'Oh, yes,' said Laura darkly, nodding at him. 'Fresh air. Oh yes.' She paused in the doorway, and gave him another cold smile, before gliding (she hoped) smoothly down the corridor to the kitchen.

'Thank you,' Mr Kowolczyk called out.

Laura reappeared in the room. 'Er, I've just realised I have to pop out in about five minutes,' she said in her normal voice. 'Will you be OK to finish up by yourself, and let yourself out?'

'Of course,' said Mr Kowolczyk. 'Going somewhere nice?'

'Yes,' said Laura, standing in the doorway. She smiled at him. 'I'm going to see my grandmother.'

'That's nice,' said Mr Kowolczyk. 'Good girl. She old lady? You see her a lot?'

'She's amazing,' said Laura. 'And, no, I haven't seen her a lot. Not for a while. I think that might be part of the problem.'

'What problem?' said Mr Kowolczyk, but she had disappeared again.

CHAPTER TWELVE

So, just before lunchtime, Laura rang on the doorbell of Mary's flat.

'It's me,' she said nervously, when the well-known, rather imperious voice of her grandmother said, 'Yes?' over the intercom. 'Your long-lost granddaughter, come to reintroduce herself to you.'

'Goodness gracious,' said Mary. 'This is a surprise. Come up, darling, come up.'

Laura had walked a lot of the way, enjoying being outside. But now she was tired, her early enthusiasm waning, and she felt naked and exposed being out in the normal world again. She kind of wanted to go back to bed, but stiffened her sinews and climbed the stairs up to the second floor. There, in the doorway, a gin and tonic in her hand and a smile on her face, was her grandmother.

Mary Fielding was still as beautiful at eighty-four as she had been thirty years before. She carried her age with an elegance that owed nothing to expensive clothes or fine airs. She could tap-dance, she could sew, she adored Elvis and cowboy films, and she spoke five languages. She was the best grandmother ever, all in all, and as Laura saw her standing there she knew she'd been right to come.

'It's been far too long,' she said, as Laura came towards her. 'You're practically a stranger, darling. Good grief,' she added, as she saw Laura's face, 'what's happened?'

'Everything,' mumbled Laura, wiping her nose inelegantly on her hand. 'I'm sorry I've been so crap, Gran. I haven't seen you for ages.'

'No,' said Mary, 'but you're here now. Let's get you a drink. Come inside and tell me all about it.'

Laura sat on the grey velvet sofa, a drink in her hand, not knowing how to start or what to say next. She was feeling infinitely calmer now she was inside Mary's flat. She looked around the room, thinking briefly how much it reminded her of all of her life – more, in a way, than her parents' house in Harrow where she'd grown up. The photos on the wall; the drawings that each of them had done as children framed in a clip-frame above Mary's bureau; the tusks and knickknacks; Guy's pipe in the corner of the room. Legacies of a life spent together crammed into this flat for one person.

'I'm sorry I haven't seen you for ages,' she said awkwardly, breaking the silence.

'Me too,' said Mary. 'Well, you're here now, darling.'

'Don't you want to know why I'm here?'

'Of course I do, if you want to tell me,' Mary said, lowering herself into the chair next to the sofa. She looked across at her granddaughter.

Laura clutched the wide base of her tumbler, feeling the ice cool her hand. She looked up, out of the window at the identical apartment building opposite, then down away towards where she had just been walking. Through the open window, the sun was shining, and the purr of early afternoon traffic sounded in the distance. From the balcony upstairs she could hear the sound of laughter.

'Jasper and his boyfriend – they've just got back from Skye,' Mary explained.

'Right,' said Laura, even then amused by the comings and goings of the inhabitants of Crecy Court.

Mary took another swig of her drink, and looked expectantly at her granddaughter. Laura shifted in her chair.

'OK. Shoot,' said Mary, who had a particular fondness for the early oeuvre of Clint Eastwood.

'Well – I've messed everything up,' Laura said calmly. 'And I don't know what to do.'

Mary leant forward in her chair, her earrings glinting in the sunlight.

'I'm sure it's not as bad as all that,' she said. 'Now, my love, suppose you tell me about it, and we'll see what we can do?'

'It is bad,' said Laura. 'The worst.'

'Well, you're still alive, I'm still alive. I got a postcard from Simon in some small village in Peru today, so clearly he is still alive, and when I spoke to your mother an hour ago she and your father were still alive, so that's not true, is it, darling? Come on,' she said, crossing her capri-pant-clad legs. 'I'll just sit here, and you tell me in your own time, how about that?'

So Laura told her grandmother absolutely everything, safe in the knowledge Mary wouldn't judge her or frown or be shocked. As she finished, culminating in the dinner at the Newman Pie Rooms, the retreat to the bedroom, and the pigeon, there were tears running down her cheeks again.

'I'm sorry,' Laura said, trying to breathe properly. 'I just . . . god.'

Mary smiled at her granddaughter. She put her smooth brown hand under Laura's chin, and wiped away a tear with her thumb.

'My darling girl,' she said. 'Stop crying. Stop it. From what you tell me I imagine you have had the luckiest of escapes. Now, dry your eyes, and sit still, and I'll get you another drink. It's over now, don't you see? Isn't that wonderful?'

'What?' said Laura, wondering what on earth she could mean. 'It's not wonderful. I feel like a complete fool. I've lost my best friend; I've lost my job; I've behaved like an idiot.'

'I think it is wonderful,' said Mary, standing up. She went into the kitchen. 'You fell in love, well, that's wonderful. All right, it was with completely the wrong man. But it's over now, and the best of it is no more secrets. No more living your life in half-shadow, which is what it seems to me that you've been doing these last few months.'

'Yes,' said Laura, staring into the gloom of the kitchen. 'I hadn't thought of it like that. But – I'm always doing it, always falling for the wrong person. I'm so stupid.'

'No, you're not,' said Mary. 'You just haven't met the right one yet. And until then, at least you're not lying to everyone you know any more.'

'I know,' Laura said. She squirmed a bit in her seat. 'But . . . I know this sounds awful, but –'

'What?' said Mary.

'I quite liked all of that,' Laura confessed. 'The secrecy. The drama of it. If I'm completely honest, I think that was partly it. Isn't that awful? That's what makes me feel so bad about it all. What a nasty person I must be.'

It was dreadful, when she thought about it with the tiniest bit of hindsight, to admit this was the case. That a small part of herself was such a masochist, so enjoyed putting herself through all of this. That she liked hearing sad songs on the radio and staring gloomily out of the window late at night. Liked the tears in her eyes as she walked home of an evening, thinking about how much she loved Dan and how great they were together. It was so adolescent.

'Laura, darling, every woman does it at some point in their life,' said Mary. 'You're not a nasty person. You're an honest person. You've absolutely shown how incompetent you are at cloak-and-dagger stuff, my love, and that's wonderful too. It's not in your nature, Laura, it never has been. You've always been honest, since you were a tiny thing. It's best that way. Let me get another drink.'

'It's boring that way,' said Laura.

There was silence from the kitchen. Laura thought her grandmother hadn't heard her.

'I mean, it's such a boring way to live your life,' she said.

Mary appeared in the doorway, holding two more gin and tonics. She put them down on the raffia mat at the centre of the table. She put her hand on Laura's shoulder.

'Darling, never say that.' She spoke quietly. 'Never say that. Living an honest life is the best gift anyone can have, believe me.'

She sat down heavily in the wicker chair.

'Really?' said Laura.

'Really,' said Mary firmly. 'Besides which, I think you may have had a lucky escape. No, listen –' because Laura's expression was mutinous '– honestly. This way, you'll come to realise you were better off without him. I promise, you will.'

'Don't, Gran,' said Laura. 'I know. I know. It's just – really hard.'

'It's true,' Mary said. She drummed her fingernails on the table. 'You never got to the next stage, thank god. The stage when you're together with him, and both of you are walking down the street, and a girl walks past who looks exactly like – whatever the girlfriend's name is, what is it?'

'Amy,' said Laura.

'Yes, exactly,' said Mary, as if this was further evidence. 'And instantly the guilt starts up in your mind. The recriminations. Is he looking at her, is it awkward, does he still find her attractive? Does he think he made an awful mistake?'

'Well,' said Laura.

'It's a life half-lived. That's what you would have had, believe me.' Mary drained her drink. 'And that, my darling girl, is not your destiny.'

'Well –'

'Trust me.'

Laura didn't know what to say, but something about her grandmother's expression told her further questioning would be dangerous. After a few seconds Mary sighed, and smiled, and the twinkle reappeared in her eyes.

'You are a very great girl, Laura darling, you do know that?'

Laura didn't know what to say, it seemed such a completely untrue remark, apart from anything else. So she was silent.

Mary watched her, and she said, 'I know you don't think so, but you are. I am so proud of you, of the way you are. Guy would be so proud to see how you've turned out, you and Simon.'

'Hardly,' said Laura. 'He'd disown us. Well, me. If you can disown your step-grandchildren, which I don't think you can.'

'You're not listening,' said Mary slightly sharply. 'I am proud of you, Laura, and do you know why?'

'I am listening. Why?' said Laura, hastily swallowing some more of her drink.

'Because the quality you castigate yourself most about – your tendency to fall in love with the most inconvenient people – is what I love about you, darling.'

'Oh, Gran,' said Laura, trying not to sound impatient. 'That's just not true. It's awful – I should get a grip, not –'

Mary interrupted her. She banged her ringed hand on the arm of her chair, as if she were Elizabeth I inspecting the English fleet. 'No, darling. You have a great capacity to love. Be careful. Use it wisely. But be proud of it. So much love in your heart. That's why I worry about you.'

She coughed. Laura listened, relieved to be talking about it at last, but not really knowing what to say.

'I worry you will walk away from that. That this will close you up, make you forget how wonderful falling in love can be. Don't.'

'Are you saying I should go out there and pull the first man I see?' said Laura, trying to make light of it.

'No, no,' Mary shook her head crossly. 'Just – promise me, darling. Don't run away from it, not now.' She closed her eyes briefly. 'I worry that you will. That's all. Now, tell me,' she said, changing the subject and lifting the glass to her mouth and holding it there. 'If you have nowhere to go on holiday next week, might this mean that you want to keep me company with your parents in Norfolk? And that you'll be there for my birthday lunch? Which, darling, I note you would have missed otherwise.'

Laura's hand flew to her mouth.

'Oh shit,' she said. 'Sorry.'

'What's that?' Mary said, alarmed.

'Holiday.' Laura croaked, then stood up. The buried memory of her financial situation came rushing back. 'Holiday. With Dan. All booked. Have to cancel. No insurance.' She sank back into her chair.

'Well,' said Mary. 'Ain't that a pretty pickle.'

'No one in a western ever said that, Gran.'

'Yes they did.'

'What am I going to do?'

'I'll lend you the money,' Mary said instantly.

'No,' said Laura, shaking her head slowly. 'No. I got myself into this mess. God. I'm going to get myself out of it. And then I'm never, ever looking at another man ever again.'

'Really?' said Mary, smiling.

'*Really*,' said Laura fervently.

CHAPTER THIRTEEN

Slowly but surely, Laura's rehabilitation had begun. When she got back from Mary's, in the early evening, slightly light-headed from the gin and wine her grandmother had pressed upon her, and full of good intentions, she cleaned the rest of her room from top to bottom, and the rest of the flat, even vacuuming in Paddy's room. She went out and bought fresh flowers, bunches of sweet peas and cheap anemones. She had long known that a broken heart takes a while to mend, but as Mary always said, flowers in vases to look at go some way to help. And she bought food. She made supper, spaghetti with clams, scrubbing them clean for ages, cooking them in white wine, garlic, lemon juice.

She didn't feel suddenly light as a feather, or much better. She felt – numb. But a little hopeful. She was just glad she was out of bed, frankly. She told herself she would take everything as it came, not try to sort it out immediately, in the old impetuous Laura way. When Paddy came back from work they sat together and ate, chatting lightly over a bottle of wine, and Paddy asked, 'What the hell happened to you?', and Laura repeated the story again that day. Everything – Dan, the baby, the job, no money. Somehow saying it all to someone her own age, who wasn't on her side necessarily, made it worse, because then it was out there, final and true, not just in her head. Paddy whistled through his teeth as Laura finished. She held her glass of wine by the stem, and looked into her lap.

'I'm sorry, love,' Paddy said. 'I'm so sorry. I wish –'

'You wish you'd been wrong, and you wish I wasn't so stupid,' Laura said lightly. 'There's no need to say anything. I just wanted to say sorry, Pads. I've been a crap flatmate. And an even crapper friend. Not any more. Things have changed now, OK?'

'Oh, right,' said Paddy uneasily. 'How?'

Laura heard the tone in his voice, but carried on regardless. 'How? How? Ha, well. New leaf, that's all. I've seen the light. No more romance. It's cold, hard facts for me from now on, and that's that. I'm not going to go on about it,' she said as Paddy coughed politely and settled back into his chair. 'Seriously! I'm not. That's all I'm saying.'

'Yeah right,' said Paddy. He smiled. 'You don't have to change, Laura. We all love you just the way you are, you know.'

'Thanks, Pads,' Laura said. 'But you don't get it. I mean it. This isn't a *thing* thing I'll forget about in a couple of weeks' time. I am Never. Feeling. Like. That. Again.' She banged her glass on the table. 'I promise you. I never want to go through that again. I will do Anything. To. Make. Sure. I. –'

'Yes, yes,' said Paddy. 'I see, I see.'

'I mean it, seriously,' said Laura. She looked at him.

'Right,' said Paddy, but she saw him hide a smile in his wine glass.

Never mind, she thought to herself. I'll just have to show them all. 'So,' she said, changing the subject. 'What about Becky? Any news?'

'Hah!' said Paddy. 'She's got a bloody boyfriend!'

'No!' said Laura. 'Oh damn. How do you know?'

'Because I effing saw him, didn't I?' Paddy said bitterly. 'I was walking down the stairs today, *really* slowly, just in case she came out of the flat.'

He paused, and looked into his wine glass, shaking his head as if wondering at the cruelty of the world.

'So?' said Laura. 'Then what happened? Did she come out of the flat?'

'Yes, oh yes,' said Paddy. 'Ha. She came out of the flat all right.'

'Yes?' said Laura. 'And?'

'With some bloke. Who she snogged for about five minutes outside. I walked past. They didn't even say *hello*,' he finished sadly, as if it was the breach of manners that really upset him about the whole thing.

'Oh,' said Laura. 'Sorry, man.'

'No sweat,' said Paddy. He raised his glass. 'Onwards and upwards, yes?'

'Yes,' said Laura, clinking his glass. 'Onwards and upwards.'

The next day, Laura got up at eight thirty. She knew what she was going to do. She showered and got dressed, putting on jeans and a strappy vest top, and smoothed her thick shiny hair back into a plait. In the kitchen, she made herself a cup of hot water with a slice of lemon and then went to the cupboard and pulled out a big cardboard box, which she stared at for a while. She went back to her room, carrying both. It was starting to look quite bare, she'd thrown so much away, and it was tidy and fresh now Mr Kowolczyk had been.

Laura took a sip of her drink, and squared her shoulders. Then she opened her chest of drawers, and from it pulled a bundle of letters from Adam – her Romantic Poets university boyfriend – a series of cards from Josh, and the tiny pathetic scraps of memories she had from Dan. A photo of him. His expired work security pass. The bill from their weekend away in the Cotswolds (which she had had to pay for). A condom packet – god, how pathetic. Yet symbolic, she thought wryly as she chucked it in the bin. A couple of cards swearing undying love and promises of disgusting things he wanted to do to her.

A bookmark – why, she had no idea. All of these went in the box. Then, with a heavy heart, she turned to her video collection, stacked up on the bookcase by her ancient video recorder. Laura was the one person who still scoured HMV for videos, scurrying home at the dead of night with a fresh cull of films Paddy would simply refuse to watch.

In went her beloved Doris Day Collection. In went *My Fair Lady*, *The Way We Were*, *Pride and Prejudice* (TV boxed set), *Breakfast at Tiffany's*, *Gone with the Wind* and *Brief Encounter*. She lingered over *When Harry Met Sally* – surely that was a comedy primarily, a fine piece of film-making, winner of an (she squinted at the case) Academy Award for Best Original Screenplay – but she was firm, and it went in the box, to be followed by *Moonstruck*, *The Truth About Cats and Dogs*, *What Women Want* and *Four Weddings and a Funeral*. Finally, with the heaviest of hearts, in went *The Sound of Music*, her own personal favourite. Yes, the songs were great, but as far as Laura was concerned, it was all about the Captain and Julie Andrews. The misunderstandings! The harsh words, the cross-purposes! The dance in the moonlight on the terrace! The – she stopped herself, and with her left hand prised the tape out of the frenzied grip of her right hand, and threw it almost viciously in the box. Gone.

She moved over to the bookshelf. Laura gulped. This was harder than she realised. She thought of Mrs Danvers again, and hardened herself. Firm. Strong. Away with childish things. She put *Rebecca* on the bed, in case she needed to consult it. But in went all her Nancy Mitford books. In went all her Mills & Boons. She hesitated over her Jane Austen collection. Surely that was proper English literature, she shouldn't be throwing it away! But no, the Mrs Danvers in her spoke again. You have never read them for academic enjoyment, Laura Foster, she said. You read them because they make you swoon and sigh and they have striding men with breeches in them. In they go.

Finally, she reached the top shelf of her bookcase. With a

shaking, heavy hand she picked up her Georgette Heyer collection. She knew it had to be done, but by god it hurt. Tears came into her eyes. One by one, she dropped each book in, watched as they slammed onto each other, the pale colours of the old paperback covers gleaming up out of the box at her. It was torture.

But no. They were wrong, and they had to go. And the box was full. Slowly, Laura taped it up, and carried it out into the hall, down the stairs. Outside, in the fresh sunshine, she squinted up at the sky as she staggered like a drunk person down the path to where the wheelie bins were kept. She balanced the box on top of one, and was debating whether to open the bin and throw everything in or whether to just give the box to Paddy for safekeeping when a voice said,

'Hello, Laura! How are you doing today, then?'

'Hello, Mr Kenzo,' Laura said. 'I'm fine. Much better than the other day, you know.'

'I'm glad, I'm glad,' said Mr Kenzo, who was carrying a balsa-wood box of fruit. He reached in, handed her something. 'Have a peach, my dear.'

'Thank you,' said Laura, and bit into it. The rasp of the skin caught on the roof of her mouth, and she pressed her tongue up to the flesh and felt the sweet, musky juice flood down her throat. 'Mm,' she said. 'My goodness! That's delicious!'

'You look well today,' said Mr Kenzo, considering her. 'Hair nice. New shirt? Much better than on Saturday. My dear, you looked – my *gahd*. Like a dead, drowned cat. Old.'

'Er,' said Laura, taking another bite, not sure how to respond. 'Thanks?'

'Let me help,' said Mr Kenzo, and before Laura could protest he had gripped the box firmly under his arm, lifted up the bin, and tipped the contents into its black mouth.

Laura gazed helplessly as videos, books, letters, all tumbled out of the box one after the other, disappearing into the dark. She'd never actually *thrown* a book away before, and she normally took her conked-out videotapes to the plastic recycling bin. It felt like sacrilege. 'Oh,' she said.

'Mistake?' said Mr Kenzo. 'Oh dear. Were you – that was rubbish, wasn't it? You did want to throw it away? Yes?'

'Yes,' said Laura, finishing the peach and slinging the peach stone in afterwards. She shut the bin lid and licked her fingers. 'Yes, I did. Thanks, Mr Kenzo. See you later.'

And she turned and walked up the path and up the stairs back to the flat. Another thing to check off the list. She was doing well. It was like having a New Year's resolution, she thought. I will get over Dan and I will sort out my life. Also, I will go to the gym and have freshly squeezed fruit juices every morning before work. Well, little by little.

The phone was ringing as she came back into the flat, and though she'd been avoiding the phone she instinctively picked it up. It was Jo.

'Hi, babe,' she said.

'Er, hi,' Laura answered uncertainly.

'Look. I know it's none of my business. But Paddy just rang me. He told me what happened.'

Her voice was echoing, it reverberated down the line.

'Oh,' said Laura. 'Right.' She twisted the phone cord around her finger and sat down on the chair by the hall table. 'Go on then,' she said, not really knowing what to say, not wanting to sound rude, but not wanting to get into it. She really couldn't cope with Jo if she was going to be sanctimonious and say, 'I told you so.'

'Well . . .' Jo coughed. 'I just wanted to say hi.'

'Thanks,' Laura said, fidgeting, feeling like a five-year-old.

There was a pause, then Jo said in a rush, 'Look. It's none of my business. I'm not going to judge. You know what I think about it all. But I've been a really bad friend to you lately. And I'm sorry.'

'You haven't been a bad friend!' Laura cried. 'My god! I'm the one who's been bad! How can you say that?'

122

Jo's voice was a bit muffled, but she chuckled and said, 'Well it's over now, isn't it? Hey.' She sniffed. 'I really, really miss you, Laura. Can we – er, can we be friends again?'

'Of course!' said Laura. She hugged herself. 'Oh, I'm so glad.'

'Me too,' said Jo. Her voice was quiet. 'Look, I am really sorry. You poor thing. Are you OK?'

'Well,' said Laura, not wanting to sound pathetic. Then she said, 'Actually, no, not really. But I will be.'

'Can I – can I pop round?'

Laura looked at her watch. It was only three o'clock. Jo should be at work. 'Course,' she said. 'Where are you?'

There was a knock on the door, three feet away from Laura. She jumped up in the air. 'Argh!' she cried.

'It's me,' came Jo's voice, from down the phone and outside at the same time. 'Hello.'

Laura opened the door. There was her best friend, standing in the doorway, her tiny frame dwarfed by her enormous backpack. She was holding some chocolates and a bottle of wine. She raised a hand and her eyes met Laura's and she smiled.

'Bunked off work,' she said, rolling her eyes in the direction of the backpack crammed with papers on her back. 'I – I wanted to see you,' and she came forward, her arms outstretched, and gave Laura a hug.

'Poor, poor baby,' she said soothingly into Laura's hair, and both of them were crying, not just for Laura's predicament, but because girls are a bit pathetic like that. 'Poor baby.'

'Yes,' sniffed Laura, wholly in agreement. 'Thanks,' she added. 'You must think I'm a complete idiot.'

'No I don't,' said Jo firmly. 'Just – no, I don't. *He's* the idiot, isn't he?'

'Yeah!' said Laura. 'But – well, I have been really stupid. And the worst of it is, you were right,' she said in a rush. 'All along. You're always saying it.'

'Saying what?'

'You know,' said Laura, looking at the floor.

Jo swung her bag onto the ground and said nothing.

'Well,' Laura said after a while. 'Just – it's not the first time. I should have learnt my lesson by now. I have. Just so you know.'

'Sure, sure,' Jo crooned, putting her arm around her friend. 'Yes, of course you have.'

'No, I mean it,' said Laura firmly. 'You sound like Paddy. I have. Well, you'll just have to see. I'm a changed person. Anyway. Forget it.' She eyed the bottle of wine. 'Screw-top, yum. Come and get a glass.'

'Great,' said Jo. 'So, tell me all about it. It happened on Friday, right?'

'Right,' said Laura, retreating into the kitchen. 'So . . .'

Laura suffered a setback on Wednesday. She knew she'd been doing so well, but it was hard being good and kind *and* Mrs Danvers-like all at the same time. She woke up with a vicious hangover (Jo had stayed till eleven o'clock, and they'd got through a lot of wine together) and the dramatic avowals of friendship and cathartic chats of the previous night seemed a little empty the next day, when her tongue was furry again and she was tired and miserable and still jobless, penniless, Danless. She made herself a cup of tea and crawled back into bed, chewing her fingernails. What was she going to do with her life now? The practical side of her started to worry. How was she going to convince Rachel to give her another chance, to trust her again? Future invented phantoms crowded into her mind, she couldn't stop thinking everything over, over and over, and she cried again, huge, self-pitying sobs. She didn't deserve Jo as a friend, or Paddy. Or even nice Mr Kenzo! He had brought them Turkish delight, and she hadn't even thanked him. She didn't think that this setback might be entirely understandable. She gave in to it, and lay in bed with the curtains closed.

She was lying there when her phone rang. Laura reached out

an arm, patted the bedside table without looking at it, feeling blindly and knocking over her lamp and book. She picked it up and brought it under the duvet to see who it was.

Amy Mob.

Laura pressed 'Busy', her fingers fumbling. She turned the phone off, put it down the side of the bed, by the wall, feeling terrified, and curled up into a ball and hugged herself. It was over an hour before she moved again, put her hand gingerly down onto the floor, squeezing her knuckles through the tight fit of the bed frame, to pick the phone up. She turned it on. It seemed to take hours. The screen lit up, the welcome message tinkled at her, and then the voicemail rang. Laura pressed 'Answer', her jaw set. Perhaps . . .

'Laura. You know who it is.' She hadn't seen Amy for so long, hearing her voice came as a huge shock. Sickly sweet, slightly rasping, scary. It didn't sound violent, or over-emotional, or hormonal. It sounded in control. 'Don't hang up on me, you *bitch*,' she hissed. 'You fat, spotty, spineless little *bitch*. Dan finally told me who he's been screwing, like I couldn't guess anyway. OK? You're too much of a fucking coward to talk to me after what you've done, aren't you? Fine. Let me spell it out for you. I know what you did. If you ever go near him again I'll find you and I'll make your life a misery. Even more miserable than it must be now. You fat, stupid *dog*. He told me how you chased after him, how you begged him, just like the ugly dog you are. Like you were at school, always begging. You're pathetic, Laura. You are PATHETIC.

'We're going on holiday next week, dog-girl. Just so you know. We're going to Florida. I would ask you along but they don't allow dogs in the hotel. So why don't you just fuck off, and think about what you've done. I hope it eats you alive. So long, dog-girl.'

Laura couldn't feel her fingers, her hands, they were shaking so much, and the mobile fell onto the bed. She deleted the message and looked at the phone, terrified of its power all of a sudden, that something so nasty could come out of it. She turned it off again and slid it under her new duvet, feeling slightly sick. She licked her lips, tasting blood. She had bitten her lower lip and made it bleed. She hadn't done that since she was little. Laura looked around the room and felt very tired. Exhausted. Would it always be like this? She could feel Amy's presence nearby, coming out of the phone, coming in through the windows. She was close, too close; so was Dan. Laura wished she was anywhere but there. She closed her eyes, but she didn't cry. She didn't know how to.

It was her mother who finally sorted her out. She swept into Laura's room on Thursday, and drew back the curtains. Laura was watching *Trisha* on her TV, and her eyes bulged with amazement at her mother's nerve.

'How . . . how dare you! Get out!' she screamed, waving her finger at Angela rather like a French aristocrat to a peasant caught wandering in his garden before the Revolution.

'Hello dear,' said Angela, drawing back the curtains. 'I spoke to your grandmother last night.'

'Oh,' said Laura, sinking down in the bed and chewing her little finger.

'She – well, she said she thought you'd been having a hard time lately,' said Angela, who wasn't half as insensible as her daughter thought she was. 'Darling, aren't you . . . needed at work at the moment?'

'No,' said Laura, her voice muffled.

Angela bit her lip.

'And . . . are you going on holiday next week any more?'

'No,' said Laura, with the sheet over her head. 'Go away.'

Angela twisted her hands together, and said, 'Listen, dear. I have a suggestion. Why don't you come to Norfolk with your father and me instead? And Granny, of course. How about it?'

'Absolutely no way ever, ever, ever,' came the voice from

126

under the duvet. 'I'd rather eat . . . I'd rather eat – er – this duvet. No way!'

The next day was Friday. It should have been Laura's last day in the office before her holiday. She should have been getting ready to go to Florida, packing her gorgeous new printed hotpants, her halter-neck bikini, her new digital camera, her cool cowboy hat.

As she was sorting through some clothes in her wardrobe, Laura found the cowboy hat. She took it down from its shelf, and looked at it wonderingly, as if it were something from another planet. She stood there, running the rim around her fingers, letting her mind drift aimlessly over the past few days, weeks, months. Yes, in another life the cab would have been coming to collect her in an hour. If it arrived now, if Dan was inside it, calling up to her, telling her he loved her, that it was all a big mistake, what would she do? She put the hat back in the wardrobe, and closed the door. She knew what she would do.

A few minutes later, Laura rang her mother.

'Mum,' she said. 'I've . . . now my plans have sort of changed, I was wondering . . . can I come to Norfolk with you?'

Angela knew her daughter far better than Laura realised. Laura could tell she was smiling into the phone. She said, 'Yes, of course you can, darling. Oh, that's wonderful. How nice. I'll start on the packed lunch right now.'

Laura put the phone down. She leant against the armchair and gazed around the sitting room. It was early Friday afternoon, too early for anyone to have left work. The air was still and out on the street not a leaf stirred on the trees. It was very quiet. She brought her knees up under her chin and hugged her legs, sitting there on the polished wooden floor, and she stayed like that, thinking, for a long time.

PART TWO

CHAPTER FOURTEEN

The Foster family had been going to Seavale for their summer holidays since before Laura was born. About thirty years ago, when Guy and Mary started spending less time living as nomadic Bedouins or travelling through South America on diplomatic missions, and more time in the UK, they had bought the bungalow overlooking the sea. The house had been built in the Twenties, a pretty, if small, arts and crafts villa, crammed with books and cushions and dancing light from the water. At the side of the sitting room was a terrace, partly sheltered, and on the other side of the terrace was a single-room structure of glass and wood – Guy's studio, where he would spend the majority of the day in his smock, chewing his pipe and looking out to sea. It was now an extra bedroom, hung with his watercolours.

Mary's eighty-fifth birthday party was to fall on the following Saturday, when the clans would gather for one day only. Because it was a momentous occasion, Angela and George were to be joined then by Aunt Annabel, Uncle Robert, Lulu, Fran, and Fran's boyfriend Ludo. Laura could only feel relief she'd already said she had to be back in London that Saturday evening (some bollocks about a party somewhere, she'd told her mother), and so was not exposing herself to the Sandersons for longer than was necessary. She could cope with the formidable Aunt

131

Annabel, just about. Robert was a boorish bore, but he was passable, he spent most of the time either drunk or asleep. It was Lulu and Fran from whom Laura wanted to run in the opposite direction. She wanted to like her cousins. She just couldn't bring herself to do it.

Lulu and Fran were famed throughout their teenage years for being creative, super-intelligent, and well-behaved, always clearing up the tea-trays, writing thank-you letters and saying 'Oh! How lovely!' about things, rather than slouching grumpily around and grunting, thinking the world was against them, which is how Simon and Laura spent their teenage years. But Simon and Laura had *quite* liked them then, because they were naughty too, and were up for things like the disco in the village next to Seavale, or having sneaky cigarettes in the sand dunes. But the years since had highlighted the gap between their respective families, and Laura now thought of them as snobbish, hyper-artificial and fake, and 'creative' in the way that rich, pointless people are 'creative': i.e. they become feature writers for *Posh Person's Monthly* or open their house once a month and sell expensive jewellery they bought for next-to-nothing in Morocco.

Lulu lived in Notting Hill and was skeletally thin and unbearable; Fran, actually, was slightly more bearable, but had gone native in Lulu's eyes. She lived in Putney with her boyfriend Ludo, was a sports physio, had thick hair and thick ankles, and spent her life either doing runs with Ludo or getting bladdered with him in an All Bar One-type pub on the river. They both made it quite clear they thought Laura and Simon were bourgeois and suburban beyond belief; that they'd grown up in Harrow was horrifying enough, let alone the fact *neither* of them had *ever been skiing*.

'Thank god they're not related to us,' Simon and Laura would moan.

'I know,' Angela once answered, in a rare display of solidarity.

132

They were just all different, and Laura didn't like the way she sensed the Sandersons were looking down their collective noses at the Fosters, just because their house was a semi, and they lived in Harrow, and only had one car. The Sandersons had two cars, they lived in Holland Park, Lulu and Fran had gone to a super-exclusive school, and Annabel sat on several committees and co-wrote cookbooks on things like *The Glorious Twelfth* and *Buffets for Debutantes*, or *Picnics for Countryside Alliance Marches*, which was ridiculous, since they lived in Zone 2 and Annabel actually didn't like meat that much.

So, Laura had one week with her parents and her grandmother to get through, climaxing in the gathering of the extended family – with guest appearance from Simon, who was supposedly returning from Peru on Friday and coming up on Saturday morning. Laura's brief was pretty simple, really. Be good, be nice, be kind. Put what's happened behind you and move on. A clean slate, a blank wall, a new dawn *and* a new leaf.

But of course, nothing ever turns out the way you expect it to.

Laura sat watching her family in her deckchair, her mouth knitted unconsciously into an expression of bitter disdain. She glared at her parents from under her sunhat, then realised she was actually *wearing* a sunhat, and threw it on the ground in a gesture of indignation – one which went totally unremarked-upon by her parents and grandmother, who were apparently blithely unconcerned with her suffering.

She looked wearily out at the view. The sea was a rough, choppy grey. The clouds loomed overhead, menacing and bulbous, as if they might burst at any moment. The sand, which should have been glowing golden yellow, was a dirty cement colour. And the huge beach was deserted, apart from a lone, tatty-looking dog who was deliriously running around in circles in the distance, almost at the tide. An empty tar barrel rolled on its side, creaking. The sea-grass rustled ominously in the wind. Why was she surprised the weather was crap? It was Britain. It was July. It was a typical summer holiday by the seaside.

George Foster was humming to himself as he carefully opened the National Trust Members' Guide out on the rug in front of him, and fastidiously turned the pages till he got to 'Norfolk's Stately Homes and Castles'. Beside him on the rug, Laura's mum was devouring her book club's selection, her mouth half-open in absorption.

Mary was half-asleep. Her tanned hands rested lightly on her lap, one half-clutching her book. She stirred slightly as Laura watched her, hitching an old shawl up around her shoulder again. Laura meanly thought about coughing sharply to wake her up, but she wasn't so far sunk beneath hope as to consider giving her beloved grandmother a heart attack just so she could have someone to talk to. She picked up *Take a Break*, which she had thrown aside in disgust, and tried to concentrate on the story she'd been reading about a woman whose husband is having it away with their neighbour, but her attention wandered, or rather marched purposefully away, after only one sentence. She put the magazine down and gazed thoughtfully out to sea.

She'd been so good so far this holiday, but now she was in the grip of an irrational anger and there was nothing she could do about it except hunker down and wait for it to pass. It was Tuesday, day four of the holiday, and acting like an angel with a blank slate, a new leaf and all that, was starting to wear her down because, much as she loved her parents and her grandmother, four days of constant exposure to them at a time when her reserves were low was not ideal. It put her in a kind of limbo – she didn't know whether she was a grown-up with a responsible place in society, or whether she was a child, a total screw-up with no job, no boyfriend, no morals, and therefore should just stop trying and give up. So she did a lot of gritting her teeth, till her jaw ached.

134

The first few days had passed by without murder being committed at least! Despite the cold weather Laura had tried to feel as if she were – well, not exactly *on holiday*, but still, away from it all. She helped her mother in the garden; Mary's hip was playing up. They all went to see a steam-train display, and Mary made best friends with the driver and got to ride in his cab, which made George jealous. They watched *Midsomer Murders* together, and Mary rolled her eyes and said things like, 'It's the vicar, you total idiot!' whilst Angela gripped the sofa and screamed every time the incidental music played.

Laura made salad dressing, she mixed drinks, and did not object to her parents' choice of television, newspaper, or plans for the week, one of which included their long-held ambition to see the Seekers tribute band, who as extraordinary luck – or ill-luck, depending on your point of view – would have it, were playing that week in the nearest resort's little theatre. She'd managed to politely decline her parents' offer of tickets. They were actually called the Seekers Tribute Band, her mother had informed her that morning. Laura felt irrationally furious with them, that they couldn't have come up with a better moniker – Desperately Seeking the Seekers, or They Seek Them Here, or something like that – it was a pure gift! This did not contribute to a lightening of her mood.

She had played Trivial Pursuit with her grandmother, who disputed the result every time the question was a modern one (*'Britney Spears?* Well, how on earth am I supposed to know that? Ridiculous question. Give me another one. That's not Art and Culture, don't be stupid. Trivial Pursuits, you should be ashamed of yourself. Honestly.') She had tried to go for a long, moody walk by herself, but her mother and father had joined her and raved for a good two miles about the progression the National Trust was making with the coastline around the area, how the litter bins were so well-placed, and how the cafés were much *nicer* than they used to be, until Laura tried walking slightly faster, ahead of them, but they merely caught up with her and carried on talking. So she had just smiled politely again, and gritted her teeth.

She had also smiled agreeably at dinner each night as George briefly outlined the agricultural and economic history of Norfolk in the eighteenth century, and asked a couple of pertinent questions, much to her father's obvious delight. She'd listened politely as her mother went through every family member in their enclave in Harrow and delineated each one, what they were doing, what their children were doing, what their children's boyfriends or girlfriends were doing – people Laura hadn't seen for years, much less cared about. And she nodded wisely as Mary, for the umpteenth time, told Laura some marvellous story of derring-do about Guy and herself, this time in Jerusalem in the early Sixties. Normally Laura loved these stories. But this wasn't normal.

Laura shifted in her chair, and pushed her hair out of her eyes. She looked around again to see if Mary was awake. Nothing doing. She checked her phone, but there was nothing. Her mind wandered again. Scary Hilary was having a party on the Saturday night to celebrate being single again; Jo had promised to let her know what happened, and what the view was from the terraces now Dan and Amy were in the States and it was clear everything was out in the open. If Dan had told Amy, which he obviously had, who else knew? And would she have to pay penance for it? She wished she could ask him, but of course she couldn't, and she had heard nothing from him, nothing at all, after their last night. It seemed Amy was speaking for both of them now. As well she might.

Thinking about Dan and Amy was all the reminder she needed. It was her own fault that here she was, on the beach at Seavale, having the same summer holiday she'd had since she was *five*. Only when she was five she'd had Simon and Lulu and Fran and various other grubby holidaying children to play with. It was fine when she was five; Seavale was a nice place to go to on summer holiday. The beach was vast, the tides were gentle, the sea was warm. There were ice creams and donkeys! And when she was thirteen, she had kissed Robert Mulligan behind the beach huts, and had her first cigarette with Lulu; and then she had gone to the disco in stonewashed jeans when she was fifteen, and gone on a long last walk with Guy when she was twenty, over the dunes, into the fields, over the river and towards the next village. It was all fine – it was more than fine, it was her favourite place in the world. But not now. If only Simon was here now, she thought, moodily wrapping her scarf around her. But no. My brother *has a life*. He's *travelling*. And I'm *here*.

A seagull croaked viciously overhead, dangerously low, stirring Laura out of her torpor. She shook her head, ashamed to find tears were in her eyes. She pulled herself together and realised she'd be better off back at the house rather than here, making the others worry about her, because they already clearly thought she was mad. And it was freezing, apart from anything else. She turned to tell her mother this, and found her grandmother was watching her. Laura met her eyes and saw that Mary was smiling with understanding.

'I'm going back up,' Laura whispered. 'See you in a bit.'

Mary nodded, gave her a quick smile and picked up her book again. Laura's dad murmured, 'Mm . . . mmm, see you then,' and Laura's mother looked up blankly and said,

'You going back, darling?'

'Yep,' said Laura briefly. 'I'm cold. I'll put the kettle on, shall I?'

'Ooh, lovely,' said Angela Foster. 'There's some of that fruit cake we bought from the craft fair in the tub, you could get that out.'

'Right,' said Laura, repressing the urge to scream, 'I hate fruit cake! You know I do!' Instead, she said, 'OK, see you in a bit then.'

'Great,' said Angela. 'Dad and I are going to write our postcards later,' she added inconsequentially, in the way that

137

parents do when you are trying to leave them, a delaying tactic of some sort.

'Look, is that a crested grebe?' said Mary from behind her book, and Angela's head swivelled round. 'Oh no, my mistake.' She carried on reading, the corners of her mouth twitching.

Laura flashed her grandmother a grin and, thankful for her escape, snapped her deckchair up and propped it under her arm. Swaying slightly in the wind, she began the trudge across the cold sand up to the path back to their house.

Her bag made a vibrating sound as Laura reached the café by the lifeboat station. She stopped, fumbling eagerly in her bag, hoping against hope that it was Jo or Paddy, that some kind of salvation from Olds World was on its way. She flipped open her phone eagerly.

'Just reminding you to stay away from me, you stupid little bitch,' she read. *'And from Dan. Why don't you just fuck off? No one wants you, dog-girl. PS Miami is gorgeous, by the way. Wish you were here – not.'*

Stumbling blindly, her eyes stinging with tears, Laura dropped the phone and fell to her knees on the dirty sand to search for it. It was hard to see, but she gritted her teeth and blinked the tears away. The café owner, Bart, watched her impassively, as Laura found her phone under a clump of grass, picked up her chair again and stood up. She breathed very deeply, and continued on her way.

'All right, love?' Bart finally asked, drawing heavily on his cigarette as Laura went past.

She turned to him and smiled. 'Yes, I'm fine thanks,' she said.

Bart put out his cigarette, looked at her curiously once more, and went back inside, casting one more glance up to the sky. Yes, it was definitely about to rain.

CHAPTER FIFTEEN

As Laura stumbled back from the beach to the house on that cold afternoon, she was trying not to crumble into little bits again, not to go back to what she'd felt like before, but she couldn't help it. She crawled up the path to her room, threw the beach bag on the bed, and cried. About five minutes later, footsteps sounded across the terrace, and a tapping sound was heard through the door.

'Darling, it's me,' said her mother's voice anxiously. 'Are you OK?'

'I'm fine!' Laura said, unnecessarily loudly, and buried her head in the sodden pillow again. She howled silently for what seemed like several hours but was in fact about fifteen minutes, feeling deeply, deeply sorry for herself, the pitiable, unattractive, unlovable, friendless girl she was.

And then, all of a sudden, she stopped and sat up. She dried her eyes, wiped her nose on her hand, and looked thoughtful.

Laura had a pragmatic streak running through her, often not in tandem with the romantic streak, but following close behind. Listen to yourself, she said firmly. You have had your lowest moment; that was last week, in bed in your room. Remember the box of stupid romantic stuff now in the bin. Remember the pigeon. Your lowest moment was then, you're not allowed any more.

You've been here four days now. OK, it's pretty duff, but actually it's doing you a lot of good, and Mum and Dad and Granny are having a great time, don't ruin it for them. This is over, now.

She suddenly felt a hot bolt of anger shoot through her at Amy's text, at her message, at Dan's total weakness, the way he was willing to string both of them along and still end up the winner. This man, whom she'd thought was The One. He wasn't. Boy, he wasn't. Waiting for Mr Right, The One, the great, great romance, was a waste of time – it had been a waste of time, and that's what she'd been getting so wrong all these years. It wasn't just Dan, it went back much further than that, but he was the one who'd totally, comprehensively stomped out her romantic strain. And perhaps she should thank him for it. She was going to be better off without it.

'Great,' she said out loud. 'Great.' And she felt a little more cheerful.

Laura swung her legs off the bed and sat there, thinking. Perhaps I should move in with Granny, she thought. I could help her, like Mrs Danvers in real life, a maiden spinster helpmeet. Hard-working and unassuming, perhaps with a touch of religious mania. Yes, she thought. OK. Then she thought about her and Paddy sprawled on the sofa with a bottle of wine and some Chinese food, laughing at *The Simpsons*. Maybe not, she thought again. Still, it was a start. She could adapt the modest, unassuming spinster helpmeet bit for something else when she was back home. Embroidery, soup lunches, that sort of thing. She'd fix Paddy up with that Becky girl from downstairs. She'd make cookies for everyone at work. If she was allowed back at work . . .

Angela knocked on the door again. 'Darling, we're having a sherry, do you want one?'

There was a silence. Then Laura said, 'Yes, please,' and jumped off the bed. She pulled her tangled hair into a ponytail. 'Just coming,' she said, and she opened the door.

*   *   *

That evening, as a storm raged around the bungalow and the leaded windows rattled and shook in their draughty wooden casements, the female Fosters and Mary sat around the table in the kitchen eating lasagne and not saying much, whilst George chatted merrily away about something. Conversation was slightly lagging, four days in, and Laura wasn't as much in the mood as she wanted to be. She knew her mother was staring at her, wanting to ask if she was OK, but she also knew she wouldn't. She knew her father was trying to jolly everyone along, but he wasn't really succeeding. And Mary, though she loved her, was always slightly hard to read, her mood hard to predict from day to day. She, Laura, had to make the effort. She looked up as her mother said,

'George, more broccoli, dear?'

'Yes please,' said George, breaking off his very interesting monologue about the great aristocratic families of the North Norfolk coast, and how they had fared during the Civil War. Angela looked at him, her face softening with affection, and Laura's heart turned over. Her father took the bowl and smiled at his wife, the corners of his mouth crinkling, his ears wagging with pleasure, and Laura suddenly felt a rush of love for her parents. Yes, maybe Dad did often discuss heraldic symbolism at the dinner table for too long, and maybe he was just a normal bloke, not a conductor or a deep-sea diver. Laura secretly, deep-down, had always thought Mary found him a bit – *boring*. Laura knew why. Angela wanted a home, a family. Roots. A back garden, a climbing frame. She didn't want the expat life, the faded glory, the cocktail parties, stucco hotels, servants, bygone eras. She was normal, sensible. *Un*-romantic, if anything. She looked up and smiled at her mother, looking from her to her grandmother.

'Is there any more mustard, dear?' said Mary.

'Gosh, you two do look similar,' said Angela fondly.

Laura stared at her mother. 'Who?'

'You, dear, you and Granny.'

141

Mary looked at Laura. 'We do, don't we.'

'It's odd sometimes,' said Angela. 'Just now, the two of you, next to each other. You looked rather fierce, Laura.'

'Just like Granny, you mean?' Laura said, laughing, and Mary looked affronted.

'Angela dear, is there some more mustard?' Angela shook her head. 'Well, can you get up and check for me, dear? Thanks.'

Angela stood up, looking from her daughter to her mother again, and went to the larder. Mary carried on eating, quietly, and Laura gazed into space, holding her fork in her hand. George was still talking as Angela returned with a new pot of Colman's.

'. . . Fascinating, that actually, he *never visited the house* again! After she died. Heartbroken, they said. Of course, Sir John's additions were anathema to him, he loathed Palladian architecture, said it was a betrayal of the old English ways . . . Still, fascinating to think that, wouldn't you say?'

There was silence. Neither grandmother, mother nor daughter replied, partly because they couldn't think of anything to say, mainly because they hadn't been listening to a word.

'Well,' said George, looking rather pink. 'That's nice, isn't it. Was no one listening?'

'I wasn't,' Mary said frankly. 'I was thinking, will Jasper remember to water my mint plant whilst I'm away?'

George scowled.

'I was, darling,' said Angela. 'I just had to get up to get the mustard, that's why I lost the train of what you were saying. Were you talking about the de Beauvoirs?'

'No,' George said huffily. 'Well, it doesn't matter. Let's talk about something else, shall we?'

Laura caught her grandmother's eye and smiled. Poor Dad.

'Pass the mustard, George,' Mary said serenely, wiping her mouth elegantly on her napkin. 'Now, I brought along the Elvis '68 comeback special. On DVD. Who fancies watching it with me after supper?'

'I'm going to mend the shed door,' George said remotely.

'In this weather? Don't be ridiculous,' retorted Mary briskly.

'The catch is very loose. Someone has to do it. I don't mind,' said George, with the air of one willing to martyr oneself for one's family. 'I can talk to myself out there. At least the deckchairs don't answer back.'

'I don't know,' said Mary. 'You carry on talking to them for long enough, they may well walk off to another shed.'

'Mum,' Angela said. 'Don't be mean.'

Mary smiled wickedly. Laura felt cross with her suddenly. It was irrational, she knew, but she wished Mary wouldn't do it. She looked at her dad. He pushed his chair back as if to stand up, in a rather defeated way.

She took a deep breath. 'So Dad,' she said suddenly. 'Where would you like to go tomorrow, then? If it's still raining? There's enough of those bor— er, I mean big stately homes around here, which one was first on your list? We could take a picnic, go for a walk, wander round the house. Make a day of it.'

'Er,' said George. He looked astounded.

'What?' said Angela, who was standing up, holding the salad servers in one hand and the bread in the other.

'Laura?' said Mary, moving forward in her chair. 'Darling, are you OK?'

'Yes,' said Laura, trying not to sound impatient. 'I'm just asking, Dad, what do you want to do tomorrow?'

George's face turned pink again, but this time with pleasure. 'Well, Laura, that's a very interesting question, love.'

'Is it?' said Mary, sitting back again. 'Is it really? Ask yourself, George, my dear man, is it?'

'Granny,' said Laura warningly. She looked at her dad again. 'Come on, where shall we go?'

'Well,' said George Foster slowly. 'If I had to pick one, to kick things off with, I'd say . . . Chartley Hall.'

'Lovely,' said Angela. 'Ooh, it's beautiful there. We haven't been there for ages, have we? Didn't they have a toy soldier festival a few years ago?'

Mary slapped her hands to her cheeks.

'Yes,' said George. 'And they used to have that lovely fete in the summer. Super. With the miniature train tracks you could ride on? You and Simon used to love it, Laura. We went in '86. And '87. Do you remember?'

'Vaguely,' said Laura. All their summers at Seavale blended into one for her these days, but her parents seemed to recall each and every one with the precision of an Exocet missile. The mention of Simon discomfited her. She missed him. She wished he was there, sitting next to her, being deeply annoying, as a good brother should. She wanted to talk to him. She thought about him, where he was, making his way through Peru, perhaps already starting the journey home for Granny's birthday lunch. Only four days to go, and then she'd see him. Only four days to go, and then she could go home, to . . .

To what? To Paddy, and a messy flat, and a job she might not have, and a group of friends who were probably sticking pins in a wax effigy of her, if Amy had got to them, and she could hardly blame them . . . It was funny, she thought. Her life in London had pretty much the same structure as it had had a few short weeks ago. And that life then had seemed full of drama, glamour, passion, excitement, agony and ecstasy. Now the thought of going back to it was mundane, boring, sad. Like a life in shades of grey. She thought then, with some relief, that perhaps it was best that way. Never mind what her grandmother had said to her the afternoon Laura had gone to find her, that she had a great capacity to love. Mary was wrong. She had a great capacity to love being in love. That was the difference. Now she had to learn to live without it.

'Laura, you remember it, don't you?' said her father, recalling her to her senses.

Laura had no idea what amazing stately home they'd moved on to, so she said cautiously, 'Er, is it the house with the loos in the stables?'

'No, no, no,' said George, almost impatiently. 'That's Corve

144

Manor. No, Chartley Hall, Laura. Well, you'll see tomorrow. It's one of the great houses of England. Of anywhere. Beautiful. Inigo Jones. Finest collection of Hogarth's work in private hands. The library – all Grinling Gibbons. And the most incredible books, a set of Austen first editions, of Henry James. The – was it the seventh marquess of Ranelagh? A bibliophile, it consumed him.' He cleared his throat. 'Landscaped grounds . . . beautiful, just beautiful. In its heyday –' his eyes glazed over, and he reminded Laura almost of St Teresa in her moment of Ecstasy '– ah, it was the great house for miles around, its own kingdom, you know. The Needhams – there was no family like them in the area, none at all.'

'Why's that, then?' said Angela, picking up the place mats.

'Well – more of everything than anyone else,' George said simply. 'They survived the Civil War, emerged with all their money intact, and they built themselves this great house to demonstrate it. They were a terrible lot to start off with. Brigands, extortionists. They made their money in the fourteenth century as debt collectors, then they married into money, then more money, then more, till they were the Needhams of Chartley Hall and everyone else had long forgotten they were thugs. Then Charles the Second's great mate, Thomas Needham – he got given the marquessdom. Mainly for letting Charlie have his mistress, I understand –' George chuckled, in an all-boys-together way, delighted at this behaviour, then realised he was on his own and coughed. 'So yes. More money, more power, more of anything. The most glittering marriages – they married well, the Needhams. The greatest prizes – there was a Michelangelo plaster cast in the Ballroom, till they sold it to pay off the – ooh, now, what was it? Which marquess? Nineteenth century, anyway. Terrible gambling debts, bad business.'

'Hm,' Mary said. 'I remember the chap who was there when we went. Flew planes. He still alive? He was getting on a bit, wasn't he?'

'Yes, died two years ago. Terrible business, what happened to him. Broken man.'

145

'Why?' said Laura, interested despite herself.

'Wife left him. Ran off with someone. Can't remember who, someone in the family. Big scandal, it was.'

'His brother,' said Mary. 'His brother Frederick.'

'Really?' said Laura. 'Blimey.'

'She was the film star. Vivienne Lash, you wouldn't remember her, Laura. She was big in the late Fifties and the Sixties. Beautiful. It was this very high-society match. The marquess and the actress. But yes –' Mary pushed her glass backwards and forwards between her fingers, then looked around at them all. 'Nice girl. I knew – I thought he couldn't have been much fun. Not a very nice chap, I hear. So she ran off with the brother, never saw her children again.'

'Extraordinary,' said Angela. 'How could she do that? To them.'

'Well, she was in love,' said Mary, slightly sharply. 'She would have done anything. And they weren't babies, they were grown-ups, I seem to remember. I met them once, several years ago. They were – lovely.'

Mary and Guy had met everyone. 'Did you?' said Angela, refusing to be cowed. 'Still.'

George interrupted his wife. 'Anyway, it's not him now. Died a couple of years ago. It's his son. Vivienne's son. Young chap. She had him rather late.'

'Right,' said Laura, wanting to say, 'Get on with it, Dad!' but instead she said firmly, 'Wow, sounds great, Dad. Tomorrow then.'

'Tomorrow,' said George, looking round the cosy room. He rubbed his hands together. 'And Mary, we need to talk about the plans for Saturday, you know. What you want to do. Angela and I are going to buy the food on Friday. We need to prepare.'

'Oh, yes we do,' said Mary, her eyes twinkling at him. 'Preparation is key, my dear boy.'

'I've got to ice the –' Angela said, and then broke off suddenly, her hand flying to her mouth. 'Oh. Nothing.'

'Ooh,' said Mary. 'The dreadful suspense, my heart is in my mouth. What can you be talking about, darling?'

'Er,' said her daughter. 'Nothing. I'm icing – nothing.'

'Great,' said Mary. 'How jolly. Just remember I hate green food-colouring with a passion. Thank you.'

George went on, 'Champagne first, then the barbecue if it's nice, then the iced nothing, then a walk for those who want it, and we thought we'd go down to the beach at sunset, have some more drinks and a game of boules, how does that sound?'

'It sounds wonderful,' said Mary. 'But I don't want too much trouble. Don't want a fuss. Let's wait till Friday and then we can get everything we need. Let's not arrange it all tonight.' She waved her hand imperiously in the air, and Laura watched her, thinking how totally, utterly great she was, like a film star at her own table, and marvelled again at her, the very *Maryness* of her.

'Right,' said George amiably, collecting the glasses. 'We don't want to let you down, that's all.'

'You never could, George,' said Mary simply. 'Bless you.'

George looked flustered. 'Hoh-kay,' he said, exhaling slowly. 'Hah. Well, I'm on for the Comeback Special, who else is game?'

'Great,' said Mary, slapping her thighs and standing up slowly. 'I could do with a whisky, who'll join me? I have a choice bottle of Glenmorangie in there. Who wants one?'

'Me,' said George.

'Ooh, well then, me,' said Angela.

'Ooh, me too,' said Laura, then realised she sounded like her parents. Strange, though, she could almost get used to it.

CHAPTER SIXTEEN

Laura woke up on Wednesday morning, forgetting where she was. She lay there in her light airy bedroom, listening to the sound of the waves breaking as the gradual rush of memory slid into her waking brain. She got up and pulled up the blinds, to be confronted with a beautiful sunny day. The storm of the previous night had blown all the clouds away and the sun was dancing on the sea. There was a faint breeze, and the beach huts were already showing signs of life, coloured doors open, wind-breakers being erected. Laura's heart lifted.

Then, out on the terrace, she heard her parents having breakfast with Mary and discussing departure times for their expedition to Chartley Hall, and her heart sank again. Oh, lord. It was one thing to cheer Dad up by encouraging him to re-enact the National Trust guide at the dinner table; it was another to actually *go with him* to one of these places just to keep the peace. Sure, she had liked them a lot when she was smaller. She especially liked the daydreaming you could do, pretending this beautiful silk wallpapered room with its enormous bed was yours; pretending this marble staircase with the huge sculpture at the bottom was what you had to descend each night, huge crinoline skirts swaying from side to side as you greeted your guests, then were danced off onto the moonlit terrace by your husband, the terribly dashing Baron of . . . something. Or was that a scene from *Regency Buck*? She couldn't remember, and wouldn't, especially now all her Georgette Heyers were probably languishing in an un-ecological landfill site somewhere.

Anyway, it was nice to imagine, quite another to have to pretend to enjoy it now you were twenty-eight, and basically thought stately homes perpetrated the myth of an outmoded class structure on British society, and kept people like her dad firmly in his place, thinking they weren't good enough for other people like the Sandersons. Apart from anything else, the idea of trailing round after her parents all day whilst they went 'Ooh' and 'Aah' over some boring carving in a library was dire, not to mention too depressingly embarrassing to imagine. She could stay at home with a good book; she had found an old Lord Peter Wimsey mystery on the bookshelf the night before and was looking forward to settling down with that for the day, perhaps outside if the weather held. No more romances for her.

She got dressed and went to the kitchen, and there was her dad, his head bobbing up and down enthusiastically as he passed his mother-in-law the milk.

'A-ha, Laura! Morning! We thought we should set off in about an hour, what do you think?' he said, munching on toast and brushing imaginary crumbs absent-mindedly off his rather bald head.

'Morning, love,' said Angela. 'Come and have some coffee, I've just made it. Do you want toast?' She stood up. 'I'll get you some, do you want some?'

'I'm fine,' Laura growled. She cleared her throat. 'I'm fine, Mum, I'll get it,' she said, rather more lucidly.

'So, Laura,' said her dad jovially. 'Looking forward to our trip today, love?' He waved his guidebook at her.

'Yup,' said Laura, reaching for a mug and pouring herself some coffee. 'Look, Dad, the thing is . . .'

'Take the A road, not the B,' George said, pressing his finger firmly down on the open road map which was on the table. 'Look, dear, don't you think?'

'Dad,' said Laura.

'But it's not that far,' Angela said. 'Only fifteen miles or so, wouldn't the B road be nicer, and just as fast really?'

'Well,' said George. 'Hm. And there *is* that interesting crafts shop in Wenlock on the way, isn't there? Perhaps –'

'*Dad!*' Laura said sharply. Both her parents looked up at her. Mary carried on reading *The Times*.

'Dad, look – I was thinking,' Laura said. 'Do you mind if . . . if I don't come today?' She yawned, in a deeply unconvincing way. 'I'm really tii-iired. Aaah. I didn't sleep well. And I don't feel well.'

Her parents looked at her.

'Also, I've got to do some work, too,' she finished. 'For the – the thing next week. My meeting. So, I really have to, actually. And . . .'

'Laura,' Angela interrupted, holding her hand up as if to prevent her from speaking further. 'Let me give you a piece of advice.'

'Sure,' said Laura meekly.

'If you're going to make an excuse, only make one excuse,' said her mother sternly. 'Don't make four. It makes it terribly obvious that you're trying to get out of something.'

'I'm not!'

'Yes, you are,' Angela said. 'Never mind, dear. If you don't want to come, just say so. We're hardly going to be heartbroken, you know.'

Laura looked at her dad. He didn't look heartbroken, of course. He did look quite sad, though. She shifted in her seat. She didn't want to go. She was twenty-eight! She didn't have to go if she didn't want to, and – she wasn't going to go, that was it.

Silence fell upon the group, until Mary said, 'Such a nice

postcard from Annabel, did I show it to you? She and Robert are really looking forward to Saturday, Angela. And she says Robert said to let George know he'll be able to give him a hand with the barbecue, too. Well, that's nice of him, isn't it? I suppose he's remembering George's slight mishap with the grill last year.'

Woah, thought Laura. Woah, woah. God, those Sandersons, they really were the pits.

'God,' George muttered under his breath. Laura could have sworn she heard him say something else much ruder than that, but – no! Not Dad, surely? She looked up at him in Foster solidarity, her chin in the air.

'Sure, I'll come today,' she said suddenly. 'I just needed to wake up a bit. Great. Great.'

'Great!' said George.

Mary smiled, and went back to her paper. 'Have a lovely time.'

Laura looked at her questioningly.

'I'm not coming, darling,' she said serenely. 'The garden needs doing and my hip's much better. You'll have a wonderful day without me, I'm sure.'

'Hm,' said Laura.

They took the B road in the end, an hour later, and it was getting on for twelve by the time they turned off for Chartley Hall. Away from the coast it was a hot, still day, the trees along the quiet lanes around the house were heavy and green, the only sound a passing car or a lazily cooing wood pigeon high in the trees. They drove through Chartley, a small village crammed with B & Bs, shops selling tea towels of the house, quaint old pubs, and a mile further along they came to the turning. A painted wooden sign, cracked and peeling, stood on a stake, partly obscured by cow parsley and trailing leaves. Laura had to peer to read:

'Here we are,' said George, the excitement in his voice palpable. 'On we go.'

They turned into the drive and crawled slowly down the potholed, clay surface, bumping along gently.

'Imagine what it must have been like in a *carriage*,' said Angela, bouncing enthusiastically up and down in her seat.

Laura gazed out of the window at the vast expanse of meadow framing the drive. No, she would *not* imagine what it must have been like in a carriage. That kind of behaviour was over for her. Of course, the old her would be busy thinking up fairytale stories, some complicated scenario which involved her and her parents being asked to stay for supper, invited to a ball in the house that evening, the young marquess her dad was so excited about asking her to waltz . . .

Well, there you go. Apart from anything else, she was wearing a faded old cotton skirt and a ribbon-strapped vest from Marks and Spencer – that wasn't ballroom-dancing gear. She'd seen *Strictly Come Dancing*. She couldn't waltz, she reminded herself. She gazed out of the window at the view unfolding before her. Surely even her new unromantic self could enjoy a view; that was allowed.

Beyond her, the landscape fell gently away, and she could see trees, and a stream rising up to some kind of temple in the far, far distance at the top of a hill. She could smell freshly mown grass, and she could hear the sound of a breeze rustling the trees, even across the wide stretch of open land. The car

152

slowed down as they got to a cattle grid, and drew up beside a tollbooth.

It appeared to be empty, but there was clearly some form of life inside. It was shaking, and muffled shrieks and growls were coming from within its narrow, dark interior.

'Morning!' said George, jauntily unperturbed. 'Three, please!'

There was silence inside, then a muted coughing noise, and a remarkably pretty girl suddenly stood up. She was about Laura's age, with milk-white clear skin, scattered with the darkest freckles, dark brown eyes that were almost black, and tousled, auburn-brown hair, which she flung out of her face as she smiled at them. She had a pretty strappy white top and a lot of jewellery on, and she played with a large thick gold costume necklace round her neck, as she said, 'Hi there.'

Her voice was strangely mesmerising, slightly transatlantic, slightly posh, slightly offhand. It was low and smoky. She smiled at George, biting her top lip.

'How are you?'

'Er . . .' George looked round wildly, as if to ask his wife for the answer. 'Er . . . I'm fine.'

'Good, good,' said the vision soothingly, her whisky tones drawing him in so that George swivelled towards her, and coughed.

'So . . . you want some tickets, yeah?'

Something in the bottom of the tollbooth made a shuffling, clunking sound, and the girl giggled huskily and stamped her feet.

'Sorry . . . sorry about that.' She glanced wickedly down. 'Naughty. Right, then, tickets. Yeah?'

'Tickets . . .' said George again.

Just as Laura was thinking she might have to get out of the car and slap her dad back into rational thought, her mother intervened.

'Three, please.'

'Great,' said the vision. 'Great. How much is that?'

'Well,' said Angela, much disconcerted by this question. 'I don't . . . well, I don't know, do I?'

Suddenly the sentry box spoke.

'House and grounds or just grounds,' it said in a low Norfolk accent.

George and Angela jumped out of their seats.

'What?' said George. 'My goodness. What?'

Angela was suddenly alert. She peered towards the tollbooth, her dark eyes flashing with interest.

'Well, my goodness,' she said. 'Have you got someone down there?'

The vision chewed a lock of her hair. 'Fuck,' she said, apparently unbothered.

'She's got *what*?' said George.

'She's got someone down there. Whereabouts down there . . . I don't know,' Angela said, showing a rare glimpse of camp humour. 'Do let him get up and let us in, dear, then you can get back to what you were doing.'

'Forty-five pounds for house and grounds please,' said the voice from within, even more quietly than before. Laura surreptitiously looked over to the tollbooth to see if she could see anything, when suddenly its back door shot open and a lanky youth was seen bolting across the grass, behind the trees and out of sight.

His former companion sighed, and tossed her hair again.

'Well, he said forty-five pounds, so I suppose he's right.'

'*Forty-five pounds!*' said Laura in a stage whisper. 'That's bloody daylight robbery!'

As ever, the stage whisper was totally ineffectual, as it seemed to her that everyone within fifty paces could have heard her. The girl shot her a look of pure dislike. 'Have you got a problem with that?' she said.

'No, no, no,' said George hastily, fumbling in his wallet. 'There you go. It's cash, there you go.'

'Great,' came the reply. 'Keep on driving.'

'Any tickets with that?' said George desperately, as the girl made to turn away. She was examining something under her fingernails.

'God, right. Uhm . . . yeah, here,' she said, and carelessly flicked four tickets out from a roll on the counter. 'Great. Have a . . . great day, then.' She peered in at Laura, her stare of curiosity verging on the rude. 'I'm sure you'll all really enjoy yourselves. Bye.'

And she turned away and, tossing her hair, called someone on her phone. As they drove on, George gazed about him wildly, expecting other titian-haired beauties to pop up in their path. Angela was looking back and saying, 'Well, *really!* Who was *she*?'

Laura gritted her teeth and scowled. She heard the girl on the phone in the distance, her smoky, cracked voice carrying on the wind.

'Sean! Hey, Sean. Get back here, finish what you started. No! I'm bored. I'm so bored . . .'

CHAPTER SEVENTEEN

They drove on, through the near-silent park, through the huge oak trees that fanned out away from the drive. They were vast, sturdy things, standing in a line like sentries, and their branches hung low, casting a velvety-green shadowy band across the landscape.

'Look!' said Angela suddenly. 'There it is. Beautiful, isn't it?'

There it was, and Laura turned her head to look. It was beautiful, it was true. The great house rose up out of the gently curving parkland it sat in, a crouching lion, noble and welcoming at the same time. The sun warmed the old stone, giving it a rich, golden glow. The windows glinted in the patchy midday sun, and the clouds that raced above the house reflected in the glass. It was a huge, gracious thing; Laura could see additional wings and flanks stretching off it again and again, almost as if it were a small town. Though it had been built by hand, it was part of its own landscape, and it was very easy to imagine how it might have been three hundred years ago. Remove that family with the screaming toddler and the buggy at the front. Take out the sign saying 'Café This Way', and the five old ladies in identical summer-print lawn frocks oohing over a guidebook, and the Range Rover peremptorily parked right outside – surely it shouldn't be there? – and replace it instead with footmen in wigs, some Mozart in the background, and Laura herself, her hair piled up, one ringlet escaping and curling over her shoulder, dressed in a gown of beautiful red and gold, the door to her carriage being flung open as she is handed daintily down onto the gravel, fanning herself with a delicate thing made of bone china. She allowed herself that one. It was a beautiful house. But as they parked in the car park, a field some distance from the house, Laura got out of the car and a new rush of gloominess overtook her as the mundanity of the situation hit her again.

'Ha ha!' said George, gripping his guidebook as tightly as if it were the key to a new Aston Martin. 'Right, let's be off then. Shall we start with the house first?'

'Great,' said Angela, fluffing her hair out of her mac. 'Then we can have the picnic, then look at the grounds. And the Orangery. Oh, George! The Orangery –'

'Yes, mustn't forget that,' George said, winking at his wife.

'What?' Laura asked.

'There's an entire re-creation of the Battle of Trafalgar in there,' George said, pleased.

'Isn't the room a bit small for that?' asked Laura, dead-pan.

George ignored her and strode on ahead. 'No,' said Angela beside him, as Laura brought up the rear, scuffing her flip-flops childishly along the dry gravel. 'A *miniature* re-creation. Toy soldiers. Thousands of them. The eleventh marquess painted them all himself.'

'Wow,' said Laura, as they rejoined the drive that led to the house. 'That is quite simply incredible.'

'The Great Hall was the first room to be fully completed, and it is here that guests would be welcomed as they arrived. This tapestry was designed especially for the Great North Wall and woven in Mortlake, which was the pre-eminent location for tapestry weaving during the 1670s. The chandeliers, mouldings and fixtures were designed as part of the overall décor for the hall by Jean-Bastide Rousseau, the pre-eminent artisan of his day in this area. This map of the county which you see above the great fireplace is very old. It dates back to 1484 and the final battle of the War of the Roses at Bosworth, in which the Danvers and Needham families both fought. On the winning side, of course. Lady Anne Danvers was betrothed to John Needham afterwards, and the two great families were joined then. This map was made to commemorate it. Thus it is central to the story of Chartley. And now we move through . . . into the Ballroom . . . do follow me. Thank you. No flash photography. Thank you.'

'Cynthia,' said George keenly, annexing the fearsome woman who was their guide, 'may I just ask why the significance of the map? It is interesting when one thinks that the Needhams . . .'

He danced alongside Cynthia, whose hair was set in tight curlers of an iron and tin hue, and whose back was as straight as a wall. She frowned at him as they passed into the next room. Laura watched, as Angela gazed around, her mother's birdlike eyes darting from one object to another, taking it all in, wondering what she should say and think about it all.

The other fellow day-trippers on this guided tour were as Laura had feared. Three clearly hysterical middle-aged women who were on some kind of day out, and who displayed such a degree of over-excitement about everything Laura wanted to tell them never to go to somewhere really *actually* exciting, like Las Vegas – the shock would kill them. Two separate, solitary, dour-looking men, one very thin, one verging on obese, cameras round necks. An overwrought family trying to pretend they were having a lovely day, whereas in fact the husband looked bored, the wife exhausted, and the children bewildered and tetchy by turns.

She seemed to have been there for about a week already – could it really be that they were still only in the first room? She spotted her mum waving at her, pulled herself together, and trotted obediently over to join her, wearing what she hoped was a pleasant smile of mutual enjoyment.

'And here is the library,' said Cynthia, opening the door and flattening herself against it, sentry-like, to allow the group to file past her well-harnessed bosom and into the final room on their tour. 'Hm,' she muttered, as the large camera-wielding man wedged himself between her and the door, and eventually pushed himself out onto the other side, spluttering. Laura followed, trying not to laugh.

'The library is perhaps the most famous room in Chartley –' Cynthia began. 'It –'

'Excuse me, Cynthia?' one of the three ladies said, waving her hand in the air. 'Hellooo.' She nodded enthusiastically at Cynthia, who looked as if she would like to have her executed for treason. 'It's so lovely to be here!'

The other ladies wobbled together in agreement.

'Can I ask you something?'

Cynthia inclined her head. 'Of course,' she said coldly. 'Briefly.'

'When was the last time you saw Lady Ranelagh?' said the first lady, as the other two looked on expectantly.

'Excuse me?' said Cynthia. 'There is no Lady Ranelagh. His Grace is not married.'

She turned to move on, but the second one stopped her. 'Sshh, Clare! Sorry. What my friend means is, the marquess's mother. Vivienne Lash. Has she never been back here? Did you ever see her?'

The rest of the group watched nervously, as Cynthia looked at the three ladies in turn.

'Oh, Frances,' the third one said crossly. 'We shouldn't have asked.'

'As I said before,' said Cynthia, turning magnificently on her heel. 'There *is* no Lady Ranelagh. I believe Mrs Needham – as she is known now – lives in the South of France. *Ai* have never seen her.'

There was silence. The three ladies looked crushed. Laura smiled sympathetically at them, as Cynthia made her way down the room.

'Now,' she went on, 'the library.'

It certainly was a stunning room, as George had said. It looked about as long as Laura's street at home. Shelves rose high on both sides, and light poured through the long, high windows on three walls – it took up the whole of the side of the house. It was like a big, glorious lantern, humming with interesting things, and although Laura desperately wanted to be interested, she was fast running out of steam. The old Laura would have cast herself as the bookish marquess's daughter, Lady Laura, creeping in here to study John Donne by candlelight whilst her brutish, unintelligent family slept on, but she simply couldn't work up the enthusiasm. She could almost block out the sight of George leaping up and down by a painting on the far wall.

'Yes, the famous Hogarth series,' said Cynthia, marching the length of the gallery as the tour dribbled along behind her. 'Har-rrem. The jewel of the Needham family's art collection. Long thought to have been unfinished by Hogarth. In fact, they were only discovered fifty years ago, by the present marquess's grandmother. Chartley Hall was used as a boarding school during the Second World War, and many of its most prized possessions were put into storage, in the attics above us here.' She stopped in front of the painting hanging in front of them. A man and a woman were holding hands, emerging from a country church, with a plethora of characters – the grasping mother-in-law, the sozzled father, a beggar and some children playing to the side – fanning out around the central bride and groom. 'Some of his greatest work is shown here. All his life, Hogarth struggled to reconcile the twin demons of narrative subject matter and what he saw as great "historical" painting in the grand manner . . . With this sequence, which shows the happy courtship, wedding and

160

subsequent life together of a young aristocratic couple, he found it. Note the . . .'

Laura's attention wandered. What was Paddy doing at the moment, she wondered. Paddy and Jo – and all of that – seemed so far away, a lifetime away. It was good to be at a distance from it all, but did she miss it? She didn't know, she didn't want to think too closely about it. She liked the fact her life was on hold, as though she'd pressed the pause button on a video of it. On a tour of stately homes with her parents. Hm. She bit her lip and turned back to Cynthia, who was still talking, her clipped tones hurrying the information along.

'. . . It was only when Amelia, the new marchioness, was taking these pieces out in 1947 that she stumbled upon a secret cupboard in the depths of the last room. There, rolled up in twine, miraculously preserved – five of the eight paintings of this series. The only one of Hogarth's series which actually tells a happy story, I am pleased to say.'

There was nodding of heads and pleased clucking from the group, as Cynthia smiled benignly down at them.

'Where are the others?'

Cynthia looked up around her. 'I beg your pardon?'

Laura, to her astonishment, found herself saying again, 'Where are the other paintings?'

Cynthia turned towards her, her smile a little more forced. 'The other paintings?'

'In the series,' Laura said. 'You said they found five all rolled up. Why's there only one up, then?'

'Oh, dear girl,' said Cynthia. 'We couldn't hang the others up. Too risky. Someone might cause them damage. They're very frail, you know. This one's the strongest.'

'But –' said Laura. 'What's – well.' She stopped, not wanting to sound rude.

'Go on, dear,' said Cynthia, her eyes glinting.

Laura looked wildly around her, regretting starting this conversation. Why? Why couldn't she just keep quiet? She felt

161

the heat of someone's gaze on her and realised her mother was staring at her, eyes silently beseeching politeness. Laura ploughed on.

'Sorry. But – well, what's the point of keeping them in storage? Why can't you put them on display so they can be together?'

'It's not as simple as that, dear,' Cynthia said firmly. 'And it's up to the trustees of the house. It's not really about putting everyone out so the general public can enjoy it, is it?'

'Why?' said Laura, feeling heat rise within her, suddenly so impatient with this sad, middle-England, middle-aged debate, setting, scene – everything. The new pragmatist in her rebelled. This wasn't fairytale, it was extortion! 'You've charged us fifteen pounds to get in, most of the rooms are roped off, the car park's miles from the house, everyone here is about eighty – no offence, Mum and Dad – no one seems particularly pleased to see us here, we're treated like cattle – I just wonder why you bother.'

'Laura!' said Angela, horrified.

There was a short silence, broken only by the shuffling of feet on parquet floor as the majority of the group trotted surreptitiously towards Cynthia and away from Laura, putting as much distance between themselves and this crazy, dangerous recidivist as they possibly could.

'*Well*. Really,' said Cynthia slowly, puffing up like a tweedy balloon. 'I mean. Really. That's not nice, now, is it?'

'Sorry,' said Laura. 'My fault. I apologise.'

Laura had been on a negotiation skills workshop a few months ago, where she learnt how to deal with reluctant, lazy volunteers, undermined, exhausted teachers, parents who were sometimes demanding, sometimes hopelessly bewildered. The key, in most situations, was to apologise. Say sorry. People love it. It makes them feel much better, even if nothing gets done. The verbal action is greater than the mental commitment, in nine cases out of ten. When rats were found in the kitchens of the local comprehensive nearest to Laura, kitchens that were

162

already riddled with damp, the Department of Education apologised (one of the parents was a well-known author with connections in the right circles; otherwise the matter would never have gone that high). And everyone felt much, much better. No matter that the rats didn't go, the school was falling apart, and the damp was spreading. No matter that the textbooks were held together with Sellotape, the computers were so old they were practically wound up by hand and one of the pupils had stabbed another the previous year. No, someone apologised, in a heartfelt way, and everyone felt reassured, right in their grievance, even though absolutely nothing got done about it. It astonished Laura, depressed her, amused her sometimes, the power of an apology.

She looked around her, down the long hall, at the sunshine which had suddenly broken into the great window at the end, the honey-coloured books lining the shelves; at the collection of flared-skirted, guidebook-clutching, middle-aged, middle-class families and groups in front of her, and just wanted to be on her own. She should never have come in the first place. She should have stayed at home. What was she doing here, arguing with some woman in a knitted raspberry tank top about car-park fees and tea-shops?

'I'm really sorry,' she said again. 'I'll wait outside, Mum – Dad – you take your time. I'll meet you back at the car, OK?'

Her parents nodded mutely. And so Laura turned and left, tripping swiftly and silently down the old wooden staircase that swept majestically down into the Great Hall. The sun was pouring through the great wide door and, with her flip-flops flapping on the black and white marble floor, she ran outside, away from it all.

CHAPTER EIGHTEEN

Laura walked briskly, pulling her cardigan down over her hands and clenching the wool in her fists. She walked away from the stable block, leaving the house behind her, the dry fern and grass crunching satisfyingly under her flip-flops as she went. Ahead of her was a glade of trees, cool and dark amongst the yellow-grey meadow. Above her in a white sky the hazy sun shone down. She could feel sweat pooling at the base of her spine.

Behind the trees was a huge field where, at one end, a mower worked methodically, making his way towards the heavy, nodding grass at this end of the field. Laura could hear the humming sound of the blades, growing louder in the distance. In amongst the edge of the trees there was a little bench. She looked around anxiously, hoping against hope not to be accosted by yet another happy family or more irritating fact-giving middle-aged people, such as those who had accompanied her here, but, happily she was alone now. She reached into her bag for her sunglasses. Her hand felt a shape, a square shape beneath the torn lining. It was a packet of cigarettes. She hadn't smoked for days, she only really had with Hilary or Dan – in fact, she was pretty sure they were Dan's this time, from some snatched moment somewhere when she'd rammed them into her bag, in the rush to be somewhere, not late. How strange. They were a bit bashed around, but there was a lighter in the packet too, so she leant against a tree and lit a cigarette, closing her eyes and listening with blessed relief to the silence all around her, underpinned only by the sound of the engine growing louder as it came closer.

Something made her open her eyes. It was a deer, moving towards the copse, at the edge of her line of vision. Its antlers were huge, fascinating to one who hadn't really seen a deer close-up since she was six on a school trip to Richmond Park. Laura stared at it in wonder, mesmerised by its proud beauty, the contours of its body. The deer stared impassively back. I must take a photo of this, Laura thought, and rummaged in her bag again for her camera. Finally, something that might actually be a good photo, after five days of snapping remarkable road signs, or Mum, Dad and Granny giving a thumbs-up sign whilst seated around a collapsible camping table.

Laura threw her cigarette on the ground. The noise from the mower was louder in her ears. She crouched amongst the grass and tried to make a cooing noise, the better to lure the deer closer, but it stayed where it was, perfectly still, gazing dreamily at her in the sun. Suddenly, the noise behind her stopped, but Laura didn't notice, or care. She edged towards the deer, crouching and shuffling, camera in place.

The afternoon scent of mown grass, the tangy, sharp smell of a bonfire crackling, filled her nostrils. In the distance, a bird cried harshly in a tree somewhere, and Laura remained as still as possible. Suddenly, the deer reared back and ran away, fleeing lightly into the wood. Laura got to her feet, disappointed, as the smell of the bonfire grew stronger. Perhaps they were burning the fields now harvest-time was here. Or something.

She turned around, and was appalled by the sight that met her eyes. The cigarette she had put out had obviously not been put out, and at her feet was a small, smoking black haze, with tiny flames that licked the brittle straw around it, which crept along the ground. It was alarmingly big, over a foot wide. Shit. Shit. Shit. She was *so stupid*! She knew you were supposed to put fires out with damp towels, where could she run and get one from? Damn! She looked down at the fire, and for one mad second thought perhaps she should throw herself on it, when someone from behind grabbed her by the shoulders and pushed her out of the way.

'What the fuck do you think you're doing?' came a furious, low voice behind her. It was a man, a tall man, and he was glaring at Laura as if she were a cockroach he'd found in his kitchen. He was wearing old jeans and a battered T-shirt, and a soft cotton shirt tied around his waist, which he pulled off, flung to the ground, and stamped on, his boots blacking out the centre of the blaze.

'Stand back,' he said briefly, not looking at her. 'You'll burn your feet in those shoes.'

'No I won't – ouch!' Laura yelled, as she stepped on a small line of flames that had crept away from the main conflagration. She stumbled back and fell over.

He held out his hand, and Laura took it, and he pulled her up to her feet with amazing ease. She realised he was furious.

'Are you OK?' he said, steadying her as she hopped backwards to put her flip-flop back on. 'Good. Do you realise how stupid that was, putting your cigarette out here? Apart from the fact you shouldn't be smoking in the first place, you idiot, we haven't had any rain for two weeks. This place could go up like a tinderbox.'

'Right,' said Laura, bending down again and picking up her bag and camera, to cover the embarrassment she felt at being told off. She caught sight of some keys in his hand and deduced, correctly, that this cross, scruffily dressed and rude man must have been the person driving the mower. She looked up at him, a ready answer on her lips, but stopped as she caught sight of him.

Mr Mower was obviously much angrier than she'd realised.

He breathed as if he had been running. He was sweaty, and there was grass or hay in his messy black hair. His dark brown eyes were glaring at her with something akin to loathing. He was broad-shouldered, tall, powerful-looking, his face tanned. Laura suddenly felt rather scared, as if he might pick her up by the scruff of her neck and fling her amongst the blades of the mower, to be shredded to small pieces.

She squinted up at Mr Mower, annoyance written on her face. 'Look, I'm sorry,' she said, trying not to feel upset. He stared impassively back at her, his only expression one of enormous disdain. 'But I'm not an idiot. It's a free country, you know, I can have a cigarette if I want. They should have signs up, if they're that against it, how was I supposed to know? I'd have picked it up afterwards and I certainly wouldn't have left it to catch on fire, not being blind or anything, you know,' she finished, with a note of triumph in her voice. 'Sorry, OK?' She swung her bag over her shoulder and made to leave.

'Typical,' said Mr Mower behind her, as she walked off. 'Typical townie. It's not your fault, is it? It's always someone else's fault. I don't know why we bother sometimes.' He stopped, but Laura carried on, pretending not to hear him. 'Here,' he said suddenly. 'Hey. You forgot your camera case.' He gripped Laura's arm lightly.

Laura turned around and smiled up at him, unable to be cross with him for long. He was nice, even if he was fairly rude, and prone to throwing people around cornfields. 'Thank you,' she said. 'I'm not doing very well, am I? Listen, thanks. I'd better get back. Good luck with the seed-sowing, or whatever it is.'

'Crop rotational eco-system, actually,' Mr Mower said. 'Listen, you haven't got a cigarette I could nick, have you?'

Laura gaped at him. 'Are you having a laugh?'

'No.'

'Why on earth . . .' Laura said. 'You don't deserve one, do you?'

'No,' the smoking farmer said. 'I could go inside, but it's just such a hassle. Takes about fifteen minutes just to get to my room.'

'Yes,' said Laura, handing over the packet, her heart sinking. She really didn't want to be treated to some long monologue about the wonders of the estate, how great Lord So-and-so was, how friendly the people were. Fifteen minutes – she looked at her watch.

'Where do you live, then?' she said.

Mr Mower lit his cigarette. 'Over there,' he pointed.

Laura followed his direction. 'In . . . in the house?' she said.

'Yes, that's right,' Mr Mower replied, laughing at her incredulous expression. 'Someone has to, you know.'

'Seriously?' Laura said, impressed despite herself. 'You actually live – there?'

'Yep,' said Mr Mower. He ran his hand over the back of his neck self-consciously.

'So – how come?' Laura said. Her new inner self was saying, 'No! Don't be impressed by this strange man just because he lives in a big house!' And her old inner self was saying, 'Wow! Cor!' She shook her head, trying to drown the voices out, then realised she must look insane, and so she smiled at him, almost shyly.

Mr Mower looked at her for a second. 'How come – what? I live there?'

'Yes,' said Laura. She couldn't help staring at him. He was – well, pretty OK-looking. In a plaid shirt, lean kind of farmer way, she supposed. The old her would have gone for him like a shot, started batting her eyelids and wondering which room was his. The new Laura smiled pleasantly at him, wondering when she should get back to her parents.

Mr Mower smiled back at her. He looked her up and down. 'Well. I look after it. So I get to sleep there.'

So that was what it was like, working for one of these places – you had to be able to make the frigging tea, sell people tea towels in the shop *and* get out and mow the fields. What a life. She looked at him with something akin to pity and he stared back at her with that glowering expression, his brows furrowed together. He drew on his cigarette and said, 'What about you? Where do you live?'

'In London,' Laura said. 'I'm on holiday here. With my . . . er.' She stopped. 'Er . . . with my boyfriend.'

'And where is he?' said Mr Mower.

Slightly nettled by his nosiness, and unwilling to entrench herself too deeply in the lie she was already regretting, Laura said, 'Er . . . looking at the soldiers. But I got bored so I went for a walk.'

An expression of annoyance strode across Mr Mower's face. 'So, you're on holiday together, then?'

'Yes,' Laura said, putting the lighter back in her pocket. 'Look, I'd better go. Sorry again about . . . you know. Don't tell your – well, whatever you call him. Or perhaps you don't see him. Don't tell whoever your boss is.'

'Hold on a minute,' said Mr Mower. 'What's your name?'

'Laura,' Laura replied. 'What's yours?'

'It's . . . Nick.' He held out his hand. 'It's nice to meet you, Laura. I'll let you get back to your boyfriend, then. Have a nice holiday. Thanks for the cigarette. Oh, shit. There's Charles. I need to speak to him.'

Laura followed his gaze over to the house. There, under the spreading plane tree by the shop entrance, stood a tall, lean man, about her age, stooping slightly as he stopped to talk to some visitors, who were drinking in the sight of him with obvious pleasure. One of them took a photo of him. He smiled, put his hands out in a semi-defensive but still polite gesture, and the couple walked away, their heads together, twittering with excitement and looking at the photo on their camera.

'Who's Charles?' said Laura. 'What does he do?'

'Er,' said Nick, scratching his cheek. 'Well – he kind of runs things. You know?'

169

Laura looked up at him. 'Oh!' she said, realisation dawning. 'I'll let you get back to your boss, then.'

'He's not really my boss,' said her companion. Charles waved over at them, and Nick waved back. Charles disappeared back into the house, via a side door, and Nick turned to her and smiled wryly. 'Well, he sort of is, I suppose. I'll catch him later. Couple of things he wanted to ask me about.'

'Oh?' Laura said, happy to delay her return for a moment or two. She leant against a tree and watched him. He looked at home there, standing almost arrogantly amongst the grass. She suddenly felt self-conscious in her pink vest and skirt. A bit flimsy. Silly. 'You are lucky. To be self-employed.' She thought of the decisions she hadn't made, the mess she'd left behind.

'What do you do, then?' he asked curiously.

'I'm a . . . I work with schools,' said Laura uneasily. She could hear her own voice, knew it sounded like a lie, even though it was the truth. 'For the council. I'm a co-ordinator. Sort of.' She cleared her throat. 'Well. It's kind of weird at the moment.'

'What do you mean?' Nick asked, looking at her rather strangely.

'Well – like I don't – I don't really know what I'm doing, even though I know it's what I want to do. Anyway.' She shook her head, and Nick stared at her again. 'That sounds stupid, forget it.'

Nick was silent. After a moment he said, 'No.' His voice was matter-of-fact. 'It doesn't. It doesn't at all. You love it, but you think you're rubbish at it. I'm the same.'

'That's exactly it,' Laura said. She stared at him. 'It sounds so stupid when I think of it myself.' She smiled at him gratefully. 'Well, I'm going to be late. My parents want to spend a long time in the shop. A long time.'

Nick laughed. 'Doing what?'

'Well,' Laura said. She scrunched her eyes up, trying to explain. 'I don't know what your parents are like in a place like this, but

170

mine like to finish a long day off somewhere like here by going to the shop, buying about fifty postcards of obscure portraits of the family who lived there, and then having a really, *really* long, intricate discussion about the merits and demerits of every tea towel. Interesting Norman Fonts of Norfolk? Or one in aid of the local RNLI lifeboat?' She ticked them off on her fingers, oblivious to Nick's quizzical expression. 'Or Narrow Boats and Scenes from the Broads? Or How to Make Cheese in Five Easy Steps, printed on some cotton so you can dry the dishes with it.'

'Right,' said Nick, smiling.

'Right,' said Laura. 'So I have to meet them to get started with –' She stopped, suddenly remembering what she'd said before. 'Them – and, and – my boyfriend, I mean.'

Nick raised an eyebrow at her. He smiled sardonically, his eyes glittering with amusement.

'So you don't have a boyfriend then,' he said, throwing his keys up in the air and catching them.

'Yes,' Laura said hotly. 'He likes tea towels, too. He's just not here. He's, er . . . oh god. Never mind.'

'Never mind,' Nick agreed politely.

There was a pause.

'Boyfriends are for losers,' Laura muttered, after a while.

'Are they?' said Nick. 'Really?'

'Oh, forget it,' Laura said defensively. 'It's not your problem.'

'Not really, no,' said Nick. 'I have no boyfriend problems. Perhaps I should, though. Perhaps I should get a pencil with a pink rubber on the end and spend ages in my room reading magazines and writing about how horrible boys are in my pink five-year diary with a padlock so flimsy and crap that a blind, fingerless newt could break into it if they wanted.'

Since this was how Laura had spent most of her teenage years, she didn't quite know what to say. She could feel herself blushing, and tried to cover her tracks by saying jovially, 'Well! I've never done that, that's for sure! But – er, I do have some friends who did. How d'you know that?'

171

'I've got a sister,' said Nick feelingly. 'Well, two. But one of them spent about five years doing just that.'

'Anyway,' Laura said, feeling the conversation was veering wildly off the point, and reminding herself not to come across as a stupid person who *had* spent their teenage years scribbling 'I love Mr Wallace' in several different languages in a pink diary, 'nice meeting you.'

'I'll walk back to the house with you,' Nick offered. 'I'm going that way. Time for my tea. We can talk about your psychological disorder as we go.'

'What psychological disorder?'

'The psychological disorder you have that means you need to invent imaginary boyfriends who like picking out tea towels with your parents.'

Laura said, in what she hoped was a dignified manner, 'No, thank you. I'll walk back this way, thanks. Goodbye.'

She stomped off again. Nick followed behind. He strode easily, catching up with her. Laura ignored him.

'Can I ask you something?' he said.

'Go ahead,' Laura breathed, increasing the length of her stride.

Nick stopped suddenly and stood in front of her so she almost fell onto him.

'*What?*' Laura said, steadying herself. 'God, you're annoying, has anyone ever told you that?'

'Lots of people,' Nick said. He put his hand on her folded arm. 'It was nice to meet you, Laura.'

'You too,' said Laura. 'Thanks. And I'm – I'm sorry about the fire thing. Really stupid of me. I *am* really stupid.'

Nick looked at her. 'I'm sure you're not.'

'Trust me,' said Laura fervently. 'I really am. Anyway, there are my parents, ho, hum. Better be off to meet them, get on with the rest of my lovely holiday.'

'Well,' said Nick. 'I'm sure you'll have a whale of a time. Sounds like the perfect recipe for a really great holiday.'

172

'Oh yeah,' said Laura. 'If you like jigsaw puzzles and going through guidebooks looking for Roman roads. And going to craft fairs. And having to see the Seekers tribute band. Which is called The Seekers Tribute Band, by the way,' she added bitterly.

'What a crap name,' said Nick. 'You'd think they could have come up with something better. "They Seek Them Here", or something.'

'*Exactly!*' Laura said, hitting him on the arm. 'Sorry,' she added, as Nick yelled with shock. 'That's what *I* said, though! That was *my* suggestion! To myself, I mean,' she said confidentially. 'Mine was Desperately Seeking the Seekers – you see, I think that's much better.'

'No it's not,' said Nick, rubbing his arm. 'Who's heard of *Desperately Seeking Susan* if you're a Seekers fan? They wouldn't get the reference. No, mine's best.'

'No way,' said Laura heatedly. 'But hey,' she continued, correcting herself. 'Let's agree to disagree. Well, agree as well. I can't believe you said that one too,' she said, musing. 'Hah.'

She was silent for a moment. 'Anyway, I'm just glad I'm not going mad.'

'Blimey,' Nick said sympathetically. 'Holiday not great, then.'

'Like I say,' said Laura, 'jigsaw puzzles, craft fairs, the Seekers. If you like that, well, great. Oh, and listening to endless monologues about some boring Marquess of Blah Blah and his ancestors and their stupid house that you have to pay millions of pounds to get into and then it's about as much fun as – as *botulism.*' She stopped, and her hand flew to her mouth. 'God, Nick. I'm really sorry! Sorry. I know he's your – your boss and everything. And you work here. I didn't mean it. This is a lovely house. Really nice.'

'What do you mean?' Nick asked.

'Not my thing,' Laura replied. She tried to explain. 'Just – well. You know how there's two sides to everyone. I used to like this kind of thing, going around pretending I was a countess, or something.'

173

'Really?' said Nick.

'Yes,' said Laura. 'But not so much now. Anyway,' she continued, remembering Mrs Danvers, 'it's a long story.'

'I'm sure,' said Nick. 'I barely know you, but I'm sure it is a long story.'

'Shut up,' said Laura. She looked around again, and said, 'Look, I'd better go. And there's the lord and master himself, coming to find you.'

Indeed, Charles had emerged from a door in the side of the vast edifice of the house and was walking towards them.

'Fair enough,' said Nick. He added, 'Look, I know this is a bit – out of the blue, but how about a drink tonight, maybe some food?'

'Tonight?' said Laura. She felt awkward, suddenly.

Nick said easily, 'No big deal if you can't. I just thought you might want a bit of time out from your family. I always do.'

He looked up as Charles approached, then looked back at her. 'So? What do you think?'

'Um,' said Laura, not really sure. What did it mean?

Then she thought of the new her, and thought, well, maybe, fuck it. Who cares if it is wise or not, it's a holiday, and it's an evening away from Mum and Dad and Granny. This is the new Laura, who dates casually and doesn't start replaying the plot of every slushy movie she's ever seen every time some new bloke crosses her path. She glanced at him, up and down, and smiled a small smile. And – well. Look at him.

'I don't know,' she demurred.

'I'm not going to ravish you,' said Nick, puncturing her pretensions. 'It's just a drink, for god's sake. I know you appear to have taken some vow of asceticism, but you look like you might need a drink with someone under the age of forty.'

'Yes,' said Laura. 'My god, yes.'

'The George,' said Nick, almost urgently, as Charles drew near. 'Do you know the George?'

She did know the George; at least, she knew of it. It was

174

the most popular gastropub in the area, booked up for months in advance, notoriously heaving with posh Londoners and those savvy enough to make their dinner reservations in January for July. She wanted to ask how on earth they'd get in there, but she didn't. She merely nodded, mutely.

'At eight?' Nick added. 'I can get a table there. Yes? What do you think?'

There was silence.

'OK, then,' Laura said recklessly. 'OK.'

She had no idea why she was agreeing to go out to supper with this total stranger, only that there was something about him she liked. She wanted to talk to him again. She was also curious to know how he was going to get a table there, but there was something about him that made it seem certain he would.

'Charles, this is Laura,' said Nick.

Charles looked down at Laura and smiled. He was a tall man, a few years older than Laura. He looked sort of how you'd imagine a marquess to look. He was handsome, in a rather gaunt way, with hollow cheeks, and a hollow sternum. But he had a kind, wistful face, and a courteous smile, and he bowed slightly as he bent over Laura's hand.

'Nice to meet you, Laura,' he said. 'Has this man here been a nuisance?'

'You could say that,' said Laura, looking up at her companion, whose expression was impassive. 'No, not really.' She collected herself. She was talking to a marquess, after all. 'This is an absolutely beautiful house,' she said.

Charles nodded, obviously pleased. 'It is, isn't it? We're very lucky.'

He talked politely, asking about her holiday so far as they crossed the grass back towards the house, Nick following a little way behind them, silent. As they reached the gate Laura saw the three middle-aged ladies from the house had gathered and were watching their arrival. As he walked towards them

175

Charles lifted his head and smiled at them courteously, as Nick lingered in the background.

'Lovely house,' said Old Lady #1, simpering and wringing her hands amongst a tea towel in a bag.

'What a lovely day out, Your Grace,' said Old Lady #2, who had a wicker basket under her arm which was crammed to the wicker gills with jams and marmalades with the Chartley logo on them.

Charles held up his hand in a gesture of thanks. 'I'm so glad you've enjoyed yourselves,' he said simply. 'Do hope to see you back here sometime.'

Nick nodded. 'Thank you for coming,' he said. 'It's wonderful you came, isn't it, Charles?'

'Oh, thank you, Lord Ranelagh,' said Old Lady #3, as Charles smiled politely at them, and they all dissolved into the near-hysterical yet deferential giggles which only affect the British public when confronted with the royal family, members of the aristocracy or people like Judi Dench or Joanna Lumley.

'Thanks again,' said Nick, steering Charles gently but firmly away from them.

Charles pulled his cuffs down from his tweed jacket, and smiled at Laura. 'Lovely to meet you,' he said. 'Enjoy the rest of your holiday.'

'Thank you,' said Laura, as he drifted away. 'I –'

'So,' said Nick, turning back to her. 'I'll see you tonight, then?'

He looked at her intently and Laura felt herself losing her nerve. 'Well –' she began.

'Look,' he broke in. 'Shall we make an agreement? I'll be in the bar at eight. I normally am, in any case. So if you're there, you're there.'

Laura didn't want to disappoint him, but she told herself it didn't seem as if he'd really mind that much either way. 'Cool,' she said. 'I'm not sure what I'm doing for the rest of the day anyway. So I'll see. Thanks.'

'Well, Laura. I hope the rest of your day here is enjoyable. Thank you for coming. Apart from the low point of nearly burning down the house and its grounds, you've had a good time, I hope?'

He was already turning away, withdrawing, when Laura said, 'Well, Nick – I know this isn't really your business, but since you ask – actually, I haven't had a very good time, to be honest. It's not much fun here, not for me anyway.'

Nick stopped and turned around. 'What?' His voice was sharp.

Laura twisted the camera strap around in her hands. 'It's just – well, it could have been better.'

'Could have been *better*?' he repeated, incredulous.

'Yes,' Laura replied firmly. 'It's a stately home, I know that. But it's a day out for most people. That's really important, you know? You can't just expect them to have to negotiate with two lunatics having sex in the ticket kiosk to get in, and then charge them a vast amount of money for the privilege of seeing some second-rate paintings in a few dusty rooms, and then round it all off with some rock-hard, stale old scones in the café. On their precious holiday. I really don't mean to be rude, I'm sure Charles is lovely, he seems very nice and it's wonderful for you that you live here and everything. But since you ask, no, I haven't had a good time.'

Nick flinched as she finished, as if someone had thrown cold water at him. 'Well, thank you for that,' he said, after a while.

Laura bit her lip. 'I'm sorry. But you did ask. Look – I've got to go now. Oh hell, look, there's my mum. She can't meet you, she'd want to meet Charles too and that'd be like suicide. Bye, Nick. Thanks, sorry about everything. I've been so rude, I can't believe it.'

'Don't worry,' Nick said. He took her hand. 'You haven't been rude. You've been very interesting. Incredibly interesting, in fact. Enjoy the rest of your holiday, Laura. If I don't see you tonight.'

'Thanks,' said Laura.

Nick touched his hand to his forehead and made a mock-salute. He smiled at her politely, slightly formally. 'Take care, anyway. Bye.'

In the car on the way back, Laura was silent as Angela and George chatted enthusiastically about the things they'd seen, what they'd done, and the postcards and tea towels they'd purchased.

'What a beautiful house. I mean, one room after the other, so beautiful. You missed the picture gallery, Laura. It was – well, beautiful. All of it was! How do you live there, I wonder? It must be strange, mustn't it?' Angela gabbled, like a six-year-old after too much candy floss.

'I agree,' said George, taking a corner slowly. 'A strange life, living there. I was talking to – hrrmph – I was talking to Marjorie, that very nice lady in the shop. She was telling me the marquess is there full-time now. He hardly ever goes to London any more. On that estate, day after day. He knows them all by name, ever such a nice chap these days apparently.'

'Of course,' said Angela. 'Yes, of course. He was the one who –'

'Yes,' said George. 'And his sister. One of them.'

'Of course, there's three, isn't there?'

'Yes, of course.'

'Of course what?' Laura broke in, unable to contain herself any more.

'We-ell,' said Angela. 'Yes – hrrm. Audrey – that's the very nice lady who was in the toy soldier display. Well, she said there was a time they were all very worried about him. The young marquess, I mean. Before his father died. Quite wild, apparently, when he was younger. Drink. *Drugs. Women.* You know, all sorts. And the sister, too. Rose. She had to go to a clinic. A rehab clinic, to sort herself out. This was after the mother left, you know. She went quite wild, Audrey said.'

'What do you mean, drink, drugs, women?' Laura said. 'That doesn't really mean anything these days, you know. I mean, we've all – well. So he went clubbing a few times and got pissed. Big deal.'

'Oh no,' said her mother, shaking her head sorrowfully, as if the Marquess of Ranelagh were the son of one of her friends from Harrow. 'Really went off the rails. Few years after his parents split up. Well, poor boy, he was only eleven when it happened. It was awful. All over the papers. Well, some of the papers. Not the *Guardian*, naturally.'

Laura couldn't work out if this was a veiled criticism of the *Guardian* for not having its reporting priorities right, or of her for reading a paper that did not concern itself minutely with lives of the aristocratic, rich and famous. So she said nothing, but a pang of sympathy for Charles shot through her. Poor Charles, poor thing. To have that everywhere, your family's misery, picked over by vultures and people who didn't know you, who made up their minds about you – it must have been bloody.

'Well, he seems OK now,' she said in a neutral voice.

'Yes, lovely man apparently,' Angela said happily. 'Audrey was telling us – he's Going Out with a very nice young girl. Cecilia Thorson. Her father is some millionaire, he's Swedish. Very grand. Married to one of the Inghams, Lady Tania.'

Laura rolled her eyes. She couldn't care less, she really couldn't. Even her old self, pre-purge, was completely uninterested in the lives of socialites and which posh person was shagging which other posh person. Maria the simple nun and Captain Von Trapp – now, that was interesting. *Had* been interesting, rather.

'That's been in the papers too, I remember now,' said Angela. She swivelled round in her seat and lowered her voice, as if there might be a *Daily Mail* reporter hiding in the glove compartment. 'I *hear* it's serious. They're all hoping she's – well. The One! You know!'

'Ooh, goody!' said Laura sarcastically, but it was wasted.

'Yes!' said Angela, nodding.

'So, when are the Sandersons arriving?' Laura asked, deftly steering the subject elsewhere.

Angela knitted her hands in her lap. 'Early Saturday, I think. Your grandmother was going to call them today to confirm who's staying and how long, that sort of thing.'

'Are they *definitely* coming?' Laura said childishly.

'If you mean Lulu and Fran, yes, they definitely are,' Angela said sternly. 'And very nice it'll be too. Yes. Annabel's bringing pudding, that's very kind of her.'

'Is Robert coming?' George asked, suddenly.

'Yes, of course he is!' Angela said.

'Oh,' muttered George.

'Look, you two,' said Angela, as the car turned into Seavale and the wheels crunched slowly over the sandy stone path, 'stop being childish. Yes, you George,' she said to her husband, who had opened his mouth to object. 'It's Mum's day, and we'll all have a lovely time, and it'll be great. Besides, Cedric Forsythe's coming up, and he's bringing Jasper.'

'Oh, great,' said George, cheering up. Beneath her father's staid exterior, Laura had long suspected there lurked the heart of a true romantic. He loved the old British glamour of Mary's neighbours in the mansion block. Especially that of Cedric Forsythe, who had starred in George's favourite film, *When Victory Comes*, a stirring black and white epic about our boys in the Second World War. Cedric Forsythe was dapper, polished; at least, his onscreen persona was. He smoked panatellas and wore silk dressing gowns; he raised his eyebrow as he talked – but he could still shoot a damned Boche at fifty paces and knew how to pull a plucky WAAF from a sinking U-boat, sling her over his shoulders, and swim four miles back to shore. In short, he was everything George Foster dreamt of being, but had long accepted was not his lot to be.

'I just hope it's what Mum wants,' Angela said anxiously.

George flashed a smile at his daughter in the rear-view mirror. Her frown lifted momentarily, and they shared a conspiratorial grin.

CHAPTER NINETEEN

There was a message on Laura's phone when she got back to the house. It was from Jo. 'Hello, Laura. It's Jo. We – I miss you. Hope you're OK. Hope Norfolk's good – what you needed. Listen, give me a call. Wanted a chat. Just wondering if you're on for drinks on Sunday. Me and Hil. Hope so.'

Laura had deliberately left the phone behind, turned it off, afraid of the power it had since Amy's text message to disturb the equilibrium of her day. It was her link with her life back in London, and she was still in two minds about it all. She missed it; she just wanted to be back in the pub with Paddy and Jo and her brother Simon and all of that. And because she couldn't see the way to do it, whilst she was here in Norfolk, being treated like a ten-year-old, she'd behave like one, renounce all responsibility for her other life. She texted Jo. '*Drinks would be great. Looking forward to it. Hope yr OK. Love L.*'

She brushed her hair, and took out her singed, blackened cardigan, hanging it out of the window in the evening sun to air and dry a bit before she washed it. How embarrassing that was, to have nearly set fire to a whole estate. Stupid her. An involuntary smile crossed her face, though. It had been funny – the aftermath. Even though Nick had been, well, really quite odd in a way, there was something she liked about him. She tried to analyse it. Basically, it was that she could talk to him. And enjoy it. She felt, in a funny way, as if she could say what she liked to him and he wouldn't care. That was the great thing about strangers. Especially quite handsome strangers. She smiled at the memory. Ah well. Nice of him to ask, but – she couldn't go. She wasn't here to go out drinking with strange but hunky farmhands. She was here to – get a life.

Outside on the terrace, George was fetching sherry for Angela and Mary, as Laura joined them to watch the sun set.

'No, it was a lovely day,' Angela was saying. 'We had a wonderful time, didn't we – ah, there's Laura. Didn't we, love?'

'Oh, yes,' said Laura, handing the bowl of crisps to Mary, and sitting down in one of the old wooden reclining chairs. 'It was marvellous. There isn't a tea towel left in that gift shop, is there, Mum?' She stretched and yawned as her father handed her a sherry.

'No, there isn't,' said Angela. 'Wait till Saturday, you'll see,' she said to her mother, nodding significantly. 'Now, talking of your birthday –'

'My birthday present is a tea towel?' said Mary, in rigid accents sitting upright.

'What?' said Angela.

'It had better not be,' said Mary.

Laura stood up and wandered over to the edge of the terrace, to look out at the sea.

'Of course not,' said Angela impatiently. 'I was joking, Mum. I'm not that bad, you know, that I'd buy my own mother a tea towel for her eighty-fifth birthday. Come off it,' she finished, rather bossily.

'No,' said Laura mischievously, turning round. 'Wait till you see the book of postcards they've got you. The First Marquess of Ranelagh, 1578. The Seventh Marquess, 1854.'

'Not true,' said George, but he was smiling in recognition. 'Here,' he said. 'I did get a collection of postcards, though, 'you're right.' He handed a small paper bag to Laura, who came over to collect them from him.

'Actually, you'll see,' he said, taking out the postcards and showing them to her. 'The seventh marquess was a great man, it's strange you should pick him. Although it was in 1846 that he inherited the title from his father, you know.'

'Right,' said Laura, grinning. 'I'll never make the same mistake again.' She wanted to say, Actually, I met the Marquess of Ranelagh today, but she knew it would prompt more questions than she wanted.

'I should hope not,' said George, but then slightly ruined the moment of levity by clearing his throat and saying, seriously, 'Look at him, Laura. He was a very extraordinary man, the seventh marquess.' He fumbled amongst the postcards, as Laura stood over him, a sinking feeling washing over her. 'Here we go. He was young, you know. And he did all these amazing things. This was just at the end of the nineteenth century. He put proper drainage in the estate, overhauled the workers' cottages, all of that. He built the pub in the village, most of the cottages there too. He added on the south wing. He's the one who collected first editions, he bought all the Jane Austens in the library. And he married his childhood sweetheart. But she died – it was terrible. Cholera. He never forgave himself. Dominic, Seventh Marquess. Amazing chap.'

He handed Laura the postcard and she took it, interested despite herself. There, in tight breeches, a viciously tailored jacket and top hat, standing rather stiffly against a country backdrop, with Chartley in the distance, was a portrait of a young man, dark hair elegantly coiffed, dark eyes friendly, amused. He was smiling, holding a book in one hand, his expression relaxed and at odds with his formal stance. Laura stared at it. It was a very immediate portrait, the young man could be someone you'd walk past on the street today. He even looked vaguely familiar.

'Take it,' said her father, and Laura put it between the pages of *The Nine Tailors*, which she slipped back into her bag.

'We'll look at the rest later,' said George. 'All very interesting.'

'Oh yes,' said Angela. 'Ooh.' She clapped her hands, and turned to Mary. 'Now then. I want to buy the meat for the barbecue tomorrow or Friday. What special meat requests do you have, Mum? It's your birthday.'

'Chicken hearts,' said Mary promptly.

'What?' said Angela.

'Chicken hearts. We used to have them when we were living in Brazil, you know. Guy loved them.'

'OK,' said Angela, in a tone that said clearly, I will say yes now, but we ain't getting no chicken hearts. 'But, some burgers? Chicken drumsticks? As well?'

'Don't mind, really,' said Mary, slapping her hand down on the wooden arm of her chair. 'Honestly, love, I really don't care. The main thing is having all my family there. It'll be so lovely. Annabel's making some amazing cake thing. It sounds fantastic.'

'Great,' said Annabel's stepsister, slightly icily.

'It will be lovely to see Lulu and Fran again, won't it?' Mary said. 'And Simon will be back then, won't he?'

'He will,' said Angela. 'Well, I hope so.' A frown crossed her face as George shifted in his seat and said, 'Hurrumph'; Simon was not exactly renowned for his reliability, nor indeed for his communication skills when away. Although this time he had been quite good – they'd all had postcards, and the usual long emails detailing people and places that meant little or nothing to Laura, but seemed to give her parents and Mary no end of pleasure, since they kept rereading them out to each other.

Laura feared for her mother if he didn't make it back in time. She knew enough to realise that in some small part of her mind Angela had obviously, fervently, envisaged a scene where Simon strode in, tall and tanned and charming, with a lovely poncho-style present for his grandmother, greeted his family and aunt and was a general hero for coming all the way back from Machu Picchu just for lunch, whilst skeletal

185

Lulu and heavy-thighed Fran looked on and contributed nothing, and Annabel had to concede that yes, for once, the Fosters had won this round.

Laura changed the subject. 'What's for supper? Anything I can do?'

'No, it's all ready,' said Angela. 'Some salady things, I hope that's OK. Something simple so we could eat by eight.' She turned to her mother and smiled brightly. 'Mum, you must be tired after all that gardening today, you've really cleared it all out, haven't you? It looks marvellous, I must say.'

'Thank you, darling,' said Mary. 'Good-o.'

'Yes, yes,' said George amiably, picking up the thread of his wife's conversation. 'I'll give you a hand tomorrow.' He paused, and rubbed his hands together. 'Sooo. Tomorrow. Where shall we go, dear? I thought the windmill at Moxham might be nice. What do you think?'

'Well,' said Angela, excitedly, 'we could try for the Seekers Tribute Band in the evening, couldn't we?'

'Yes, we must!' said George. 'Tasks for tomorrow, Angela! Now. Let's get the guidebook, and decide what to do, eh?' He loped over to the table and picked up the guidebook. 'Hm.'

He bent his head in concentration, as Angela looked out happily to sea, and Mary downed the rest of her drink. Laura glanced at her watch. It was seven fifty. She looked up, out across the lawn. The sun was crowning the sea, casting long, golden shadows across the water. It was very still. Suddenly she stood up.

'I'm going out,' she said.

Her parents looked up at her, bewildered.

'What?' said Angela. 'Where? Going out where?'

'Just out,' said Laura. 'Can I take the car?'

'Er – no!' said George. 'You can't suddenly announce you're taking off just before supper. Where are you going?'

Laura bit back a reply, and instead said, 'Sorry. I just want a drive. Someone I used to work with – well, she lives up here. Naomi? Do you remember her?' Her parents' faces were blank. 'She works for the Wetland Trust now. Well, I got a text from her earlier. She's over at the George. I thought I might join her for a drink, but it's rude of me to leave without having supper –' she ploughed on, aware she was laying it on a bit thick but hoping against hope it'd work '– so, perhaps I shouldn't go, you're right. I just fancied a bit of a change, getting out, seeing some friends.'

Laura's parents looked at each other, and Laura held her breath. She knew they were thinking, *She's been through a bad time. Not sure how bad. But something's not right. Perhaps this is a good thing. Young people ought to get out and about on holiday. Shouldn't they?*

They must have managed to convey these thoughts to each other by ESP, because they both nodded at each other at the same time. George produced the car keys and dropped them reluctantly into his daughter's hand. Laura pocketed them, and turned to go. 'Thanks, Dad,' she said, as she disappeared into the sitting room. She grabbed her handbag, her book and a wrap, and ran out onto the terrace again. 'I'll take care of it, I promise.'

'Don't be back too –' Angela began, then silenced herself as Mary shot her a warning look.

Laura ran across the gravel and jumped into the car. The bushes on the path up to the house were already greeny-black in the early dusk. She turned on the engine and drove away, leaving the house behind her. As she sped through the lanes in the evening air with the window open and her hair blowing in the breeze, she found herself feeling not like Mrs Danvers for the first time in days, but more like Mrs de Winter herself. With a bit more spine, hopefully.

When she arrived at the George, twenty-five minutes later, it was well after eight, and there was no sign of him. It was extremely crowded, as if the whole populace of Norfolk,

187

indigenous and tourist, were having a drink there. Laura pushed through the throng, avoiding their glares of disapproval, as she made her way to the lounge area, where people were sitting with drinks, the doors flung open out into the pub garden. She walked amongst them, looking left to right, but couldn't see him.

Standing there in the busy pub, she suddenly wondered if he'd meant it or not, this casual invitation he'd thrown out at her. What would she and Nick the farmer, groundsman, estate-manager person, *whatever* it was he did, talk about? They had nothing in common. Why had he asked her for a drink? And why had she come?

She breathed deeply. She couldn't go home just yet; it was too embarrassing. Apart from that, she would prefer to stay here and look like the loneliest person in the room rather than spend another evening with her parents. And she realised she quite liked it in a funny way, being here by herself, no ties, no responsibility, no dragging feeling of guilt about what she was doing. It was a drink with a nice strange man, no ties, nothing. She was a free agent, after all, she could do what she liked. Her new self rather appreciated that. She'd stay here, damn it, and enjoy herself, whether he showed up or not.

So Laura went up to the bar and got herself her one unit of white wine, then went and sat outside on one of the tables by the French windows and opened *The Nine Tailors*, but she couldn't read. She fingered the postcard portrait of the seventh marquess and gazed into the distance for a while, thinking about lots of things. At the image of her parents' expressions if they could see her now, she allowed herself a small smile. Her sense of the ridiculous, which had lain dormant for a while, suddenly resurfaced, and she laid the book down on the table and grinned broadly. Here she was, basically having a date with herself, and it was the best evening she'd had in quite some time.

So she sat there, till it was nearly nine, reading her book and occasionally looking up to take in her surroundings. She felt perfectly content, enjoying her own company for the first time in a long while. But then a deep voice behind her said, 'Excuse me, are you waiting for anyone?'

At last. Laura looked up, a quick retort ready on her lips. But standing in front of her was a tall, large man with a rather fleshy face, whom she'd never seen before, tucking his shirt into the back of his waistband and looking impatient.

'Sorry?' she said, taking a moment to recover.

'Are you expecting some friends?' the man said again, putting his pint down on Laura's table.

'Er,' said Laura warily. She really wasn't in the mood to be chatted up. Good grief, men were incredible. Just because she was on her own and reading a book! Six months ago, perhaps she would have smiled and said, 'No! Sit down!' and then developed an inappropriate crush on him, but now . . .

'Well –' she said, trying to let him down gently, and grimaced. 'You know . . .' and she shrugged her shoulders.

The man looked at her as if she were a half-wit, and Laura felt even more uncomfortable. Something in the City, Laura thought, nodding to herself. She glared at him rather crossly but he said, unheeding, 'Look, it's just there aren't any other tables and we're having food. There's five of us.'

'Eh?' said Laura.

'Is there any way you'd mind moving –' he pointed in the direction of one of the sofas, where there was a small square of squashy leather free '– over there, so we can sit here?'

Highly embarrassed, Laura shot up out of her seat. 'Ha ha! No! I mean, yes, of course you can! Ho!' she practically yelled, and then felt like an idiot.

'Thanks a lot, seriously,' said the large man, heaving himself onto the bench. 'I should buy you a drink.' He slapped his wallet and drink down on the table, and as he did the beer slurped up, out of the glass, and over Laura's skirt.

'Oh shit,' said Laura, wanting to be irrationally cross and shout at him all of a sudden.

189

'God, I'm sorry,' he apologised. 'Are you OK? Can I buy you another drink?'

'No, don't worry,' said Laura, in a tone meant to convey that she was not OK and he should buy her another drink; moreover he should get a towel.

'Really sorry,' he said. He patted ineffectually at the table with large, meaty hands, and looked at her skirt as if he should do the same there. 'I'm such an idiot.' He ran his hands through his hair. 'Big, stupid idiot. So sorry.'

'It's fine, honestly,' said Laura. She turned round to smile magnanimously, and found herself humiliatingly talking to thin air, as the man nodded gratefully, glad to be released, then turned back to his friends, who huddled together, waiting for her to leave.

'Great,' said Laura out loud, feeling suddenly exposed, rather like someone whose skirt has been ripped off, like they did in Bucks Fizz.

She threw an evil look at the tall man as she turned to go, her good mood evaporating as she pushed her way back through the throng, which seemed to have grown in the intervening hour. The queue for a table was still there, potential diners lounging in a bored fashion, waiting for the bills of the previous occupants to be paid. She pushed politely past them, and stumbled as she stepped out into the car park. She headed for the car and fished for her keys. Definitely time to go home.

'And where do you think you're going?' came a voice from behind her.

Laura froze, her key in the lock of the car. She turned slowly around, and there was Nick, striding easily towards her across the floodlit gravel. He looked smarter; he'd changed out of the T-shirt and jeans and was wearing a worn but clean, freshly ironed shirt and khaki trousers. He was tall, she remembered now, taking in his close-cropped hair, the almost harsh contours of his face, the strong cheekbones, the dark eyes. She almost didn't recognise him. He looked – different, somehow. Like a different person.

'Where have you been?' he said, as he came closer. 'I thought you'd stood me up.'

'Me!' Laura squeaked. Her voice was unrecognisable to her own ears. 'I waited for you for –' she looked at her watch, it was after nine '– for forty-five minutes! How dare you!'

'So you got here at eight thirty. Hm,' said Nick easily. 'And you're surprised that, having said I'd be there at eight, by eight thirty I'd assumed you weren't coming and went upstairs to say hi to someone in the office.'

'You said you'd be here *from eight*,' said Laura accusingly. 'I didn't – I wasn't going to come – I – anyway, well –'

She turned back to the car and stabbed ineffectually at the lock with her keys.

'Oh, calm down,' said Nick. 'Look, you're here now. Why don't we have supper? Come on, you might as well, and I haven't eaten yet – I'm hungry.'

'Ooof,' said Laura, staring helplessly up at him. 'I – god. I'm tired.'

'Me too,' said Nick. 'Look, Laura – I'm apologising. Come and have some food and then go home. You can't not eat, for god's sake. The food is amazing, I promise you. What were you going to have with your – with your boyfriend back at home, instead?' He smiled mockingly at her.

'Oh shut up,' said Laura, but she smiled back and put her keys into her bag. 'Thank you, that'd be lovely. I'd love to have supper with you.' She looked him up and down. 'You look smart.'

'There was a reception at the house,' he said easily. He looked down at her. 'Let's go inside. They won't keep the table forever.'

'Great,' said Laura. She stared at him.

'Get a move on,' said Nick unemotionally. 'There's a bloke over there I don't want to spot me. We'll be here for hours if he does.'

'Where?' said Laura. Nick pointed at the table-nicking, pint-spilling large man, who was guffawing loudly with some friends of his in the corner, past the bar.

191

'Ha,' said Laura. 'I know him.'

'You do?' said Nick, slightly surprised. 'City chap – can't remember his name. Works for a bank. Sorry, I didn't realise he was a friend of yours.'

'God no,' said Laura, slightly hysterically in case Nick thought she was consorting with strange, annoying men whilst waiting for him. 'He split a pint over me. Spilt, I mean, he spilt a pint, and I was all like –'

'Look,' said Nick. 'Mind if you tell me this story upstairs? He's looking over.'

'Right,' said Laura. 'Sorry.'

'No problem. Looking forward to it. It sounds great.'

He held the door open for her and they stepped through into the pub.

CHAPTER TWENTY

They threaded through the crowded pub in silence. Safely out of view of the table-stealer in the corner, Laura watched as Nick shook hands with various people and had his back slapped. She hung back a little, not wanting to announce herself to a roomful of strangers who obviously all knew this man well. It was his local, after all, and who was she? Some girl he'd met that afternoon who he'd asked for a drink. But why?

Stop it. *Stop it*, she told herself. This, this is why you're always getting into trouble! Your imagination runs away with you. She looked at Nick, who was shaking off some old fellow farmer bloke. He looked rather uncomfortable, and he pushed her gently ahead of him, through the rabble, almost as if he were in a hurry to leave them all behind. Laura liked the feel of his warm, firm hand on the small of her back, then brought herself up short. Remember, Laura, she said to herself: he is NOT Prince Charming. He is a nice, good-looking man and you are going to have a drink with him. Just because he made an amusing joke about the Seekers, *don't* go casting him in the role of romantic hero. You don't know him. He is a virtual stranger, he's not Rhett Butler. It's completely unedifying, it's sad. You HAVE to remember that, otherwise we will cut to two weeks' time when you're sighing hopelessly about some fictitious version of him in your head and making replicas of Chartley Hall and Nick's tractor with your new corn-dolly set. Reality. Reality.

She pinched herself on the arm, hard, to remind herself, as Nick got waylaid again, and she looked up to find him staring at her across the old wizened farmer who was droning on about something to do with his family. His eyes met hers, and he jerked his head towards the stairs. 'Come on, Laura,' he said. 'Sorry, Mr Withers. I'd better get on,' and he took Laura's arm and steered her lightly upstairs.

Mr Withers glanced happily at Laura, looking super-pleased for her, muttered something about how grateful he was and crept backwards, almost bowing, towards the door.

'Nice old chap,' said Nick, holding the door open as they reached the first floor.

'He seemed very keen on you,' said Laura, impressed.

'He said he was glad I was having supper with such a pretty-looking girl,' said Nick. He nodded as Laura looked at him sceptically. 'It's true,' he said lightly.

'Aah,' said Laura, self-conscious. 'That's nice.'

'It is nice,' said Nick. 'Very – er – nice. Right, let's get some drinks. And the menu. I'm hungry, aren't you?'

'God yes,' said Laura, who was completely starving. 'I'm completely starving.'

She thought with relief how relaxing it was to *not* be thinking of this as a proper date, worrying about whether it was seemly to be quite so actively gagging to wolf down some food. She was hungry. She wanted to eat. That was it.

Nick smiled at her. 'Steak OK? They do a great one here. Fantastic béarnaise sauce. With chips.'

'Thin chips?' said Laura.

'Absolutely,' Nick replied. 'I wouldn't come here if they weren't. Fat chips are wrong, I think.'

'Me too,' said Laura. 'Like half a potato each. They're impossible to eat. And they're always cold in the middle.'

'Yet again we agree,' said Nick. 'Never trust someone who says they prefer fat chips to thin chips. That is my motto.'

'I concur,' said Laura. 'Strongly concur.'

'Great,' he said.

Nick ordered a bottle of wine, and soon the food arrived. The steaks were as he had predicted, delicious, tender, melting, juicy, drizzled with garlic and parsley butter.

'God, I love garlic butter,' said Laura. She rubbed her hands together. 'I could drink it.'

'Please don't,' said Nick. 'And I sincerely hope you're not going out on the pull later if you're planning to scarf garlic all evening.'

'Why?' said Laura. 'Where does one go on the pull around here?'

'Well,' said Nick. 'There's a nightclub about thirty miles away. Champagne's, it's called. Actually, appropriately enough, there's usually a glassing there about eleven thirty every Saturday night. If you eat quickly, you can get there in time to pull *and* watch a fight.'

'There's a club like that in Harrow, where I grew up,' said Laura. 'Called Ballyhoo. I used to love it there. Till it got shut down.'

'No, really?' said Nick. 'Why?'

'The loos got blocked one night and it flooded and the electrics fused. Permanently.' Nick raised his eyebrows. 'I'm sorry. We're eating.'

'Well. If you want a trip down memory lane, I'd be more than happy to drive you to Champagne's and leave you outside, so you can revisit your misspent youth, you know,' said Nick politely. 'Sound nice?'

'I'm OK, I think,' said Laura, laughing. 'I'm going to scarf away instead.'

'Good,' Nick replied. 'Right decision.'

Laura *was* starving, and she ate happily. And as she ate and they talked, she found she was genuinely enjoying herself for the first time in ages. Nick was good company – compared to the company she'd been keeping all week most people would have been to her by then, but she couldn't help thinking he really was. He was his own man, he wasn't in Charles's pocket. They found common ground almost immediately, as any two strangers can if the basic ingredients are right. They discovered they both loved *The Sopranos*, that they had both stayed in the same hotel in Edinburgh, a day apart, and that their birthdays were both in May.

'So, Laura Foster,' said Nick, several glasses of rich, velvety red wine later. 'Why did you come tonight? I'm curious.' He wrapped his long fingers around the stem of his glass and smiled at her. 'I must say, I didn't think you would.'

'Why not?' said Laura curiously.

'Just thought you'd think it was weird.'

'I know,' Laura agreed. She opened her hands out to him in a gesture of disclosure. 'But I just thought well, why the hell not. It's got to be better than another evening at home with the parents.'

'Well, thank you.'

'You know what I mean.'

'Actually,' he said, 'I don't, really, no.'

'Well. Have you ever been on holiday with your parents?' Laura asked. 'After the age of sixteen, it's a pretty terrible idea.'

'So – why are you on holiday with yours, then?' Nick asked, taking a sip of wine. 'If it's such a bad idea.'

'Long story,' said Laura. 'I – ah.' She looked down, not really knowing how to go on.

Nick poured her another glass of wine. 'Doesn't matter, though, does it?' he said, his voice light. 'Right. Do you want some pudding?'

Laura looked up gratefully. 'Oh. I'd love to. But I shouldn't, really.'

He laughed, and said, 'Go on. Have one if you want to. No one's going to stop you.'

'No, I know,' said Laura. 'But I won't, honestly.'

'You sound like my sisters,' said Nick. 'Women! You go mad if someone tries to say you're all the same, but that's the exact same response my sisters always give if anyone asks them if they want pudding. And they couldn't be more different. You'd barely know they were related.'

'Really?' said Laura.

'Yes,' said Nick. 'One of them lives in London. She – ha.' A cloud passed over his face. 'She's ten years older than me. She used to be rather wild. Quite good fun, always turning up off her head on something, with someone. She – yes. Anyway, now she's married to a very uptight businessman. She's gone all grown-up and boring. Wears suits, sits on committees, that kind of thing. She's a real snob these days. Whereas Lavinia – god.'

'What's wrong with Lavinia?'

'Oh, she's a liability,' said Nick. 'She moved back here a few months ago, and she's shagging this bloke on the estate. Does the tickets. Sean. She basically stalked him into submission. He has no choice in the matter. Not that he seems to care that much, he's – god, he's almost as thick as her.'

Laura thought of the red-haired beauty they'd encountered on their way in to the estate earlier that day. 'Do you know, I think I met her today,' she said.

Nick groaned. 'Oh god. Where?'

'In the ticket box. With Sean. They –'

'Don't tell me,' Nick stopped her, holding up his hands. 'Oh god,' he said suddenly. 'They're the lunatics having sex in the kiosk you were complaining about earlier. Aren't they?'

'No,' said Laura, blushing. 'I was just being rude.'

'Don't spare my feelings, Laura.' He looked resigned. 'She's a nightmare, and I've got to do something about it now she's living back at the hall. At some point.'

'It's very nice of Charles to let her stay there,' said Laura.

'What? Oh, yes,' said Nick. 'He's always been fond of Lavinia, too. Think he has a crush on her, actually.'

197

'He seems lovely,' said Laura. 'It must be a weird life for him, though, I suppose.'

'Why do you say that?' said Nick, and there was a note of defensiveness in his voice.

'Well,' she said carefully. 'I just mean, it's a big responsibility, that house, all those people. And it's not like he's married with loads of kids and a wife, or he has someone to share it all with. It must be weird.'

'It is,' said Nick.

'Would you want to be him?' said Laura.

Nick looked blank for a second.

'I mean,' she said, trying to explain, 'would you want to swap places, be the marquess? Do you ever think that?'

'No,' said Nick slowly. 'You know, I sometimes think I wouldn't be him for all the money and estates in the world.'

'Well, he's lucky to have you as his friend,' said Laura.

Nick was silent. Then he cleared his throat, and said, 'I'm not so sure about that. More wine? Here, have the rest.' He poured the last of the wine into her glass, and his hand touched hers momentarily as he set the bottle down again. Their eyes met, and they smiled at each other. Laura sat back in her chair, relaxing a little more. There was something so comfortable about him, about his company. Her mind flew back to the mess of tangled friendships and relationships she had left behind in London, and she thought suddenly that it was funny, but here in this pub, with this nice, strange man, she felt calmer, like she was breathing properly, like she could see the vista of her life stretching out over the next few months more clearly than she had for . . . she didn't know how long. That for the first time she was looking forward to it.

'So, when do you go back to London?' said Nick.

'Saturday,' said Laura. 'Yeah.' She gazed reflectively into her glass. 'Got a big birthday lunch for my grandmother on Saturday. All the relatives coming up.'

'Oh god,' he said, looking at her with amused sympathy. 'If they're anything like mine –' He trailed off.

'They're a bit grim, to be honest,' said Laura. She finished her glass of wine, and Nick poured her some more. 'Thanks. They mean well, I'm sure.'

'What does that mean?'

'Well – take my Aunt Annabel. I'm sure she's not *evil*, but if you were stranded on a desert island and she rescued you after six months, she'd criticise you for not tidying up the grains of sand. And she'd say the jungle was out of control and you should have pruned it back.'

Nick looked at her, trying not to laugh. 'Right,' he said. 'That's some aunt.'

'She's not really my aunt,' said Laura. 'Actually, she's like my step-aunt. You know.'

'Er,' said Nick politely, after a pause. Oh no, Laura thought, I'm gabbling. She opened her mouth to ask about his family, but he said, suddenly, 'So. Do you have brothers and sisters?'

'A brother,' said Laura. 'It's just me and him. He's called Simon.'

'Are you close?'

'Yes we are,' said Laura. 'I miss him. He's away at the moment, in –' she scrunched up her face, trying to remember the location of the last postcard. 'He's in some mountain village in Peru, anyway. But he's coming back for Granny's lunch on Saturday. I haven't seen him since March. Hurrah!'

He smiled at her enthusiasm. 'Hurrah indeed. You sound like a close family.'

'Well,' said Laura. She looked at him. 'We are, but – you know.'

'What?'

'Well, families. It's all complicated, isn't it? We are close, but we're all quite weird at the same time.'

'How so?'

'My aunt, and her lot. That's why I – I –' She fiddled with her napkin again, 'I'm not looking forward to it much. We're all quite different.'

She was silent then, and took a gulp of wine. 'Sorry,' she

said, meeting his gaze. His eyes were warm, understanding. 'I don't mean to gabble on.'

'You're not,' said Nick. 'Really, you're not. That's families for you. It is, as you say, complicated.'

'How about yours?' said Laura. 'Same thing?'

'Yes,' he said, standing up. 'All very complicated, and it's not on the surface, is it? Give me a moment, I'll settle the bill and then I'll walk you to the car.'

He left her, and Laura watched him go. She felt as if he were holding her at arm's length, and she didn't know why. She looked around the pub, and drained her glass. Then she told herself not to be so silly, not to jump ahead again. She'd only just met him. And it was strange, how she felt as if she could tell him anything and it wouldn't matter. For the first time in ages, no judging, no agenda, nothing. Just a friendly stranger in a warm summer's room, a glass of wine, and a proper conversation.

CHAPTER TWENTY-ONE

They settled the bill and walked outside, onto the moonlit gravel path, out of the floodlighting. As Laura approached the car, she had that sensation of two sides of her brain, the subconscious and the conscious, rushing together for the first time that evening. The subconscious had been hiding something from her, and it suddenly hit her with the full force of an oncoming train.

'Shit!' she said suddenly.

The violence in her voice made Nick stop in his tracks. 'What?' said Nick. 'Laura?'

'Shit, shit,' said Laura, turning around and banging her fist on top of the nearest car. Luckily it was her car. She turned back to face him. 'I can't drive!'

'You can't drive?' Nick said, perplexed.

'No, not that! I completely forgot. I've had –' She quickly added up how many glasses she'd had, and gave up in despair at three. 'I've had far too much to drink. At least three glasses. Argh.' She banged her forehead gently on the roof of the car and let out a muffled groan.

How could she have been so *stupid*? How could she have forgotten she had the car outside? She'd relaxed, let herself enjoy the evening – and this was what had happened.

'It's OK,' said Nick calmly. 'Don't worry. You can – stay with me.'

'No!' said Laura, so loudly both of them took a step back. 'Sorry,' she continued in a quieter voice. 'Oh, stupid! Stupid me! How could I have forgotten I drove here?'

'Do you make a habit of this kind of thing?' said Nick. 'Drinking nearly a bottle of wine and forgetting you drove to the pub?'

'No, never,' said Laura. She was cold all of a sudden in the night air. 'I don't, in London. I don't have a car. So I always drink when I go to the pub.'

'Well, there you are then,' said Nick. 'It's different up here, you know.'

'I know,' said Laura miserably. 'I was – enjoying myself, that's all.'

Nick watched her for a moment. 'Don't look so tragic about it, Laura. It's not a crime to enjoy yourself, you know.'

'Yes it is,' muttered Laura, feeling as if she were in some biblical parable, the one where the Lord wreaks vengeance on the stupid girl who is a foolish wanton by removing common sense in her brain.

'No,' said Nick firmly. 'It's not. But it will be if you drive. Look, Laura, come back to the hall with me. It's five minutes away. You can either stay the night or call a cab. But at this time of night, a cab's going to take over an hour to get here.' Laura shifted from one foot to the other, unsure of what to say. 'Which is why you might as well stay.'

'Oh,' she said eventually. 'But – look, Nick –'

'This isn't a come-on,' said Nick in amusement. 'Seriously, this isn't my dastardly way of taking advantage of you.'

He laughed at her, his voice soft in the velvety darkness. Laura stepped away from him, feeling embarrassed. She didn't want him to think – she couldn't bear the idea he thought she might be angling for something, that this was some ploy of hers. Especially not when they'd had – well, the perfect evening,

202

she thought. She didn't want to spoil it, the memory of it, and now she had.

'I know – of course. Really –'

She couldn't see his face still, but his voice said in a kindly tone, 'Look. I'm your only friend in Norfolk, aren't I?'

'You are actually my best friend in Norfolk,' said Laura.

'Well, there you go,' said Nick. 'Come back, and we'll get you a cab or find you a room.'

'It won't be a problem?'

'I shouldn't think so,' said Nick gravely. 'There's about thirty-five bedrooms. I'm sure we can find somewhere for you to sleep for the night.'

She shook her head, smiling. 'I didn't mean that! I meant, you won't get into trouble, will you? It's OK for you to – to ask some – some random gi— person back and give them a room for the night?'

'Yes,' he said. 'I promise you it won't be a problem.'

She shivered. Nick put her wrap around her shoulders, and said, 'Come on, then, new best friend. Come back to mine. You're getting cold and I'm not standing here all night. You can pick the car up in the morning.'

Laura was mightily amused, and said so. '"Come back to mine", eh? You make it sound like you live in a flat next to the Post Office. And how do I explain what happened to my parents? And how do I explain I'm staying the night without them getting totally the wrong end of the stick?'

Nick started walking ahead of her. He said shortly, 'Well, you could make something up. What did you tell them tonight?'

'Is it really only a five-minute walk?' said Laura, following him. 'I don't believe you. The bloody driveway alone took ten minutes.'

'We're round the back, this is the edge of the estate to the north,' said Nick, leading the way. 'The fields over there are corn – the combines are arriving soon, in a couple of weeks, you know.'

He strode ahead in silence, Laura following behind. It was funny, she thought, admiring his rear view dispassionately, what a curious mixture he was. In person, face to face, he was diffident, closed-off, the polite man who could make you laugh and was endlessly flippant, never serious. In repose, or when he thought he wasn't being watched, he was a different person: the broad-shouldered, outdoorsy country boy who talked enthusiastically about animal husbandry, whose face and attitude was quite different, more relaxed, more human, almost. It was hard to believe they were the same person, and it was strange she felt so comfortable with him.

'Thanks,' she said suddenly. 'I'm sorry. About this.'

'My pleasure, Laura,' said Nick.

'If we bump into Charles –' she said abruptly.

'I'll make something up,' Nick told her. 'Don't worry. I'm not a slave there. I'm allowed to bring people back, you know. But you're right. Best if no one sees. People will only gossip.'

They had reached the gate beyond the pub's garden, and Nick unpadlocked the bolt and drew back the tall, solid wooden door.

'OK?' he asked.

'OK,' said Laura, but as he said, 'Mind the –' she stumbled into a tiny ditch, a hollow the other side of the door. Nick caught her hand.

'Sorry,' he said, putting her on her feet again and releasing her. 'Must get that sorted out, you know, I keep meaning to talk to the guys about it. You OK?'

'Absolutely,' Laura replied.

Their feet made scraping sounds along the dry earth of the pathway. An owl hooted in the wood to their right. Ahead of them the path swung round by the trees, and as they walked past them Laura drew her breath in.

'The house. Look. It's –'

There, in the moonlight, the side view of Chartley Hall appeared in front of them. The stone gleamed in the moon's light, but the windows were dark. Ahead of them lay a formal garden, knotted with rows of black yew. It looked old, forbidding, magnificent – and nothing like someone's home.

'Nearly there,' said Nick. 'I love this view.'

'It's beautiful,' Laura said simply. 'Beautiful. You must –'
She stopped.

'What?' said Nick.

'Well, it must be quite lonely, sometimes.'

'It is,' said Nick. 'Yes, it is.' He was silent, standing still. 'Right,' he continued, after a moment. 'Here we are,' and they walked down the gentle slope past the woods to the monolith in front of them, towards a side door in the centre of two wings. It was as if the house was swallowing them up, taking them in its jaws, Laura thought, and she craned her neck, looking up to the roof as Nick unlocked the door and held it open for her. They stepped into a small hallway with a staircase, wooden panelled and painted green, ghostly in the night-time light. It was tiny, incongruously small given the vast shell that lay beyond it.

'God, this is weird,' said Laura.

'What do you mean?'

'Well, when I stagger back from the pub late at night the walk home is slightly different,' said Laura. 'More wheelie bins in my way. Lots more empty fast-food wrappers. A few people lying in the kerb, you're not sure if they're alive or dead. That kind of thing.'

'Well, this is weird for me too,' said Nick, leading the way up the stairs. 'When I stagger back from the pub I don't usually have some pyromaniac girl with me who keeps hitting me, and can't drive because she drunk so much she forgot the car right outside the pub that she drove there in.'

'Oh –' Laura cast around for the appropriate response. 'Shut up.'

'Well done,' said Nick. 'Excellent comeback.'

They reached the top of the stairs. There ahead of them was a prim, neat, very long corridor. Laura looked around, almost disappointed not to be confronted with some magnificent vista, a sweeping staircase, a vast, airy ballroom, or some such. Nick could obviously sense this, because he said, 'Sorry. I should have given you the guided tour, shouldn't I, rather than just rushing you up the back stairs. This is my front door, you see.'

'Oh, no,' said Laura. 'Please, don't worry. I had the guided tour today.'

'And you hated it. I remember,' Nick murmured, then he put his fingers to his lips. 'I can hear something. Come this way.'

They walked down the long corridor, and the unmistakable sound of someone coming up the stairs behind them could be heard, echoing towards them. Someone was down below, then a rather tentative voice said, 'My lord? Is that you?'

Laura looked at him in alarm and, without warning, Nick opened a door and virtually pushed Laura inside.

'This is my room,' he said apologetically. 'Charles is just down there, they must think it's him. Sorry about that, don't want anyone to see us, don't want you to have the third degree and all that.'

'Goodness, yes,' Laura agreed.

'OK,' said Nick. He glanced around the room, ran his hands through his hair. It was big, high ceilinged, painted white, virtually without any decoration or personal touch whatsoever. There was a clock radio, a portable radio, a mahogany chest of drawers, and a door leading to a bathroom. A dressing gown hung on the back of the door. It was, in short, a very typical boy's room.

'Look,' he said. 'I think what's best is if you sleep here, and I'll kip somewhere else. I don't want to plonk you in another room only to find someone trying to hoover you up tomorrow morning. They're pretty fascist around here about hoovering. But they don't ever bother me in my room. Is that OK? Can you sleep here? Sheets are clean on today.'

'Yes, of course,' said Laura, giving herself up totally to the

206

adventure of it all. 'No problem.' She was suddenly very tired, and she reached up to take her wrap off. But Nick leant forward and unwound it from her shoulders. It slid off, and he handed it to her, and then he kissed her on the cheek.

It was a strange moment, it felt like a strange gesture, intimate yet not intimate, and there was a silence as both of them stood there, rather embarrassed. Laura looked up to find his dark eyes on her, his expression unreadable. There was a silence.

'OK, best friend in Norfolk,' she said after a while. 'Thank you, thanks a lot. I'm sorry about this.'

'No problem at all,' said Nick. He walked over to the dresser and took out a big old T-shirt, which he handed to her. 'Here. You can borrow this.'

'Thanks,' said Laura.

'I'm sorry this is all a bit cloak and dagger. I just don't want you to have any hassle. I'll knock on the door after eight sometime, is that OK?'

'Great,' said Laura. He raised his hand in a gesture of farewell. 'All right,' he said. 'Sleep well. Don't rifle through my personal possessions, and if you do, ignore the hardcore porn.'

'Sure, sure,' said Laura. 'No judging. Night.'

'Night,' he said, and smiled at her as he shut the door behind him.

The wine, the walk, the unexpectedness of the day – Laura barely managed to text her parents and take off her shoes and skirt before falling onto the bed and into a sleep so deep she didn't think till afterwards how strange it was that she was there, and how strange it was that it didn't feel strange.

When she woke, funnily enough Laura knew exactly where she was. She opened her eyes and looked around the room, taking in its appearance in the daylight which shone through the thin curtains at the far end, opposite her bed. She sat up and rubbed her eyes, feeling deliciously relaxed, then looked down at the baggy blue T-shirt Nick had given her. It said 'Thorson

Technologies' in huge red letters – trying to read it made the letters dance in front of her eyes. Out of the window she could see pine trees in the distance, a mass of greenish black to the north of the house. A wood pigeon was cooing somewhere nearby. Other than that it was completely quiet. She snuggled down again, and pulled the duvet over her. The bed was huge, the sheets were smooth and clean. Laura stretched her arms and legs wide, and still couldn't feel the edge of the bed. She made a star shape with her limbs, moving like a windscreen wiper under the sheets, and she was laughing to herself at the sheer randomness of it all when there was a knock on the door.

'Laura?'

'Yes,' cried Laura in a strangulated tone, getting tangled in the sheets.

'Er – are you decent?'

'Yes, yes! Come in!' Laura said chirpily, as if she were June from *Terry and June*.

The door opened about half a foot, and Nick's head appeared around the door, his short, thick hair sticking up in tufts. He looked in, obviously rather afraid of what he might find. 'Ah,' he said with relief, as he saw Laura was sitting up in bed, her arms crossed, under the duvet. He came in and shut the door behind him. She suddenly had a pang of fear – after all, it was a weird situation to be in. Perhaps this was all really embarrassing, perhaps she had in fact made a total fool of herself last night? Was there something she wasn't remembering, some repressed memory where she'd licked him, or broken a Sèvres vase?

'Hello there,' Nick smiled at her in a friendly way. He looked younger in the morning light. 'You sleep well?'

'God yes,' said Laura gratefully. She looked at her watch. 'Blimey. It's nine thirty! I didn't realise it was so late.'

She hadn't slept for nine straight hours since – she couldn't remember when. Over a year ago. She stretched again, smiling at him. 'Thanks so much, Nick. I'm so sorry about last night – how completely emba—'

Nick cut her off, raising his hand to silence her and saying, 'Really, Laura. Don't apologise. It's as much my fault as yours, I should be apologising.'

'I threw you out of your room, though,' said Laura.

'No, I did,' he said. 'I'm a big boy. And it's a big house, you know. I found a study further down where I could lay my weary head. Two chairs pushed together will do me fine.'

Laura's hand flew to her mouth. 'Oh no! Really?'

'No, not really,' said Nick. 'The guest bedroom next-door-but-one, actually.'

'Oh,' Laura said. 'Ha ha.'

There was a pause. Laura was suddenly aware of what a strange situation it was. She slapped her hands on the duvet and said, 'Well. Thanks again. I'd better be going.'

'I've asked for some coffee to be sent up,' said Nick. 'Thought you might like some before you go.'

'Oh great,' said Laura. 'Thanks a lot.'

'No problem.'

'I'm going to get dressed,' Laura announced.

'Oh,' said Nick. 'I'll avert my gaze, then.'

'Well, it'll only take a minute or so,' said Laura, as he turned around politely. She hopped out of bed and slipped the T-shirt off, put her bra and skirt and cardigan on, then her flip-flops, and pulled her tangled dark-blonde hair into a messy ponytail.

'Are you decent?' Nick said after a while.

'Yup,' said Laura.

Nick turned round, amused. 'That's your daily toilette, is it?' he said. 'Very extensive.'

'Absolutely,' Laura said. 'It just saves time. Wear the same pants for a week and they double up as pyjamas. It's very handy. You get so much more done.'

'I bet,' said Nick. 'Wow, you must be popular.'

She raised her eyebrows at him. He grinned, and then came a knock at the door and the sound of something on the floor outside. 'Coffee, sir.'

'Ah,' said Nick. He waited a second for the sound of footsteps walking away before going to the door. Laura was amused to see that, whilst everything was utterly relaxed between the two of them, he was not quite so relaxed about anyone else knowing he had had a strange girl in his room last night. What would Charles say, she wondered, as Nick put the tray on the bed. She thought he was probably more austere about these things than his friend. Might not like it, even though it couldn't be more innocent.

Nick handed her a cup of coffee. 'Pastry?' he said politely, indicating a plate of delicious-looking croissants.

'It's like a hotel here,' said Laura. 'Wow!'

Her host was pouring some more coffee. 'Yes,' he said. 'Slightly different, though. You can check out any time you want, but you can't leave. Like the song.' He looked up and smiled that disarming smile.

Laura didn't quite know what to say. She looked out of the window. 'What's that?' she said suddenly, standing up and going over to look out.

Nick followed her pointing finger. 'What?' he said.

'*There*. Jesus, what *is* that?'

'Oh,' said Nick. He came and stood behind her. 'Fuck.' He gazed out of the window. 'That's a helipad. And that – *that* – is a helicopter. Help, I'd forgotten. Rose is coming for the weekend.'

'Rose?'

Nick ran his hands through his hair. 'Yes. Er – the sister. Charles's sister. With her awful husband. Bloody Malcolm. There's a thing on Saturday evening, a dinner for . . . Shit. I should go and –'

He groaned, and looked out gloomily. 'Damn. She *has* brought Malcolm. Help.'

There was a light tap on the door. They froze, as if caught in the act. Nick was the first to relax. He smiled ruefully. 'God, this is ridiculous. Yes? Who is it?'

'It's Charles,' came the calm voice from outside. 'Man, Rose is here. I was wondering where Mrs Hillyard is, I can't find her. Can I tell her?'

Nick leapt up, went to the door, opened it, and had a muffled conversation with Charles in the hallway, leaving Laura realising suddenly that she really should go, she was getting in the way. She looked out of the window, high up on the top floor of the house. How strange it must be to wake up here, even if you've known it all for years. The countryside sloped gently away from the grounds, the woods of the estate to the north merged into pine woods, which stopped abruptly, and there, beyond, was the sea. There was a fresh breeze, and Laura breathed in, catching the scent of pine and seawater. She felt calm, awake.

'It's a lovely day,' she said, as Nick came back into the room.

'It is,' he replied. He was looking at her, his hand on his forehead.

Laura inhaled again, closing her eyes. It was gorgeous, air you could taste. She sighed, and shivered suddenly.

Nick watched her. 'Goose walk over your grave?' he said.

Laura nodded. 'Something like that.' She paused. 'Right, I'd better go.' She allowed herself one last glimpse out of the window, and said dreamily, 'The beach looks so lovely from here, doesn't it? You must want to spend all day there when it's like this.'

'I suppose so,' said Nick. 'I – where? Oh, I've never really been.'

'What?' said Laura, gaping. 'You've never been to the *beach*?'

'Not really,' he said, looking out of the window again.

'Nick, sorry, sorry,' said Laura, holding up her hands. 'You live overlooking that beach, the beautiful sea, and you've never been there?'

'Yes, of course I have,' he said impatiently. 'I used to go, but when I was small. I mean, I haven't been – you know, since –' he waved his arm vaguely. 'It's always too crowded. With. People. You know. And I don't really have time to go. Since I came back.'

'How long ago was that?' asked Laura.

'Two years ago.' Nick backed away, walked across the room. He chewed a nail. 'I moved back two years ago.'

'Oh,' said Laura. She asked, curiously, 'Why did you come back?'

Nick scratched his head. 'I had to, when my father died. Before that I didn't come here much. I was . . . being stupid, mainly. Pissing my life away in London. That's why I hate London. And I love it here. It saved me, basically. Charles did, too. And – I'll do anything – well.' He stopped suddenly, and sat on the edge of the bed. 'That's all.'

'Well, you should go to the beach,' Laura said, following the thread of the conversation, not really knowing what else to say. She slung her bag over her shoulder. 'Right. Well, I'd better be off.'

'I should, I know,' Nick replied unexpectedly. Then he stood up and said casually, 'Listen. What are you doing later?'

'What, later today?' said Laura. 'God, no idea. Going to a windmill. Or a buttery, or something, I expect.'

'I meant tonight,' he said.

'Oh,' said Laura. 'Oh.' She wanted to see him again, she knew it, but . . .

'Not that that doesn't sound lovely,' he said. 'Well – give me a call if you need rescuing or you fancy a drink or whatever.' As Laura involuntarily opened her mouth, he said, 'Relax, old chum. I feel it's my duty, since I'm your best friend here, to make sure your holiday goes well.'

'Well, thanks to you,' said Laura, 'it's actually much better than I thought it was going to be.'

'Cool,' said Nick.

'Cool,' Laura agreed.

They said goodbye by the back door, the one they'd entered by last night, a few minutes later. It was nearly eleven, and the sun was climbing higher in the sky. Nick had offered to walk her to the car, but Laura said no, she'd be absolutely fine. He'd given her his number, too. They stood in silence for a moment, suddenly awkward, and then Laura saw Charles approaching them, skirting around the formal garden at the back. Laura pushed her sunglasses on her head, held out her hand and said, 'Thanks. I'll – I'd better go.'

He took her hand in his, and shook it firmly. He smiled down at her, a smile that was so familiar to her now.

'Remember what I said about tonight,' he said, casually.

'Yes,' said Laura, equally casually. 'Thank you.'

'Fine,' said Nick. They grinned at each other. 'Are you going to tell your parents where you were?'

'Nope,' said Laura. 'They'll just get over-excited. I told them when I texted last night. You're Naomi. You're a friend from my first job, and you work for the Wetlands Trust.'

'I do, do I?' said Nick in amusement, as Charles appeared. 'Hello there again. It's – Laura, isn't it?'

'Good morning,' said Laura, resolved not to be embarrassed or obsequious. She smiled at him, turned back to Nick and said, 'Maybe I'll see you later, Naomi.' She reached up, and kissed him on the cheek. 'Thanks for a lovely . . . er . . . thanks for a lovely evening.'

As she walked away her heart was beating strangely fast. She looked back, but Nick had already turned and was heading across the front lawn, his tall, rangy frame solitary in the vast expanse of grass, towards a voice saying, in strident tones,

'Nick! You're there. Hello. Where's that useless sister of yours? Lavinia not up yet? The roses have got ash-rot, you've been over-watering them, you must tell Fletcher . . .'

Nick answered back, his voice inaudible, and the sounds of greeting, familiar exchanges, gradually faded away, as he slipped back into his life and Laura continued on her way, across the lawn, up to the path she'd taken on that strange previous night. She was in no hurry. She'd slept so well, the tired feeling behind her eyes had gone, and she could feel the sun on her arms, on her hair, as she walked away from that strange world back to her own. She turned and looked at the house as she reached the gate. It looked so different in the morning sunshine, gold and glittering, with green all around it. She could hear the hum of a tractor in the distance, and the coo of the fat pigeons in the dark trees to the north.

CHAPTER TWENTY-TWO

As Laura walked round the side of Seavale over an hour later, dodging the deckchairs, she could hear her parents and Mary making polite conversation over what was clearly an early lunch.

'Pass the ratatouille, would you, Angela dear?'

'Yes, Mum. Would you like some more water?'

'No, thanks. Is there any wine left in the bottle?'

'George?' said Angela. 'George, is there any wine left?'

'No,' said George. 'Oh well.'

'Hm,' said Mary.

Silence fell as George and Angela Foster carried on eating. Laura watched them through the window, mesmerised by her own family, and the contrast to the scene she'd left behind.

'How about opening another bottle?' said Mary. 'I think I'd like another glass.'

George looked up aghast, as Angela frowned. 'Really, Mum? Do you think . . .?'

She trailed off as Mary gave her a stern look. George and Angela were not great drinkers, but Simon and Laura took after their grandmother. The idea that three people could get through more than a bottle at lunch clearly appalled George, whereas the idea in reverse appalled Mary. But George was a good son-in-law, and so Laura watched him fondly as he dabbed at his mouth with a napkin, stood up and said,

'Of course. I'll just see if there's any . . .'

'In the wine rack, the Hamilton Russell,' Mary said firmly. George crossed the sunny dining room and disappeared into the tiny kitchen, through the corridor.

'Lovely.' Mary looked pleased. 'You know, after lunch I think I shall sit outside and do the crossword for a little while. It's such a beautiful day.'

'Yes,' said Angela, though it was clear she was actually thinking, No, you should have a nap and a glass of water. 'I wonder where Laura is,' she said out loud. 'Her text message did say she'd be back from Naomi's by lunchtime, didn't it?'

'Naomi. Yes,' said Mary, musingly. 'Funny. I've never heard her mention Naomi before. Have you?'

Laura hurried across the lawn and through the French windows. 'Hello,' she called, putting her bag on the floor as her father appeared with the wine.

'Laura!' said Angela, her face alight with pleasure. 'Here you are, and there's still some lunch left. Ratatouille, you like that, don't you? Would you like some ham? Here, have this sandwich.'

They looked at Laura expectantly, as one.

'Did you have a nice evening, darling?' Angela asked. 'How was Naomi?'

'Er.' Laura cleared her throat, and stared at them.

'Bread?' said George, proffering the breadbasket at his daughter.

'Wine?' said Mary, pushing a spare wine glass over towards Laura.

Laura cleared her throat again and ran her hands through her unruly, half-dried hair. She was starving again – why was she so hungry all of a sudden? – but felt like a savage come amongst civilisation and did not trust herself to form a full sentence.

'Thanks,' she said, and sank into the chair her grandmother pulled out for her.

216

'So,' said Angela. 'We were surprised to get your text message. But how nice. Did you and Naomi get to chatting then? Reminiscing about old times?'

'Yes,' said Laura. 'Yes we did.'

In answer to her mother's curious stare, she tried to expand. 'It was nice to see her.'

'Great,' said George, talking to his ham. 'Well, you missed the windmill this morning, Laura, but we've got some great news!'

'What?'

'Laura, we've managed to get tickets to see the Seekers Tribute Band! The box office just rang to confirm they're holding them.'

'For me?' said Laura, in a slightly strangulated voice. 'Oh – well – I –'

'Come on, love,' said George. 'It'll be terrific fun. Oh, I know, they're not that popular with you lot –' he waved his hand in the direction of Laura and Mary, leaving Laura unsure as to whether he meant not popular with young people, old people, or merely people with ears. 'But, I promise you'll have a good time.' He stood up. Laura swallowed a remark in her throat.

'Mary, are you sure you don't want to come? Tickets are still available, you know.'

'What are the odds?' said Mary, to her plate of ham. 'Amazing.'

'Yes,' agreed George happily.

'No thanks,' Mary answered. 'Just fantastic you can go, of course, and Laura, I'm so jealous. But at my age – whew. I think the excitement might be a bit too much for me, you know. I think I'd better stay in and get an early night.' She smiled serenely at her son-in-law.

'Excuse me a moment,' said Laura, pushing her chair back and getting up. 'I'll be right back.'

She went outside, plucking her phone out of her bag, and texted, '*You were right. Going to Seekers Tribute Band tonight. Help.*'

Mary was standing up when she got back. 'I'm going to sit in the sun for a while,' she said. 'Enjoy the calm before the storm tomorrow.'

'Why?' said Angela, who was collecting the plates. 'What's tomorrow?'

Mary gave her a look. 'My birthday, Angela dear. Don't be silly.'

'It's on Saturday, Mum,' said Angela.

'Oh.' Mary smoothed her grey hair. 'Oh. Of – course it is. It's – it's Thursday today, isn't it? Yes.' She looked rather uncomfortable, her hand clutching the back of the chair. 'Silly of me.'

'Let me give you a hand,' said Laura, coming across to her. Her phone rang in her bag. 'Oh,' she said, starting forwards.

'You get that, darling.'

'No,' said Laura, thinking it could be Amy. 'Let's go outside. If they leave a message I'll hear.'

'So, you had a nice time yesterday,' said Mary, walking slowly, her grip on Laura's arm tight as they went outside. She relaxed a little in the sunshine, pushed her sunhat on as she sat down again.

'Yes,' said Laura uncertainly.

'Did you go to the Wetlands yesterday?' asked Mary. 'They're not that special, are they? Personally I've always thought they were rather dull.' She fixed a beady eye on her granddaughter.

Laura breathed in as she met her grandmother's gaze. She could have just told the truth. There was nothing to be ashamed of, she was a grown-up, she could do what she liked with whom she liked. And it was hardly as if she'd actually *done* anything, anyway. She could just say, 'I met this nice bloke yesterday, he lives at Chartley Hall and I stayed in his room, but nothing happened.'

But something stopped her. She didn't know what. She breathed out again.

'It's funny,' said Mary. 'Guy and I, when we used to come here, do you know what we'd do?'

'No,' said Laura. She sat down next to her grandmother. 'What?'

'We'd read. And go for long walks. And watch films. Eat lots. Listen to the radio, do the crossword.'

'Nice,' said Laura, because it was, and she loved hearing Mary talk about Guy.

'He loved fish,' said Mary, her eyes closed. 'Grilled fish. That barbecue,' she waved in the direction of the barbecue at the edge of the garden. 'We'd use it every night, just the two of us, some wine, some music from the Proms on the radio, sitting out here, watching the sunset.'

She was silent.

'Your parents don't go in for that sort of thing, though. They like being told things. Seeing things. Cramming as much in as possible. Your grandfather and I – well, we liked doing our own thing.'

'Your way's the best way, I think,' said Laura. Because of course, it was still Guy and Mary she looked up to more than anyone else in the world, not her parents, and it was Mary's approval she craved all the time, rather than her mother's.

Mary looked up sharply. 'There's no right or wrong way, Laura,' she said, sticking her neck forward and tilting her hat up so she was looking at her granddaughter. 'That's not what I meant. I mean, each to their own. What's sauce for the goose, and all that.'

'What?' said Laura, confused.

Her grandmother lay back in the chair again. She said quietly, 'You're twenty-eight. Aren't you?' Laura nodded. 'My memory's so terrible these days. Darling, all I'm saying is – you're not your parents' age. Yet. Or mine. You should enjoy yourself whilst the going's good.'

'Right,' said Laura. She stared out across the sea, wanting to ask more, but when she turned to her grandmother to say, 'Do you know where I was last night, then?' she was asleep.

She picked up the sandwich her mother had given her, and

219

munched it happily, then she dozed for a bit in the sunshine, her mind stretching lazily back across the previous twenty-four hours, sifting through everything that had happened. It was refreshing, really, she decided. For so long her life had been so narrow, so confined to what one man was doing, when he could see her, and the blinkered view she'd had about everything else, that to be here, to have met Nick – and Charles, of course, and the house – it was all really interesting. Yes, that was it, nothing more than that.

Yes, it was true, of course Nick was attractive. In fact, he was gorgeous. It was also true he lived in a huge house, the greatest house in the country. And there was also the other stuff, the stuff that actually mattered – how easy it was to talk to him, how funny he was, how she felt she could tell him everything even though they had nothing in common. She thought of the previous night, sitting high up in the soft glow of the dining room overlooking the darkening woodland, each of them leaning into the candlelight, their elbows on the table, drinking wine and talking, talking, and laughing. It was a great Brief Encounter, that was all, and Laura told herself that it was a really good sign that she could get out there, and meet someone as nice as him. It boded well for the future, even if she wasn't going to see him ever again. She wasn't. It was just too weird. Leave it at that, a perfect evening, a nice experience, an amusing story to tell Jo and Paddy when she got back, to show them she was over Dan, everything was OK, and all of that – yes . . .

Her phone rang again, and, without thinking, she picked it up out of her bag. *Nick Mob.* Well, just to be polite.

'Hello,' she said softly, not wanting to wake Mary. She got up, and walked to the low wall on the other side of the garden.

'Hi,' said Nick. 'Get home OK?'

'Yes, thanks,' said Laura. 'Thanks again.'

'It was – a good evening, wasn't it?' said Nick.

'Really good,' Laura agreed, wanting to say more but not wanting to go too far.

'I mean it,' he said. 'I really enjoyed myself, Laura.'

'Well, I did too,' she replied. 'I mean it too.'

She smiled into the phone. There was silence, and she knew he was doing the same thing.

'You know,' said Nick. 'It's a real shame about tonight.'

'The Seekers?'

'Yes,' he said. 'I'm sorry.'

'I am too,' said Laura. 'You have no idea.'

'Do you have to go?'

'What?'

'Can you get out of it?'

'No,' said Laura. 'They've got me a ticket and everything.'

At that moment, her father appeared at the French windows and called, 'Laura?'

Mary shifted in her chair, and lowered her hat even further.

'Laura, we're going for a walk,' her father said, bending down to brush something off his Gortex sandals. 'Come with us? We're going to look at the marsh, about two miles away. Marvellous birds.'

'Oh,' said Laura.

'Wait a minute, George,' her mother called, disappearing back into the house to fetch something. 'My binoculars.'

'Oh god,' Laura whispered into the phone. 'Help.' Then she realised Nick was still there, and said, 'Sorry.'

'Don't be,' he said, and she could hear laughter in his voice. 'So, you're going to the marsh and then to the Seekers Tribute Band concert for the rest of the day, and you're not going to let me take you out for a drink?'

'No,' said Laura sadly. 'I've said I'll go. I can't get out of it.'

'Right.'

'Right.'

'Of course,' he said, 'I'm not the kind of man who'd ask you to lie to your parents and get out of an evening so I can see you again.'

'No,' said Laura. 'You're not.'

221

'And you're not the kind of girl who'd agree to lie to get out of the evening in the first place.'

'No, Nick,' said Laura again. 'I'm not.'

'So –' he said. 'I'll meet you at six thirty then?'

'Where?'

'The north gate of the estate. You can't miss it.'

'See you there,' said Laura, smiling into the phone again, as her mother emerged from the house.

'Ready?' her dad asked.

'Oh dear,' said Laura, putting down the phone. 'Mum, that was Naomi again. Her boyfriend. He's just dumped her. She was really upset.'

Beneath her hat, Laura distinctly heard Mary chuckle softly as she walked across the lawn to her parents, but she ignored it, knowing she would pay for it on Judgement Day, but also knowing that, as lies go, this one was *almost* excusable. Almost.

CHAPTER TWENTY-THREE

'. . . That's why you don't seriously like them. Name one single player.'

'Theo Walcott.'

'Well, OK,' said Nick. 'But he's never actually played for them, you know.'

'But he's Arsenal,' said Laura. 'And the French bloke. Thierry Henry. There.'

'Right, right,' said Nick, pushing aside a protruding branch and waiting for Laura to pass by. They were walking through the wood to the south of the house, having met at the north entrance. 'Yes, of course, so you can name two members of one of the most famous clubs in the world, so that makes you a really big fan of theirs.'

'I like them,' said Laura obstinately.

'I'm sure you do. I'm just saying, you like them because you live in North London and you're deeply middle class and think you have to support Arsenal as a result.'

'That's not true, and don't be rude to your guests,' said Laura. 'Ouch,' she added, as her foot came down on a twig. She put out her hand to steady herself; he caught her arm, and said,

'Yet I never understand why people who move to, say, West London never feel this overwhelming urge to support Queens

Park Rangers. Or Brentford. Both of which are actually quite decent teams, with proper players.'

'That's rubbish!' Laura said, but she was laughing. Nick leant against a tree and thought for a moment.

'What's the name of Arsenal's new stadium?'

'Oh,' said Laura vaguely. 'Well, it's nearly finished.'

'No, that's not it.'

'I don't know,' said Laura, knowing she was beaten. 'Arsenal's New Stadium. I don't really care.'

'I thought you said you were their biggest fan.'

'Damn,' she said, and leant against the tree next to him. The evening sunshine was filtering through the branches creating a kaleidoscopic effect of hundreds of tiny flecks of light shimmering over them in the slight breeze. 'Where now?'

'I thought we'd walk over towards the pond, then out to the village. There's a nice pub there, too, we can have a drink.'

'Great,' said Laura, following her host as he walked ahead along the path. Even after a summer of sunshine it was dark and damp, and the way was cool after the heat of the day. It was deliciously green, the air mossy and moist, in contrast to the already parched, yellowing land outside, dry and brittle now summer was so far advanced.

'So,' said Laura, breathing deeply, enjoying the cool on her arms. 'What did you do today?'

'Today?'

'Yes,' said Laura.

'Why?' asked Nick, fiddling in his pocket for something.

'Well,' said Laura, slightly taken aback. 'I wasn't being nosey. I just wanted to know. I have no idea what someone like you does all day.'

'God no, sorry,' said Nick. 'I was – thinking of something I forgot at the house. Sorry. Of course. Right,' he said. He took his hand out of his pocket, picking a switch off a tree as they passed. 'Today – well. I spent the morning in the kitchen garden with Fletcher – he's the head gardener. Talking about what our

224

yield will be this year. What we're likely to get, where we'll put it, and so on. How much we can use. I want the estate to be as self-sufficient as possible, you see.'

'Right,' said Laura. 'Is that possible?'

'Not really, no,' said Nick, laughing. 'Although we do make all our own jam and scones for the tea-shop, which I'm very proud of. All Chartley products, which is good, isn't it?'

'That's great.'

He picked a flower out of the mossy bank growing nearby. 'Here. Have a white campion.' He handed it to her, and she took it, startled. 'Especially when you realise how many damn cream teas we sell on a day like today.'

'Must be hundreds,' Laura said, tucking the flower behind her ear.

'Hm? Oh yes, it is. Hundreds and hundreds. We have nearly a hundred thousand visitors a year, did you know that?'

'Oh my god,' said Laura. 'Seriously?'

'Absolutely.' Nick tapped a tree with the branch he was holding. 'All of them wanting a slice of heritage. They come, they have their cream teas, they see the tapestry and the Hogarths and the staircase and they wander round and hopefully buy a tea towel and then they go home.'

'It's bizarre,' said Laura.

'No,' said Nick. His voice was determined. 'It's not. It's great that they want to come, and it's our job to make sure they have a good time. I feel – we need to make it somewhere people feel genuinely welcomed.'

'And do you think it is?' said Laura, remembering how she'd criticised it yesterday.

He read her thoughts. 'Well – yes and no. I've been thinking about what you said, you know.'

Laura looked down at her feet as she followed the path. 'I'm sorry. I was really rude.'

'No, you were honest. Which, believe me, people usually aren't.'

'Honesty's not always the best policy,' said Laura ruefully.

225

'It is,' said Nick. 'Really, it is.' He stopped. 'Anyway, I – it was helpful.'

'Are you going to talk to Charles about it?' said Laura.

'Charles? Oh – yes. Yes, I suppose I am.'

'That's nice of you!' said Laura, laughing.

'Ha,' he said. 'Yes. You're right, though. I – we should do something about it.'

'Get the sign repainted,' said Laura.

'The what?' His face was blank. 'What sign?'

'When you arrive, outside,' Laura explained. 'The sign looks awful. It's the entrance to the house, and it's cracked and peeling, and it just looks like the place is falling apart. And your sister and that bloke in the ticket booth,' she said, getting into her stride. 'Sorry, but I don't think that's what Charles would want people's first impression of the house to be. Especially when you're paying fifteen quid for the privilege. You need some friendly, nice, welcoming person, who says they're just completely delighted you're there and gives you a guidebook and is sensible.'

'That flower suits you, in your hair,' Nick said. 'You're pretty when you rant, did you know that?'

Laura felt herself going red. 'Am I?' she said, rather stupidly.

'Yes,' he said solemnly. 'You are. Well, don't get distracted. I take your point. You're saying a randy young woman and some confused, exploited, sex-mad youth isn't the right way to say "Welcome to Chartley"? Well, I can't think why. Look, here we are. Here's the pond.'

They had come to the edge of the wood, and he stopped, Laura next to him. In front of them was a wide expanse of water, surrounded by thick grey reeds waving gently in the breeze. Over the other side was a tiny bridge of golden stone, and a stream flowed under it, cutting through the grass. They were high up, Laura realised – she looked over in wonderment and there, as the land sloped away, was Chartley Hall below them, a hundred metres or so in the distance. They were looking at the south side and the back view, with the formal gardens stretching out behind the house. The dark green of the tiny formal hedges looked like perfectly drawn letters of the alphabet on the ground; a secret message to someone. The stream ran away through the landscape, following the contours of the hill until it reached the formal gardens, where it became part of the layout, flowing into the fountains at the foot of the terrace, sparkling in the setting sun. The stone from the house glowed. Around them was the green of the landscaped park, the dull grey-yellow of the shorn fields, rolls of hay puckering the view and, in the distance to the north, the thin blue band of the sea, behind the wood. The people looked so small, incongruous compared to the breathtaking size and grandeur of the house and its surroundings. Laura turned to her companion, to say this to him, and found him watching her, a strange expression on his face. He leant towards her, and then very slightly stepped back.

'You like it?' he said.

Laura laughed. 'It's OK.' She looked out again, not wanting to move. 'You are lucky, living here, you know.'

'I know,' Nick said. 'I'm very lucky.' He checked his watch suddenly. 'Right. Shall we get a drink? It's not that long to Chartley village. Have you got time?'

'Oh yes,' said Laura. It was nearly eight. 'I told my parents I didn't know when I'd be back.'

'Don't you feel horrible?' said Nick gravely. 'Lying to them, making them think some imaginary friend of yours is in trouble.'

'She's not imaginary,' said Laura. 'I used to work with her.'

'Naomi. Excellent. Poor Naomi.'

'She doesn't even know I'm here,' said Laura. 'I shouldn't think she's losing sleep over it; she wasn't even that nice. She –' She trailed off.

'What?'

'Nothing.'

Laura felt a bit embarrassed. In fact, Naomi had stopped speaking to Laura when she'd finished with Josh – they'd all worked together. She'd told Laura she was a bitch, and that Josh deserved much better than her. She'd then got really drunk at Rachel's birthday do a couple of months later – god, they were fun, those evenings, especially Rachel's birthdays – and thrown herself at him. Josh had politely said no, and then no again and again, as she virtually started to stalk him. People at work said that was why he'd moved to Australia – to get away from her – and she'd moved to Norfolk – to try and live down her stalker shame. So it was hardly likely she'd be that overjoyed to hear from Laura, really.

'Go on,' said Nick, putting his finger on his chin. 'I'm all curious now.'

So Laura told him about Naomi. He was highly amused, and let out a yelp of laughter. 'She sounds lovely.'

'She was pretty awful. I feel sorry for the Wetlands, you know, being looked after by her.'

'Well, I love her,' said Nick firmly, as they turned their back on the view and walked south, towards the gate.

'Don't.'

'I owe her a lot,' he said. 'Thanks to her, I'm your best Norfolk friend. Right,' he said, walking swiftly on. 'What will you have when we get to the pub? Let me guess.'

'You won't be able to,' said Laura, walking fast to keep up with him. 'I bet.'

Nick looked at her. 'I guess you'll *want* a Pimms, but you'll actually *have* a glass of white wine.'

'Oh,' said Laura, severely disappointed.

'I know you better than you think. Evidently,' said Nick.

'That's eerie,' Laura told him, genuinely surprised.

'It's not that eerie,' said Nick. 'Girls like Pimms. Girls like white wine.'

'Don't be sexist.'

'I'm not,' said Nick. 'It's a fact. In any case, that's not sexist. I guessed right, as is clear from your expression.'

'Well, yes,' said Laura, unsure of her ground. 'But you shouldn't generalise.'

'Neither should you,' Nick retorted.

'I'm not!' said Laura. 'What am I generalising about?'

'Well, you're not at the moment,' he said. 'But you do. I know. You're a snob. An inverted snob.'

'I'm not!' Laura yelled, in amused outrage. '*You're* a snob.'

'No I'm not,' he said. 'Don't hit me! Stop hitting me. You're violent.'

'No, *you're* violent—ly wrong in your assumptions,' said Laura, breathless but laughing.

'No, you are.'

'No, *you*.'

The conversation continued in this vein as they walked across the high, wide downs at the top of the park. As they reached a gate which led them out of the grounds onto the road, they dawdled, Nick chewing bits of grass and telling Laura the names of the various flowers along the wild banks as they walked. Laura picked a bouquet of flowers in the hedgerows, hedge parsley, goose grass, and pale pink dog roses, already in bloom. They chatted, not really saying much, walking easily, soaking up the evening sun as they approached Chartley village, skirting around the edge of the village, until they came to the Needham Arms at the top end of the high street.

The interior of the pub was small and dark, and though it was nearly empty, Laura noted, impressed and amused at the same time, that Nick was greeted like a young prince, rather than the bloke from the estate.

'What do you want?' he asked Laura, looking down at her as they stood by the bar.

'I'll have a pint please,' said Laura firmly.

'You don't want any –'

'No, thanks,' said Laura. He nudged her. 'Oh, all right then,' she said, giving in.

Nick turned to the barman. 'Sorry. A Pimms, please. No, make that two.'

'Good choice,' said Laura, and they nodded at each other, smiling, as the barman watched them curiously.

They were ushered to a quiet parlour at the back, and Laura was touched to be given a wet napkin to wrap her flowers in by the barman.

'Does Charles ever come in here?' Laura asked, as Nick was halfway to finishing his pint. She was more and more curious about the elusive, shy marquess, and how he coped with his role. He seemed too – well, *old-fashioned* to actually be able to keep up to speed with the needs of the estate, more like someone who'd be happier in the library deciphering obscure Latin texts.

'No,' said Nick. 'Not really his scene.'

'It must be difficult for him, too.'

'How?' said Nick.

'Well,' said Laura. 'Because he's –' She trailed off.

'Tall? Got pustulating boils on his face? Two noses?' said Nick. 'What?'

'Well, because of who he is. The *marquess*.' Laura spoke in a whisper.

'Why should it make any difference?' said Nick. He sounded impatient. 'Why shouldn't he come in here?'

'All right, all right, don't get shirty with me,' said Laura, trying to make a joke out of it.

'Well, he's a person,' said Nick, and his voice was still sharp. 'He's not an alien, you know. It says "No Dogs" outside. It doesn't say, "Don't come in, You're too Posh", does it?'

'You're impossible,' said Laura.

He relaxed, and smiled at her. 'You're right. One more drink?' he said, draining his glass.

'One more,' Laura agreed, standing up, 'and I'll get them. I'll watch out for any aristocratic-looking people trying to get in and eject them. Don't worry.'

'Thanks,' said Nick. 'That's a weight off my mind.'

She came back bearing the drinks, and sat down. Nick took a sip from his pint and said suddenly, 'So, Laura. Can I ask you something?'

'Anything,' said Laura recklessly.

Nick paused. 'Well . . .' He looked carefully at her, and put his pint down on the table. 'What's your favourite film?'

'Ha,' said Laura. Her heart, which had been beating loudly, slowed down again. 'That's a hard one, you know. What's yours?'

'*Raiders of the Lost Ark*,' said Nick. 'Seriously,' he added, as Laura looked surprised.

'I agree,' said Laura, 'I'm just surprised you think so.'

'Why?'

'Well,' she paused, 'I'd have thought you were more of a . . . *Godfather*, *French Connection* kind of guy. Serious. Heavy. Lots of themes.'

Nick obviously found this amusing. 'I like that. You think of me as this serious, grown-up man who relaxes by reading biographies of Hitler, don't you?'

'Er, a bit,' said Laura. 'And I don't know why, when –' she broke off, not wanting to sound rude. When your life on the estate is quite easygoing, even if it is hard work, and Charles is obviously a good boss, and you seem to have quite a nice life, so why are you so closed off and prickly about so many things?

'When – what?' said Nick.

'Nothing,' she replied, smiling at him. 'Nothing.' She put her hand on his arm, impulsively. 'It's my favourite film too.'

'Really?'

'Yes,' said Laura. 'Didn't used to be. It used to be, er – *The Sound of Music* or *Four Weddings and a Funeral*. When I was into all of that.'

'All of what?' said Nick. 'It's not crack cocaine, they're just films.'

She shook her head, trying to explain without explaining, not wanting to give herself away, and then realised she was doing exactly the same thing as he was, closing herself off, and it was weird, but OK.

231

'Ah . . .' she said. 'When I was younger. And more stupid. Than I am now.' She looked down.

'OK,' said Nick, nodding as if he understood. He stroked her arm gently, just once. 'I'm going to ask you something else then.'

'Yes?' said Laura, staring at the table.

'So . . . why are you here?'

'What do you mean?' Laura looked at him, over her Pimms.

'I mean here on holiday. I still don't quite understand it. You said yesterday something about how your job was weird at the moment. And you keep darkly mentioning how you've apparently fallen out with various people, which I don't get either – I mean, you keep hitting me, but you don't seem like someone who's constantly making new enemies.'

'I –' Laura began, but she didn't know what to say and trailed off.

Nick said lightly, 'So – what happened?'

'Ah.' Laura looked at him, not sure how to answer. She said tentatively, 'Well . . . it's complicated.'

'Complicated. I see,' said Nick. He paused, holding the matches. 'Don't tell me if you don't want to. I don't mean to stick my nose in.'

'No, no,' said Laura, relieved his curiosity was that, nothing more. 'Well – it was . . . well, it was just this bloke – this bloke I was seeing. That's all.'

'Right,' said Nick. He tore one of the matches off. 'It is none of my business, don't worry.'

There was silence.

'He had a girlfriend,' Laura said in a rush, unable to bear it. 'We had an affair, he was – Dan – he was still with his girlfriend. I got it wrong, I got a bit – er, ah – I fucked it up, basically. Big time. Kind of got everything out of proportion a bit.' She cleared her throat, and said in a small voice, 'I thought he loved me. It's stupid. Anyway, that's it. It's over.'

'And where's Dan now?' said Nick, in a neutral tone.

Laura chewed a fingernail, looked up and said, 'With his girlfriend. Pregnant girlfriend. On holiday in Miami. We were – supposed to go away together. But – I found out about her – being pregnant.'

'When?'

'Two weeks ago,' Laura said, smiling ruefully. 'Lost the money on the holiday. Been suspended from my job, too. Oh yes,' she said, meeting his eye, almost enjoying the surprise on his face. 'I've really screwed it up. At the moment, anyway.'

'So you came here to get away from it all?' Nick said.

'And so I came here.' She looked up and said definitely, 'It's over. That's it, end of story. I'm getting over him.'

She smiled at him, over her glass. And suddenly something clicked inside her. She *was* getting over Dan. She wasn't there yet, but it didn't actually hurt so much, suddenly the whole thing didn't. She hadn't thought about it, couldn't bear to, and now she said it she realised it seemed – a million years away.

'Good for you,' said Nick, and he smiled at her, the hard lines of his face softening as he patted her arm. 'Sounds pretty rough.'

'It was – a bit.' Laura looked at him gratefully, surprised at how much the gesture meant; he knew she didn't want sympathy, just a bit of human understanding. 'But you're right. I'm here to get over it. This is the "turn over a new leaf" approach, this week. So far, not too bad. Well, now I've met you, that is. So thanks.'

'Well,' Nick said, raising his glass. 'Thank you too. Here's to the "new leaf" approach. Or the Norfolk Outreach Programme for Mental People. After you leave I'm going to start hanging around the train station for the London train, to pal up with the next unstable person on holiday and in need of a friend.'

'Well, that's really kind of you,' said Laura.

They were silent; both took another sip of their drinks. Laura looked at her companion from under her eyelashes, until his eyes flicked up towards her and she looked elsewhere, at the old photos, the dried flowers in baskets on the windowsill, the clock on the wall. But she could still see his face in her mind's eye, like she had taken a snapshot. The close-cropped, curling black hair, the bony face with its rather harsh expression, tanned by the summer sun. The expression in the eyes that gave away so little, and occasionally so much. It was strangely familiar, that face, and he reminded her of something, someone, but for the life of her she couldn't remember what.

'When do you go?' he said suddenly.

'What?' asked Laura, still lost in a dream. 'Oh.'

'No, I mean back to London,' he said quickly. 'When do you go?'

'Saturday evening,' she said. 'But I have the birthday lunch all day on Saturday, so –'

'So – what are you doing tomorrow?' he asked, shifting in his seat on the wooden bench.

'Evening?'

He nodded, his expression inscrutable.

'Nothing,' said Laura. 'Well –'

She felt a bit guilty, suddenly. Shouldn't she be spending some more time with her parents? With Mary? But she saw them all the time, a voice inside her said. And it was the lunch on the Saturday, after all – she'd see them then. Surely that was –

Laura jumped suddenly. She glanced down. Nick had put his hand on hers. He said quietly, 'I know you have to go. But tomorrow. Do you fancy a picnic at the beach? Since it's your last night?'

Suddenly Laura didn't know what to say to him, which was weird because up till now she'd felt she could say almost anything to him. She looked anxiously up at him, into his eyes. They were narrow, watching her almost like a hawk, the old expression of kindness, humour, arrogance and sarcasm mixed with – something else, something indefinable. His grip tightened slightly, then he released her hand and sat back.

Laura said, slowly, 'Yes, of course.'

He nodded, and they looked at each other again, strangely, blankly, until he said, 'Meet me there at seven. I'll bring the picnic.'

'Really?' said Laura. 'No, I'll bring something too.'

'No, it's my pleasure. Someone in the kitchens owes me a favour.'

'Right,' said Laura.

'How are you getting home tonight?' Nick asked, as he took another sip of his pint. He watched her over the glass, as Laura said,

'I'm getting the bus.'

His expression was bemused. 'Seriously,' she laughed, wanting to reassure him she wasn't making it up. 'There's a timetable at home. I checked it before I left. It goes from just outside here. Every half hour. So I won't have to force you out of your bedroom again. I've planned ahead.'

'Great,' said Nick. 'Well – that's great.'

There was silence between them then, and this time it was awkward. Something had shifted, imperceptibly. Nick said nothing. He looked down at the table. Laura wanted to say something, but she couldn't. In the end, she said,

'So, I'd better go soon . . .'

'You don't have to,' he said abruptly. 'You could –'

'No,' said Laura softly. She drummed her fingers on the table. 'I –'

They were alone in their tiny alcove, the murmur of the other drinkers in the pub was faint. Nick slid his thumb under her hand, and wrapped his fingers around hers, stopping the tattoo she was beating on the table. They stayed like that for a few seconds, her hand in his. Laura looked up at him, her heart beating now, so loudly she was sure he could hear it. He was watching her, with that strange, familiar expression. His face was pale under his tan. She noticed how plump his bottom lip was, how biteable it was, compared to the sharp

235

lines of the rest of his face. And then he put his other hand behind her neck, and gently pulled her towards him, and kissed her.

His lips were soft, his arm was wrapped around her, and she could taste fine, salty sweat on his skin, as she kissed him back and they pulled apart. She looked at him, drinking in the sight of him, and they said nothing again, but smiled at each other in understanding. Nick was still holding her hand; he squeezed it, and then put his other hand up to her mouth. He touched her lips gently with his fingers, and his hand dropped to his side again.

'Well,' he said, his voice noncommittal, but he was smiling at her.

Laura smiled back. A feeling of happiness was washing through her, like sunshine after a cloudy day. She looked into his eyes. 'Well,' she agreed, and tightened her grasp on his hand as they stared at one another.

'What's your surname?' she asked suddenly.

He laughed, and stroked her cheek with his index finger. 'How very Victorian of you, Laura. I didn't know you were so old-fashioned.'

She blushed. 'I just meant . . .'

'It's Needham,' said Nick. He paused, his eyes on hers. 'Better now? Any more questions?'

'No,' said Laura dreamily. 'Not at the moment.'

So he kissed her again.

'I'll see you tomorrow, then,' said Nick, as they walked along Chartley high street. It was a warm, dark evening, the sky a deep royal blue colour, not quite night yet. 'Are you sure you –'

'I'm sure,' said Laura firmly. Mrs Danvers told her in no uncertain terms that she had to get on that bus, much as she wanted to stay in the Needham Arms and carry on making out with Nick for the rest of the night. She looked at her watch. It was nearly ten. She was suddenly tired, and moreover, she'd promised her mother she'd help her with the shopping bright and early the next morning (it was one of Angela's great obsessions, going to the supermarket at the crack of dawn, to avoid any possible danger of having to queue). And she couldn't hang around two nights in a row and invade this poor man's house, which wasn't even his. No, with regret, she knew she ought to leave him, and whatever this unexpected lovely thing was between them.

'So.' Nick took her hands in his, so she was facing him, still clutching her rather bedraggled posy of flowers. The air was still, the horse chestnuts lining the road heavy and scented, stirring faintly. She took a deep breath.

'Thanks,' she said. 'A lot.'

'No,' said Nick. 'Thank you. You have no idea.' He held her hands tightly, but his face was in shadow under the tree and she couldn't see his expression.

'You neither,' she said.

'Well, let's just agree we're both total screw-ups, and we won't fight about it,' he said.

'What are you a screw-up about?' Laura asked, curiosity getting the better of her.

'Trust me, Laura, we don't have time for that now,' said Nick. 'I won't bore you with the many ways in which I've screwed up. You wouldn't want to see me again.'

He didn't sound self-pitying, merely detached, amused. It was impossible to gauge his real meaning, so Laura said cautiously, 'Nick, about what I said earlier.'

'About what?'

'About that guy – the one I –'

He kissed her. 'Forget about it.' His hands tightened on hers again; there was hardly any gap between them as they stood, facing each other, her hips pressing into his. 'That was then. This is now.' He stopped. 'This *is* what this is, isn't it?'

He threw the question out snappily, as if it didn't really mean anything. Laura said hesitantly, 'Nick –'

237

'I know,' he said, his voice full of laughter. 'Let's worry about that tomorrow. Or whenever.'

'Absolutely,' said Laura, as the sound of a heavy engine grew louder, coming towards them. She turned her head – there was the bus, incongruous primary colours, out of place in that lovely old street, this perfect, perfect evening.

'See you tomorrow.'

'Seven o'clock,' said Laura. 'Tell Charles thanks for letting you out another evening.'

'I'll tell him,' he said. 'The Marquess of Ranelagh says thank you.'

'I'm honoured,' said Laura, as the doors shuddered open.

He leant down and kissed her again, hard and swift. 'Bye, gorgeous,' he said casually, stepping back onto the pavement.

The bus driver gave him a salute, doffing an imaginary hat. Laura sat down by the window and smiled at this piece of faux courtesy. She waved at Nick as the bus rolled gently down the road, out of the village, back towards Seavale.

She put her head on the glass and found she was smiling insanely, grinning ear to ear. She pulled her book out of her bag and tried to read, but couldn't concentrate. Nick. Nick. Nick! She couldn't stop smiling, and she told herself she had to calm down, that Mrs Danvers would not be pleased at her schoolgirlish behaviour. She pinched herself on the arm. Good grief, she was almost having a relapse. No. No more old Laura again. She carried on looking out of the window, thinking how sudden, how strange the whole thing was. She *mustn't* start being her old self again, the person who had taken up running to impress a boy at university and sprained her ankle. The person who had convinced herself that the man who'd painted the office, Julian, was her future husband, because they both had grandmothers called Mary.

The book fell from her lap as the bus swung around the corner. Laura put her hand over her mouth and yawned. She ran her hand down, over her lips, her neck, to her breastbone, wanting to remember how it felt to kiss him, touch him. She bent down to pick the book up, and saw the postcard her dad had given her had fallen out and had skidded across the scuffed lino floor. Smiling with recognition, glad Nick hadn't seen it, she picked it up, turned it over, and her mouth fell open with shock.

The seventh marquess smiled up at her from the card, his dark, intelligent eyes boring into hers. She gasped.

It was Nick. It was the spitting image of him. How could she not have seen it before? The hair, his eyes, the bony, rather arrogant face. Just a hundred years earlier. She turned it over again, as if wanting to check she hadn't picked up another postcard that happened to be lying on the floor of the Coastal Hopper. She read the caption on the back. '*Dominic, Seventh Marquess of Ranelagh, Earl of Albany Cross, 1867–1928. In 1895, the* Illustrated London News *called him "England's Most Eligible Bachelor".*'

Dominic. Nick.

CHAPTER TWENTY-FOUR

'Is it OK if I need to stay with Naomi tonight?' Laura asked casually the next day, as she was pushing the trolley around the supermarket with her mother.

'Again?' Angela said, scanning the fresh vegetables. 'But you saw her last night. And the night before.'

'I know.' Laura laced her fingers together.

'So why tonight, darling?' Angela looked distractedly at her daughter. 'Did you two have a row? You were in a very strange mood when you got back yesterday.'

'Not a row,' said Laura. 'More like I found out something.'

'Gosh, Laura.' Angela began rapidly repeating ingredients under her breath. 'It's like the two of you are having a holiday romance. Ha!'

She turned her attention momentarily away from the bag of onions she was holding, and squeaked slightly as someone pushed past them.

It was lunchtime, it was Friday – they'd got there too late for Angela's liking and now the supermarket was packed full of locals and holidaymakers alike, stocking up for what promised to be a boiling hot weekend – perfect barbecuing weather. Laura didn't know what to say. She was tired, and hadn't slept well. Her head ached.

Perhaps she should ring Nick when she got home and tell him she couldn't come tonight. Keep it simple, don't get involved, one side of her was saying. Walk away. But the other side was saying, But I want to see him again. Not because he's a Marquess, because I liked him. That was why her head was aching. Should she go?

'Lulu doesn't eat meat, does she?' Angela said, breaking into her thoughts.

'Lulu doesn't eat anything, Mum,' Laura said, prising the onions from her mother's frenzied grip and picking up a smaller bag. 'Here, Mum, you wanted red onions.'

'Oh . . .' Angela had wandered down the aisle and was looking at crisps. 'Annabel's always so snooty about these,' she said, brandishing a huge packet of semi-posh crisps. 'Says they're full of E numbers. But I rather like them, what do you think?'

'I think they're great, and Gran likes them too, remember? She asked you to get that exact flavour,' said Laura patiently.

'Oh my goodness,' said Angela. 'My memory.'

'Mum!' said Laura. 'It doesn't matter what Annabel thinks. Or what she wants. Gran's *your* mum, isn't she? And this is *her* birthday! Isn't it!'

'Yes!' said Angela, slamming her fist down into the crisps section. There was a loud crunching sound as several packets burst.

'Oh dear,' said Angela, looking amazed at her own strength. 'Good grief.'

'She winds you up,' said Laura. 'Don't worry about her. Simon's coming back tomorrow, it's Granny's birthday, the sun's shining and everything's fine.' It was true, she thought. Go for it. She pushed the trolley on, blocking her mother's way. 'Now, *is* it OK if I stay with Naomi tonight? I – er – may not. But if I do, I'll be back early tomorrow to help you before the others come, I promise.'

'Yes!' said Angela. 'Bless you, darling. You're quite right.'

'Yes to Naomi?' said Laura, hopping from foot to foot with frustration.

241

'Naomi?' said her mother, as if hearing the name for the first, not the fourth, time. 'Oh. Again, dear?'

'Yes,' said Laura, extremely patiently. 'I'm sorry, but tonight is my last night, and it's been so lovely to meet up with her again.'

'You've really enjoyed it, haven't you?' said Angela, stopping to look at her daughter.

'Yes,' said Laura. 'Yes, I have.'

'Do you think you'll stay in touch?'

Laura gazed into the distance.

'Not sure,' she said. 'We need to talk about that tonight. About a lot of stuff.' She came back into the present with a sudden jolt. 'I – er, I mean, Naomi needs to sort all that out. With her ex. She's got a lot of things to sort out.'

'Ah,' murmured Angela sympathetically. She picked up a bag of salad. 'What about this? Looks nice.'

'It's washed in tonnes of chlorine, and it's really ecologically unsound,' said Laura, throwing the offending bag of salad back. 'Oh, Mum,' she said in a rush of confidence. 'I don't know what she's doing, to be honest.'

'Why?' said Angela, her head on one side. 'Oh dear. Why, what's the problem with her boyfriend?'

Laura was silent for a moment, then she said slowly, 'She's only just met him. But she thought – she thought he was great. That they were really good together. But he's kind of lied to her.'

Her eyes filled with tears; she turned towards the bags of salad again. 'Oh look,' she mumbled in a muffled voice. 'Watercress.'

Angela wasn't really paying attention, having moved on towards the vegetables. 'Oh dear. That's a shame,' she said vaguely, covering her tracks, her eyes scanning the shelves like an SAS operative. 'Carrots, ooh yes,' she said, moving on. 'Leeks.'

A night of sleepless tossing and turning, of reaching out

242

to grab her phone, wanting to text him, to say, 'I know who you are', of wrestling with the knowledge she had now acquired, had brought Laura no more answers. She liked him; he liked her – wasn't that enough? It didn't matter, did it? she told herself, through the long night, as the sky filled with light and the morning came. Surely this didn't really change things?

Then came the doubts, the questions. Was it really true, that he was this person? Someone she felt she knew, and now just didn't know at all? She couldn't reconcile the two: Nick, who loved thin chips, made her laugh, kissed her as if it was just right – and the Marquess of Ranelagh, this symbol of ancestry and wealth, of formality and duty – this person whom she realised she had heard so much about as a thing, rather than a living, breathing man. She had turned over and over in bed, till the sheets were loose and crumpled, trying to make sense of it, desperate for some calm. That house – the treasures inside it – the history – the family, Lady Rose, Lady Lavinia . . . The mother who left him, the scandal. The publicness of a life like that. Then she knew why he hadn't told her, and she felt a cold feeling start inside her, that this was stupid, doomed, that she shouldn't take it any further.

After all, she'd only just met him. Perhaps even worrying about it was stupid. Perhaps thinking about it was the last thing to do. She wasn't angry with him, or even with herself, for once. She just wanted to see him again, to be with him, and perhaps then she would know what happened next. Because at the moment, she wasn't sure.

'Naomi's boyfriend lied to her as well, did he?' Angela said vaguely, putting some leeks into the trolley. 'Oh dear.'

Laura shook herself out of her reverie, gathered herself together and followed behind. 'Well,' she continued, not really minding whether her mother was listening or not, 'Er . . . yes. She knows he's lied. But he doesn't know she knows.'

'What did he lie about?' said Angela, looking curiously at her.

Laura said sadly, 'About who he is.'

'What, is he a convict?'

'Kind of. The opposite. Sort of.'

Angela looked at her daughter as if she were mad, and Laura said hurriedly, 'Well, she doesn't know what she should do about it now. And that's not even the biggest issue,' she continued, warming to her theme, as Angela made sympathetic noises and moved around the corner to the condiments. She bent over slightly, humming, and putting her finger to her lip as she ran her gaze over a row of mustards. 'The biggest issue is, now she knows he is what he is, that makes *everything* different.'

'What would your grandmother say?' said Angela. 'Dijon? Or wholegrain?'

'Dijon,' said Laura, plucking a jar viciously off the shelf and throwing it into the trolley, where it clattered loudly. Angela frowned, obviously rewinding the sounds in her head so she could respond to her daughter's last sentence.

'How is everything different?' she said, with astonishing clarity. 'Does him having not told the truth about who he is really make that much of a difference? If she feels that strongly about him? Doesn't matter if he's a convict. Unless it's for something *really* awful, of course,' she said, lowering her voice. 'But it doesn't, does it?'

Laura stopped still in the aisle. 'Don't know,' she said, chewing her lip. 'I'll have to see. See her and see.'

'It is Dijon she likes, isn't it?' said Angela, moving on. 'Ask your grandmother when we get home, just to make sure.'

'I'll ask her,' said Laura. 'Good idea.'

Before lunch, as Angela stood in the kitchen, chopping, dicing, preparing marinades, getting things ready for the next day, and George crouched down by the barbecue, oiling it, speaking tenderly to it as if it were a temperamental dressage horse, Laura wandered out onto the terrace, carrying a huge bowl and a massive bag of broad beans to shell under her arm. Mary was crouched over a flower bed, dead-heading a pink scented rambling rose that clung to the side of the house. She was wearing sunglasses, and had tied an old printed scarf over her hair.

'Ah,' she said, standing up with a groan as Laura approached. 'Come and talk to me.'

'I will,' said Laura, pulling a chair up to the table and sitting down.

Mary brushed the dead leaves off her gardening gloves, and winced as she bent down again. 'Got everything you needed this morning?'

'Absolutely,' said Laura. 'You like Dijon, not wholegrain, don't you?'

'Oh yes,' said Mary. 'Loathe wholegrain. Those little bits. In fact, I was thinking we should have some mayonnaise, too. Guy used to make garlic mayonnaise, you know. Delicious, it really was. When we were in Morocco, he –'

'Sorry, Gran,' Laura said, wanting to steer Mary's thoughts in a different direction. Mary looked up, rather crossly. 'Can I ask you something?'

'Of course,' her grandmother said. She leant against the slatted wood of the house and undid the scarf covering her hair, shaking it out. 'What's on your mind, darling?'

'You – you said you'd met the marquess's mother,' Laura began. 'Vivienne something. Didn't you?'

'Golly,' said Mary. She patted her cheeks. 'Vivienne Lash. Yes, ages ago. Guy and I met them both, when we were living in the South of France for the summer. Saw quite a bit of them, actually.'

'Have you met her son?'

'No,' said Mary. 'The new marquess? Oh, no. She was the outcast, you know, darling. She left his father when he was – ooh, still only a teenager, I think.'

'Right,' said Laura, not really knowing what to ask next, or what she was hoping to get out of this conversation, all of a sudden. 'So – did she talk about her children?'

'Vivienne?' Mary sat down next to Laura, and lifted up her sunglasses. 'Not much. Think it was too painful for her. We knew all about it, of course, though. Everyone did.'

'How come?' said Laura.

'Well, it was a huge scandal. Massive. Kept the tabloids busy for weeks.'

'Really?' said Laura. 'Why on earth? People run off with people all the time.'

Mary smiled at her. 'Oh darling. You are naïve sometimes. Just because it doesn't interest you, you'd rather read about it in the pages of a novel, doesn't mean it's not endlessly fascinating to the rest of the public. Or the newspapers, at least. No, it was all rather juicy to them. For a variety of reasons.'

'Like what?'

'She was terribly famous in her day, you know, Vivienne. Real A-list British star. When she married the Marquess of Ranelagh, it was like a real-life fairytale. Beautiful actress marries richest peer in the land, that sort of thing.'

'And they are – that rich, are they?' Laura said, in a small voice.

Mary flexed her right hand, squeezing the secateurs tightly together. 'The Needhams? I should say so. Laura, they're the great aristocratic family, you know. Vast wealth. That house is only the tip of the iceberg, you know. There's the place in Grosvenor Square, that castle in Scotland – and they own half of Belgravia, too.'

Something caught in Laura's throat; she breathed in the wrong way and started choking, coughing violently. 'God,' she rasped, when her breathing had returned to normal.

A seagull flew overhead, croaking loudly. Mary looked up, and followed it as it flew out to sea. She said distantly, 'Yes. You know, though, it wasn't enough for her. She shouldn't have married him. I think she loved him, but it was Freddy she really loved.'

'Freddy?' Laura asked, breathing deeply.

'The brother. I think William – was that it? William? Guy would remember, he – oh well,' said Mary, her face clouding. 'Anyway. Yes, it was *the* scandal for a while. Because she was so well-known. And the Needhams were so rich. And she was running off with his *brother*, you know, that's really not on in some people's eyes. And then there were the children, they were still quite young.'

'Really,' said Laura, her heart beating wildly. 'How young?'

'I can't remember,' said Mary, slightly impatiently. 'Guy would have known. There were three of them, though. Yes, that was it. Rose was the eldest. Then there was Lavinia, yes, that was it, gosh, I'd forgotten. And then the little boy. The heir. She did worry about him. He was only – what? Eleven? Twelve? Still quite young.'

The seagull squawked in the distance. Laura stayed very still, her arms around the bowl, not wanting to disrupt anything. She gave a tiny, polite nod, willing her grandmother to tell her more. Mary sighed, and stretched out her arms. She cleared her throat.

'Yes,' she said. 'I loved her. But she did suffer about leaving that boy behind. Dominic. Nick, she called him. The heir to the whole damn thing. What a life. Can you imagine?'

'No,' said Laura. 'Absolutely not.'

'Can't imagine it. Losing your mother like that.'

'Well, but she didn't die,' said Laura.

'No, but they weren't allowed to see her. Or she them. She missed them dreadfully, you know. I sometimes wonder –'

She stopped, and looked out across the lawn, over the wall, down to the sea.

'What, Gran?' said Laura.

'Was it worth it? But they were so in love. And she was so miserable with her first husband, you know. Still.'

247

'Still . . .' Laura said encouragingly.

'I think she hated herself for it, for doing such damage. Still does probably. I haven't seen her for years, you know. She was lovely.' Mary sighed. 'But she was punished for it. She didn't deserve it, I think. She was only human. We all are, you know.' She put her hands lightly on the arms of her chair.

'Yes,' said Laura. 'We are.' She patted her grandmother's hand, and nodded at the bag of beans. 'I'll get on with these, then.'

The rest of the day passed as if she were sleepwalking, counting down the hours till she saw him again. Against the backdrop of preparation for the next day, as the sun shone down on the Fosters as they put up bunting, cleaned and cleared everything, tidied the house, put the newspapers outside, Laura worked almost silently, still tossing it all over in her mind, like the mounds of salad she washed in the spinner, still thinking so hard her head hurt, without ever reaching a conclusion about what to do. She only knew she liked him, more than she could say, that it felt so right.

But that's exactly what was terrifying her. Because she'd been there before, and been proved utterly wrong, and if she'd thought Dan was someone who wasn't entirely coming clean about his life, Nick could win an Olympic gold medal in the same event. She had to see him, to talk to him, to try and work out why, yet again, this had happened to her. And why it mattered so much.

CHAPTER TWENTY-FIVE

He was waiting for her when she arrived at the beach. The last of the day's holidaymakers were leaving in dribs and drabs, brightly coloured nylon windbreakers rolled up under their arms, clutching towels, goggles, rubbish – the paraphernalia of family holidays. Laura passed one such family as she made her way down to the beach, past the rustling sea grasses and beach huts. There was something real and comforting about them, about the way the father held his son's hand, the little boy quiet and dirty after the day's exertions; about the way the other son, about five, Laura guessed, trailed behind his parents, his face tear-stained, his mouth lolly-stained, the excitement of it all obviously too much for him. That was real life, she thought again. This, the thing she was walking towards, in a red sundress, the silver bangles on her wrists jingling as she walked, this wasn't real, was it? But here, now, with the sun setting ahead of her and the calm of evening falling on the sea, she just didn't know. All she knew was she couldn't wait to see him again.

Nick turned at the sound of her step. He frowned slightly as he recognised her, his eyes squinting against the evening sun. There was something intensely familiar about him, Laura realised. Not because he looked like some postcard of his ancestor. Not as if it had only been two days. She watched, like a neutral observer, as he straightened up from the post he was leaning against, his tall, muscular frame moving easily under his shirt, his tanned, dark face, so distant, almost arrogant in repose, now smiling quickly at her as she drew near. How comfortable he looked here, in this landscape. Laura knew she looked like what she was – a tourist. Utterly different.

'Hello,' he said, taking the bottle she'd brought and catching her hand. 'My name's Naomi, great to see you again.' He shook her hand, grinning at her. 'Can I show you some interesting bog weeds?'

'Hello,' she replied, her hair blowing behind her in the breeze. She looked up at him, suddenly shyly. She'd forgotten how attractive he was, how *nice* to look at he was. Marquess or no marquess. He was still holding her hand, and he pulled her towards him and kissed her. She remembered with a jolt how much she enjoyed being with him, how kissing him was something she wanted to do all evening. She broke apart from him, and stood back.

'How are you?' she said abruptly.

'Fine, I'm fine,' Nick replied, scanning her face. She could see a note of uncertainty in his eyes. He was still holding her hand, his face inches away from hers. 'I'm glad you could come.'

'Me too,' said Laura. Their eyes met, briefly, and suddenly she wanted to put her head on his chest, stay like this forever. But she shook her head, released her hand and stood back a little.

'Shall we go this way?' said Nick, jerking his head to his right.

'Great,' said Laura. This was strange, it wasn't working out the way she'd expected. He was still the same. She'd expected to notice the difference in him, now she knew, and there was none. The same distant, detached amusement at the world, the same politeness and kindness. The feeling that she could totally be herself with him – it was still there. She did not move as he set off, and he turned back to find her watching him, the knuckles of her hands pressed against her cheeks.

'Everything OK?' Nick said easily.

'Well,' said Laura, suddenly feeling a bit sick. 'Not sure, really. Nick, why didn't you tell me who you really are?'

A tiny muscle ticked in Nick's cheek. He was silent for a moment, and gave a harsh, short laugh.

'I see,' he said, putting the cooler box down. 'I assume you're referring to the title I happen to have, rather than to my unbeaten record as Chartley District Junior Darts Champion in 1985.'

'Don't joke, Nick,' said Laura. 'I'm serious. You – you lied to me.'

He looked as if he were about to protest, then he said quietly, 'Yes. Yes I did.'

'Nick –'

'I lied about a couple of little details, Laura. That's all they are. I promise you. They're unimportant to me.'

'But they're not to me!' said Laura. 'You're – you're a freaking *marquess*, for god's sake! How could you not tell me? Do you do this to people all the time?'

'No,' he said, holding out a hand to stop her. His voice was low, his expression serious. 'Laura, listen to me. Listen. This is important. It is not a big deal. I promise you. The person you met. That's me. You know my name, you know what I do all day – that *is* what I do all day, mostly. You – you – I didn't want to tell you the truth, because you got the wrong end of the stick and then I found, well.' He smiled at her. 'I found I wanted you to like me for myself, more and more. So I didn't tell you.'

'You should have.'

'Yes,' he agreed. 'I should have. 'But –' he stepped forward and grabbed her fingers, enclosing them in his strong hands. 'Laura, I swear to you this doesn't make a difference to us. Whatever this is between us, it mustn't make a difference.' His hands tightened. 'It already does, too much, to other things. It's not going to, to this.'

The pressure of his hands suddenly hurt. She winced. He

released them, and said, 'I'm sorry. It's just – my life is odd. Extraordinary. And when I'm with you – it seems more normal. And believe me, that's quite rare.'

He shook his head, and made as if to turn away. 'Look, I'm sorry.'

Laura suddenly saw how comic the situation was, in a funny way. 'Don't apologise for being a multi-millionaire aristocrat,' she said. 'I should be impressed, I suppose, not having a go at you.' She smiled at him, to let him know it was OK, not wanting to tell him what she was really thinking.

'Shall we go and eat?' said Nick. 'And we'll pretend it's yesterday, and you still think I'm your local friendly farmer, or whatever it was you assumed I was doing when you started shouting at me and trying to set my estate on fire.'

'I thought you were unbelievably rude and a big bully, and I still do,' said Laura.

'Great,' said Nick. 'Glad to see you're still the same charming girl I took a chance on and asked out. Nothing's really changed, has it?' She smiled at him. 'Has it?' he asked, more seriously, looking at her for the answer, and Laura shook her head.

He picked up a cooler box, handed some bottles to her, and they walked down towards the beach together in silence, casting long shadows in the setting sun.

'Potato salad, some biscuits – ah, there's some cheese in here too. Crisps. Some ham. And mustard. Great.'

'You didn't make this, did you?' said Laura, leaning forward on the sand to peer inside the box.

Nick paused as he lifted a bottle of wine out. He said, 'Er, no.'

'So, who did?' Laura said mischievously, genuinely curious. She stretched her legs out on the rug, feeling more relaxed.

Nick lay on his back, looking slightly embarrassed. 'Um . . . the housekeeper.' He scratched his face.

'Who is called . . .?'

'Mrs Hillyard.'

'And does she have a scrubbed red face and wipe her hands on her apron all the time and say things like, "Ooh, I say, Mr Hudson"?'

'No,' said Nick, trying not to smile. 'She's a very elegant lady from a very expensive agency, and I'm terrified of her.' He handed her a glass of wine. 'Charles persuaded me.'

'To ask her to do a picnic?' said Laura incredulously.

'Yes,' said Nick. 'I know. Pathetic.'

'A bit,' said Laura. She laughed. 'I don't get it.'

'What?'

'Your relationship with him, I really don't.' Laura smiled at him. 'If I was him I'd have cleared out long ago.'

'He's the estate manager,' said Nick. 'And he's my best mate. I suppose.' He looked surprised, as if he'd never realised this before. 'Well, relationships are funny things. Now, have some wine.' He clinked her glass.

'Talking of relationships,' said Laura carefully.

Nick looked up. 'What?' he said.

'It's stupid of me to ask,' said Laura, hating herself for remembering in the first place. 'My mum mentioned it – when we were coming back from Chartley, after I'd just met you.'

'Yes?' said Nick. He put his hand on her ankle, which was the bit of her nearest to him.

'She read it in the paper,' said Laura. 'Believe me, I don't read that kind of thing. She loves it. It's none of my business anyway.'

'What on earth are you talking about?' said Nick, rolling over so he was facing her.

'You've got a girlfriend, haven't you?' Laura asked.

'A what?' Nick shook his head, and then realisation dawned on his face. 'Oh, for god's sake. You mean Cecilia Thorson. Look – it's not true.'

He drank some wine. Laura said, uncertainly, 'But Mum said she saw a picture of Cecilia Whatsername and the Marquess of

Ranelagh in the paper, and it said they were going to get engaged.'

'That's what she thinks,' said Nick quietly. 'Let's not talk about it, please, Laura?'

She was silent, a worm of fear crawling through her, turning the wine in her stomach into vinegar. This was how it was going to be, wasn't it? Did she really not matter at all to him, was she just a holiday fling whilst his posh girlfriend was away? Already things were different, were altered, because of who he was. It was unfair – and, most of all, it wasn't right.

'No, Nick,' she said suddenly. 'Tell me. I can't help knowing it, can I? You owe me that much, after all. Come on. I know it's hard for you – but it's hard for me too, having just found out. And really,' she flung up her hands in a fleeting gesture, 'it's not as if we're married. We've only just met.'

His face softened. 'You're right,' he said. 'It's ridiculous, I'm sorry. I shouldn't even be bothering you with all that stuff.' He put his hand on her ankle again, and she put her hand on top of his, and moved closer.

'Cecilia – she thinks she's seeing me. But she's not.'

'Right,' said Laura, confused. 'What the hell does that mean?'

Nick sat up. 'It doesn't mean anything. I'm single. I swear to you. But she – we were set up. By my sister, Rose. Her husband, Malcolm – he works in the City. He knows Cecilia's parents, the Thorsons. When Dad died two years ago – he was very helpful when I had to move to Chartley, take over the house.'

'How?' said Laura.

'Dad – well, he hadn't been the same since my mother left. You know. Things were starting to slide, and we were in debt. Malcolm was very helpful, and so was Lars Thorson. They gave me advice, helped make some investments, so I could get things on an even keel again, or begin to.'

Laura felt a rush of admiration for him, again. 'It's only been two years?' she asked.

'Yes,' Nick said. He waved it aside. 'Anyway. Cecilia. They set us up, we went out on a few dates, to a few parties in town, that sort of thing. Charity dos, you know. But that's it.'

Charity dos. Parties in town. It sounded hilariously unlike Laura's life, the gap was so wide she could have laughed. Perhaps if she did it would get rid of the sick feeling she had. 'So you haven't slept together or anything,' she said, trying to be calm.

Nick looked uncertain. 'Well,' he said. 'Yes, we slept together, of course.'

Boys, Laura thought. I love the way their idea of not going out with people is completely different from girls'.

'Right,' she said.

'But she's – um. I finished it with her, last month. Not that there was anything to finish, but I didn't want her getting the wrong idea.'

'The wrong idea?'

'We're not compatible,' Nick said. 'She's obsessed with the house, all that. Having a title. And I can't stand that kind of stuff. It's tacky.'

'Oh, I don't know,' Laura said, feeling some sympathy for Cecilia. 'The old me – wow, I'd have loved that.'

'Who's the Old Me?' said Nick. He topped up her glass. 'Is this something else you haven't told me? Do you have two personalities?'

'No,' said Laura, trying to think how best to explain herself. 'No, it's stupid. Just – the old me, well . . .' She ran her hand through her hair. 'Nothing.'

'Go on,' said Nick. 'I won't laugh, I promise.'

'Well, I was a bit – head in the clouds,' Laura said. 'Fairytales, and all that. I wanted to meet Prince Charming. It got me into a lot of trouble.'

'Really?' said Nick.

'Yes, it did,' Laura told him. 'I told you about it. Well, not any more. I threw away all my videos. There,' she said fervently. 'I haven't told anyone that.'

'What videos?' asked Nick, bewildered.

Laura reddened. 'Forget it. Just . . . stupid films and stuff. And books and things. I only read improving books now. And I watch interesting foreign-language films.'

'You do?' said Nick. 'What interesting foreign-language films have you seen recently?'

'Er. I haven't yet,' Laura admitted. 'But I'm going to when I get back to town. You know what it's like. Well, you don't,' she said, wondering if Nick ever went to the cinema. Perhaps he had his own private cinema. No, he didn't seem the type, really. Suddenly a mental image of him, dressed like the postcard of his ancestor, all medals and morning dress, striding into the King's Lynn multiplex popped into her head and she laughed. The wine in her glass slopped over onto the rug.

'Sorry,' she said quickly, and knelt up to reach for a napkin.

'Here,' Nick replied. He leant over her, caught her arm and wiped it with a cloth, rubbing the bare skin gently. They looked at each other, saying nothing, and Laura sat back down again.

'So,' he said. 'We're OK, then? The Cecilia thing? I'm not avoiding it, it's just it's nothing.'

'No, I know,' said Laura. 'It's just a bit weird. I don't want you to think I'm making a big deal about it either. It's just there's lots I don't know about.'

'I know,' he said, after a moment's pause. 'And I'm sorry. For being uncommunicative. I don't like talking about myself much. As you may have noticed.'

'Just a bit,' said Laura.

'Even to you,' he said.

'But –' Laura was taken aback. 'I hardly know you.'

'Yes and no,' said Nick. 'Does that make sense?'

'It makes a lot of sense,' said Laura. 'When I think a week ago I'd never met you – that's weird.'

'It is,' he said. 'It's almost unbelievable.'

They looked at each other, and were silent.

* * *

256

Nick produced a bottle of whisky as it grew colder, and poured some into Laura's glass.

'Here, have this, it's getting colder,' he said, and threw her his jumper.

Laura took it gratefully, and put it on. She didn't want to move, or dispel the magic charm of the evening, knowing that when they left more things would be said, things would change. She wanted to leave it like this, perfect, suspended in a bubble. She was silent, and wrapped her hands round the glass, gazing contemplatively out across the sand.

'It's getting late,' said Nick's voice after a while.

'Yes,' Laura murmured, looking out at the dark petrol-grey of the sea.

'You're not driving, are you?' he asked, laughter in his voice.

'I brought the car, yes,' said Laura. She rolled over on the rug, so she was facing him.

'So —' Nick said. He put his hand on her shoulder. His skin felt warm against hers.

'But I don't think I can drive it home.'

'Ah,' Nick said softly, and she could feel his breath in her ear, on her neck. 'I was kind of hoping you'd say that.'

'So —'

He sat up and leant over Laura in one fluid motion, his hands either side of her arms. She said nothing, just lay there and looked up at him, watching him and, behind him, the stars in the black sky.

'Laura —' he said.

'Yes?' she asked softly.

'You are coming back with me, aren't you?'

'Yes,' she said, reaching up and putting her arms around him. He lowered himself gently onto her and kissed her once. Then he groaned and sat back. 'Let's go home,' he said. 'Let's not waste any more time.'

He stood up and held out his hand, pulling her up. 'It's definitely your last night, isn't it?'

'Yes,' said Laura. 'Nick – don't let's –'

'I know.' He nodded. 'No big deal. You can't stay for one more night, can you? It's just –'

'No,' she said firmly. 'I can't.' They were still for a moment, and Laura felt incredibly sad, and she didn't know why.

'Here,' he said, suddenly practical, handing her an old jumper from the hamper. 'Take this. And oh, I'd better warn you. Just – watch out for my sister.'

'Lavinia?' said Laura.

'I'm not worried about Lavinia so much. No, Rose. We don't want to bump into her. Disaster if she saw us.'

'Right,' said Laura, brushing away the feeling she was a sluttish scullery maid being seduced by the master in *Upstairs Downstairs*. 'I'll be careful,' she said, standing up and brushing the sand off her dress.

CHAPTER TWENTY-SIX

They walked back, talking quietly, until they reached the edge of the house again, as they had done last night. Laura felt as if she were in *Groundhog Day*, or *Groundhog Day* meets *Gosford Park*. She said so to Nick, who laughed. He reached over to kiss her, but broke away, looked up and said, under his breath, 'Damn.'

'What?'

'Rose is still up – look, there's her light.'

'I don't mind –' Laura began, but Nick took her hand.

'It'll be a real pain if – she sees us.'

'Yes, of course,' Laura said automatically, wondering if she should offer to fold herself up and climb into the cooler box.

'I know,' said Nick suddenly. 'I've got an idea. Come with me.'

He led her down the path, through the trees, so that they skirted the house, which was almost entirely in darkness. This is his *home*, Laura thought as she followed him, shaking her head in disbelief.

Finally they came to the front of the house, their feet crunching quietly on the gravel.

'We'll go in through the front door,' said Nick. 'Rose is at the back, she won't hear, and the people who live here won't notice. They'll just think it's Sam, one of the footmen, doing his rounds.'

'Er . . . through the front door? Right,' said Laura, bemused by mention of footmen and suchlike.

They walked up to the centre of the great façade, up the steps, which Laura had climbed up only a few days before, dragging her heels behind her mother's exclamations of pleasure and her father's comments about Doric columns. Outside the small, balustraded terrace with its black panelled door, almost twice the size of Laura's whole sitting room, Nick paused and rummaged in his jacket.

'Keys. Ah, here they are.'

He slid a huge brass key into the lock, turned it smoothly, and pushed the door open. He smiled sardonically, as if he were aware of the strangeness of the situation, and inclined his head.

'After you, madam.'

Through the ghostly, dark house they walked, as quietly as possible. Through the Great Hall, where Laura looked at the huge map of the county and smiled, past the Ballroom, where George had got his digital camera stuck on pause, precipitating a mini-crisis, up to the Grand Staircase, where their feet slapped on the cold, hard marble and the immense chandelier which hung down over them was dead and still, its crystal pendants dull.

They reached the library in silence, and Nick stopped, put his hand on her arm. 'Nearly there,' he whispered in her ear. 'I'm sorry about this, this is ridiculous, but we'll have to go through the house. Quietly – I don't want James to hear. He's Sam's night-time partner in crime. Or not. '

'It's fine,' said Laura, hissing in a stage whisper that made both of them jump apart a little. 'It's fine,' she repeated. Nick gave her a strange look.

'You OK?' he said. 'Not having second thoughts?' He walked into the room, and she followed, as she came towards the painting.

Laura wasn't having second thoughts, she rarely did once she'd got to this stage with someone. She was, however, trying not to freak out about everything else to do with the situation. Who were James and Sam, for starters? Normally when she was climbing up the stairs of someone's house in silence it was to avoid a sleeping flatmate or a drunk friend passed out on the sofa.

'Yes, yes,' Laura whispered again. 'I'm not very good at whispering, that's all – sorry . . .'

'That's OK,' said Nick. 'I'm not surprised, knowing you as well as I do. You're a bit too much of a ranter to be able to whisper particularly well.' He smiled, and took her hand in his. 'Hold my hand. I've just got to check they've locked up.'

He walked towards the library door, Laura following him. She watched as he grasped the old brass handle and looked in. His gaze ran down the long room, where moonlight was starting to creep onto the carpet through the slivers left by the blinds.

'*The Happy Marriage*,' she said out loud, looking down towards the two lonely paintings at the end of the great room.

'Yes,' said Nick, almost to himself. '*The Wedding*. It was my mother's favourite.'

'Really?' said Laura.

'Yes. She loved it. She used to dance along the room with me when I was little, doing a jig. And then my sisters used to make me re-enact it with them when we were small. I had to be the bridesmaid.'

Laura laughed quietly.

He smiled. 'And now we're advised that we can't afford the insurance to have them all out on display during the summer. Pathetic, isn't it?'

'It's beautiful,' said Laura inadequately, feeling foolish.

'Beautiful,' Nick repeated slowly, looking around him. 'Do you think so? Yes. Of course. It is.'

She caught the fleeting expression on his face, and it disturbed her. It was dark, ugly, his mouth curling in an unhappy smile.

'It's all yours,' said Laura impulsively, saying something to break the silence. 'Isn't that weird?'

'It's very weird, especially when you find yourself getting used to it,' said Nick quietly. 'You start to think this is what a normal life's like. It's not. I have to keep reminding myself of that, otherwise I'd go insane.'

Laura didn't know what to say. She agreed with him.

'I'm sorry I lied,' he said frankly, almost to himself. 'It's just you get in here, and *this* becomes the big deal.' His gesture encompassed the room, the fields outside. 'Not the important stuff, and I don't want you to think –'

'Stop worrying,' said Laura. 'I mean it. I'm not here because of all of this. I'm here because of you.'

She looked around the big, beautiful room. It was completely still, not a sound within or outside. As if it was just the two of them, nothing more in the world, in this room alone. Nick took her hand and held it. She watched him; the skin on her palm was creamy white in the moonlight streaming through the great windows. He raised her hand to his lips, and kissed the tips of her fingers, gently.

'I just keep thinking perhaps you're made-up,' he said softly.

'Me too,' said Laura. 'Me too.'

They stayed like that, in complete silence, staring at each other, in the centre of the long, silvery room.

'Are we still friends, then?' he said, his voice light.

Laura looked up at him. 'Oh Nick,' she said. 'I don't think we're friends any more, do you?'

No one disturbed them, and it was almost a relief to reach the strangely familiar surroundings of his room, a comparative haven of normality tucked inside this great shell of a home.

Nick dumped the cooler box and the rug on the floor, and took off his jacket, his back to her, whilst Laura took off her shoes. She felt suddenly ill at ease, and the white noise of questions she had about all this and him, how strange it was, how something was bothering her about it but she didn't know what, started to rise within her. But then he turned around, and she wondered how she could have thought he was anyone else, how she could have thought she didn't know him, because she did.

He walked towards her. 'I've wanted to do this since the moment I laid eyes on you, you know that?' he said, and he calmly put his hands on her hips, and kissed her again. As his lips met hers, Laura felt as if she was melting into him. He kissed her slowly, wrapping his arms around her, so that he held her tightly. As she returned his kiss more urgently, his tongue inside her mouth, pushing, sliding slowly into hers, she could feel the strength of his body against hers, but strangely so, as if they were breathing together, as if they were in their own world. She stopped thinking for the first time in days, weeks. She simply felt, in her heart and head, and soon she barely knew where she was.

Nick's eyes were black. He gave her that old, sweetly familiar smile, half-mocking, half-comforting. She knelt on the edge of the bed and wrapped her arms around his neck, and he buried his face in her skin.

'Don't go tomorrow,' he said, his voice husky. 'Laura – don't go . . .'

Laura put her finger to his lips, and he pushed her back. They fell on the bed together and Laura remembered fleetingly how big it had felt when she had got into it alone, two nights ago. How strange that was now. Nick was on top of her; she could feel he was hard, and her last thought before she gave herself up to it, to him, was how strange it was, too, that it should feel so right, like she had known him for years. Her very own romantic hero, and yet it turned out who he was couldn't have mattered less to her; all she wanted was to feel him, to be joined to him, to stay like that forever.

CHAPTER TWENTY-SEVEN

Laura dreamt that she was back at home in her flat with Paddy that night. She dreamt he was walking towards her, smiling, pleased to see her, and behind him were Jo and Chris, Simon plonking his backpack down on the ground, Hilary and Hamish. Rachel was there, with a picnic hamper, looking overjoyed, and they all had a picnic, until Dan appeared, with Amy and three small children, and suddenly all their friends dispersed, like pale, insubstantial ghosts, leaving her alone in the sitting room as Amy advanced towards her, holding a child in each hand, screaming at her, whilst Laura called out for help, but no one came, and Dan stood in the background, wringing his hands . . .

She woke with a start in Nick's sparse, light bachelor bedroom. She sat up, realising where she was, and her heart lifted at the view of sun out of the window. Nick wasn't there. She lay back again, remembering the previous evening, the night, Nick's hands on her body, all over her, the two of them together, and she stretched again, smiling. Funny to be alone in the bed, when the two of them together . . . Almost the perfect date, she thought, and she put her hand to her breast, to calm her heart, which was fluttering most alarmingly.

She sat up again and bit her lip, turning her thoughts to

more pragmatic matters, to the day ahead. She was in charge of meeting and greeting when the relatives arrived for Mary's lunch, handing out drinks and crisps, almost like a maître d'. Oh yes. She looked at her watch. It was ten, she realised with horror. At this very moment the Sandersons were on their way, getting closer and closer. As was Simon – she was going to see Simon, hurrah. She had to go, she had to help Mum. Right, she told herself. Get dressed, find Nick, and say goodbye.

Say goodbye. At the thought, though, of doing just that, her heart turned over itself and sank. Goodbye. She couldn't. She wished he was here, so she could ask him – so she could convince herself it was the same for him, that she wasn't this convenient fling. That this whole sleeping-with-a-marquess thing wasn't a really bad idea. It didn't seem like it, here in the relatively comforting surroundings of his room. It hadn't seemed like it the previous night, as they lay together, tightly entwined, his hands stroking her hair, whispering softly to her as she fell asleep. But today . . .

There was no point in reliving it, not just yet, she told herself. She got dressed, pulling on her sundress and gathering her things together. She opened the window, straightened the duvet cover. She was pragmatic, organised. It was what Mrs Danvers would do. Then she sat on the edge of the bed to wait for him to come back, feeling rather marooned, not knowing why she wanted to cry, why suddenly this all seemed much sharper, more real, with more potential to hurt, to cause her pain.

She was just admiring her post-bed hair, which looked like a tousled bird's nest, in the mirror, when there was a knock at the door. Laura grimaced. What should she do? Pretend there was no one there? She was silent, hoping they'd go away.

The knock came again, and there was a pause. She could hear a light cough. 'Nick?' came a low, tentative male voice.

The door opened slowly. Laura froze on the other side of the room, not sure where to go or what to do, feeling insanely English all of a sudden.

It was Charles. He caught sight of her and stopped at the threshold, looking horrified.

'Ah. Oh, my goodness. Laura? I'm so dreadfully sorry. I had no idea.'

'Hello,' said Laura, feeling very unsure of herself. Did Charles know she was here? Did he know anything about the situation? Argh! It was embarrassing, she thought, then collected herself. Was it against the law? No, of course not.

Charles advanced a little way in, and leant against the thin edge of the door, in an attempt to look natural and casual. It didn't really work. He was nervous, she noticed.

'I was – I was just going,' said Laura, picking up her things.

'No, no,' said Charles, looking alarmed. 'Please, don't go on my account. I was looking for – for Nick. Do you know where he is?'

'No,' said Laura, shoving her knickers into her bag and standing up straight. 'I don't, I'm sorry. I woke up – er, he was gone. I was wondering where he was, too. Shall I give him, give him a message if I see him?' She leant nonchalantly against the side of the bed, misjudged its height, and nearly fell over.

'Ah,' said Charles, somewhat discomposed as she flailed around trying to right herself. 'Well, it's a couple of things, really, that's why I thought I'd better –' He looked at her, his pale blue eyes smiling shyly at her. 'His sister's looking for him. Lady Rose, you know, she's staying here.'

'Right,' said Laura. 'I don't really want to –' She looked up rather helplessly at him.

'Stay there,' said Charles decisively. 'He is useless, abandoning his – er, guests. I'll go and find him. You must want to – be on your way. Er.' He coughed, mortified. 'Not that I mean you're not welcome – ah.'

Laura laughed. 'Please don't worry, Charles. I do need to be off, though, I should find him.'

'Of course,' said Charles. 'You know what he's like, starts

talking to someone about something and he has to listen to all their problems for hours. That's Nick, though. You know how passionate he is about it all. The estate,' and he waved his arms vaguely.

'Yes,' said Laura, not feeling she could tell the truth, which was, No, I don't, actually.

'It's the big dinner tonight,' Charles confided, relaxing slightly. He folded his arms and leant against the wall. 'Phew. That's why Lady Rose is down. Hordes of Needhams gathering from all round the country.'

'Oh,' said Laura. 'Why? What's the occasion?'

'Well,' Charles said with enthusiasm. 'Sir Guillibert Danvers, in – gosh, thirteen-something – anyway, some ancestor of Nick's, a knight in service to Eleanor of Aquitaine. Old boy got stabbed in some plot to oust the king. They got the Pope to make him a saint by way of thanks. It's his feast day today. The whole family always gathers for it. It's a great evening.'

Laura suddenly felt as if she were having a conversation with her father, so she said politely, 'How interesting.'

'Yes,' said Charles. 'Yes, yes. And it's rather a big do. Lady Rose does like everything just so. You know how these family gatherings can be, it's the same the world over.'

Since there was no way Laura could reply, 'It bloody well is not the same, I'm telling you,' she smiled instead. 'Well,' she said. 'I bet they couldn't do it without you.'

Charles looked shocked. 'Oh yes, they could,' he said. 'Absolutely. It's Nick, you know. He takes it all very seriously, the tradition of the thing. He's been up since the crack of dawn, discussing it with Mrs Hillyard, sorting out everything.'

'Oh,' said Laura.

Charles coughed delicately. 'Are you – er, are you coming tonight?'

'God no!' said Laura. She looked around her wildly. 'I mean – you know. This is – just a casual thing, you know. We've only just met, I don't think he'd invite me tonight, seriously.'

'He asked for another place setting on his table,' said Charles doubtfully. 'That was yesterday. Perhaps –'

Perhaps Cecilia Thorson's suddenly available, Laura thought miserably to herself, assailed by doubt and fear and hating it. This had to stop, it was ridiculous. She looked up at Charles. 'Well, if you're off to look for him then –'

'Yes,' said Charles, collecting himself. 'Sorry to have kept you. Laura, it's so nice to see you again.' He walked to the door. 'I'll send Nick up to you. Ah – see you soon, I'm sure.'

'Thanks,' Laura replied.

The door banged behind her, and she gathered the last of her things together, feeling even more like a guest in a B & B, a very posh B & B, but still. Outside, a seagull called loudly. She walked to the window and looked out, taking in the view, thinking how beautiful, how unreal it all was, and it was her here, not a film. Which was why it was so awful that it was all starting to feel so wrong. She closed the window, slung her bag over her shoulder and left the room.

She walked quietly down the stairs, trying to remember in this huge labyrinthine maze of doors and corridors how best to find her way out without bumping into a tour party, a relative, or the man himself. She didn't want to go without saying goodbye, but what else could she do? It was the coward's way out, but then she was a coward, not up to living this life. She reached the bottom of the stairs, and opened the door that she was sure led out to the rose garden at the side, when suddenly a voice called from above her, 'Laura!'

It was Nick, coming down the stairs towards her. He breathed as though he had been running. 'Where are you going?'

'I'm – I have to go,' said Laura, standing in the doorway.

'You were going to leave without saying bye?' he asked, his tone light, but his eyes dark in his tanned face. He stepped outside, motioning her to come with him, and shut the door. 'You know, it's polite to thank the host for the lovely evening.'

'I know,' said Laura, blushing in the sudden sunlight and

feeling horrible. 'I know, thank you, thank you so much.' She allowed her eyes to meet his. 'I didn't know where to find you – and I didn't want to come barging in – then Charles said you were busy – I thought I'd . . .' She trailed off, knowing it sounded pathetic.

'Laura,' Nick said. He took her hands in his, folding them into his clasp. 'I'm so sorry. You were asleep. I tried to wake you, but you turned over and ignored me. Then you hit the pillow and said something, and I thought I'd better clear out in case you tried to attack me in your sleep. I had a few things to do, boring things to sort out for tonight. So I came downstairs. I checked on you but you were still out for the count – I should have come back earlier, I'm sorry. Do you have to go right now?'

'Yes,' said Laura. 'I really do, I'm afraid. The relatives are descending any moment now – and from what Charles tells me, the same's true for you.'

'Yes,' he said. 'Look –'

'Thanks,' said Laura. 'Thanks again, Nick, it was a wonderful night. All of it.' She stood on tiptoe and kissed his cheek. 'Look – I hope – it'd be nice to . . .'

He didn't say anything, just stood there staring at her. A muscle ticked in his cheek. Her heart sank, though she didn't really know what would be best. And at that moment a sturdy blonde with rigid hair appeared from around a corner, talking to Charles. 'Nick must know I wanted to discuss the apples with him – Good god! Hello?'

She glared at Laura as if Laura were wearing a black and white stripy top, an eye-mask, and carrying a bag labelled 'SWAG'.

'Nick!' she said, still staring at Laura. 'There you are. I've been looking absolutely bloody everywhere for you.'

'Rose,' said Charles, collecting himself first. 'Rose, this is Laura. She's a friend of Nick's. She's just – are you going?'

Rose's eyes bulged, and she smoothed her rather strained,

269

correct shift dress over her hips. 'And how do you do?' she said, nodding at Laura.

Since Laura hadn't been addressed like that by anyone since she had met Father Christmas on a Brownies trip in 1983, the shock of the situation meant she let out an involuntary snort of laughter, which she tried to disguise as a sneeze. Nick was staring at her in bemusement, and she realised how strong the family resemblance was, as she turned from brother to sister and said, 'I'm so sorry – lovely to meet you. I must go, I'm afraid.'

'Laura,' said Nick. 'I'll –'

'Nick, the roses really *are* a frightful mess,' said Rose, turning to her brother, and almost blocking Laura out. 'Sam says he's started on them, but how, I want to know. And about the apples. I want to give you a recipe. And Great Aunt Teresa's arriving by train, can someone please be sent to pick her up? I particularly asked, but no one seems to know anything about it.'

Laura was waiting for Nick to say something else to her, but he didn't. He stared distractedly at her, and then at his sister, and said, 'Oh god, Rose. I don't know. I –'

'Bye, then,' said Laura. 'Thanks again, Nick. Bye Charles. Bye – er, Rose,' she added uncertainly, not sure how you addressed someone like Lady Rose Balmore; and that, if anything, was surely a reason she shouldn't stick around much longer. She raised her hand in a gesture of farewell, and walked briskly around the back of the house, up towards the woods to where she'd left the car, by the beach, and she didn't look back once.

CHAPTER TWENTY-EIGHT

By the time Laura pulled up in front of Seavale, it was after eleven, and there were two new cars in the drive. She sat in the car for a moment, pulled the mirror over and looked at herself. She didn't look any different. Tired, maybe, with dark smudges under her eyes. Not older or wiser, which wasn't surprising, since she still hadn't learnt anything, it would seem. She rested her head on the steering wheel briefly, her mind racing back over the past eighteen hours or so.

Was she *so* stupid that she still hadn't learnt a thing, despite everything she'd been through? The dreadful thought that Nick was just another one to add to the list, the most spectacular cock-up of all Laura's failed romantic endeavours, was almost too much to handle. It looked like it could be, she had to admit. Meet some guy, fail to spot he's the ideal romantic hero to beat them all, spend all your holiday with him, fall for him, sleep with him, and never mind the fact that a) he's one of the richest people in the country, b) he owns more land than is covered by the distance from Mum and Dad's house to your titchy flat in North London, and c) you have nothing in common, he's a *marquess*, for god's sake, you work for the local council, and, finally, d) he has a *girlfriend*. Well, he claims he doesn't, but really – Laura banged her head against the steering wheel softly – it's clear that's what *she* thinks she is.

No, she thought. Best that it ends like this, a lovely memory, a beautiful summer interlude, like something out of a book. Leave it there, recognise it for what it is. And now, go inside, smile brightly, and help your mother with the Foster family's equivalent to Nick and his Sir Elephant Something or Other evening. At the thought of how hilariously disparate those two gatherings were, she smiled, realising she was right to be putting it behind her, and pulled the keys out of the ignition. Her heart ached, a stab of something, but she said briskly out loud, 'Indigestion', and got out of the car.

'Mum, Mum! It's me, I'm back!'

Angela had appeared on the lawn, rubbing her hands on a tea towel. She smiled thinly. 'Oh, Laura. There you are. At last!'

'Sorry, Mum,' Laura called, as she walked across the gravel. 'It was all a bit complicated. I'm really sorry. Here now, what do you want me to do?'

'Well, set the table, maybe,' said Angela, still rather frosty.

'Are they here?' asked Laura in a whisper. 'Simon? Is he here?'

'They're outside, having drinks. Robert and your dad are doing the barbecue,' said Angela, unbending somewhat at her daughter's apology. 'Fran's brought Ludo, that's nice, isn't it.'

'Best news ever,' said Laura, heartily. She threw her bag into the corner of the room. 'What can I do?'

'Get Annabel another drink, I think,' said Angela demurely. 'She had a somewhat – *fraught* – journey up here, I think. Cedric and Jasper were rather – boisterous.'

Since the last time Laura – who was too young to recognise Cedric Forsythe as the demigod he was to George and a generation of impressionable young British schoolboys – had seen him, Cedric had taken her and Mary to see *Anything Goes* and had alarmed everyone by breaking wind violently and deliberately throughout, Laura was not surprised. And since she knew he and Jasper were incredibly naughty when they were together, she was even less surprised when a voice came booming down from the lawn,

'Is that Laura? Is that gorgeous Laura? Ha ha, hahahaha. Come here, beautiful.'

Laura found herself being swept into Jasper Davidson's navy besmocked chest. He kissed her on the head. 'You're too thin, gorgeous. Far too thin. Ah, Cedric, look who's here.'

'Dear girl,' said Cedric Forsythe mellifluously, advancing towards her with a happy smile on his face. 'I am truly glad to see you here.' He handed her his glass of champagne. 'Come and find your grandmother. God, your cousins are awf— Ah, Annabel! Dear lady, how are you?'

Aunt Annabel, obviously hearing the commotion, had arrived in the doorway and was regarding Laura with minimal warmth. Laura went over and kissed her, feeling rather like she was in some kind of random Thirties farce. Annabel was wearing a strangely formal all-in-one button-through housecoat, in striped khaki, with fake cuffs, adorned with several pieces of carefully understated – but nonetheless ever so slightly ostentatious – gold jewellery. She was about fifty-five, but she was suspended in time. She could have been seventy, or thirty – one never really knew. She was so correct, seldom betraying any emotion. Laura couldn't remember her ageing or acting any other way. Where Angela waved her arms, worried, dropped wooden spoons covered in batter on the floor and generally despaired of herself, her husband and her children, Annabel had, Laura thought, probably never suffered a moment's self-doubt in all her life. And at that moment, she kind of wished she was Annabel.

'Ah, Laura, you're here,' she said. 'Goodness. You have been ages, haven't you? With your friend from the Wetland place, dear me. Angela,' she redirected her steely gaze towards her stepsister, 'your mother's getting rather hungry. How long till we eat, do you think?'

'Grrmshowalla,' said Angela, muttering something as she turned towards Annabel. 'Not long, Annabel, shall we all go outside and finish our drinks?' She made a sweeping motion that included everyone within it, and Cedric and Jasper turned away from the drinks cabinet and shuffled towards the door.

'Yes, but –' Aunt Annabel said, looking over towards the kitchen.

'I suppose it depends on how long it really takes for Robert to get the barbecue going,' Angela said serenely, and sailed away.

Round one to Mum, thought Laura, settling back into her normal life, and she raised her glass to George as she stepped out onto the terrace. It was hot, almost too hot, and George was slaving over the barbecue, sweat forming perilously on his jaw, whilst Robert lounged next to him, chatting negligibly about something, a bored expression on his large face. Laura's father glared at her as she appeared, then his expression softened and he rolled his eyes, and flipped a burger in a fluid motion that impressed his daughter deeply.

'Where's Simon?' she said again.

Annabel made a moue. 'Oh dear.'

'Not here yet,' said Angela tightly. 'I'm sure he'll call, though. He knows it's today.'

Laura knew from long experience that the phrase 'he knows it's today' absolutely meant the person concerned did *not* know it was today, or was *not* going to turn up.

'Oh, man!' she muttered as she followed her mother into the kitchen, unreasonably cross with her absent brother, although deep down she had never seriously thought he might turn up on time. She was cross because she missed him, and the thought of a normal person here had been sustaining her these seven days. 'Shall I call him?' she said.

'I've tried,' Angela replied. 'His phone's switched off.'

'It's always switched off,' said Laura. 'I don't know why he took it there. I'll try him again, anyway. Perhaps it's just because he's in a tunnel on his way to King's Lynn. Don't worry, Mum, it'll –'

'*Lawww-Rah!*' came a booming voice behind her, and Laura turned around to be snaffled in a headlock by Fran, and patted painfully on the back by Fran's indecently hefty boyfriend Ludo.

'Lululu! Laura's back. Hi, Laura! Wow, how are you?'

Fran stepped back, bouncing on her huge trainers, her stubby ponytail wagging behind her head like a pug's tail.

'Wow!' she said again. 'You're here! We thought you'd just decided not to bother! Lululu thought you'd pulled, but I said "God, no *way*, Laura never pulls, can you imagine!" Hey Ludo, get Laura a drink!'

'Hey Laura,' said Ludo, who was a huge human man-mountain. His bulk momentarily blocked out the sun as he stood facing Laura, his hands on his hips. 'Hi. *Really* great to see you. What do you want? Some poo? We bought a couple of bottles.'

'Argh,' said Laura, disentangling herself from her cousin's grasp. 'Can you just – give me a moment. I just want to dump my stuff.'

'LULULU!' screamed Fran, even louder than usual. 'Come and say hiiiiiiiiiii to Laura!'

'I'm not going anywhere,' said Laura desperately. 'I'll be back in two seconds, I promise – oh, hi, Lulu.'

'Hiiiiiiiiiii Laura,' said Lulu. 'Great to see you.'

Lulu and Fran were like Jack Sprat and his wife. Where Fran was totally exhausting because she twitched with excitement and boundless enthusiasm ('like being beaten repeatedly about the head with a shovel', as Cedric told Laura and Simon once when they were teenagers, much to their delight), Lulu was exhausting in a different way. She looked like an advert for Nytol, for a start. She was sepulchrally pale, tall and thin, spoke in a soft, languid voice, seemingly with great effort, and affected the air of a Pre-Raphaelite muse, about to drift away because of consumption.

Like their mother, neither Fran nor Lulu admitted self-doubt – none of the Sandersons did, in fact. It was obviously a family trait.

'So, Laura,' said Lulu, as Ludo handed Laura a glass of champagne, 'where have you been? Really great to see you.'

She said this with the enthusiasm of one who has just been given a present of a dead rat.

'Mum said she thought you weren't going to show up, just like Simon!' squeaked Fran behind her. 'Wow, Laura, we've got loads to fill you in on. Ludo and I are buying a flat! In Battersea, well, it's kind of Battersea, towards Clapham. It's *really* lovely. You're still sharing, aren't you?'

Laura cast an anguished look about the patio. She didn't know what to do, how to react. Her father was still slaving over the barbecue; Mum was talking animatedly to Annabel, who was looking bored; Jasper and Cedric were throwing olive stones over the hedge into the sand dunes, trying to hit day-trippers. Suddenly she caught sight of the person she'd been looking for.

'Sorry, give me a minute,' she said briskly. 'I just want to say hi to Granny.'

Leaving her cousins slightly gaping behind her, Laura strode over to where Mary was sitting in her wicker chair, watching the progress of the olive-throwing, and nursing a gin and tonic.

'Hi Granny,' she said, and bent down to give her grandmother a kiss. Mary's cheek felt cold and papery, beautifully soft to the touch. She patted her shoulder. 'I'm so sorry I'm late. Happy birthday. Are you having a good time?'

'Oh, yes darling,' said Mary, opening her blue eyes very wide. 'You're here, then. Thank goodness; I'd given you up.'

'God, Granny,' said Laura. 'I didn't mean to. I overslept. I'm so sorry.'

Mary bent her index finger, motioning for Laura to come closer. 'It's fine,' she said. 'You're here now.'

'I know, I know. I feel – I feel terrible. Anyway, we're all here, and it's such a lovely day,' said Laura manically, feeling like a children's entertainer, wanting to don a stripy jacket and some huge clown's shoes.

'Go and see if your mother wants any help,' said Mary. 'I'm afraid your aunt rather puts her on her mettle.' Laura nodded obediently, and turned to go. 'And – Laura?'

Laura turned back to face her. 'Yes, Gran?'

'Will you tell me who he is one day?'

'Who who is?' Laura said stupidly, blinking in the sunlight.

'Whoever he is you've been spending all your time with.' Laura gaped. 'I know you, darling. Now go.'

'Er,' said Laura, feeling that since she arrived home all she'd done was speak in a series of grunts. 'Ur. Argh. Well – it's complicated.'

'I'm sure it is,' Mary smiled. 'It always is.'

'It's nothing,' said Laura, standing firm. 'Nothing at all. Part of my new rule.'

'We shall see,' said Mary. 'Darling, be a dear and get me another gin and tonic,' she said, holding out her glass.

'You don't want any champagne?'

'Loathe the stuff,' said Mary cheerfully, glaring balefully at Ludo, who was flexing his muscles and showing them to Fran and Lulu, amidst screams of delight. 'Some ice and a –'

'Thick slice,' Laura finished. 'Sure, be right back.'

They were everywhere, these Sandersons, blocking her way to the kitchen, making loud noises, cheerfully insulting her father – 'No, old man, that burger's charcoal on the outside, but you've left it raw inside, look' – and subtly digging at her mother – 'Angela, your salad was rather small, so I've taken it out of the fridge and added some spinach.' Laura leant against the wall of the kitchen and breathed deeply. The events of this morning seemed an age away already. She would have time to digest them all when she caught the train home that night and said goodbye to all this. Tonight she would be back home, back in the flat with Paddy watching TV, flicking pistachio shells into the bin, having a beer, telling Jo all about her holiday on the phone. If Laura wanted to tell – she thought she probably didn't. She checked her phone. There was a text message from Paddy.

Need your help asap. Please advise return time. Having romantic crisis with Becky downstairs. She is single. Think we're going on date tonight. Not sure. Need you to be laughing flatmate who thinks am great. V important. Love to yr gran. Y x

The phone in the hall rang, and she ran to answer it.

'Hello?' she said uncertainly.

'Laura?' came a distant voice, accompanied by what sounded like someone waving sheets of metal in the background. 'It's —mon.'

'Simon!' Laura yelled. 'You're here! Where are you? Ely? Cambridge?'

'Callao,' came the distant voice.

'Where?'

'It's near Lima.'

'Simon –' said Laura. 'Oh god. Why aren't you here?'

'I . . . chew . . . amazing!' Simon's voice said happily. 'Can I speak to . . .?'

'Who?'

'Um!'

'Mum? Hold on.' Angela appeared in the corridor, a squeezed lemon in her hand. 'So you're not coming back?' Laura yelled unnecessarily.

'Isst my . . .' Loud metal sheet waving in the background. 'Ing to see the . . . gasts!'

'Oh good grief,' Laura said, turning to her mother.

'Give me the phone,' Angela said crossly. 'Silly boy. What happened?'

'Tell Granny I . . . her!'

'What?'

278

'Yes!'

'Simon! Are you –' Laura began, but the line went dead. Laura banged the phone hard on the cradle in annoyance.

'He's gone?' Angela asked.

'Yes.'

'Where was he?'

'Somewhere called Callao. It's near Lima. That's all I could get out of him,' said Laura. 'Sorry, Mum. He sounded OK, though.'

'Hm,' said Angela. 'It's just as well I didn't speak to him. I'd have said something unforgivable.'

Laura reflected with some amusement that the safety and wellbeing of her son came a very distant second to Angela's desire for him to fulfil his family commitments. She looked at her phone again; there was a text message from Paddy.

PLS REPLY re return time to flat. P. PS Just had call from Simon. Not coming back till next month. In Callao. Is near Lima apparently. Sounds nice.

'Argh!' Laura growled, surprised only that she was still surprised at the crapness of blokes. From the garden George said loudly, 'Lunch is ready', and Laura followed her mother outside, with a heart as heavy as Aunt Annabel's mashed potato.

They sat down to eat a few minutes later, and as the others tucked into their food, Laura sat there, staring at her plate, half-expecting it to talk to her. She felt suddenly very weary. As her father munched happily away on his burger, equilibrium briefly restored as Sandersons on both sides ignored him, she gazed around the table, unsure of what to say or do.

She speared a leaf of salad, looked at it, then put it back on the plate. She wasn't hungry.

'You all right, dear?' said Cedric Forsythe.

'Ye-yes,' said Laura. 'Just tired, that's all.' She pulled herself together. No, not again. She'd be home this evening, ready to advise Paddy on Becky from downstairs. That sounded

279

promising. It was the hearing at work on Wednesday, she reminded herself. She had to get through that. That was what she'd focus on. That, and the shape of the lettuce leaf she was eating. Focus, focus. Don't let this become a thing, like all the other times. Just don't think about it, she told herself, and second by second, minute by minute, the lunch went on its way, as Mary relaxed, the sun shone, and this odd assortment of quasi-relatives concentrated on trying to have a good time, unconscious of their nearest neighbour's most fundamental hopes and dreams. It was ever so.

CHAPTER TWENTY-NINE

The clock ticked on, nearer the time she'd be able to get away
and go back home, and whilst Laura nodded and smiled and
said things like 'Yes, I love rugby' to Ludo and 'Yes, I love
sushi' to Lulu, Annabel held court at one end of the table,
ignoring George, and batting her lashes at Cedric Forsythe in
an alarming way. Cedric, in turn, was making overt eyes at
Mary, who was frankly not repelling them as she might, whilst
Robert was locked deep in conversation with Jasper, expounding
upon the art market and its relative value in recent months.
Jasper's eyes were drooping, and he stifled a yawn. Ludo and
Fran joined in – they knew someone, a guy who'd been travelling,
who'd taken some really wonderful wildlife photos in Africa,
he should contact Jasper, shouldn't he? Wasn't Jasper's gallery
looking for young new photographers too?

When the conversation moved on to Lulu's latest career path
– in this case her burning desire to be a singer-songwriter, Laura
tried not to let her incipient hysteria overwhelm her.

'So what kind of thing?' Angela asked politely, piling up the
bowls.

'Lululu's had a lot of interest already, haven't you, Lulu?'
said Annabel, a fond smile cracking across her wintry expression.
'She made a demo tape – that's a demonstration of her songs,

Mary. At her friend Barrett's house. Some record producers are *very* interested, apparently. She'll have to pick and choose who she goes with.'

'It's like – it's kind of my own stuff, my own message,' said Lulu, coming alive a little. 'Like – like Dido, but she's so kind of – you know, *commercial*. Really hackneyed. It's sad, really. I don't want to be a sell-out, you know. I just wanna do my own stuff, really say something with it. Stuff – that's happened to me. Really personal stuff, you know. Just for me, not for anyone else.'

'So – you don't want to sell any copies,' said Laura acidly, as Angela disappeared into the kitchen, followed by Jasper and Cedric.

'Yeah, of course I do. Obviously, if people like me –' She smiled coyly. 'But –' Lulu's eyes glazed over and she ran her finger around the rim of her glass, so it made a chalky, whining sound. 'I don't want to be on *Top of the Pops* or any of that shit. I don't want to be on magazine covers. I really don't want that stuff. I just want to write, songs and stuff.'

'Right,' said Laura. The sound of Lulu's long fingers on the glass was excruciating. 'So, who's asked you to be on the cover of a magazine, then?'

'No one,' said Lulu, staring at her as if she were talking to a moron. 'I just won't do it when they do ask.'

'Right,' said Laura, getting up. She said in a friendly tone, 'I really hope no one's interested then. Good luck, fingers crossed for you.'

'How's the job, Laura?' Annabel called from the other end of the table. 'I've hardly said two words to you so far. How is everything? Mum says she hasn't seen much of you lately.'

'I didn't say that,' said Mary patiently. 'I said it was lovely to have her here and spend all this time with her.'

'Yes,' crooned Annabel, as if she were talking to an imbecile. 'I know. *Lovely*.' She swept on, holding the table. 'And, that reminds me,' she said inconsequentially, 'I did a talk to a lovely group in Bexleyheath the other day. On preserves and the larder, and guess who was there?'

'Who?' said Mary, as Laura picked the plates up.

'Lady Rose Balmore,' said Annabel.

'Who?' said Mary again, as Laura put the plates sharply down on the table.

'You know. The Marquess of Ranelagh's sister. *Lovely* woman. Chartley Hall.'

Cedric was standing by the French windows, watching the group with a detached air. He said, 'Vivienne Lash's daughter.'

'Who?' said Annabel sharply, turning round to see who had interrupted her so rudely. 'Oh, Cedric! Hello! Er – well, we obviously didn't talk about *that*, of course.'

'I did a few films with her,' said Cedric reminiscently. 'Stunning creature. Flighty, though. Pretty mad. Still, gorgeous. Beautiful breasts.'

'Belle, old girl, you remember,' said Robert, hurrumphing a cough into his big fist. 'Actress. Nice looker. In all those Fifties comedies. Ran off with the brother, 'member?'

'Yes, of course I remember,' said Annabel.

'Who, Ma?' said Fran. 'Ludo, don't do that.'

'Oh, it was *years* ago,' said Annabel, pronouncing it *yi-arrrz*. 'Well, twenty-five years ago, I suppose. Huge scandal. There they are, up at the hall, the Marquess and Countess of Ranelagh –' She paused, rolling the words around on her tongue, as if she loved saying them, as if it brought her closer to the aristocracy, Laura thought with distaste. 'Married, three children, etcetera. And then one day, she simply ups and runs off. Says she's been in love with – the brother, whatsisname –'

'Frederick,' Laura repeated, aware her grandmother was eyeing her rather strangely.

'Whomever. Anyway, says she's been in love with him since day one. Married the wrong brother. Should never have married him.'

283

Annabel's expression was animated. Laura realised that, like most people who affect to be repulsed by any displays of vulgarity, she actually liked nothing more than a big old bitching session about anyone who had fallen from grace.

'Can't remember where they live now,' she went on. Laura was silent. 'I met her once, at a ladies' luncheon. Strange woman. Rather standoffish, I thought. That girlish affectation – and rather a lot of see-through chiffon. Not really appropriate for a lunch in Epping, I thought.'

'I liked Vivienne,' said Cedric. 'Couldn't understand why she married the marquess fella myself. But there you go. Big whisky drinker. Could hold her drink, too. Not like some people. Good girl, she was. Like you, Mary darling.'

Mary was playing with her napkin ring, sliding the bone ivory in and out of her fingers, but she looked up at this. 'Oh, thank you, Cedric,' she said, her eyes twinkling. 'You are kind. And a terrible flirt. I don't believe a word of it.'

'Anyway,' said Annabel. 'Lady Rose Balmore. I had the chance to meet her, a most interesting woman. We discussed Chartley, you know –'

'Yes,' said George, coming alive abruptly. 'We went there on Thursday, had a great day, didn't we, Laura?'

'Ah,' said Annabel, not particularly interested. 'Well, we talked about Chartley. I asked her – I hope she didn't mind! – how her brother was getting on. He's younger than her, you know. Dominic. And she said very well, and then I told her the apples at Chartley were perfect for jelly, gave her a recipe tip, you know. Well, I said, she must be sure to make some this year. She said she would pass it on. Well!'

With a lightning flash of certainty Laura knew, as sure as the tide was coming in, that Annabel's tip for apple jelly was what Lady Rose had been coming to find Nick about less than two hours ago, and the cosmic certainty of this made her want to laugh out loud, but of course she didn't. She sat down again, rather weakly, and poured herself another glass of wine. There was some dead dry skin on her feet, and she bent down to pull it off, a small act of bad manners directed at her aunt.

'Anyway, I mentioned – only in passing – that my stepmother had a house on the coast nearby, and she was most kind about it, very nice. She even asked –'

'There's a car just pulled up in the drive,' said Jasper, wandering out onto the terrace, drying a glass with a tea towel. 'I wonder who –'

On the stone stairs by the side of the terrace, the sound of heavy footsteps rang out, and a deep voice called tentatively, 'I am – I'm sorry to disturb you. I just wanted a quick word with – is this where Laura's staying? Is she – here?'

Laura sat up sharply, or rather tried to, and banged her head hard on the table. 'Shit,' she muttered, and turned around.

There, walking towards the table, walking towards her, was Nick. Right there. A real-life marquess, the most eligible man in the country, and he was looking for her.

Opposite her, Aunt Annabel's jaw dropped so low that a bone clicked loudly in the silence.

CHAPTER THIRTY

'Can I help –' Robert began, half rising, but the words died on his lips.

'Oh my god,' said Lulu. 'I know who you are! You were in *Harpers* last month! You're –'

'It's you,' breathed George.

Aunt Annabel tried to pull herself together. 'Good lord,' she said. 'You – you're –'

'Ah,' said Mary. 'Of course! It's you.'

'Hello,' said Nick. 'I'm Nick.'

'Oh my god!' said Angela, appearing on the terrace with a summer pudding in her hand. 'You're –' She regained her composure remarkably fast, and said, 'Pudding?'

Dominic Edward Danvers Needham, twelfth Marquess of Ranelagh, Earl of Albany Cross, returned the gaze of those grouped around the table. Lulu giggled and turned towards him, her huge eyes even more enormous than usual.

'Er, no thanks,' Nick said. 'I'm so sorry to interrupt your lunch.' He moved towards them. 'I just wanted a quick word with Laura here –' He stared at her intently, across the table. 'Laura?'

Laura, meeting his gaze, stood up instantly. 'I'll be back in a minute,' she said. 'Er – start pudding without me.'

'Fine,' said Cedric, hugely enjoying the street theatre going on in front of him. He took out his pipe. Annabel looked at it disapprovingly.

'We're having pudding now,' she said firmly, her eyes following Laura. 'You can do that later.'

Laura escorted him away from the goggling family group, down the stone steps which led onto the beach.

'Sorry about that,' said Nick, as Laura shut the gate. 'I hoped you might have finished.'

She turned to face him.

'Hello,' he said.

'Hi,' she replied, uneasily. 'I –'

'Look,' said Nick, scratching his cheek. 'I won't disturb you for long. I just wanted to see you again. You were so strange this morning. I wanted to make sure you were OK.'

'Yes, of course,' said Laura, reaching her hand out and putting it on his chest impulsively. 'I'm sorry, really sorry. I know you've got loads on today – I knew I was in the way.'

He held her hand, pressing it against his ribcage. 'That doesn't matter, Laura. Seriously. You're not – I was worried you might have regretted it. Last night.'

'God no,' said Laura, rather too frankly. She clapped her hand to her mouth as he smiled. 'I mean . . . No, of course not. It was –' She met his eyes, and smiled back. 'It was great. You know it was.'

'It was,' he said. He was still holding her hand. 'I'm glad. I thought you might have had second thoughts. About it all.'

'No,' she said. 'No, I haven't.'

Nick looked up at the sky. He was suddenly serious. 'It's getting late,' he said, switching gear. 'I can't stay long, either. I wanted to ask you to come tonight.'

'Tonight?' said Laura, not understanding. 'But you've got the –'

'Yes,' said Nick. 'It's the family dinner thing. It's good fun.

Charles'll be there. And Lavinia,' he grinned quickly. 'You've met her, remember?'

'Yes,' said Laura. Her head was spinning. 'Yes, but – Nick – me? Come tonight? Why?'

'I want you to,' he said simply. 'I want to have you there. Please.'

'Nick, it's a family thing,' said Laura uncomfortably. 'I wouldn't want to –'

'It's lots of people,' said Nick. 'Laura, I keep thinking I've short-changed you this week. Not telling you who I was.' He shook his head. 'I thought perhaps you might like an evening at Chartley, just one more night. I don't want you to think I didn't tell you because – of some stupid reason.'

'Go there – with you?' said Laura.

'Yes, absolutely,' said Nick. 'And I won't leave you on your own. I promise.'

Laura felt slightly sick, like before a big meeting at work. How could she say no? How could she say she didn't want him like that, that she *didn't* want to be his date, the one everyone was staring at, like Prince William's new girlfriend or something? That she just wanted him, by himself, them together, nothing else . . . Oh, this was ridiculous, it was getting out of control. 'Er –' she said, not knowing how to say that she couldn't, she didn't want to, that they weren't meant to be together at things like that.

But then she was saved. Her phone, which was in her pocket, rang.

'Hello?' she said, whipping it out and jamming it up to her ear, turning away from Nick, who stared at her, obviously rather taken aback.

'Laura?' came a jagged voice, cracking over the sound of the sea and the wind.

'Paddy!' Laura said. 'I've missed you! How are you? I didn't reply, did I – I've . . .'

'*Why* didn't you reply?' Paddy's voice was aggrieved. 'Laura,

I'm freaking out, man. Becky's coming up here! She's coming up here at eight.'

'I can't believe you finally asked her out,' said Laura. 'Well done, man. What happened to the boyfriend?'

'I didn't ask her out!' Paddy practically shouted. 'She asked me! And before I could screw it up, I said yes, without thinking! What am I going to do? She says she thinks I'm a lovely guy!'

Nick walked away, out towards the sea. Laura watched him, the cast of his dark head, his wiry frame, the way he walked, his slightly stiff bearing.

'No!' she said, not paying attention. 'She never said that, seriously?'

'Thanks,' said Paddy. 'Thanks for your support.'

'Sorry.' Laura tore her gaze away from Nick, and swivelled round, towards the dunes.

'So, when are you back tonight?' Paddy said. 'You need to be here, to have the nuts in bowls ready, and all of that. Whilst I'm cooking.'

The last time Paddy had cooked for a girl on a date, he'd made salmon and cucumber mousse, which he'd whipped up in the food processor so much it looked like grey foam. He'd served it with some carrots, and that was it. Not again.

'Why are you cooking?' said Laura. 'Don't cook. Take her out! And why do I need to be there?'

'To talk me up!' said Paddy, his voice rising. 'You have to say things like, "Hey, Paddy, man! Did you mend that cupboard whilst I was away? How did you reach it?" And I'll say, "Well, because I'm a big strong —"'

She was standing on the edge, on the edge of the precipice, and she couldn't stop herself, didn't want to . . .

'Paddy,' Laura interrupted. 'I'm not coming back tonight.'

Nick heard. He turned around.

'Laura! No!' said the voice on the phone, crossly.

'I'll be back first thing tomorrow. Promise. We can have a debrief then. I've got lots to tell you.'

'Really?' Paddy sounded dubious. 'So, sorry to be a bad flatmate. How are you? How's it all been?'

'Great, actually,' said Laura, as Nick walked towards her again. He raised his eyebrows. She put her finger to her lips, smiling gently at him, trying to breathe normally, pushing aside any voice that told her she was in too deep, she was vulnerable. He was there, in front of her, looking at her with those eyes, nothing else mattered – for the moment.

'So,' Paddy said, recalling her to herself. 'What are you doing tonight? Something mega-exciting, eh? Night at the pub with Ange and George?'

'No, a ball at a stately home with a marquess,' said Laura, and Nick wrapped her in his arms, and kissed her neck. She could feel his stubble, rasping on her skin.

'Absolutely,' said Paddy on the other end of the phone. 'Me too. After I take Becky for a drink at the Cavendish, we're going on to dinner at Buckingham Palace.'

'Well, there you go then,' said Laura. 'Ow.'

'You sound muffled, is something in the way?'

'No, just bad reception,' said Laura. 'I'd better go. See you tomorrow.'

'Bye,' said Paddy, as Laura dropped the phone on the ground, and Nick kissed her again.

'Who was that?' he asked, after a minute or two.

'My flatmate. He's having a romantic crisis,' said Laura, twining her arms around his neck. She said, trying not to sound anxious, 'Nick – tonight. Am I mad? It is going to be OK, isn't it?'

'I promise,' said Nick. 'You'll have a great time. Don't worry about any of the other crap.' She scanned his face, and he pulled her against him, tightly. They stayed like that, and he whispered in her ear, gently, 'Honestly, Laura. I'll be there, won't I? We'll be there together.'

She looked at him then and smiled, and at that very moment Fran, leaning over the fence back up at the house, yelled down in her best decibel that they were cutting the cake, and was Laura coming back up again or not?

Aunt Annabel appeared next to her, and boomed graciously, 'Your Grace, you are of course *more* than welcome to – to eat the cake with us.'

Laura's toes curled up in their flip-flops. She and Nick stepped back, holding hands, and glanced at each other. She saw his lip curl, too. 'Sorry,' she said instantly.

'Don't be,' said Nick. 'Thank you,' he called, his voice carrying up to Annabel. 'I'm leaving, thank you again, though.'

He turned to her. 'You'll stay the night, Laura?' His eyes were on her. She remembered it all; she felt dizzy, she wanted him so much.

'Yes,' she said.

'So can you get to mine for eight?'

'Absolutely,' said Laura, pulling herself together and ignoring his request that she make her way to his thirty-five-bedroom, five-thousand-acre Grade One listed estate for eight o'clock as 'Can you get to mine for eight?' She smiled to herself, something she thought she might be doing a lot of before the evening was over and she got to be alone with him again. 'I'll drive, then.'

'That OK? I can send someone if you want.'

'No,' said Laura, smiling. 'You are funny.'

'God. I really have to go,' he said, looking at his watch. 'Why am I funny?'

'Nothing,' said Laura. 'I'll see you later.'

'It's going to be great,' said Nick. 'I'm so glad you're coming.'

CHAPTER THIRTY-ONE

She should have listened to herself when she was getting ready that evening, thanking the God of Odd Packing that she'd brought a simple little black dress along. She had wondered why on earth she'd seen fit to pack it, but thank god she had. It was nothing special, but she could just about get away with it tonight. What did you wear to something like this, anyway?

As she put on her make-up, as she brushed her hair, there was a voice in her head telling her to be careful, to watch out, not to go too far too fast. To make sure she could get out of this thing, this falling feeling that she had, without hurting herself again. Mrs Danvers kept telling her to be careful, as Laura looked at herself in the mirror and dried her hair. She kept telling her she should go back to London, that she shouldn't go to Chartley.

You'll be going there as his girlfriend. You'll roll up that driveway, in your car, get out, and you'll see yourself running up the stairs, the voice in her head said. *You'll imagine what it'd be like to live there. All that good work you've done, not daydreaming, not believing in that stuff. Gone.*

Laura said impatiently, to her reflection, 'I know. I know. But it's too late now, isn't it?'

No it's not, said the voice. *Look at you. You're doing exactly*

*what you always do. Paddy needed you tonight, and you were
too busy snogging some bloke on a beach to go home and be
there for him.*

'But this is different,' said Laura to herself. 'It is different,
isn't it?'

No it's not, the voice said again. *This is like Dan all over
again, Laura.*

Dan. Dan Floyd. Dan. Laura said his name out loud as if it
were a foreign word on her tongue, amazed at how neutral it
sounded. Dan. When was that? When had it been? It seemed
to have happened months ago. The last three days, four days
– they, in turn, seemed like years.

She put her hand in her sponge bag, looking for mascara. There
at the bottom were two diamante scallop-shaped clips, pretty
things Jo had bought her for Christmas. She'd never had the
chance to wear them, much as she loved them. She slid one on
each strap of the dress, feeling rather glamorous suddenly, excited.

Oh, Laura, said the voice in her head as she looked at herself
in the mirror, her hand on her breastbone, trying not to get too
nervous, trying to tell herself not to care as much as she did.
Then suddenly she felt utterly defenceless, like the day-old baby
chick she and Guy had rescued from the street of the house in
Oxford when she was small. It had fallen from a tree and
shattered its shell. It was ugly, tiny, totally exposed, and though
they gave it water, though Guy stayed up to look after it, it
died. Being out in the open, too soon out of its shell, with no
protection was just too much for it. It had upset her so much,
the ten-year-old Laura. She remembered how distressed she had
felt, now, watching herself.

She shook her head, her eyes dark, her pupils huge, her
reflection in the mirror strange to her, like someone she didn't
know. 'Oh. Just be careful.'

She should have listened to the voice as she drove along the
winding lanes, her palms sticky on the steering wheel in the

warm summer's evening. And as she turned into the drive, and crawled along in solitary, splendid isolation, suddenly feeling self-conscious in her parents' Rover. What did posh people drive? Not Rovers, probably.

As she reached the house, she could see a figure was waiting for her on the steps. She looked up expecting to see Nick's face, and found it was Charles, in black tie, hands behind his back, hair combed. The machine was in operation.

'Leave the car there,' he called, as she wound down the window to say hello. 'Someone'll take it around the back for you.'

'Oh,' said Laura. 'Cor.' She coughed. 'Thank you so much,' she added. She wondered if she should say, 'What about my overnight bag?', lying so neatly packed on the back seat, and then decided that would complicate things Far Too Much, so she left it where it was, got out of the car, and climbed the steps to meet Charles, who gave her a kiss. 'Jolly nice to see you again, Laura,' he said. 'So pleased you're here.'

'Oh, well,' said Laura. 'It's great to be here.' She looked down at her silver, strappy evening shoes; they were worrying her. She normally wore them with jeans. They were high, but not too high, in fact strangely comfortable. But the heels were scratched, the silver covering torn. They looked rather shabby, and she wished with all her heart that she was in something glamorous. She clicked her heels together. Perhaps they would magically transform into gorgeous new shoes. But no.

'Jolly nice diamond clips, those,' Charles said as she looked up. 'Very pretty.'

'Oh, thanks very much,' said Laura, fingering them. She smiled at him. 'Jolly glad. Don't want to let the side down,' she added, then stopped, alarmed by the role she was giving herself, which was, she realised, Virginia McKenna in *Carve Her Name with Pride*. She'd cried over that film one long Saturday afternoon a few weeks ago, during a particularly low moment with Dan, but really, there was no need to start talking like her.

'Hey,' said Charles, patting her arm. 'Shall we go in? Everyone's here, pretty much.'

'Really?' said Laura, taken aback. 'I'm not late, am I?'

'No, no,' said Charles. 'They've been having drinks for a while. In the Great Hall. Most of them arrived in the afternoon, you see. Staying the weekend, and all that.'

'Ah,' said Laura. She looked past him, past the porticoed balustrade, into the Great Hall. 'Er . . . Right. Where's – er, where's Nick?'

'He's in there,' Charles said. 'Shall we go and find him?'

It was pathetic to say, Can you get him to come out here whilst I wait, I'm scared, I don't want to go in? It was, wasn't it? Laura pulled herself together.

'Yes,' she said. She slid her arm through Charles's. 'Let's go in.'

'So,' said Nick's Great Aunt Teresa, five minutes later, 'Laura. Where are your people from, then?'

'Oh,' said Laura. She took a nervous sip from her heavy champagne glass. The alcohol was chalky, the bubbles rasped in her throat. Over on the other side of the room, Nick was talking to Olly and Penelope, two cousins from Somerset. Laura had said hello to them both briefly, and Nick had squeezed her arm, and whispered, 'I'll come and find you in a minute, OK?'

The room was crowded; fifty or more relatives, of varying ages, but tending towards the forty-plus, were talking loudly, laughing, greeting each other. Ripples of amusement, of shared jokes or reminiscences, floated to Laura's ears as she stood there, trying not to feel too like an outcast:

'Well, hello there! Terrific to see you again, old thing.'

'Minty's in Cornwall.'

'John? Wife died few months ago. No, he's up at Balmoral.'

'Damn nag fell at the first fence. I know.'

In front of her stood one such specimen, Nick's great aunt, well over ninety, clad in upholstered purple velvet, wearing a small diamond brooch, with beady eyes that bored into Laura in a most disconcerting fashion.

'Sorry?' said Laura, who felt as if all she could hear was a loud buzzing noise.

'Hello? I said, your people. Parents. Where are they from, dear?'

Laura dragged her gaze away from the back of Nick's head to Great Aunt Teresa, who was regarding her intently. 'Oh,' she repeated. 'Sorry. My parents? They're from Harrow.'

'How lovely,' said Great Aunt Teresa, politely but vaguely. She grimaced, sucking her lips into her mouth. 'I don't know it very well, I must say. Although my brother was there. Beautiful.'

'Oh, Harrow boys,' said Lady Lavinia. She was standing next to Charles, who was gazing at her like she was an exotic princess. 'Gosh. Lucky you, living so near them.' She smiled, her little pink tongue darting out between her tiny white teeth, and tossed her golden-red hair over her shoulder.

Charles scowled, and rubbed his face; Laura had never seen him so discomfited.

'Not really,' said Laura, trying to explain. 'I mean, the school – it's not that near where I love – I live, I mean.'

'Right,' said Lavinia. She smiled at Charles from under her eyelashes. He blushed rosily, and Lavinia lapsed into vacant silence, which seemed to say, 'I've done my bit.'

Great Aunt Teresa picked up the gauntlet. She peered at Laura's dress. 'Those clips,' she said. 'Very pretty.'

'Oh, thank you,' said Laura. 'My friend Jo –'

'The diamonds are lovely. What is the setting? Platinum, or silver?' Great Aunt Teresa peered at one of them, her beaky nose almost jabbing Laura's arm.

'Oh no,' said Laura, laughing. 'They're not real. They're fake. But they're pretty, aren't they?'

'Fake?' said Great Aunt Teresa loudly. 'Oh. I see.'

'My friend Jo,' Laura said again, weakly. 'She gave them to me.'

Nick left the cousins and moved across the room. Her heart leapt, then sank again as she watched him shake hands with someone else, a dark-haired, bearded man.

'So, Laura, you're off back to London tomorrow,' said Charles, turning to her.

'London?' said Great Aunt Teresa. 'Whereabouts do you live, then?'

'North,' said Laura, noncommittally.

'Regent's Park?' said Great Aunt Teresa. 'Near there?'

'Er – yes,' said Laura, reasoning that, in relation to, say, Newcastle, her flat *was* near Regent's Park. 'Lovely, isn't it?' she said politely. 'Where do you live?'

She felt with unease that she should know how to address Great Aunt Teresa, whom she felt sure was a lady or something, and moreover not *her* Great Aunt, but, like Lady Rose earlier in the day, still wasn't sure enough to ask.

'Where do *I* live?' said Great Aunt Teresa, in tones of astonishment. 'At Dearden.'

'Dearden Hall,' Charles murmured in her ear.

This meant nothing to Laura, not even Charles's kind clarification, it only made her feel even more gauche, were that possible. 'Right,' she said politely, hoping that was contribution enough to the conversation, knowing it wasn't, really.

Great Aunt Teresa of Dearden Hall, and Lady Lavinia moved off, in different directions, to be greeted with shrieks of joy by their respective new companions, and Laura was left standing next to Charles, trying not to feel like a shorter, fatter Audrey Hepburn in *My Fair Lady*, that she was failing some subtle, silly test. This was the twenty-first century, what the hell did it matter who was who and where they lived and all that? It didn't make them important. It didn't matter that she was from Harrow and lived in Tufnell Park. She was here because of Nick, because of how she felt about him. The rest of it wasn't a big deal.

Why did it *feel* like a big deal, though? Why couldn't she

shake the idea that she was about as welcome tonight as a cockroach infestation? She glanced across at Charles gratefully. He was watching her, and smiled as she looked around the room again for Nick, who was talking politely to the same man and a couple of other people her parents' age. One of them said something, and Nick nodded seriously. He was so handsome, she thought. The white of his shirt gleamed against his dark hair, black tie, black dinner jacket, stood out in the cavernous gloom of the Great Hall. He looked grown-up. Remote. Different. Very different from the Nick she knew.

Of course, he was, though, Laura thought, and her hand flew to her cheek, because thinking that upset her, though she knew it was stupid. He was a marquess. He was an important person, not just because he was so rich, so posh, so well-connected. But also because he was the employer of hundreds of people, the person who ran the estate, who had investments, who sat in City boardrooms whilst people presented to him. She didn't know that Nick at all, and it was all very well for him to say it didn't matter, that the two of them was all that mattered, but she couldn't help feeling it mattered more than he could see, or she had realised.

Then she thought, you stupid girl. You think he's wonderful, don't you? You've fallen for him, for this handsome marquess in his huge stately home. You've convinced yourself you know him, that he knows you, you've had three wonderful nights together. And you've bloody fallen for him. And then she heard Mrs Danvers loud and clear, and this time Laura listened.

It's been three days. You met him three days ago, Laura. How could you let yourself do this again? Haven't you learnt anything?

But, Laura said to herself, staring into her empty glass, it's Nick. He's not like that.

Laura, Laura. Come on. Three days. How can you possibly know? Of course he's nice. He's lovely. He's kind, he makes you laugh, you get each other really well. But isn't that just

*because of circumstance? Isn't it something to do with the fact
that he was the first person you'd had a normal conversation
with in days when you met him? Because he's tall, and so
handsome, and looks at you with those big dark eyes like he's
falling in love with you? Oh Laura. It doesn't mean he is . . .*

Her throat hurt, she didn't know why. She wanted to be
alone, but she knew she was just being silly. She smiled, and
pulled herself together, taking a deep breath. She turned to
Charles, still standing there politely, carefully, nicely.

'What about you, Charles?' she said, trying to get onto
something approximating common ground.

'What about me?' said Charles, smiling at her.

'Well,' said Laura, waving her hands vaguely, and trying not
to sound like the Queen asking someone questions in a line-
up. 'What do you do? Er, in your spare time, I mean?'

'When I'm not running after Nick, or sorting out the house,
or his crazy family, you mean?' Charles nodded. 'Ha. Well, that
leaves about five minutes in the day.'

'Really?'

'Oh,' said Charles. 'No, not at all. I'm very lucky. Don't
really want any spare time, to be honest.'

Laura didn't believe him. That didn't sound like luck, it
sounded about as much fun as botulism, but she pressed him
again, genuinely curious.

'No,' she said. 'I mean, if you had a night off, could do
anything. What would you do?'

'Well, I'd potter around the garden, I suppose,' said Charles.
'I've got my own bit, out the back, by the kitchen garden.'

Oh good grief. This was awful. Laura nodded politely. 'Still,'
she said gently. 'Like, a night out. If you could do anything at
all.'

'American sitcoms,' said Charles, unexpectedly. 'I'd watch
them all day if I could.'

'Really?' Laura said incredulously.

'Yup,' said Charles. 'Love 'em. I've got a digital box in my room. *Seinfeld. Larry Sanders. Curb Your Enthusiasm. Arrested Development.*'

'Seriously?' said Laura, feeling as if she was in a weird trip. 'Wow. I love *Arrested Development.*'

Charles's face lit up. 'Isn't it amazing?' he said. 'So clever. So hilarious! Did you know, Ron Howard's the person who narrates it?'

'No!' said Laura. 'Really? I always thought he sounded familiar. That's so cool! I must tell Paddy that.'

'Paddy?' said Charles.

'My flatmate,' Laura explained. 'He . . .' She trailed off, suddenly remembering that at this moment Paddy would be having a drink in the sitting room, on A Date with Downstairs Becky. How she wished she could be there . . . She looked around the room, thinking again that this was odd. This was effectively Nick's sitting room. She cleared her throat. 'Anyway. He's the executive producer, isn't he?'

'Yes,' said Charles seriously, and Laura realised she was the only one finding it at all incongruous, out of place, this conversation. In fact, this whole situation. Perhaps because it was just her who was out of place. Incongruous.

CHAPTER THIRTY-TWO

Five minutes later, the gong sounded for supper and Laura felt unease creep over her again. She could talk about telly for hours, and she enjoyed talking to Charles, who was so lovely, and whom she genuinely liked, with his pink and white face, and sweetly intelligent, shy manner. But at the same time, she knew he was looking after her, and that he probably had things to do, or people he wanted to talk to. She knew he'd rather be talking to Lavinia than to her, or discussing the harvest, or something, rather than having to be her bodyguard.

Charles said, 'We should go through, ah, just here,' as a swarm of unknown relatives bustled past them, seemingly unconcerned with Laura and Charles, though a couple looked back at her as they passed through, and gave her rather appraising stares, as if to say, You stand out. What are you doing here? Charles put his hand gently on her back, and steered her towards the Ballroom, when suddenly she felt another arm steal around her waist, and Nick kissed her lightly on the neck, and murmured,

'I am so sorry, Laura. Here you are. You look beautiful. Thanks, Charles.'

He took her hand and they walked in to dinner together, and Laura's heart sang at the feel of his fingers entwined with hers, the reassuring press of his heavy dinner jacket against her bare arm. The crowd parted, as if they were Cleopatra and Mark Antony, and people stared and whispered, heads bent together, as the combined Needham family suddenly realised who that bland, uninteresting, unglamorous girl was talking to Charles. She was Nick's date. From the look of open-mouthed shock on some people's faces, Laura could tell this news wasn't exactly welcome to them.

They entered the Ballroom, and Laura glanced around, thinking how strange it was that the last time she'd been in there her father had been asking Cynthia about dynastic successions, and her mother had been saying, 'Do you think they have a lampshade similar to that in the shop? I should ask, shouldn't I', and Laura had never even met Nick, and here she was now, standing next to him, his hand squeezing hers. It all felt slightly unreal, like a dream, as if she were watching a film about someone else.

The room was a mass of dinner jackets and brightly coloured taffeta. Scanning the long table, set in the middle and laden, glittering, with crystal and flowers, silver cutlery, snowy-white tablecloths, Laura looked at the row of Needham relatives ranged opposite her, and saw there was a family resemblance; a faint one, but there nonetheless. It was something in the cheekbones; the high, rather narrow face, the dark hair. It was extraordinary, she thought – centuries of interbreeding, all in one room, and she looked down at her hand, tangled with Nick's. He squeezed it again, reassuringly, and then held out her chair for her to sit down.

'Thank you,' said Laura formally. He touched the bare skin of her shoulder lightly, and sat down next to her.

'So,' he said. 'Bearing up OK?'

'Yes,' said Laura, smiling at him. 'Just about.'

'I kept meaning to come over and introduce you to people, and every time I made a move, someone would annex me,' Nick said. He turned towards her and smiled, the Nick she knew, even in a dinner jacket. 'And then you looked like you were having such a good time with Great Aunt Teresa and Lavinia – I'm glad.'

'Yes,' said Laura. She stared at her lap, feeling rather helpless. Strange though it was to think it when he'd lied to her for most of the time she'd known him, she hated lying to him about this now. It felt – like everything was wrong. But she had to, so she did. 'Yes,' she said again, as his hand stole onto her lap and squeezed her thigh gently. 'It's been just great, Nick, thank you.'

A waiter unfolded a napkin and waved it gracefully onto Laura's lap. Nick moved his hand, and they were both silent until he'd moved on.

'Well,' he said. 'I don't know about that. I don't really like these things, you know. But I have to do them and we all actually quite enjoy seeing each other.' He scratched his head, and a shadow crossed his face, briefly. 'The one thing to watch out for is . . .' He trailed off.

'What?' said Laura.

'Well, someone's bound to bring up my mother. They always do, after a few glasses, and then . . .' He shook his head. 'Forget it. That's an even longer story. Do you –' He looked unsure, then angry. 'I hate this. It's so stupid, asking someone you – if they know about how your mother ran off with your uncle. Because it was in the paper every day for about a year.'

'I know,' said Laura. 'My grandmother told me, yesterday. She met them.'

Nick looked amazed. 'My mother?' he said rather loudly, and next to him his cousins Clare and Ann stopped talking, and looked appalled, as if Nick had just made a Nazi salute, or punched a waiter, or something.

'Yes,' said Laura. She added softly, thinking she sounded like *her* mother, 'Shall we talk about it later?'

'Yes, let's. You're right,' said Nick. His fingers gripped his napkin, screwing it into a ball, and he looked up and down the room impatiently, his gaze travelling the length of the table, until it came to rest on her. 'Oh, Laura. I'm sorry. This – perhaps this was a bad idea.'

'What?' said Laura, feeling sick again.

'Asking you tonight,' Nick explained. 'Thank you. White, please,' he said to the waiter. 'I don't mean – you know. I just mean perhaps it's a bit rich, expecting you to get all of this, so soon.'

Feeling slightly like a disease-ridden barefoot chimney sweep, Laura tried to smile reassuringly at him, but his attention was claimed by an old lady next to him and he turned away. The last of the guests were being seated. Across the table, Charles sat down opposite her. And next to her, a chair was drawn back, and a voice said, 'Good evening. It's nice to see you back at Chartley so soon.'

It was Lady Rose, corseted in pale brown lace and silk, looking exactly like Queen Mary, a cool smile on her face. She saw Laura's place card next to hers; Laura turned around, and caught the look on her face. She turned back and looked across the table and concentrated on the huge bowl of flowers in front of her, trying not to eavesdrop.

'Nick,' Rose said softly to her brother. 'I wasn't supposed to be sitting here.'

Nick smiled. 'Hello, Rose. Well, you are now,' he said. 'I moved things around a little, hope that's OK. Malcolm's next to Lavinia, he's fine. You're next to Laura.'

'But –' said Rose. Her voice grew louder. 'I always sit next to you.'

'Rose,' said Nick firmly. 'Sit down, please.'

Laura, trying not to listen to this exchange but unable to avoid it, was torn between wanting to stand up and offer Rose her seat back, and sliding gently under the table and crawling out of the room.

There was a pause; the tension was palpable. And then Rose sat down next to her, and smiled graciously.

The doors closed behind them, and Nick stood up and waited

for the babble to subside. Down the long room, the noise fell, and fifty or so faces turned to look at him expectantly. The only movement was the glint of diamonds in the light of the chandeliers.

'Just a minute, please. Thank you. Hey!' Laura jumped as he banged his hand on the table. He called down the room to two old men who were still talking. 'Alec! Geoffrey! This won't take long. I just want to welcome you all. All of you.'

He paused, infinitesimally. His voice was softer, and she did not dare look up at him, but she felt as if he were talking to her.

'We're all family, aren't we? And it's rare that we are all together. So perhaps we should drink to that. To this evening. I'm so glad you're all here tonight. To the Needham family.'

There was a shuffling of chairs as the assembled company stood up. 'The Needham family,' they chorused, in a monotone accent.

Laura looked around the room. If my friends could see me now, she thought. Imagine if I called Jo and told her where I was. Or Paddy. They'd never believe it. She looked at the offending Geoffrey and Alec, stout and bespectacled; at Great Aunt Teresa, leaning heavily on a stick, staring beadily into space; at Charles, Lavinia, and Malcolm Balmore, who was short and squat and looked very disgruntled about something. At the massed ranks of Needhams, along the row until her eye rested on Rose, stately and gracious, nodding at someone opposite her, and then she turned to Nick, her Nick, so tall and grave in his dinner jacket, and felt overwhelmed. She didn't know what she was doing there at all.

CHAPTER THIRTY-THREE

Dinner was not a nine-course gourmet affair; it was a huge roast dinner for all, with the toast to Sir Guillibert Danvers scheduled to happen halfway through the evening, followed by more wine and pudding. Laura smiled inanely at no one as the roast beef was served, as if she were having a simply fantastic time. Around her the Clan Needham talked amongst itself, and Rose inclined her head graciously towards Laura from time to time. And of course Nick was next to her, chatting politely to some ancient aunt and uncle opposite him, occasionally turning to her to see if she was OK, and looking so pleased when she would smile, and simply say, 'Yes, I'm having a great time, thank you.'

As seconds were being served, Rose swivelled her attention around to Laura. She leant forward and reached for her glass. 'So, Laura. I hope you're enjoying yourself tonight?' she asked, in polite tones.

'Oh, yes, thank you,' said Laura. 'I'm very glad to be here.'

Rose said nothing, but gave a thin-lipped smile.

'It's beautiful here,' Laura continued, knowing this was a pathetic thing to say, but not sure how else to break the silence.

'Yes. Yes it is,' said Rose. 'Tell me something, Laura.' Laura nodded. 'How did you meet my brother? I'm so curious.'

'Er, well,' said Laura. She toyed with the idea of saying 'at the Sandy Lane Resort, Barbados', or 'St Tropez last year'. What did it matter how she'd met him? Why was it important?

'I was here on Wednesday with my parents, for the day,' she said. 'I bumped into him then – we got talking, and we ended up going out for a drink in the evening.'

Rose's expression was indefinable. 'Your parents?' she said.

'Yes,' Laura replied carefully. 'We're here on holiday. We were going round the house.' She took a deep breath.

'How nice,' Rose said eventually.

'Yes,' Laura said. 'I go back to London tomorrow, so Nick was kind enough to ask me tonight.'

Rose nodded. 'I see,' and then she was silent.

Laura found herself gabbling, 'Which is rather weird, because I know it's a family night, and I'm a complete stranger! But I'm incredibly touched to be asked.' She knew she sounded like a fourteen-year-old, that she wasn't saying the right thing, but with no idea of what that right thing might be she thought she'd better keep talking.

Rose raised her glass. 'Well, so here you are then.' She paused. And then she smiled brightly. 'Forgive me. It's rather a surprise, that's all. My little brother is rather useless, isn't he?'

'Yes,' said Laura, blindly agreeing. 'Well,' she amended hurriedly, 'no, I don't think –'

'You see,' Rose said, unheeding. 'I rather thought he had a girlfriend. That's why I'm surprised. He *was* seeing a girl called Cecilia.'

'Yes, he told me,' said Laura, refusing to be ruffled.

'Oh, you know? Of course,' said Rose. 'She's terribly nice. I don't know if you know her. Her father's a very good friend of Sir Malcolm's. We've known the family for ages. The Thorsons.'

'Right,' said Laura.

'They were terribly kind when – my father died.' Rose cleared her throat. 'You see, there were debts when Nick inherited two years ago. And the Thorsons have been so helpful, advising him, all of that. So kind. We thought he and Cecilia would get on. It was going rather well, I'd heard.'

'They're not seeing each other any more,' said Laura. 'We talked about it.' She sounded rather gauche and schoolgirlish, she realised.

Rose looked pleased, like a cat. 'Oh you did, did you? Well,' she said, and her tongue darted out of her mouth; she looked like her sister for a fleeting second. 'I'm sure if that's what he told you . . .'

'Yes, it is,' said Laura. She felt she ought to distance herself a little from this. She didn't want to sound like a stalker. 'But of course, I have only known him for a very short time, so . . .'

'Yes,' said Rose, almost purring. 'You're quite right. So.'

She smiled and waved at someone further down the table. 'Ah, there's Emily. Dear thing. I must say hello to her afterwards.' She cleared her throat, as if that was the line being drawn under the conversation, now her point was made. 'Well, I'm glad you're enjoying your time here.'

'Thank you,' Laura replied.

'We're all family here tonight,' Rose said. She ran a short, plump finger around the rim of her glass. 'Except you, of course.'

'I'm very lucky.'

'Yes,' said Rose. 'I'd say you were.'

And with that, she turned back to her neighbour, leaving Laura staring down at her plate, not knowing what to say.

It's almost impossible to have a relaxed conversation with someone when you know everyone else is looking at you, appraising you, judging you. And, in Rose's case, wishing you weren't there. After this, Laura felt even more exposed, and when Nick turned to ask her how it was all going, she found herself making small talk with him, as if he were one of her mum and dad's neighbours at a barbecue in Harrow. She didn't

308

know what to say to him, all of a sudden, how to talk to him. She wanted to be alone with him, on the beach, or in his room. As if it were last night, or the night before, or the one before that. Before real life got in the way – and what a reality it was!

Because it was different now, all different. Amongst Laura's opening salvos to Nick were:

'Do you have job-share schemes on the estate?'

'Is the soil good for growing potatoes, then?'

'Who handles the insurance for the paintings?'

'That's an interesting chandelier, how old is it?'

What she didn't say was:

'Can I punch both your sisters?'

'How do you cope with this, all the time?'

'Why can't it be just the two of us, like it was before?'

And:

'Do you realise I think I've fallen for you?'

Eventually, the plates were cleared away after the first course, and Charles stood up to announce, in his polite, soft voice, that there would be a break and then the toasts to Sir Guillibert Danvers would begin. Nick turned to her, and put his napkin on the table.

'Why don't we go for a walk?' he said, smiling at her, just her. 'Outside, for a couple of minutes. I don't really feel like I've been a very good host to you tonight.'

'I'd love that,' she said, gazing up at him, thinking how perfect he was to her then in that moment. How much she wished they could just leave this evening behind, forget it. Perhaps they could, perhaps the feeling that was growing inside her, this feeling of doom, perhaps she was wrong about it. Perhaps it would be OK.

He touched her hand lightly. 'Right. Let's go. I'll –'

'Nick! M'boy! Damn good to see you.'

'Leo, hello,' said Nick, turning around and standing up.

Laura turned to see a large, purple-faced man, whose dinner jacket strained alarmingly at the buttons. 'Hello,' Nick repeated, shaking his hand. 'Leo, this is Laura,' he said, holding Laura's elbow and pushing her forward.

Laura shook Leo's hand. 'Nice to meet you,' she said.

'And you,' said Leo, looking at her breasts and not at her face. 'And you, m'dear. Good that you're here,' he said to the breasts again, before coming to with a start. 'Before I forget, Nick. Need a small word with you in private. Now?'

'Now?' said Nick. 'I just –'

'Can't stay afterwards, m'boy. It's about Pickleton. The cottages. Now Ned's dead. Really think we should discuss it –' Leo looked rather anxious. 'Not sure what to do, if the truth be known.'

'Of course, of course,' Nick said, patting his shoulder. 'Laura, do you mind? Why don't you wait here? I'll only be a minute.'

'I'll go outside and wait,' said Laura, who didn't particularly want to be left alone. 'I'd love some fresh air. See you on the steps.'

He raised his hand and smiled briefly, turned away and walked out. She could see his retreating back, and Leo's, as they disappeared through the Great Hall, into a room off to the side.

Laura sat down, and drained her drink. She looked for Charles, but couldn't see him. Across the way from her, various old ladies chattered happily amongst themselves. She thought how like her grandmother they were, and how Mary would get on beautifully in this situation, would take to it like a duck to water, in fact. She stood up, trying to look inconspicuous, and headed out to the Great Hall. She didn't feel inconspicuous, though. She'd never felt more out of place in her life.

She went outside and waited on the steps. The landscaped grounds were in near-darkness now, with only the glow from the floodlit house illuminating the gravel, the drive, and a little

310

of the way beyond down to the fountain in the distance. A few people from the dinner – she didn't know their names – walked past her, or came out and saw her, but they didn't bother her. The stone was still warm from the heat of the day.

So she sat and waited, and thought about the last few days, and how she had come to be there. She thought about Mary's birthday, about how stressful family affairs were, but how it was worth it to see her grandmother surrounded by her family and friends, to realise how lucky she was to have her parents as her parents. How funny this afternoon had been; she suddenly saw Lulu and Aunt Annabel's incredulous faces as Laura said goodbye to the assembled group and drove off in her black dress to Chartley Hall. She thought about Paddy, on his date, how it was going, and felt a sharp pang as she found herself wishing she was there, so they could sit up and chat about it over a late-night drink. She thought about popping round to Jo's; sitting at her and Chris's kitchen table, reading the Sunday papers, laughing and drinking coffee, being normal.

Tomorrow was Sunday; when she got back home she knew there would be a letter waiting from Rachel confirming her meeting about coming back to work. A job. A life again, on an even keel. Now the madness of the previous few months was over. She thought about Dan, and shook her head, her hand pressed to her heart when she remembered how blindly she had loved him, wanted to love him, to be with him, and how utterly different the reality was, the cold, hard facts of daily life.

She looked behind her, to the house. It was funny, wasn't it. This was reality now, right this minute. The last few days with Nick, just being with him, just the two of them, walking, talking, kissing, making love, they hadn't been real, because they weren't the truth. This was real, sitting on the steps now, waiting for her romantic hero to come out of the door to meet her, and the irony was that it was like something out of one of the novels she'd wanted to live in so much.

As she sat thinking, sifting all these thoughts through and

through, gradually Laura realised what she had to do. The idea of it was awful, she didn't know how she would get through it, but she knew it had to be done. She looked down at her dress, her feet in their strappy sandals, light brown against the dark stone. She wanted to remember it, remember being here, preserve it, so she would always know what it felt like to know he was here, on his way out to find her, that he wanted her.

It seemed as if hours had gone by, but it was only a few minutes later that she heard his footsteps behind her, and he came and sat down next to her.

'Hello,' he said, and he slid his arm around her waist. 'Sorry to keep you waiting.' He kissed her. 'Leo does go on rather a lot. He's a great chap – he was my dad's cousin, you know. He runs the estates in Lincolnshire, does a fantastic job. But he's rather – wordy, you know. I'm sorry.'

'Don't worry,' said Laura. 'Honestly.'

There was silence between them.

'We should go back in a minute,' said Nick. 'I have to make the toast, and wear this ridiculous hat. I'm sorry. And there's a rhyme thing. God, it's ridiculous, but it keeps them happy for another year, and –' he trailed off, as Laura stood up.

'I'm going, Nick,' she said, trying to keep her voice neutral.

'What?' said Nick blankly. He looked up at her. 'Inside?'

'No,' said Laura. 'I'm going. Going home.'

'But it's –' He stood up. 'What are you talking about?'

She knew she had to play a part.

'I'm not staying here,' said Laura, in the tone of offended, stroppy girlfriend. She had her bag with her, and held it up. 'I'll get the car myself. Thanks for a lovely evening.'

'Laura!' Nick caught her by the arms. He was almost laughing, but there was panic in his eyes. 'What are you talking about? You can't leave, it's – we haven't had pudding yet.' He shook his head, as if aware of how silly that sounded. 'You know what I mean. We haven't spent any time together. I want – I thought you were staying with me. Tonight, I mean.'

She shook free from his grasp, looked away, took a deep breath, and then faced him.

'Stay here? And be treated like this? You must be joking.' Her voice was shriller than usual. She let the muscles in her face form into an ugly expression, and she smiled at him spitefully. 'Who are you kidding, Nick? I've had a crap evening, and you've treated me like dirt. You've barely spoken a word to me! You let your sisters be rude to me!' Her voice rose. 'I'm not used to it, OK? I'm used to being treated politely by my date. Like a lady.' She thought, feeling sick, that that might be going a bit too far. She didn't want to sound like Sybil Fawlty. But he had to believe her. She stopped, and put her evening bag over her shoulder.

'I'm really sorry, Nick,' she said. 'We had a laugh, didn't we? But I'm going to go now.'

Nick was staring at her, shaking his head. 'No – no,' he said. He moved closer towards her. 'Laura? Why are you being like this? I don't – aren't you glad to be here? I thought you wanted to – I thought you didn't mind all this . . .' He trailed off, his eyes beseeching her.

'What, you think I'm going to be on my knees with gratitude because the big lord's invited little old me to his stately home? Eh? Like a fucking geisha, is that what you think: thanks so much, Sir, I'm nothing and I'm so grateful.' Laura was trembling, shouting as she said it. It was horrible. She couldn't imagine it could hurt this much. 'Well, I'm not. So perhaps you'd better look around for someone else who's more up your street. OK?'

She ran down the last two steps.

'Is this about Cecilia?' said Nick, coming after her. 'Rose has just cornered me and asked me lots of stupid questions about her, about why we broke up. I'm *not* seeing her, Laura, Rose is just trying to bully me into marrying some fucking millionaire's daughter so she and Malcolm can have the proprieties observed. Is that it? What did she say to you?'

Laura saw her chance and took it. 'How am I supposed to

believe you?' she said, making sure she kept her voice shrill. 'Your sister didn't know you'd broken up with her, how am I to know if you're still seeing her or not? You lied to me about being a marquess, Nick, you could lie to me again.'

He was staring at her, his expression totally bewildered. 'I don't understand you, Laura. I thought we – I thought you . . .'

Laura turned and walked away, so she didn't have to look at him any more, because she was on the verge of losing her resolve, and she was nearly there, it was nearly done, and she couldn't believe how hard it was.

'Just leave me alone, Nick,' she said, her voice breaking. He followed her around the house, towards the stables at the back, and grabbed her hand. She snatched it away as he swung her round to face him. They were standing on the gravel, in the shadow of the huge, dark stables. The trees behind them sighed in the night-time breeze.

'This isn't you,' he said quietly. 'Laura, why are you doing this?'

She looked at him, and her shoulders heaved. A sob welled up in her throat.

'I can't do this,' she said softly, her voice breaking.

He drew her to him, holding her tightly. His buttons pressed into the thin fabric of her dress, digging into her ribs. He kissed her hair, and murmured, 'Laura, oh Laura. What's wrong?'

She drew back from him slowly, wiping a tear away from her cheek.

'Nick,' she said. 'Please. Don't try to stop me. Just let me go. I'm not pissed off, I'm not pretending any more.'

'Good,' he said, with a glimmer of humour. 'I didn't know who you'd turned into back there. I thought –'

'Nick, I mean it. This is never going to work.'

Two lines of annoyance appeared between his dark brows. 'Come on, Laura. We've talked about this. It can work.'

'No,' Laura said, her voice rising. 'We *haven't* talked about this, Nick. And it can't work. Look at us. Look at tonight.'

'Why?' he said. 'Come on, I know they're a bit hard to take, but –'

'You don't get it, do you?' said Laura, trying not to shout at him, to cry, to hit him. 'Can't you see? You're them. They're you. You're part of this,' she waved her arms around her. 'The whole thing, the house, the history, all your family. All of it. It's massive. And you're trying to pretend it doesn't matter, but it *does*, Nick. You talk about it as if it's something abstract, or as if it's a condition, like being allergic to apples, or having a fear of spiders, as if it's just a vague inconvenience. And it's not, it's the whole damn thing with you.'

'It's not,' he said, taking her hands, folding them in his, like he always did. He shook his head blindly. 'Laura. If I can't have a normal life outside it, I'm doomed. Of course all this is important to me, it has been since Dad died and I had to come back here and start looking after things. It's been the most important thing. But there are other things too,' he said, and he leant forward and kissed her.

His lips were on hers, insistent, hot against her cool skin, and her heart physically ached, in a way she didn't realise it could. Even her. She would never forget how it felt when he kissed her, what it was like. How it felt to hold him, to feel him on top of her, inside her, his hands on hers. Perhaps that was all that mattered.

And then she remembered the expression on the faces of his relatives as they walked in. She remembered the portrait of the seventh marquess, proud and handsome. Of Cynthia, the tour guide, telling her rapt audience that the Needhams had fought in the Wars of the Roses. Nick and his sisters re-enacting their own personal Hogarth paintings as children. The gardeners, the servants, the houses, the lands . . . it all whirled around in her mind, Rose's voice telling her how lucky she was, when Laura knew she wasn't, she'd probably just got it wrong. Again. And she had to get out, before she hurt Nick more than she'd already hurt herself.

She pulled away from him, and saw George's trusty, beloved Rover lined up in the darkness next to the battered old Range Rovers and a Rolls-Royce.

Nick stepped back, his arms falling heavily by his sides, and looked at her in disbelief.

'You're actually going to throw this all away because you're an inverted snob,' he said angrily.

'If you like,' said Laura, keeping all her emotions in check with one last herculean effort.

'You're a coward,' he said, his voice harsh, his fists clenched. He shook his head. 'Coward.'

She turned and walked towards the car, and when she reached it she took the keys out and, trembling, tried to unlock it. Her hands were shaking. He watched her as she opened the door.

'You know, I actually thought I might be falling in love with you,' he said quietly. He stepped away, turned around and walked towards the house, and didn't turn back once.

Laura drove out of the stables, onto the long, wide driveway, not daring to look in the mirror in case she caught sight of Chartley behind her, or the figure climbing the steps at the front to disappear inside. Tears rolled down her cheeks; she gripped the steering wheel and put her foot on the accelerator.

'The trouble is, I'd already fallen in love with you,' she said softly to herself, as she reached the end of the long, long drive, and turned onto the main road, back towards home.

PART THREE

CHAPTER THIRTY-FOUR

'So, what's she like?'

'What are they like together?'

'I heard she stayed the night, did she? God. So has she seen him being himself yet?'

'Yes, you know. Has she seen him being really Paddyish. Awkward and yet bizarrely self-confident,' said Hilary, stubbing her cigarette out in the ashtray, her long, elegant fingers squashing the butt like a helpless insect. She wiped her fingers and looked up expectantly. Next to her, Jo nodded patiently.

'I don't know!' said Laura, holding her hands up in protest. 'I haven't seen them together yet.'

Jo moved the crisps into the centre of the table. 'But you have *seen* her, though, right?'

'Becky? Of course!'

'So, she's not . . . imaginary?'

'No!' said Laura. 'Poor Paddy. Of course she's not imaginary.'

The three of them were sitting in Jo and Chris's newly designed garden, enjoying the warm evening and Jo and Chris's John Lewis garden furniture table and chair set, a wedding present of which Jo was inordinately proud. The French windows were flung open, music was playing softly in the kitchen and, way back in the sitting room at the front of the house, Chris and his brother Jason were watching telly.

It was Sunday evening, and Laura had arrived back from Norfolk early that morning.

She had crept out of the house at Seavale, waking only her mother, saying she had a lunch to go to that she couldn't miss. She had left a note for Mary, and had already embraced her inner guilt about not saying a proper goodbye. But she couldn't stay there any longer. She had to come back to London, or else go mad with thinking about what she was leaving behind.

Here, in Jo's tiny, welcoming back garden, sitting with Jo and Hilary and a bottle of Sauvignon Blanc, she could imagine it had all been a dream. She knew she would think about it later, that it would hurt, that she would think about him; but here, right now, on a warm July evening, she asked nothing more than to sit with two friends and chew the fat over a few glasses of wine.

'So,' said Laura. 'What's happened whilst I've been away?'

Jo and Hilary looked at each other. 'Nothing, really,' said Jo. 'Paddy having a date with someone is the most exciting thing that's happened to me for a long time.' She paused. 'Ooh, though. Me and Chris are going to Australia next month! I forgot that bit. And, we bought some lovely eggshell paint for the bathroom.'

Hilary looked disgusted at this, and rolled her eyes at Laura, but Laura said, 'Right – eggshell, that's great, but – Jo! You're going to Australia, wow!'

'Yes,' said Jo, clapping her hands. 'I'm so excited I can barely speak! It's like a delayed honeymoon, and we weren't going to go, but we had three weeks booked off anyway, and we got these flights, and . . . so we're going!'

'You lucky things,' said Laura. 'I'm going to miss you! Three weeks, my goodness.'

Jo took her friendship responsibilities very seriously. 'I know,' she said, patting Laura's hand. 'Perhaps I . . . well, obviously

I'm not going to *not go*, but we should talk. If you need me. You know.'

Laura laughed. 'I'm not that hopeless, you know.'

'Yes you are,' said Hilary. 'Look at the mess you got yourself into when you and Jo weren't speaking back in the spring.'

'Thanks,' said Laura. 'Charming.'

'Sorry. But you know what I mean,' said Hilary, as Jo held Laura's hand. 'Talking of which, I hear all is not well in paradise. Or Miami, to be more precise.'

'Miami?' said Laura, pouring Jo and herself another glass of wine. She looked up to see Jo making cut-throat gestures at Hilary. 'What do you mean?'

'Miami?' said Hilary. 'Who's there at the moment, do you remember?' For a split second Laura looked blank, and then of course recognition flashed across her face. 'There you are. I bumped into that ghastly friend of Amy's yesterday. Camilla? The fitness instructor?'

'She *is* ghastly,' said Jo loyally.

'Anyway, she let slip that Dan and Amy were on their way back. Early. They've had a massive row.'

'Really?' said Jo. She looked at Laura anxiously. 'Oh, Laura . . .'

Laura smiled at her. 'It's fine, really.'

'Oh Laura,' Jo said again, staring at her. 'He'd better not . . . Ooh, if he tries to get in touch with you, I'm going to tell Chris to Have a Word.'

'Have a fag,' said Hilary unemotionally. She gave Laura a quick smile. 'Thought you'd want to know, anyway.'

'Thanks, Hil,' said Laura. 'But no thanks. Look . . .' she shook her head, trying to explain. 'I can't explain why, but it really is OK. Good luck to them. I hope they work it out, seriously.' She rummaged in her bag as displacement activity, looking for her lip-salve. As she was holding her phone, it beeped, a text message. It was from Nick, but she didn't open it to see what it said. She stared at her phone, almost in disbelief. No, no. This was her real life now; that was a dream.

'Who's it from?' said Jo, mildly intrigued by Laura's sudden silence.

'Er –' said Laura. 'No one.'

Jo looked at her.

'Why didn't you see Becky last night?' she asked.

'What?' Laura took some more crisps.

'Becky. You came back last night, didn't you?'

'No,' said Laura. 'This morning.' She was still looking down at the phone; she felt Jo's eyes on her. She put it away, shoved her bag under her chair. 'I stayed up an extra night.'

'Why?' said Jo doggedly.

'I . . .' Laura faltered. 'I wanted to. Granny's birthday, you know. We – er, I . . . in the evening I . . . '

Hilary was watching Jo with something like impatience. 'Great,' she said. 'Back to the main event though, Jo.' She grabbed her friend's arm and jerked her head in the direction of the house. 'Tell me. Is Jason still single?'

Jo was still watching Laura. Laura looked back at her uneasily, until with horror she saw something like realisation dawn on her friend's face. 'You met someone in Norfolk, didn't you?' she said slowly, in an aghast tone. She shook her head. 'My god. You did.'

'What?' said Hilary. She swivelled her head around. 'You've met someone? Already? Laura!'

'She has, hasn't she,' said Jo, nodding at Hilary. 'Who's the text from?'

'I haven't read it. No one,' said Laura, only half-truthfully.

'Good grief, Laura . . .'

'It's nothing, I promise,' said Laura.

Laura didn't feel surprised or annoyed or patronised or cross, or any of that. No. She ran her finger up and down the stem of her glass and she felt glad, glad that she could justify her behaviour on the previous night to herself. It meant that she knew she had made the right decision, to leave him, leave it all behind, even if at the moment it was still raw. Even if, at the moment, it seemed – had it really only been last night that she was there? With him?

'Who is he this time?' said Jo, shaking her head.

She tried to imagine Jo and Hilary's reactions if she told them the truth, here in the garden. 'You're right. I did meet someone. He's a marquess. He owns a huge stately home. He's a millionaire. He's really handsome. Oh, and I actually think I love him, I'm not just falling for him because I'm me and this is what I always do. You don't believe me? *Really?* Why on *earth* not?'

No, she wouldn't say anything. Even if Jo was looking at her with her big brown eyes, and even if more than anything she wanted to tell her about it, talk to her about what had happened, try and make sense of it all. She'd flirted with being the girl who cried wolf too many times.

Taking a sip of her wine, she shook her head again. 'I swear, honestly,' she said. 'Nothing happened in Norfolk. Very boring. We saw some really interesting windmills, though.'

Hilary cracked a smile, then Jo, and Laura tried to persuade herself that she'd got away with it, even though there was something in her best friend's expression that told her this was not over. Jo blinked rapidly, and stood up with the bowl of crisps. 'Let's have something to eat. How's Simon?' she asked, clutching the bowl – varnished beechwood, part of a set of three, also from the wedding list – to her chest.

'Who knows,' said Laura. 'He didn't make it back in time for the party,' she explained to Hilary.

'Typical,' said Hilary.

'I know,' Laura agreed, but she added dutifully, 'I'm sure there's a good reason.'

'Some Brazilian pole-dancer called Evita,' Hilary said. 'One night only.'

Jo nodded in agreement.

'I know,' Laura repeated. 'Well, we'll see.'

'When's your thingy at work?' asked Jo.

'What thingy?' said Hilary.

'I have to go in and, kind of, er – re-interview for my job,' Laura explained.

'Oh,' said Hilary, looking embarrassed. 'Course. Sorry. When is it?'

'Wednesday,' said Laura. She stood up as well. 'I have to do my homework before, though. That reminds me,' she said, putting her bag over her shoulder. 'I think I'm going to head off.'

'But I was going to make some food,' said Jo, astonished.

'Yeah, Laura, stay,' said Hilary.

'Thanks, thanks,' Laura replied. 'I'm just really tired.' She kissed Hilary. 'Thank you so much for tonight.'

'But –' said Jo. 'I want to talk to you!'

Laura ran her hand over her forehead. 'Sorry, Jo,' she said. 'I'm really sorry. I – I need an early night. I'll call you tomorrow. Can we go over what they might ask me on Wednesday, maybe?'

'Course,' said Jo.

She kissed Laura goodbye, and walked her through the kitchen to the hall.

'Bye Chris!' Laura shouted, but there was no response.

'He's useless,' said Jo. 'Honestly,' but she smiled.

Laura looked at her. 'Thanks again for tonight,' she said. 'It's been great.'

'I'm glad you had a good time in Norfolk,' Jo told her. She shifted from foot to foot. 'Are you sure there isn't something you're not telling me?'

'Absolutely,' said Laura, trying to keep the tremor she felt in her voice from coming out too much.

'Don't want you making the same mistakes as before, that's all,' said Jo. 'I'm allowed to say that, I'm your best friend and I love you,' she added, patting Laura's cheek as if she were her mother.

As Laura walked down the path, she heard Chris shout to Jo from the house, 'What's up with Laura? She gone?'

'Yep,' she heard Jo call back.

'She OK?' Chris said.

'I don't know,' Laura heard her best friend say. 'Not sure.'

Laura walked down the road, back home, back to the flat, down the dusty, quiet Sunday streets. She pulled her phone out of her bag.

Laura, still think last night was a bad joke. All of it. Reply to this. Tell me I'm right. N

She pictured Jo's face leaning over her lovely wooden garden table, asking in tones of dread, 'Who is he this time?'

She saw Hilary's sympathetic expression – which in itself was rarity enough.

She remembered her mother's worried stare that morning as she knocked on her door and told her she was leaving, there was a cab waiting outside, she was sorry.

She thought of Paddy's blissful smile when she'd got back to the flat at lunchtime, to find he'd just waved goodbye to Becky from downstairs, eighteen hours after their date originally commenced.

There were dry leaves on the dry street; they crunched under Laura's feet as she traipsed home, dog-tired. As she thought about it, it gradually became clear to her: that the only way this would work is if she did precisely what she'd never done before. If she just blocked it out. Blocked him out, and tried to forget the whole thing as soon as possible.

Usually, when Laura broke up with someone, she almost enjoyed the post-split wallowing. She embraced the playing sad songs, getting rid of shared possessions, crying to friends over wine. The post-dumping analysis of subsequent texts and emails. The His Friends Think He's Mad conversations – all of that could, at times, be immensely soothing to a hopeless romantic like her, someone who needed to believe that the person she'd just split up with was actually The One, and thus worthy of weeks more lolling around sighing, chewing moodily on biros at work.

She knew this about herself, post-Dan, and this was where it had to stop. She looked down at Nick's message, and thought again about how she would explain to Jo that she'd fallen in love with someone, and how she'd explain who he was. Of course it was ridiculous. Of course she had to get over it, as quickly and painlessly as possible, because they couldn't be together, and that was that.

Ahead of her loomed the mansion block. She pressed *Delete*, and put the phone back in her bag slowly, rummaging for her keys and trying not to think about him, about him typing that text message. The thought of Nick standing there in the stables, his expression bleak and angry, tall and dark but yet so oddly comfortable and easy to be with, made the breath catch in her throat. She couldn't bear to think of him in pain, couldn't bear to think she had upset him. She wanted, more than anything else, for him to be happy, and, well, to be able to get on with doing what he had to do.

She climbed the front steps and let herself in. *That*, she reasoned, as she leant against the door for a moment, was why it was better this way. He was better off without her, without a doubt.

Paddy had left her a note. '*Your mum called! I'm EXHAUSTED! What a weekend! See you tomorrow!*'

CHAPTER THIRTY-FIVE

'So, Gareth, do you have any questions at this point?' asked Rachel, turning towards her colleague politely.

'Hharm . . . yes,' said Gareth, crossing his arms and leaning forward on the table, a biro in one hand. 'Laura. I accept that you were going through a difficult time personally which led to your work suffering as a result. What I have yet to be convinced of is that the same thing won't happen again in the future. What I mean is, I suppose, without prying too far – can you assure us this was a one-off?'

He paused, as if he was trying to gauge how far he could go, and drummed his pen on the table. Next to him, Rachel shifted uncomfortably in her plastic seat.

Laura sat opposite them, ankles crossed neatly under her, hands clasped lightly in her lap. She looked from Rachel to Gareth, and gave a tiny smile, which didn't quite reach her eyes.

'I assure you it was,' she said. 'There's no reason for you to believe me, I quite appreciate that. All I can say is that I look back on my behaviour over the last six months or so, my conduct and my attitude to work, and I'm horrified. I don't recognise myself and I'm appalled that I let it go that far.'

She cleared her throat and said calmly, 'I understand I've let you down. I let myself down too, massively. I'm incredibly sorry.'

Rachel nodded at her, looking mollified, but Gareth said, rather sternly, 'That's great, Laura. But we can't just let it lie there. Can you be more specific?'

Laura didn't get rattled. She just said, 'How so?'

'Well,' Gareth looked around Rachel's tidy, bright office, as if seeking inspiration. 'If you were to get your job back – if – can you tell me what areas of your job you'd need to focus on, if there are any projects you'd like to implement, stones being left unturned, and so forth.'

'Gareth, I don't think it's quite fair to ask her –' Rachel began, but Gareth shot her a warning look.

'Just let her answer, Rachel.' He turned to Laura, and looked at her sternly. 'Laura, you have to convince me this is a job you take seriously, that you're committed to it. Not that it's just something you come into the office and do from nine till five and don't give a moment's thought to outside of work.'

That's rich, coming from you, Mr Pass the Buck never there on Fridays or Mondays because he's in his rich wife's chateau in France most weekends, Laura thought. But Gareth sort of had a point, she could see that. Rachel was looking anxiously at her, and Laura paused for a moment.

They waited, expectantly.

'Well,' Laura said. She breathed in, collecting her thoughts, remembered what she and Jo had talked about on the phone the night before. Don't get rattled, don't.

'Our fundraising scheme isn't working,' she told them calmly. 'I know I haven't been paying enough attention to it. But it's more than that. We need a special initiative. Something new.' Rachel was nodding furiously. Laura took heart, and went on, 'And, I had been thinking we don't do enough to involve local businesses with schools. That we should be acting more as an introduction agency, if you like. Our catchment area of businesses is incredibly diverse. It's big city firms and small local businesses, shops, and so on. And lots of them want to be more involved with the school nearest to them. We get these lawyers or people from the banks or some café going to read with children in these schools, and yet we don't do anything else with that link. It's often just four people in a company of a hundred. We should empower that company a bit more. Get them more involved in the school. And we could get them to donate to that school. Specifically.'

'Right,' said Gareth. He nodded expectantly. 'Give me an example.'

'Well,' said Laura, leaning forward a little. 'We need money, that's one thing. The funding this year's way under –' She hesitated, not wanting to be seen to criticise Gareth's cronies, and went on instead, 'We should find alternative sources for it. And we need to strengthen the link between businesses and local schools. We should appoint a special co-ordinator in each company. Assign them each a school. So it's not just reading they're doing with them. They could have them into the office, show the children what a working environment's like. Do sponsored events, half-marathons and so on, to raise money if they liked. Give them talks about different things. Show and Tell, as it were. They could be governors, if they want.' She was excited, her eyes shone. 'You know as well as I do, a lot of children in inner-city schools, they're never likely to go into a flash law firm, see what it's like. It's out of their realm of experience. Well, we should bring it into their realm of experience. Give them something to aspire to.' Laura collected herself and leant back again, realising she was speaking rather fast.

'Great, great,' said Gareth, smiling at her enthusiasm. 'What do they get out of it, though? The person working at the local high-street bank or the person in the law firm. Why would they want to do it?'

'The call of altruism is a powerful thing,' said Laura wryly. She sat up in her chair. 'If you're some big lawyer, and you go and read with some six-year-old kid, show a class round your company, and then you get to go to their carol service, or their

329

school concert, and these children are coming up to you going "Hello Gareth" or whoever, you know it makes them feel good. Like people who wear those plastic wristbands. All in a good cause.'

'You're right,' said Gareth, with emphasis. 'Most of those people – pathetic. If you're rich, you have no idea what it's like. Big nobs. How the other half lives. Gah, it makes me so angry.' Laura swallowed a smile. Gareth Lunn was the original Red Islington phony who still liked to think of himself as Old Labour through and through.

Gareth stared ruminatively into the distance, lost in a world of thought, and Rachel caught Laura's eye. Laura met her gaze nervously, still unsure of how Rachel felt about her, and was immensely relieved when Rachel gave her a sweet smile, and winked confidently.

'Right,' said Gareth, snapping out of his reverie. 'Time, time. I have to go. Meeting other side of town. With –' he tapped the side of his nose '– contacts.' He stood up, shuffling his notes.

'Ah,' said Rachel politely. 'Sounds interesting, Gareth.'

'Yes, yes,' said Gareth sternly. 'I can't go into it in any detail, I'm afraid. Suffice to say, the Deputy Prime Minister's office has requested we discuss – ah, a few things.'

'Oh, well. You'd better not say any more than that, eh, Gareth?' said Rachel gravely. 'Before you go – can we have a quick word?' She looked significantly from him to Laura, who was still sitting in her chair.

'Yes, yes, of course,' said Gareth, collecting himself. 'Laura, wait outside for a moment, will you? This shouldn't take long.'

Laura stepped out into the main office, wondering what that meant. She felt it had gone well, but who knew? She looked round and leant against the wall, taking in the scene. Nasrin was reading a magazine, as per usual, Shana was on the phone, arranging something, and Tim had just come back from a training session, because he was loading the videos

330

back onto their shelves. He caught sight of Laura, and smiled shyly at her.

It was very strange, being back in this place she knew so well she didn't even think to look for the light switches or the filing cabinet by her desk – it was second nature to her, to march through the day on autopilot. Perhaps that was where she'd gone wrong. She didn't like it, standing here in her smart suit, feeling like a fish out of water in her own office, whilst her colleagues, her friends, looked uncertainly at her, unsure of her status, unsure whether to commiserate, ask questions, ignore her.

It didn't feel like it was nearly three weeks since she'd run out of there. She felt as if she'd been away for months, in a different world.

'Laura?' came a voice from Rachel's office, and Laura stepped back inside.

Rachel and Gareth were looking serious. 'Sit down,' said Gareth.

Laura sat down obediently, and found to her annoyance her legs were shaking. Please, please don't let this be it, she prayed.

'Look, Laura,' said Gareth. 'I'm going to level with you. OK? I was all for letting you go, to be honest.'

'Right,' said Laura, nodding earnestly, feeling she should agree with him, anything to keep him on side.

'But Rachel persuaded me, and I'm really glad I came today. I think you're good, Laura. I think you've got potential. The education authority needs people like you.'

'Thank you,' said Laura, but too soon – Gareth raised his hand in a gesture of impatience.

'But I have to say, you're lucky to have a job. We're giving you the job back, but on a three-month probation period, subject to review at that time.'

Laura looked down at her skirt, and saw there was a creased rosette at its centre, where she realised she'd been clutching the fabric in a frenzied, clammy grip. She smoothed it down and looked up. 'Thank you. Thank you so much,' she began.

Gareth said, 'But you have to be aware, Laura. You have done some damage, and you're going to have to sort it out. Pull something big out of the bag. Rachel tells me you haven't heard about Linley Munroe.'

'What about them?' Laura asked sharply.

'You remember Marcus Sussman?' said Rachel. 'The one Mrs McGregor complained about?'

'Oh, yes,' said Laura, searching through the fog of her Dan-skewed memory of the year so far. 'Goodness, yes.'

'She had a real go at him a few months ago. He's gone mad. Furious. Says it's a two-bit operation. Turns out he's quite important there. Anyway, he's told the co-ordinator to pull the plug on the whole project. It's a real shame, Laura. They were a big firm, they wanted to play a part. They were looking to sponsor a school – perhaps plough some serious money into the local community. And now it's not going to happen.'

'God,' said Laura. 'That's awful. Right.' She scrunched her face up, trying to work out what had happened, how much of a part she had to play in this. They were watching her expectantly, waiting to hear her response, and Laura looked at each of them in turn, trying not to panic. She wasn't ready for this, was she? Ready to go back into this world, ready to take up the reins again, to prove herself, when she felt she had nothing to offer. Perhaps it was all too hard.

And then she stopped herself. Took a deep breath. She put her hand gently on her ribcage and nodded at them. This *was* who she was now. She could do it, she knew she could. She knew what she needed to say.

'Leave it with me,' she said, looking from Rachel to Gareth. 'I'll get them back.' She smiled at them, nervously but candidly. 'I'll get them on board. And the whole company'll be at their Diwali festival in a couple of months' time, you mark my words.'

Even Gareth grinned a little at this. He stood up, as did Laura and Rachel. He held out his hand.

'Well done, Laura. Good luck. Great to have you back.'

Laura shook his hand. She found herself saying, as if she were in *LA Law*, 'It's great to be back, sir.'

Rachel took one of her hands in both of hers, and leant over the desk. She kissed Laura, and whispered, 'If you fuck this up again, I'll kill you.'

Laura laughed, and shook her head.

'See you tomorrow,' said Rachel. 'Bright and early, remember?'

Laura nodded emphatically, slung her bag over her shoulder and walked out behind them. A small part of her wanted to shake her head in annoyance, to ask Rachel: couldn't she tell, couldn't they all tell, how different she was from that Laura person of before, who was late and careless and self-obsessed and useless, that reminding her to be on time was totally pointless? Could she really not see? She was new, different. That Laura had gone, gone forever.

But of course she said nothing, merely smiled gratefully and left, waving to Nasrin and Tim, who both had eyebrows raised and were grinning. She was on the way, back on the way.

CHAPTER THIRTY-SIX

Outside the office, Laura stopped and got her phone out of her bag. There were text messages from Jo and Paddy, both asking her how it went, to call them, good luck, and a message from her mother. 'Hello darling! Just wondering how everything . . . er . . . went today!' as if Laura had been at the circus, not interviewing to be reinstated at work.

She dialled Jo's number, and turned away from Kingsway into the Victorian redbricked backstreets of Holborn, dawdling as she walked and talked, her bag scraping along the dusty road.

'Yes . . . I know! I know. Can't believe it. All good now. Well, I don't know about that. Yes, they have. Tomorrow! I know. Oh, thanks, love, thanks for your help, seriously –'

The battery on her phone was low, so Laura turned it off and threw it back in her bag. She threaded her way through the tiny warren of roads behind the Law Courts tucked behind the roar of central London, past the gown-makers for the judges, the minute little pubs, the rambling small bookshops tucked into courtyards. Eventually she came upon the wide leafy space of Lincoln's Inn Fields, and she headed to the north side of the square, looking for a diminutive figure outside the Soane Museum. She was there.

The Soane Museum was Laura's favourite in London. Mary used to take her and Simon there as children, and they would walk down to Simpson's in the Strand afterwards and have tea. It was the holiday treat of their childhood. Laura loved the higgledy-piggledy nature of the house, the way it had been meticulously assembled by its creator for an atmosphere of chaos and sensation. It was the kind of place you could look around for hours and still find something new to surprise you. When Simon was little he loved the remains of Egyptian, Roman and Greek sculptures in the mausoleum, how creepy and dark it was, even on a summer's day, and he and Laura would snoop cautiously round, terrified of disturbing an ancient ghost.

'Granny!' Laura called as she approached.

'Hello darling,' her grandmother said, lowering her huge sunglasses and pushing her headscarf back a little. She looked like a daintier version of the later Gracie Fields, the Capri Years. 'You're here. How did it go?'

'I got my job back,' said Laura, nodding her head up and down and smiling with pleasure.

Mary clasped her hands together, and brought them above her head. 'Oh, that is marvellous,' she said. 'Just marvellous. Oh my dear, I am so relieved. You must be, too, hm?'

She put her head on one side. 'You could say so,' said Laura grimly. 'Thank god. Seriously.'

'Never mind,' said Mary. 'All that's over now, yes?'

'Yes,' said Laura, slightly apprehensively, and then she added, 'And now I have to find a way of persuading some company that hates us to donate thousands of pounds to their local primary school.'

Mary rolled her eyes at this. 'Golly.'

'Yep,' said Laura. 'But, you know, I'm going to do it.'

'Well, the main thing is the job's yours again,' said Mary. 'It's just wonderful. Tell me exactly what they said. Tell me what you have to do. Let's go inside.' She indicated the steps up to the Soane Museum.

'Right,' said Laura, hesitating.

'I want to see the Hogarths,' said Mary. 'They've been re-hung back in the picture gallery. Last time I was here – oof. In some cramped little back room. My favourites, don't you know. Shall we go?'

'Gran,' said Laura. She stroked her grandmother's arm. 'Do you mind if we don't? It's such a lovely day, after all. Can we go up to Lamb's Conduit Street, get a coffee, sit down instead?'

'You don't want to see the Hogarths?' Mary asked. 'I thought you liked them. Didn't you do that sweet project on them in school about Marriage à la Mode, do you remember, darling? You had to make a costume, and Guy found you that wonderful piece of material for a dress. Where did he find it?'

Laura pretended to hunt in her bag for something, not trusting herself to speak.

'In the attic, wasn't it? Wasn't it from a ballgown of mine, something I had in Cairo?' Mary smiled happily at the memory. 'Yes, I'm sure it was. You were a countess, weren't you? Anyway. Are you sure you don't want to look at them?'

'No, not really,' said Laura, her face still in her bag. Mary looked at her, and then suddenly said,

'How stupid of me. Hogarths. Oh darling, how stupid of me. Let's go and get a drink. Let's talk about it all.'

'I don't –' Laura started to say, but her grandmother put her arm firmly through hers, and said, 'Sshh. We're going to have a little chat.'

They found a pretty little pub in Lamb's Conduit Street, and sat down outside on the cobbles. When Laura appeared back from the bar with two gin and tonics and sat down, Mary said,

'Darling. Cheers. Congratulations. Well-deserved.'

'Well, hardly,' said Laura, taking a sip. 'I wouldn't have had to go through all this if it wasn't my fault in the first place.'

'Maybe not,' said Mary, putting her glass down gently on the wooden slatted table. 'But still, you obviously proved to

336

them just why you're the great girl you are. Well done, darling. Have you rung your mother?'

'Not yet,' said Laura. 'My mobile's dead.'

'Eh? Oh, I see. Well,' said Mary, patting a ring of condensation on the table. 'Do call her later. She's worried about you.'

Laura said nothing.

'We all were, a bit.' Mary looked at her from under her eyelashes.

'It's fine now,' said Laura after a while. 'The job's OK, and all that stuff with Dan – it's over, honestly.'

'I don't mean that,' said Mary. 'I mean that handsome young man who appeared so dramatically at lunch and was clearly so terribly, terribly keen on you.'

Laura sometimes wanted to tell her grandmother to lay off sounding like a film dialogue school run by Noël Coward, and never more so than now. She peered into her glass. 'Don't worry,' she said, sticking her plastic swizzle stick into her slice of lemon. 'It's nothing.'

'Really?' Mary said. 'Hm. It didn't seem like nothing.'

'Holiday fling,' said Laura. She felt that if she said as few words as possible, she might be able to convince her grandmother, she might not have to stop and take a deep breath.

Mary said frankly, 'Well. It doesn't seem like nothing when you come back at ten o'clock at night, go straight to your room and lock the door,' she said, knocking back her drink. 'And when your mother knocks on the door, you tell her you've gone to bed and are very tired. And it doesn't seem like nothing when you leave the next morning at the crack of dawn, without saying goodbye to anyone.'

'I'm sorry, Gran,' she said honestly. 'I really am.'

'Don't apologise, darling,' said Mary. 'You missed your aunt's face at breakfast, and that was something quite special.'

Laura loved it when Mary was rude about her stepdaughter; it was all too rare, considering how rude Annabel was ninety-eight per cent of the time. She grinned. 'Really?'

'Absolutely,' said Mary. 'Your mother did her best, you know. She told Annabel you had severe hay fever and had to go home early before the pollen count rose during the day, and you had to get back for a very important birthday lunch in town.'

Laura thought of her mother chiding her gently for using too many excuses to get out of going to Chartley. 'Seriously?' she laughed.

'Yes, I quite admired her for it. But I fear your aunt will have told everyone she knows her niece is going to be a marchioness anyway.'

Laura looked down at her drink again. Mary pushed her large sunglasses into her hair. 'So Laura. Tell me, darling. Why did you leave so early?'

'I had to,' Laura said quietly, viciously jabbing the lemon slice.

'Why?' Mary asked.

'You wouldn't understand,' said Laura.

'I would,' said Mary. 'More than I think you know.'

'You always find these things easy,' said Laura in a rush. 'You know the right thing to say, Gran, you get it right. I just – screw it up. I wish . . . Oh, never mind.'

'What are you talking about?' said Mary with asperity. 'What exactly happened? What did he do?'

'I can't explain it,' said Laura. She knew it sounded weak. To set out exactly why she had to leave that night would take too long, it was too complicated, it was too bound up in everything to do with the past and the person she had been. She shook her head. 'Gran, it was never going to work, that's all. Trust me.'

Mary didn't say anything for a moment. She pulled her glasses back over her eyes.

'Was it the title? Did all of that rather scare you off?'

'Yes,' said Laura fervently. She wished she could tell her grandmother about it, about all of it. 'We're too different. I – oh, let's not talk about it.'

'But,' said Mary, 'those other days, when you were supposedly dancing off to see that strange lesbian girl in the marshes. What was her name?'

'Naomi,' said Laura patiently. 'She wasn't –'

'Never mind. You were with him then, weren't you?'

Laura nodded.

'Just the two of you?'

She nodded again.

'And, well, it was jolly good then, wasn't it?'

'Yes,' Laura said. She smiled, despite herself. 'It was . . . perfect. When it was just us. Oh Granny . . .' she said, and she felt sunshine flood over her again at the memory of it, until she clenched her fist and said, 'It was perfect. He was perfect. But we realised it was never going to work. In the real world. It's just too hard. He's too different. I'm not what he needs. And he's –' She couldn't finish the sentence.

'That's what you think, is it?' said Mary.

'Yes,' said Laura, looking at her grandmother, hoping for her approval, praying she would understand.

'What rubbish,' said Mary.

Laura stared at her. 'What?' she asked, in shock.

'What total rubbish, Laura. I didn't think you'd ever be like this. Not you,' Mary said, waving her glass at her. 'Darling, you fall in love all the time. You can't run away just because it doesn't quite fit into your exact romantic dream world, you know.'

'I'm not,' said Laura, so surprised she didn't know what to say. 'Gran, don't say that. Please.'

'I mean it,' said Mary. 'Honestly, I'm surprised at you. If you love him, it's worth it. And from the way you were acting about him, it seems to me it is worth it. And,' she laughed. 'good grief. It's not as if he's a warder on a convict ship bound for Australia, or a vivisectionist, or anything. He's a marquess, for god's sake! I know it's a little different from what you're used to, but goodness! He's a multi-millionaire, he's got a

339

beautiful house, and – well, even an idiot like your Uncle Robert could see he was mad about you, darling. So what if you're *a bit different*?' she said, impersonating Laura. 'So what if his family were stuck up? Who cares? If you loved him enough, it wouldn't matter.'

Laura put her hand to her throat and sucked air into her lungs, slowly, calmly. She imagined she was somewhere else, far away, walking by herself down a long road, away from all of this. Clear blue sky over her, completely alone. 'Well,' she said. She looked at her grandmother. 'It *does* matter, it just does, and that's why it's over.'

'Let me say something,' said Mary. 'Just one more thing, and then I shall stop, and we'll finish our drinks and go into Persephone Books and buy something nice to read.'

'Yes,' said Laura.

'I nearly didn't have your grandfather. Guy, I mean. When we met, it was all . . . rather complicated. During the war, and all of that.' She coughed. 'I'll tell you one day. Not now. But you know, don't you, darling, that he was the great love of my life?'

Laura nodded.

There was silence for a moment, nothing to be heard but a bird calling in a young tree behind the pub. Mary said softly, 'If I imagine how life had been without him, Laura – what would have happened, carrying on living for all these years, not knowing what it feels like to be with the one person you love –' She leant forward and put her sunglasses on the table. Her beautiful eyes were bright with tears but Laura thought, with shock, how old she looked all of a sudden. Mary clutched Laura's hand. 'I've never said this to you before. Now I say it to you. Don't run away from it, just because it's difficult. Don't.'

Ever since she was little, Laura knew she had been getting it wrong, because all she'd ever wanted was the perfect romantic hero, the man who would rescue her from everything. She couldn't tell her grandmother why it wasn't that it was difficult,

340

or too hard, or that Nick wasn't right for her. It was that, on that evening, not even a week ago, as she had watched him with his relatives, in that vast ballroom, she had realised that they couldn't be together. She didn't want to make a romantic drama out of it, she didn't want to sigh and mope or scream hysterically to impress others with how awful it all was, even though she felt as if something fundamental, deep within her, had been taken from her. She was simply trying to cope, to get on with her own normal life. Which, she knew, was something he could not be part of.

So she smiled, and squeezed her grandmother's hand. 'Thanks, Gran,' she said. 'I promise you I'm not running away. Not this time. It's not this one.'

Mary gave her a look as if she didn't understand her, and swallowed the rest of her drink. 'I need a present for your aunt,' she said eventually. 'It's her birthday next week. Shall we go?'

'Yes,' said Laura. She felt she should try and qualify it all a bit. 'It's good it happened, you know,' she said. 'I needed to get it out of my system.'

'Get what out of your system?' said Mary, sounding like Lady Bracknell.

'My Mr Darcy Prince Charming complex,' said Laura. 'And now I have.' She faced down her grandmother, who was pushing her bag along her arm. But her grandmother didn't look at her.

'If you think so, darling,' she said.

Later, after she had deposited her grandmother back at Crecy Court and walked on to Baker Street, Laura stopped and looked around her. It was early evening, and there was a freshness in the air that belied the August heat. She didn't want to get into a cramped, airless tube carriage, not on this, her last day of freedom. She crossed the hectic Marylebone Road, walking briskly, and headed into Regent's Park. She would walk home.

It was quiet, pastoral even, in the park. Because of the time of year, many of the commuters who walked through it every day on their way home were on holiday, and the majority of tourists who wandered in didn't manage to penetrate their way into the centre. She walked past the early theatre-goers sitting on the grass outside the Open Air Theatre up into the sloping meadowland that led north. They were drinking wine, chatting easily in the long shadows and the warm sunshine. Laura lifted her face to the sky, feeling the warmth on her skin, trying to relax.

When she thought about Nick, it was as if too many thoughts were all crowding in on themselves, jostling for attention, jumping up and down in her head, and she couldn't fit them all in. When she recalled his face, his smile, the way he made her laugh, how she felt when he touched her, she simply couldn't bear it, and so she thought it best not to think about it at all. Leave it as a summer dream, the last fling of a girl addicted to romance.

Laura reached the edge of the park and crossed over into Primrose Hill. She climbed up the steep incline, puffing, going as fast as she could. She wanted to tire herself out so she slept well that night, didn't toss and turn and worry before her first day back tomorrow. Towards the top of the hill the gradient grew harsher, and Laura stepped off the path and slumped to the ground, panting, resting her hands on her knees and looking at the view across London. Two rather good-looking blokes were cooking burgers on a disposable barbecue nearby, and she looked across, inhaling the sweet smell, and caught their eye and smiled. One of them smiled back. He was wearing jeans, a stripy T-shirt, with tousled hair. He looked – nice. The old Laura would have smiled back, rather naïvely, and then been surprised and flattered when he raised a can, and said, 'Hey. Do you want a beer?'

The new Laura put her head down and walked past them. A child ran past with a dog, a bee droned nearby. Below her the city shimmered, pollution and heat rising from it, the river running through it like a silver ribbon. She felt removed from it all, as if she were watching on a nearby cloud.

Since she'd returned from Norfolk, three days ago, she kept having this sensation, of being shrouded in cotton wool, distant, separate from the emotions and engagements of everyone around her. As if she were watching herself and her life, as if nothing could touch her. She liked it, she liked that layer, it was comforting. She had watched her dad once in the attic helping the builder lay down yellow, fluffy insulating material along the floorboards, and her father had explained it was an extra layer that would keep the cold out. She thought of that now, looking out of the city, feeling as if that insulating layer was part of her. As if it was preventing her from feeling and thinking with that raw emotion. She had locked her heart up somewhere, and no one could get to it. Not Mary, after this, not her mother, not anyone who knew what had happened in Norfolk, and she wasn't going to talk to anyone else about it. She welcomed the feeling without stopping to consider whether it came at its own cost.

Somewhere in a tree nearby a bird called softly. Laura stood up again, and walked the last mile home, rather bedraggled, but enjoying the sensation of physical weariness that assailed her. She told herself she felt a true, honest contentment she hadn't for a long time.

When she reached the row of shops before her flat, Laura went into the mini market and bought some lemons and a fat, frothing bunch of coriander. She was making supper. She picked up a paper and a couple of light-bulbs, which she'd been meaning to buy since Sunday – two bulbs had blown, one in the loo, one for her bedside lamp, and the sense of achievement in finally remembering this purchase was incredibly satisfying. Paddy wouldn't have remembered, she was absolutely sure, and she climbed the steps up to her flat, tired but happy, swinging her string bag beside her, and picking out bits of grass from her top.

When she opened the door, she could hear the stereo was

on, and the sound of low conversation. Paddy said, 'Is that you?' and appeared in the hallway, breathless, his feet bare, a strange expression on his face.

'You OK, loverboy?' said Laura, putting her keys on the table. 'Did you get my message? I turned my phone off. I got the job back! Hey. Did Becky call you?'

'I got your message, yes, yes,' said Paddy, looking agitated. 'I tried calling you – Laura – I thought you wouldn't be back till later . . .'

'Laura?'

A voice came from the sitting room, so familiar to her, yet so alien, but Laura knew exactly who it was. Her hand flew to her mouth and she dropped the string bag. The lemons rolled out, trundled across the floor.

Dan appeared in the doorway. 'Hello, Laura,' he said, and he smiled that same old smile. 'I'm back.'

CHAPTER THIRTY-SEVEN

The only noise for a few seconds afterwards was the sound of one breakaway lemon coasting across the floorboards. Paddy bent down and picked it up.

'Laura, mate,' he said, as if Dan wasn't there. 'I'm really sorry. He turned up about an hour ago, I couldn't get him to go. He wouldn't leave.'

'Right, right,' said Laura, in a detached tone. She looked at Dan, drinking in the sight of him again. It wasn't possible that it was only three weeks since she'd seen him. It seemed like a lifetime. Here he was, this onetime figure of myth, this fantasy, this ideal man, in front of her, every detail of him as familiar to her, as obsessed over by her as any one could ever have been, and she felt nothing, just curiosity. How fickle she was. If anything was proof of that, this was.

'Er – hi. Why are you here?' she said, in what she hoped was a polite voice.

Dan flicked a glance up and down at her, and shifted slightly nervously. Laura followed his gaze, and realised what a sight she must look. She plucked some more grass out of her top, and shook her skirt. There was dried mud on it, from sitting on Primrose Hill. Moving across to the mirror in the hall, she looked at herself and shuddered. She had mascara panda-eyes, and grass in her hair too, and she was definitely *glowing* with the exertion of her walk back. Dan smiled, as he watched her reflection.

'You look fine,' he said quietly. 'You look amazing, actually. Have you been away?'

Laura was suddenly overtaken with the urge to laugh. She nodded, and said again, 'Dan – why are you here?'

Paddy was hovering in the doorway to the kitchen. He said, 'I'll get a beer . . .' and disappeared.

'Come and sit down,' said Dan.

'I will,' said Laura. She couldn't help feeling slightly annoyed that she was being made to feel like a guest in her own home, and then she remembered that about Dan – that he was always in control, that he made himself the focus of the energy in a room. She had loved that, had adored the unexpected feeling of surrender it gave her. Now it made her want to say childishly, 'I'll do the stage directions around here, thank you.'

She sat down on the sofa, Dan next to her, and she stared at him, as if he were an alien. He was tanned, but there were dark circles under his eyes. He cleared his throat, rather awkwardly, and sat up. 'Listen. Laura. This isn't a big deal, and I tried to call you but your phone was off.'

'OK,' she said, looking at him, trying to remind herself of how she'd felt about him. Nothing.

'I felt shitty that I hadn't spoken to you. Since – you know. I came because I just think I should pay you back. For the holiday.'

'What?' said Laura.

'The holiday. You must have had to lose the booking, me dropping out like that.' He said it as if he'd been prevented from going because of a flu bug, rather than because of the termination of their relationship and the appearance on the scene-slash-ultrasound screen of his firstborn by another woman.

She said, 'Oh, well – you know. There's no need.'

'There is,' said Dan. 'Seriously, Laura, I won't take no for an answer.'

Since Laura had had, the day before, a fairly unpleasant conversation with her credit-card company, she had to admit this was welcome news.

'That's really kind of you,' said Laura practically. 'It'd be – helpful, let's say.'

'Of course. I mean it,' said Dan. 'The whole thing. I'll pay.'

'No, no,' said Laura seriously. 'Honestly. Just your half, that'd be great.'

'I want to.' He pulled his chequebook out of the back pocket of his jeans. 'Look, I've been a complete dick.'

'You have,' said Laura, handing him a pen from the table.

Dan laughed. He took the pen and started scribbling. 'I'll make it blank, so you can work out what it cost. The whole thing. Please, Laura. Let me pay for it all. It was my fault, totally my fault.'

Laura said slowly, 'No, it wasn't. It wasn't all your fault, you know.' She patted his hand. 'Just half. That's all. You need the money for the baby, for god's sake. It was me too. I should have – been a bit wiser.' She stared out of the window. 'I've learnt my lesson.'

Things are different now, she wanted to say. It'll be a cold day in hell before I lose my heart to you again or get hurt by you again. Or someone like you. And by the way, your girlfriend's a complete psycho.

She looked at him, knowing he hadn't really heard what she'd said anyway. He signed the cheque with a flourish, tore it off and gave it to her.

'Here,' he said. 'And let's – let's be friends, shall we?'

'Right,' said Laura, taking the cheque. 'So,' she continued, taking a deep breath. 'How's Amy doing? How's she feeling?' she asked politely, wanting to sound as if they were fellow parents outside the school gates, not people who a month ago were in the throes of a torrid affair.

Dan shifted on the sofa. He said blankly, 'She's fine, thanks. Fine. Yes – Miami was, er, great, thanks. We had – a great time.'

347

'Really?' said Laura.

'Yeah,' said Dan. 'We – don't know if you heard? We had to come home a few days early. Amy's not feeling so good, you know.'

'Oh, I'm sure,' said Laura.

Dan said in a rush, 'It's an amazing place, South Beach. The Art Deco hotels, wow. They're wonderful.' Laura nodded politely. 'The weather was great, too – we were lucky apparently. And the food's incredible.' His voice rose a little. 'And loads and loads of designer shops and boutiques. So Amy was delirious, as you can imagine. God, I'm dreading the next credit-card bill. I kept saying to her, what's the fucking point when you won't be able to *wear* any of this stuff for the next six months. But apparently that's the wrong thing to say. You know how touchy she is.'

'Yes,' said Laura. Several responses to this rose to her lips: Yes, I know how touchy she is, you were always going on about it, and anyway, she's pregnant, give her a break. Or, yes, I know she's an acquisitive little cow, but you're the one who wouldn't leave her, mate. Or, do you actually think it's appropriate to blithely be having this conversation with me?

But she said nothing, and took his arm gently, and, getting up, steered him towards the door. 'Thanks so much for coming round, Dan. And thanks for this –' She waved the cheque, then looked at him, and smiled gently. 'You really didn't have to. I –'

'No sweat,' said Dan. 'It's the least I can do.' He bent down, kissed her on the cheek, and she felt nothing, it was strange. Or strange that it wasn't strange.

'So – I'll see you soon,' he said.

'Well,' said Laura. 'Probably not, I expect.'

'You're right,' said Dan, nodding vigorously. 'Yep. Uhm – where are we, then?'

'You and me?' said Laura. 'We're – we're nowhere, Dan.'

'I know,' said Dan. 'I just – well. I'm sorry, that's all.' She

348

inclined her head; he looked at her curiously. 'You OK?' he asked.

'I'm fine,' said Laura. 'Quite tired, I've had a long day.'

'You – you're different,' said Dan. 'You seem different.'

He was standing in the doorway, leaning against it with that old air of confidence she used to love so much. 'Am I?' she asked him. 'I don't think so.'

'More – grown-up,' said Dan, nodding. He looked at her soulfully. 'Oh, Laura.'

'More – over you, actually,' said Laura. 'That's it. I promise.' She patted him on the shoulder. 'See you soon. Bye then.'

Dan looked slightly startled, and then he smiled. 'Yeah. Right. Bye, Laura.'

'Bye, Dan.' She nodded her head.

'Well.' He shoved his hands n his pockets. 'So – good – good luck with everything.'

Amazing, thought Laura, as she closed the door quietly behind him and leant against it, her hands flat against the cool, painted wood. It was more than she'd expected of him. But that was Dan, she thought. It didn't occur to him that it was at all weird for him to be chatting merrily away, signing away cheques for holidays, pressing himself just *slightly* too long against her as he said goodbye. That he couldn't see that he hadn't been in love with Laura at all; he just didn't love his own girlfriend and was looking for some kind of way out, or some penance to pay for not wanting to be with her. Laura knew clearly now that it wasn't that he should have been with her, Laura. No, he just should not be with Amy, and that was all there was to it. She didn't feel relieved, or justified, or sorry for either of them. She didn't know what she felt, other than a curious blankness about it all.

There was a strange acidic smell coming down the hallway, and in the kitchen Paddy was hopping around in an agitated fashion, cutting up the coriander. He'd cut it with such nervous energy that it was in tiny, tiny slivers, only millimetres long.

'Ah,' he said as he saw Laura watching him from the doorway. 'Hello, old girl. Are you – are you OK? I started on the supper.'

'I'm fine,' said Laura. 'Absolutely fine. He was sweet, actually.' She smiled.

'Oh god,' said Paddy to himself.

'No, no,' Laura hastened to reassure him. 'Nothing like that, I promise. He wanted to pay for his half of the money I lost. Cancelling our holiday.'

Even saying 'our', like there ever had been 'our' as in her and Dan, sounded weird. She walked over and looked into the pan, glad to change the subject.

'Jesus. What's that?'

Paddy looked over her shoulder into the pan. He said with pride, 'I'm frying the lemons. In butter.'

'Fried lemons?' said Laura. 'Why the hell are you frying lemons?'

'Don't worry,' said Paddy reassuringly. 'I'm adding the coriander in a minute.'

'Er – right,' said Laura. 'What else are we having with them, then?'

'I thought –' Paddy paused, he clearly hadn't thought at all. 'I thought, a bit of bread.'

'Fried lemons, some small chopped-up bits of coriander, and a bit of bread,' said Laura. 'Wow, sounds really great.' She reached out to the shelf in front of her and randomly plucked a jar off it. 'How about we add some honey?'

'I don't think so,' said Paddy kindly. 'I think it'd ruin the flavour.'

'Wine,' said Laura decidedly. 'I'll open some wine. Er – Paddy, there's some chicken in the fridge. How about you cut that up small and add it to the lemons? With some garlic, a bit more butter and stuff.' Paddy was looking hurt, so she added hastily, 'The chicken has to be eaten today, you'd be doing me a real favour.'

'Sure, then,' said Paddy, mollified. Laura threw some butter and garlic into the pan, added the chicken, then opened the wine and collected the glasses. It was still light outside. As Paddy cooked the chicken, sloshing in some wine, and found some crusty bread on the side, Laura set the table. She went to the window and threw it open, breathing in the evening air. Across the treetops, streets, houses, more houses, cars, big roads, shops. She looked north, to the horizon.

Somewhere, in a huge house a hundred miles away, was Nick. Sitting there, eating supper by himself in an empty room, a great rattling house stuffed with treasures and relics of the past. But nothing that was actually *his*, his own personal stuff, until he climbed those long winding stairs up to his room at the top of the house, a room with a radio, his own clothes, some paperbacks, that bed – and another, very different view out of the window over the treetops. Was he on his own? Was anyone with him? Did he have someone to talk to, like Charles? She stared out of the window, willing herself to see more, if only for a second, before the picture left her mind.

'Ready?' came Paddy's voice behind her. Laura spun around.

'Yep,' she said.

Paddy looked at her. 'Sit down, and pour that wine,' he said. 'You've had a lucky escape.' She looked confused, so he said, 'Dan.'

'Oh,' said Laura. 'God, yes. You know, it's fine.'

'I'm sure,' said Paddy cheerfully over her plate. He spooned out some chicken and lemon onto the salad he had thrown together and handed her some bread. 'The madness has lifted, Laura. I can tell.'

She raised her glass. 'Cheers, Pads.'

'I mean it,' he said. 'You're different since you came back from Norfolk. Bit of a fresh start, eh?'

'Oh,' said Laura. 'Yes, I'm sure. Thanks a lot.'

'Cheers,' said Paddy.

They clinked glasses.

'Tell me what's happening with Becky,' said Laura, switching tack. 'So, she hasn't replied to any of your texts yet?'

'Right,' said Paddy.

'Have you seen her on the stairs or anything?'

'Noo,' said Paddy. 'Not since she was coming outta my place early on Sunday morning. Oohoo.'

'You said she fell asleep on the sofa and nothing happened,' Laura reminded him.

'Er,' said Paddy, deflated. 'Er, yeah.'

'So,' said Laura encouragingly. 'What have you done about it?'

'I've taken action,' said Paddy, looking pleased.

'Oh no,' Laura murmured.

'I thought, OK, perhaps she didn't get any of the texts. Her phone *was* a bit dodgy on Saturday, she said. Well, I think she said. So I'm on my way back from school today, and I think, I'll go round to where she works. You know that little gift shop in West Hampstead?'

'Oh god,' said Laura.

'Yes, absolutely,' Paddy agreed, unheeding. 'I get there, it's about six-ish. I can see her clearing up and stuff. And when she comes out I say, "Hi Becky, how are you, OK?" And – god, I don't understand girls, I really don't.'

'Why?' said Laura.

'She pretends she hasn't seen me, and runs back into the shop! And I follow her and say, "Hey, look, I only wanted to make sure you got my text messages. And by the way, do you want to go out next week?" And she said she was really busy, but she'd think about it and let me know. I feel confident, though. Strangely confident.'

'How come?' Laura asked, trying not to grin.

'Er . . .' said Paddy. 'Not sure, really.'

'So . . .' Laura said after a pause. 'When are you seeing her again then?'

They both cracked up, and then Paddy said, 'Seriously, Laura.

I'm really proud of you. Norfolk did you the power of good. You're so much better off without him, you know. I'm not just saying that. It's the truth. And –' he looked slightly embarrassed. 'I don't want to sound pervy, but you look amazing at the moment.'

'Really?' said Laura. 'I must have lost weight during my period of pigeon-flying-into-my-room madness.'

'Hm,' said Paddy, and she knew he was thinking, Yeah, but you ate crisps and chocolate for a week, how is that possible? 'Whatever it is, you look – er, very nice. Really well. And you know, you're better now. Time for a fresh start, eh?'

'Yep,' said Laura. 'Fresh start.'

'Got your eye on anyone then?' Paddy asked, helping himself to the chicken and avoiding her gaze.

It was as if someone had asked her if she was an ironing board, or if she liked drinking raw meths – a completely outlandish, freakish question. 'God no,' Laura said. 'Me?'

'Yes, you!' Paddy said, chuckling. 'Don't look so amazed! You've always got someone you're mad about, haven't you? Come on, Loz. Who is it?'

It was so alien, that idea. So completely wrong and strange that she didn't know how to answer. Can't you see, she wanted to say to Paddy, just as she had with Rachel earlier that day. Can't you see I've changed, that everything's different. Of course you can't and you don't know why. But it has. It was an uncomfortable thought.

'No one, honestly,' she said after a bit. She pulled the bottle towards her.

Paddy waved his wine glass at her and nodded, in an ancient-sage-like way. 'You should get back out there, Laura. Get over him, get under someone else, you know.'

Laura flared her nostrils. 'I'm not sure.'

'My god, woman, who are you? Woah.'

Laura opened her mouth to say, 'Leave it', but then Paddy said sweetly, 'You're the best, Loz, so don't leave it too long before you fall in love again, OK?'

353

She said nothing, but smiled. Paddy raised his glass. 'All better now. To fresh starts, eh?'

'Fresh starts,' Laura echoed, knowing he was right.

Paddy was right, it *was* a fresh start. And she wasn't going to screw it up again. She was in work an hour early the next day.

'It's lovely to see you again,' said Rachel, who was waiting for her as she walked through the door. She handed her a bunch of tulips.

'Oh my goodness,' said Laura. 'That's so sweet of you.' She kissed her. 'Thank you, Rachel.' She bent down, put her bag on the floor, and switched the computer on.

Shana waved at her across the large table they shared. She was eating a doughnut, and after a minute she said, 'You OK?'

'Fine, you?'

'Yeah. Good to see you again, Laura.'

'Thanks.'

The phone rang, and Shana grinned at her and picked it up.

'Come into my office when you've sorted yourself out,' said Rachel. 'We'll talk about what you're going to be working on next. This major fundraising drive's about to take off, and I want you to work on it.'

'Thanks,' said Laura. She tapped Rachel's arm as she turned to leave. 'I mean it. Thanks.'

'Don't let me down,' said Rachel quietly. 'That's all I ask, Laura. Show me you've turned over a new leaf.'

'Trust me,' Laura said. 'I mean it – I have.'

And she had. For the next month, work became her obsession. She loved throwing herself into it, proving to Rachel that she'd changed. And she started walking everywhere. There were fresh flowers in the flat each week, and Laura's room was always tidy, her clothes sorted and hanging neatly, freshly ironed. She remembered birthdays, she coached Paddy on how not to stalk Becky, and cooked a meal for them (that he could pass off as

354

his own), she organised a picnic for Hilary to celebrate her promotion at the museum where she worked, and helped Jo paint her bathroom whilst Chris was away. She couldn't undo the way she'd behaved in the past, she knew that, but there was a small grain of comfort from realising as she looked around at her friends that she was back in her old life in some small way.

For the short remainder of the summer, Laura felt the zeal of someone on New Year's Day, trying to suppress their deep depression about it being cold and dark and having to go back to work by distracting themselves with a new keep-fit regime, some bulbs in a window box, learning to cook, taking tap lessons – anything rather than give in to it. This was her life, she knew it and recognised it for what it was. At last she felt she was being a proactive, organised, serene person. The feeling of emotional isolation, of being able to look back at her life, her mistakes, and feel nothing, or virtually nothing, continued. And if she occasionally had to bite her lip when an involuntary memory of those brief few days flew back to her with a sharp stab of pain – when she remembered walking down a leafy country lane, sitting on the beach at night-time, creeping through the Great Hall, lying quietly holding hands with him in bed, looking at him, or his face when she said she was leaving – well, she simply told herself to add it to the box, the box of memories of the past.

CHAPTER THIRTY-EIGHT

Early in September came the return of the prodigal son. Simon Foster arrived home from Peru, where he had learnt to acclimatise to altitude, to speak Quechuan, grown an impressive beard, and bought or made a selection of brightly coloured, simply woven garments that hung, Guevara-like, about his person. What does someone, having acquired all these skills and possessions, do with such a trove? Move back in with their parents in Harrow, of course. He arrived back on a damp Saturday afternoon, and Angela phoned, delirious with excitement, to ask Laura – and Paddy too, of course – round for Sunday lunch.

Though she couldn't wait to see her brother again, Laura was reluctant about going to her parents'. She hadn't seen them since she got back from Norfolk. It wasn't that she was avoiding them, it was more that she . . . she'd been busy. Her mother called fairly often, wanting to 'chat', and Laura always managed to steer her off the subject. She felt awful, but she just couldn't talk about it and she knew Angela would never ask directly.

Angela wasn't the only one Laura was trying to avoid, little though she liked to admit it. There was also Mary. She felt guilty about her, too; she hadn't seen her for weeks either. But

Laura pushed that to the back of her mind, along with everything else. The trouble was, she was working very hard these days, and was not in a love-lorn frame of mind, she told herself. It was all very well going round to Mary's and listening whilst her grandmother told her about the time she and Guy stayed in a palazzo in Venice and met Nancy Mitford, or how they had visited a maharajah in Jaipur and been woken by the sound of fighting tigers. She just didn't have the time now. A voice in her head was telling her that was rubbish, that she could talk to Mary about anything, always had done. But Laura consoled herself with the thought she'd call her. Soon.

The third member of the trilogy Laura was holding at arm's length was Jo, and now Jo had gone on her trip of a lifetime with Chris to Australia (Paddy and Laura referred to it as their Trip Before They Get Pregnant). It was a fortnight since they'd left, and Laura felt guilty about Jo too, but a slight sense of relief she was out of the country for a while, because Jo knew something was up, and Laura knew Jo knew something was up, and this gave her some breathing space. She just wanted control, she wanted to keep a lid on it all. Maybe that way it would just go away. Jo, Mary, her mother – she loved them all, but whilst they were capable of concern, she wanted to keep them at bay. Just for a while.

'I know what it'll be like,' said Laura gloomily as she and Paddy walked up Heathcote Road towards her parents' house. 'Me sitting there like a spare part, or tidying away, being a good daughter, whilst Mum has kittens because Simon's back and you're there too.'

'Well, so she should,' said Paddy reasonably, though slightly smugly. He was secure in his knowledge of Angela Foster's deep and lasting affection for her children's oldest friend. 'He's been away for nearly six months now, Laura. Remember those two weeks when you didn't hear from him? She thought he was dead.'

'He wasn't dead!' Laura exclaimed, impatiently.

'Well, obviously,' said Paddy.

'You know what I mean! He just couldn't be frigging bothered to drop his own parents an email saying, *Hello, I'm still alive!* He's a lazy bastard!'

'You don't know that,' said Paddy. 'Your poor mum.' He coughed self-consciously and increased his stride, looking bashfully down at the bunch of tulips he was clutching in his hand.

'You are such a suck,' said Laura, reverting to the behaviour of her teenage years. She strode ahead, staring crossly at the Wilsons' new conservatory over the road (a source of great consternation to her mother). Simon brought out the childish side in her, and she knew it.

'Laura! Hello, dear!' cried her mother, flinging open the door. 'And James! So wonderful that you could come, we're all so pleased. Darling,' she said, hugging her daughter. 'How *are* you?' She phrased the question delicately.

'Great, thanks,' said Laura, thrusting a bottle of wine at her. She gave her a kiss. 'Where is he, then?'

Simon appeared in the doorway to the kitchen, and Laura had to stop herself from running towards him. She smiled. 'All right?'

'Yeah,' said Simon, leaning against the cellar door. 'You all right, sis?'

'Yeah,' said Laura, coming forward and giving him a big hug. 'S'nice to see you.'

'You too.' Simon squeezed her tight, and punched her on the arm.

Laura kissed him. 'Where's Dad? I'll go and say hi. Back in a min.'

'Out the back.' Simon was hugging Paddy, patting him on the back. 'Hey, man.'

Laura wandered into the kitchen, which was, as always, immaculate. The white surfaces spotless, the plants in little tiled bowls on the windowsill, the childish nursery drawings by her and Simon in clip-frames. Their last dog Tugie's lead, folded up and hung under the cupboard. The National Trust calendar by the fridge, annotated neatly by both George and Angela. She looked at it. September had a picture of a beautiful garden in a stately home in Shropshire. She grimaced.

'SIMON BACK!' it said on the Friday, covered with stars and underlined. Then, the following weekend, '*The Real Inspector Hound*, Harrow Am Dram Soc, 7.30 p.m.' 'Dentist, 1 p.m.'

From the door out to the little conservatory at the back George Foster emerged, wearing his gardening gloves. He looked up and saw his daughter, and smiled. 'Oh, hello love,' he said. 'How are you?'

'Fine, Dad,' Laura replied, watching him. He took his gloves off gingerly, hung them on the pot by the conservatory door, then carefully wiped his weekend loafers on the doormat, and shook out his dark blue corduroy trousers.

'All OK with you, love?' he asked.

Laura wondered what her poor dad must make of her over the past couple of months, lurching from one crisis to another. She nodded emphatically. 'Yeah. Really good. Thanks, Dad.'

'Good, good, ha-ha, good,' said George, visibly relieved he didn't have to say anything more. He rubbed his hands together. 'Well, hello James,' he said, advancing into the room with the jerky, slightly adolescent motion that he and only he had, and he shook Paddy's hand, put his arm briefly around his daughter's shoulders.

'I'll get the drinks,' he said, smiling with pleasure as he went over to the fridge. 'Nice to have everyone here, isn't it?'

Laura nodded happily, and sat on the seat watching her dad take a new lemon from the bowl.

'Slice this for me, love, will you?' he asked.

In the corridor, Simon was saying earnestly to a rather scared-looking Paddy, 'I *am* well, mate. Peru – it changed my life. I can't wait to tell you all about it, you know.'

'Lunch in five minutes, darling,' her mother said, bustling into the kitchen. 'What's this! All this mess.' She stared at the lemon Laura had taken from the bowl for her drink. 'Remember to use the small paring knife if you're cutting lemons, Laura. And be careful.'

Laura growled internally. No, she thought. I won't be careful, I will deliberately slice my thumb off with the vegetable knife, just to annoy you. She glanced at her watch. 12.50 p.m.

'How's work, darling?' said her mother.

'Fine, Mum. Great, actually.'

'Oh . . .' said Angela, pleased. 'That's wonderful. I'm so glad. And you – you're . . .' She waved the knife in the air vaguely, and Laura had to duck to avoid her. 'About that chap, you know. The *marquess* – I haven't liked to ask, but . . .'

'Oh, it's absolutely fine,' said Laura. 'Good grief, I've totally forgotten about it, Mum, really.'

'Your granny said that –' Angela began.

'Granny likes to gossip,' Laura improvised wildly. Her mother looked hurt. 'Sorry, Mum, but I promise you, I'm fine.'

Angela didn't say anything. She just looked rather quashed. 'Oh love. I know you like talking to Granny about it, but you know I'm here if you ever want –' she began timidly.

'Yes, of course,' said Laura, feeling guilty, and that guilt making her even angrier. 'Come on, Mum, let's go.' She grabbed the glass and went back into the sitting room, Angela following slowly behind her. As they entered, her brother looked up.

'Now she's here. Hurrah. My favourite sister. And my darling Mum. I just want to make a toast. To being back home again, with all of you.' He raised his glass in one hand, and took his mother's hand in the other. 'I've felt very far away from here the last few months, you know. But this is where I come from. It's home. And it's just great to be here. Cheers. Thanks, Mum and Dad. Cheers.'

'My boy and girl, under one roof,' Angela said, with a catch in her throat. 'Oh, it's so nice.' She caught sight of Paddy, looking rather left out. 'Oh, James. And you too.'

'Chocolate, James? Go on,' said Angela. She waved a plate under Paddy's chin, so it loomed in his face and his eyes squinted to focus.

'Oh, thank you, Angela,' said Paddy.

Angela smiled and spun brightly round. 'Well,' she said, rubbing her hands. 'Everyone having a good time? You all right, Simon, dear?'

'Yes, Mum,' said Simon patiently, for the fourth time. 'I'm fine. Sit down.'

Looking at him, Laura realised Simon was indeed transformed. He didn't look like her younger brother. He looked huge, tall, imposing. It was as if Aragorn had suddenly turned up in the lounge in Harrow and was drinking the remains of a glass of Waitrose best pinot noir on the sofa next to Laura and George after a nice lunch of roast chicken. The conversation over lunch had been chit-chat, Simon telling them a few stories here and there, but never really going into detail. However, Laura could feel he was gearing up for it, for something.

'So!' said George.

'We want to hear *all* about it!' said Angela.

'Yes,' said Paddy, more noncommittally.

'So,' Laura said weakly. 'Tell us all about it then . . .'

She loved her brother and she really did want to know how he'd got on, but Laura was one of many who was bored rigid by tales of other people's holidays, especially of the six-months-travelling variety. She could ooh and ahh over a beautifully presented album of photos of Ayers Rock with the best of them, but sometimes she did slightly want to put her head in a cushion and scream loudly, and say, Why the hell couldn't you just pick ten of the best and show them to me? I wasn't on the holiday, why do I care who else was on your very long train journey through India? And don't try to impress me with pictures of the remote beauty of Koh Samui and the completely weird, freakish coincidence that you bumped into someone you were at university with there. It is an absolute fact that you are more likely to bump into someone you know on some beach in Thailand or in some bar in Sydney or in some olive-oil shop in Tuscany than in Birmingham city centre on a Tuesday morning in February. So don't try and make out you're some crazy pioneer, I really don't care. She sank further into the sofa cushions, knowing she was being mean.

'Try and contain your indifference a bit more successfully, sis,' Simon said. He gazed around the room, and Laura watched him taking in the Fifties majolica fireplace, the symmetrical bookshelves with framed photos of Simon and Laura getting their degrees, George's mother, who had died a few years before, the bay window, the sun shining weakly in. Simon leant back against the sofa, and sighed a deep sigh of pleasure.

'Well, it was great,' he said. 'But it's really nice to be back now, I must say. I really wanted to see you all. I've got a lot to tell you.'

'Oh great,' Laura said. 'Highlights?'

Paddy nudged her. Simon smiled. 'Highlights. OK. Being attacked by a wolf. Nearly getting shot during a drugs raid. Um – the mountains early in the morning. And dancing round a campfire with the girl of my dreams.'

'Oh!' said Angela. 'How lovely!'

'Eh?' said Paddy. 'Who's that, mate?' He looked curious.

'Jorgia,' Simon said, an expression of great serenity creeping across his tanned face. He turned to his parents and opened his arms wide. 'I'm in love, Mum and Dad. She's the most wonderful girl and I can't wait to bring her home to meet you.'

'Are you being serious?' said Angela, whipping her head round. 'Who is she, Simon, darling?'

'Oh Mum,' said Simon, taking his mother's hand again. 'She's just amazing. She's from a tiny village, high up in the mountains, near Machu Picchu. She – she – well, I want you to meet her.'

'Right!' said Angela, smiling slightly mechanically. 'My goodness. Ha! She sounds wonderful.' She winked significantly at her husband. 'Doesn't she, George?'

'Er . . .' said George, twirling his wine glass round in his hand. 'Great. Really great. So, what does she do?'

'She lives with her parents at the moment,' Simon said, smiling broadly at them. 'Her father's a doctor, in the village! Simeon Questodora. Jorgia is his only daughter, he has two sons. He's a good man, a wise man. He has welcomed me into their family.' Simon nodded, half-bowing, as if Dr Questodora might be watching him via secret camera in the vase of dried flowers on the mantelpiece. 'Anyway,' he went on. 'I'm going back there, Mum and Dad. I want to live there.' He coughed as his parents gawped at him. 'I want to marry her. Not now – I know it's all very sudden. I want to see if we can have a future together, the two of us, and how we can make it work.'

'Eh?' said Paddy.

'It may not work,' said Simon. 'I'm fully aware of that.' He cleared his throat again and said quietly, 'But I've never been happier. You know me. I didn't used to believe in fairytales. Well, now I do.'

Sitting on the sofa, Laura could barely believe her ears. Yes, of course this was happy news, but Simon was the man who shagged identical twins at university (Paddy had told her this), who had had an affair with his boss for a year and managed not to get fired but promoted. Simon was kind, he was charming, always honest – but he had never wanted a serious relationship. This was incredible!

Besides which, even setting aside Simon's historic aversion to falling in love, surely, she thought, if you claim you're about to marry some random Peruvian villager you've known for three minutes, you must have gone mad. You shouldn't be talking about it in a mature, balanced way. She could see,

363

too, that this was affecting their parents deeply, and that instead of saying, My God, have you gone Completely Mad, they were instead likely to – yes, there it was . . .

'Congratulations, son,' said George, striding across the room, clutching Simon's hand. 'That sounds – er, wonderful.'

'Oh Simon,' said Angela, tears in her eyes. 'You're sure? Well, that's just, just lovely.'

'I am sure,' said Simon, standing up and putting his arm round his mother, as Laura watched in amazement, scowling at both of them. 'I'm sure she's the one for me. I love her. But we have to think about what to do next. Jorgia – she –' he looked down, and blushed, then smiled shyly at them. Laura felt slightly nauseous. 'She wants to come over to meet you all, as soon as possible, but she is very proud. She won't let me pay. She is saving up herself for the flight.'

'How long will that take?' said Laura. Paddy gave her a sharp look.

'A few months at least. She is very proud, like her father, like her family. So – until then –' he ground to a halt, rather uncertainly '– I'll be here, if that's OK. You see, you see – I've handed in my notice at the charity.'

'Oh,' said Angela and George together. Angela reached out and clutched the enamel box that stood on the mantelpiece for support. 'That's great, dear,' she said faintly, and looked at her husband.

'They wanted me to go to India next month, and I can't if she's coming here. I had to say no, and when I did, well . . .' He held up his hands rather helplessly. 'I know it's a bit reckless – but it just seemed like the only thing to do. I couldn't let her get away, you know.'

Reckless? Laura wanted to shout. I should say so! Jeez Louise, the world has gone mad.

Her father said, 'Well. You had worked there for five years, it was probably time for a change, eh?'

'I'm pleased for you,' said Paddy, nodding wildly.

364

'Yes,' said Angela. 'Well! Travel really does broaden the mind, doesn't it!'

'So, Laura, what do you think?' Simon said, coming up to her and putting his hands on her shoulders.

Good grief, thought Laura. The world has gone mad. Here am I being a sensible person, and what reward do I get? Whereas Simon has clearly got some brain disease, causing him to lose all grip on reality. No job! No home? A girlfriend halfway up a mountain on the other side of the world? And this is good news??

Simon was looking at her expectantly, and she found it hard to breathe all of a sudden, though she couldn't have said why. And she felt a bit sick. Well, she reasoned, it was a lot to take in, for anyone. She gripped his wrists with her hands, and said, 'It's fantastic, Simon. Great. I just hope – you know, it's a big step.'

'I know, I know,' said Simon, nodding seriously, as if she'd made a great point, and Angela and George echoed him. 'That's why Jorgia and I don't want to take it further until we're completely sure. That's why I have to be here for a while. But I relish that. Dad, I must be able to help you round the house with some things, what can I do? There's a great tradition in Peru. The son waits for instructions from his father, who gives him orders, and it is considered a great honour for the son to carry those instructions out. A test of character.'

'Wow,' said George simply, bowled over.

'Oh, that's lovely,' said Angela, deeply moved.

'Can't wait to meet her,' said Paddy gruffly.

'Being in love,' said Simon. 'I'm a changed man. It's just wonderful. Jorgia is my sunshine. She's my moonlight.'

'Good times, boogie, boogie,' said Laura, cracking up on the sofa. After thirty seconds and no reaction, she said, 'You know, like the song.'

The others turned to look slowly at her, as if she'd just broken a puppy's leg.

*　　*　　*

'For fuck's sake!' Laura ranted to Paddy, when they were safely on the tube back. 'He's gone completely *mad*, and I'm the one they think's the bad guy! Jesus!'

Paddy said nothing. He looked up at the tube map.

'Seriously!' said Laura, warming to her theme. 'The hypocrisy! Bloody Simon! He misses Gran's birthday, he's lost his job, he waltzes in after months away and announces he's shacked up with some Peruvian gypsy from the mountains, and Mum and Dad! God! They just smile and say wow, that's great!'

'But it *is* great, isn't it?' said Paddy.

'No!' cried Laura. 'Well, yes,' she said, amending herself hurriedly. 'Of course, it's fine, whatever. But really, has he lost his *mind*! Have they? Why don't they care? It's Mum and Dad! They live in Harrow! Dad drives a Rover 45! They –'

'I think it's really brave of him,' said Paddy, noncommittally. Laura turned to him, eagerly sensing a potential ally.

'You agree, don't you?' she said. 'That it's mad. He can't be in love with her, can he?'

Paddy looked at her, then turned away slowly. He pointed at a TV guide littering the floor of the tube. 'Look, cool. *The Truth About Cats and Dogs* is on tonight. Good-o. I love that film. Perfect Sunday-night TV.'

Laura's attention was momentarily diverted. *The Truth About Cats and Dogs* had been one of her favourite films. Then she said, 'It's OK. It's not actually that good. Next stop us, Paddy.' She slung her bag over her shoulder.

'It's nice,' said Paddy. 'I love Janeane Garofalo.'

'It's crap. That whole Janeane Garofalo thing – why's she so stupid, why doesn't she just get over Ben Chaplin and his big dog and stop mooning around? And why does she bother being friends with Uma Thurman? She's never going to get any attention, being friends with someone who looks like that. It's stupid.'

'It's great,' Paddy insisted. 'You're wrong.'

'I'm not,' said Laura, getting off the train. 'It is, it's stupid. It's a waste of time, watching that kind of thing. Trust me.'

They were walking down the tube platform towards the stairs, when Paddy stopped. He stamped his foot on the floor and said, 'Oh, just shut up, will you?'

Laura gaped at him. 'What?'

'Yes!' Paddy said, and there was real disdain in his voice; disdain mixed with anger. 'Just shut up! What's happened to you, Laura! I know you're on this No Romance kick, ever since Dan, and I know you hate men, and I know all of a sudden your job's the most important thing to you since – since sliced bread, but god! Sometimes –' He trailed off.

Laura was completely bewildered. 'Sometimes what?' she said, trying to make sense of what Paddy was talking about. She'd never seen him quite this cross.

'You're – you're just so – so weird about everything these days!' Paddy said, coming towards her. Other people on the platform were walking past, looking at them. Laura avoided their gaze. Tried to pretend she wasn't there. 'God,' he said. 'You've been like this ever since you came back from Norfolk.'

'What do you mean?' said Laura, her heart hammering in her chest.

'Well!' Paddy threw his hands in the air. 'I thought it did you good, but you've changed, Laura, you're just . . .' He shook his head, bewildered. 'You sit there in front of the TV and you don't concentrate, you're in a world of your own. You work all the time. You don't go out any more. You're really negative about everything, you don't want to do anything. You won't look at another bloke, every time Jo or I mention some guy you might like, you look as if we've just thrown up over you.' Paddy twitched his nose and scratched it. 'Look, mate. I know Dan hurt you, but what did he do to make you this fucked up about everything?' he said sadly. 'Here's your brother, OK, yeah, sure, he's gone a bit mad, and he thinks he's in love with some girl he met travelling. But you're his sister! Just support him, OK? Don't be snide, don't think you know it all. You don't.'

'I know I don't,' Laura whispered. 'I know.'

367

Paddy looked horrified. 'Listen, I didn't mean –'

Laura pulled away from him and turned towards the stairs. She ran up them two at a time, Paddy following her. 'It's fine,' she said as she reached the top. 'You're completely right, I'm sure.' She got out her Oyster card and went through the barrier, walking as fast as possible. She was appalled, she hated Paddy for what he'd said, but a tiny part of her knew he was right. She just couldn't tell him why he was right, and she hated realising he had a point.

'Sorry,' said Paddy, as they reached a zebra crossing. 'I shouldn't have had a go.'

'S'fine,' Laura replied.

'Really,' said Paddy. 'Sorry.'

'You're right,' said Laura. 'Totally right. Just forget it, OK?'

Both were silent all the way back to the flat. They sat on the sofa together, not really saying much, for the rest of the evening. They didn't watch *The Truth About Cats and Dogs*; they watched some thriller mini-series instead, and all the while she was pretending to watch it, Laura was wishing she could just hit Paddy on the knee and say, 'Oh, fuck it, you're right. It's a great film, let's watch it.' But she couldn't, so they didn't.

CHAPTER THIRTY-NINE

The Simon situation rankled with Laura, though she didn't understand why. Over the next week, she kept thinking about what Paddy had said on the way back from Harrow. Sometimes she thought he was mad, totally out of order, and she would feel a calm within herself that she-was-right-he-was-wrong, and no action was required on her part. And sometimes, the peeling away of that layer, beneath which lay all her insecurity, made her numb with fear. She didn't want to have to think about anything else, anything big and scary like that. She wasn't going to think about it. About him. She couldn't. So what if she was working hard, and she wasn't as much fun as she had been? So what if she thought it was crazy that Simon spent two hours on the phone each day to his Peruvian girlfriend, and Mum and Dad thought it was the cutest thing ever? So what if Mum had rented a CD Rom from Harrow Library, 'Peoples and Places of South America', and she and Dad were studying it each night together? *They* were bonkers, not her. She was the sensible one, working hard, moving on.

Perhaps Paddy had a point about not going out enough, though. She had been a bit of a hermit since she'd got back. And she should be trying to meet someone else, she knew. But where was she supposed to pull someone, even if she wanted to, which she didn't? Laura started thinking to herself, how did I used to do it? Fall in love like that at the drop of a hat, how did I used to meet men so easily, so happily, be so relaxed about it all? It seemed completely alien to her now. She would no more look at a man next to her on the tube in the mornings than she would pole-dance around the pole in the middle of the carriage. And of course, she couldn't tell Paddy why.

Still, she hated not having things right with Paddy, just hated it. The following Saturday evening, she was in on her own when her flatmate returned from an afternoon out with Becky, walking along the canal by Regent's Park. He was mysteriously silent on the subject, which Laura assumed meant nothing had happened, but instead he suggested a 'casual' dinner the following Saturday, to welcome Simon back. Laura knew this was in reality a chance for Paddy to drop round and ask Becky if she wanted to swing by for supper (nothing special, just a few friends coming over, no pressure). She was glad, because it meant things were OK again, so she sounded enthusiastic about it, and waited for Paddy to talk about Becky for the next ten minutes. But he didn't. Again, this was strange.

'I'll cook,' said Laura, as she opened a bottle of wine.

'No, *I'll* cook,' said Paddy firmly. 'You call Simon, get him to come. And Jo and Chris are back next week, can you text her on her mobile, get them along.'

'Fine,' said Laura, conceding defeat happily. 'That'll be great. Have some wine.'

'Love some,' said Paddy. 'You in tonight, then?'

'Yep,' said Laura firmly. 'Just a quiet one.'

'Great,' said Paddy. 'Me too. Let's drink lots and tell each other sad stories of the sea.'

'Er . . . OK,' said Laura. 'How's it going with the girl downstairs, then?'

'Great,' said Paddy, nodding. 'It's early days, you know. But – she's just fantastic. That's all there is to it.' He shrugged his shoulders and smiled simply at her.

Laura felt panic shoot through her, and she didn't know why.

'Come on, Pads,' she said, struggling to find the joke in it. 'Haven't you got some funny story about it to tell me?'

'Not really,' said Paddy. He yawned, stretched his lanky body and reached up to get two glasses out of the cupboard. 'We had a good chat yesterday, you know. We're going to take it slowly. But – it's just going really well. That's all.'

Laura watched him, amazed. 'That's . . . great,' she said, hating herself for not thinking it was great. 'Wow. I'm really pleased.'

At eight thirty the next morning, Laura was – like most right-minded people at eight thirty on a Sunday – fast asleep. But gradually she stirred, for something was ringing in her ear, and it kept on ringing. It would stop, and then start again. Stop and start. It took a good few minutes before she lifted her heavy lids cautiously, looked around her and realised where she was, and that the sound was the phone in the hallway, ringing, then stopping when the answering machine kicked in, then ringing again.

'Shut up!' Paddy croaked, from his room down the corridor.

Knowing that whilst they were both lazy, Paddy would happily ignore the phone whilst it rang for a good few hours yet, Laura fell out of bed, cursing, and shuffled down the corridor.

'Hallagh,' she growled into the receiver.

'Laura? Hello, dear. It's Annabel,' came a voice down the phone, disconcertingly close by.

Instinctively, Laura looked slowly around her, to make sure Aunt Annabel was not lurking in the fuse box.

'Eh?' she said. 'Er.' She cleared her throat. 'Hello.'

'Hello, Laura!' said her aunt, sounding as if she'd been raised with not one but fifteen silver spoons in her mouth. 'How are you, dear?'

'Er . . .' Laura coughed. 'I'm fine. Are you – is everything OK?'

'Yes, of course,' said Aunt Annabel, sounding astonished. 'I rang to say hello. So – how are you, dear?'

Waking up more and more by the second, Laura shook her head and ran her free hand through her hair. 'Yes, well, like I said. I'm fine. It's – it's a bit early for me, though. How are you?'

'Well, I'm fine too,' said Aunt Annabel. 'Really very fine.' There was a rather tense silence for a few seconds.

Laura shook one leg of her pyjamas, which was ruched up above her knee in an attractive manner, like she was a Freemason. She rubbed her eyes to get the sleep from them, waiting for her aunt to speak, because she wasn't really sure what to say next.

'So, Laura. Have you seen the paper today?' said Aunt Annabel.

It's eight thirty in the morning, of course I haven't seen the paper today. Go away! Laura wanted to yell, but instead she said, 'No, why?'

'I think you should,' said Aunt Annabel. 'I was really ringing to say hello, of course. But I did just want to check you'd got a copy!' She cleared her throat, and said almost reverentially, 'To see *him* in it. Number three! No less, my goodness.'

'The what?' Laura asked, her mind beginning to whirr.

'Britain's Most Eligible Bachelors,' said Aunt Annabel. 'You Know Who, dear!'

Annabel had never called her 'dear' before, nor rung her at home before, nor indeed ever expressed much interest in any aspect of Laura's life before, and it was this that struck Laura first, before the mist cleared and she realised what her aunt was talking about. 'Oh,' she whispered, clutching the receiver with both hands. She leant against the wall. 'What is it?' she said, trying to keep her voice normal. 'Nick?'

'Well, I think you should read it for yourself!' her aunt said gaily. 'But we knew you'd want to see it, so we thought we'd better let you know.'

'Right,' said Laura, wondering who 'we' was.

372

'I'm sure everyone else will be calling to say they've seen it too, but it's quite something to say you're an item with the Marquess of Ranelagh, especially after this!' Annabel said, in tones of delight. 'And you were so *mysterious* about him in Norfolk, I didn't even say goodbye to you. Lulu and Fran were *so* sorry to have missed you, you know. So sorry!'

'Me too,' said Laura, crossing her fingers. 'How are they?'

'Good, fine, wonderful. Fran and Ludo are in Singapore at the moment! Having a wonderful time, back in a few days' time. And Lulu's in the South of France. It's just little old me and your Uncle Robert, you know. On our own! Very lonely! So when your uncle saw the article this morning he said, "Annabel, you must call Laura." And I thought gosh, yes, I must.'

Since Uncle Robert was notorious for saying nothing, contributing nothing, and only engaging with the newspaper, which he would a) read, b) use to light barbecues and fires, or c) put over his head for a nap, Laura found quite a lot wrong with this assertion. In fact, if Annabel had said, Actually, I have killed Uncle Robert, because he always hogged the newspaper, and so I am idling away some time waiting for the police to arrive and arrest me, so I thought I'd call you, Laura, she would have found it more believable.

But she merely replied, 'Thanks, Aunt Annabel – look, I'd better . . .'

'Yes, yes,' said Annabel. 'I'll let you go – you know, it's marvellous. That's all. And Laura – do hope to see you soon. Both of you, maybe?' she said coyly.

'Both?'

'Well,' said Annabel. 'You . . . and the marquess, of course . . .'

'Aunt Annabel,' said Laura. 'Really, there's nothing going on with me and Nick.'

'Oh, really?'

'Really,' Laura said firmly. She forced herself to sound blithely unconcerned. 'In fact, I'm sure he's forgotten all about me. It was just a fling, seriously. I'm afraid if you're thinking we're an item . . .'

'Oh, no!' said Annabel, backtracking hastily. 'Actually, it says, you know. In the article. It says he's got a girlfriend.'

Laura's knees turned to water; she swayed against the doorframe. 'Oh,' she said. 'Right, then.'

'I just thought that was probably rubbish, you know these newspapers,' said Annabel, blissfully unconscious of any irony. 'And – he did seem awfully – *keen* on you, you know . . .'

'Annabel!' came a voice gruffly in the background. 'Any more tea?'

'Oh, there's Robert,' Annabel trilled. 'Must go. Lovely to chat, Laura!'

'What?' said Laura, then hastily, 'Of course, thanks Aunt Annabel, sorry, I'm not really awake . . .'

'Please don't worry! Goodbye!' Annabel said, and the line went dead suddenly. Laura stood in the hallway, her big toe gingerly touching a hole in the worn carpet. She shook her head, confused, and then she went into her room and pulled on some clothes. Was she going to buy the newspaper? Of course she was.

Ten minutes later, Laura smoothed open the Sunday paper on the kitchen table. 'Britain's Most Eligible Bachelors', ran the headline. She pulled the cuffs of her jumper over her fingers, and read rapidly.

Number Three: Dominic Edward Danvers Needham, Twelfth Marquess of Ranelagh, Earl of Albany Cross. OK, so the Princes have to be at Nos 1 & 2, but many are more intrigued by the deb's delight, Dominic Needham (above). Thirty-five, single, handsome, worth roughly around £300m, the Marquess of Ranelagh is the matrimonial jackpot for almost every ambitious mother with a socialite daughter to marry off – and the heartthrob of a generation of boarding-school girls. And of course, there's also the house.

374

Chartley Hall is regarded by many as the finest stately home in England. Built by Inigo Jones, nestling next to the wild North Norfolk coast, it is full of the most fabulous treasures (the Hogarths, the greatest collection of Renaissance drawings in the country, the Grinling Gibbons woodwork throughout, the magnificent library, and the notorious toy soldier collection begun by his father). Visitors flock there year round. But does the notoriously private marquess have anyone to share all this with?

'Oh god,' Laura whispered to herself. She stared at the photo of Nick, scowling up at her. 'Poor bab – this is dire.'

Happily, girls, the answer is – for the moment – no. For beneath the glittering surface all is not well in the House of Needham. Rarely has there been a great aristocratic family so rocked by scandal in recent years. First came the notorious affair between the present marquess's mother, the beautiful British actress Vivienne Lash, then eleventh Marchioness of Ranelagh, and her husband's brother, notorious gambler and playboy Lord Frederick Needham. They ran off together when the present marquess was just eleven, and now live in the South of France. The eleventh marquess forbade all contact between his ex-wife and her children, and to this day Nick and his two sisters, Lady Rose Balmore and Lady Lavinia Needham, have made no effort to keep in touch with their mother, who now, in her late seventies, is said to be in ill-health.

Her children have fared little better. Her eldest daughter, Lady Rose, seemed set to follow in her mother's footsteps when, in 1978 at the age of eighteen, she eloped with Gareth Ringwood, a drummer with the heavy metal band Roxattax. It was a tempestuous marriage which ended in divorce in 1980, and coincided with her heroin addiction reaching its height. After an overdose which nearly killed her in 1982, she entered rehab and six years later married the multi-millionaire

industrialist Sir Malcolm Balmore. They have two young
children, Francis and Elizabeth, and Lady Rose is active on
many committees, tireless in her work for various charities.

'My god!' said Laura, unable to stop herself from grinning.
'Who'd have thought it?'

Lady Lavinia has not taken the same path as her elder sister.
She might be called rootless, in fact. She spent several years
in India, on various ashrams, and ran a stall in London's
Portobello Road market, selling leather goods she had sourced
herself. She spends six months of the year in Thailand, where
she has a house – paid for by her family, it is presumed,
for she has never worked a day in her life. Ethereally
beautiful, she is as famous for her love life as anything,
having dated several rock stars and actors. She is currently
living with her brother in Chartley Hall, where sources close
to the family say she is having an affair with the marquess's
oldest friend and estate manager, Charles Potter.

'He wishes,' Laura thought. 'God, what a load of rubbish.'
Nevertheless, she read on, mouth open, chewing her jumper
as she did.

So what of our handsome romantic hero, Dominic (known
to all as Nick)? Until recently, friends said he was increasingly
remote, shunning the London society that was once his
lifeblood. A regular on the smart London social scene, where
young, rich aristocrats regularly pay £1000 for a bottle of
champagne in the nightclubs of Mayfair and Chelsea, he
withdrew almost entirely from public life after his father died
in 2003, when Nick came up to Norfolk to take over the
estate. His father was much-loved in the county for his
management of Chartley and its lands and properties. His
son, who has made a few attempts to alter the running of

the estate without any great success, is often regarded as standoffish and arrogant by those who don't know him. Friends say loyally that he is merely shy, growing used to the role he must play as one of the highest peers in the realm.

In recent weeks, however, his behaviour has changed, and the gossip on the circuit is that he has finally fallen in love. Since June, he has been seen several times in town with Cecilia Thorson, trust-fund daughter of millionaire financier Lars Thorson and his wife, notorious socialite and Seventies beauty Lady Tania Ingham. The Thorsons are well-known in fashionable circles, seen as the A+ of the A list, and Nick could look no higher for a future wife. Friends say he is very much in love, spending more and more time in London and increasingly absent from his post at the estate, where he still has much to learn.

Is this true love? Is this an apprenticeship? Or is the marquess too wrapped up in himself to find the solution to his problems – a wife – and provide an heir for one of our greatest national treasures? Many would like to know – and many girls would love to be that solution.

'Who was that?' came Paddy's voice blearily from his room. 'The phone?'

'Nothing important,' Laura called back. 'Coffee?'

'Yes please.'

Laura stood up straight, arching her back and stretching. The kettle was boiling. She got the coffee out of a cupboard. She screwed up her eyes, as if trying to stare into the distance. They stung with tears. Stupid to have any kind of proprietorial feelings about him, she told herself. You haven't heard from him in over a month and that was your decision, you know it's too hard, that you can't be together, you haven't let yourself think about him, so that's why it's so weird to read about him now. Just recognise that, you'll be fine. He's not for you, this life is not yours, the whole thing is ridiculous. She knew all that rubbish about Cristal-drinking toffs was idiotic, but at the same time she also knew that there was no smoke without fire. He *was* different, she knew it. And apart from anything else, he was obviously going out with that girl, the millionairess Cecilia. Laura tried to feel noble. He may have pretended otherwise, but this was obviously what he wanted. A blue-blooded, blonde, millionaire's daughter, that was absolutely what he needed.

It couldn't be further away from what she was, an ordinary girl making coffee in a slightly scuzzy kitchen in North London on a Sunday morning. So what if it still hurt – that was the way it was. She looked down at the article again. Best thing would be if she were to chuck it, straight away. She poured the coffee, biting her lip as she read it all through again.

CHAPTER FORTY

'I'd love to, Laura. But I'm not sure. Really. Don't have a go at me.'

'Simon! But it'll be great! Jo and Chris will just have got back from Oz, they really want to see you. And Paddy's invited the famous Becky, you'll meet her too.'

Simon said apologetically, 'I'll try, Laura, but I'm just not sure. I have to speak to Jorgia on Saturday too – we've got a lot to sort out. And it's so far . . .'

Laura said, 'Whatever, Simon. Fine.' She crouched over her desk at work and started tapping on her keyboard loudly, to try and let him know that she was a Very Busy Person. It was a waste of time speaking to Simon these days, she thought crossly. Of course he should be coming over on Saturday, to catch up with everyone, but was he? No. He wanted to stay in with Mum and Dad, knitting tea cosies and cooing down the phone to his girlfriend. Pah. It was ridiculous, even Paddy was starting to think it was ridiculous, a grown man living at home in Harrow with his mum and dad, helping them out, going to the supermarket, taking care of all their recycling – he'd even hunted down their old mobile phone and gone through his old wardrobe, and theirs too, and then made them both take the bus with him to the recycling depot so they could familiarise themselves with the recycling opportunities on offer. There'd be virtually nothing left in the house if he carried on like that. And he kept going to see Mary, too – that was practically the only time he left Harrow, to travel up to town and spend time with her. He'd take her out to lunch, go to the flat, play canasta, for god's sake, with Mary and Cedric and Jasper. He was twenty-six! It was wrong!

'It's just . . . it's such a nightmare coming all the way in from Mum and Dad's, you know.'

'If you weren't living with Mum and Dad it wouldn't be a problem,' said Laura pointedly. But Simon didn't take the bait.

'But I am,' he said, as if Laura was a bit slow. 'I have to stay with them, Loz. I can't afford anywhere else till I go back to Peru and see Jorgia again.'

'Oh yes. I know. I know that's a full-time job,' said Laura, in what she hoped was an icy tone, conveying a) the futility, and b) the immaturity of her brother's current life plans. But again, Simon didn't rise to it. He simply sighed and said, 'I miss her.'

Laura was finding Simon increasingly irritating; simple conversations were impossible with him any more, all he'd do was sigh about Jorgia and how much he missed her, or go on about Mum and Dad. He didn't even have the decency to complain to her about them. No, no. It was all Mum and Dad are being so wonderful, Mum and Dad are so great, didn't Mum and Dad provide an amazing upbringing for us and aren't we lucky as a family? And Mary. What an amazing role model. What a fantastic woman. Laura wanted to scream when he said that, it was all so touchy-feely and dire. Where had her brother gone? The useless, lazy, charming one, who was messy and smelly and annoying, but in a predictable way? And why did this transformation make her so cross?

'We had such an interesting conversation today, about her being in Cairo after the war, before Suez,' Simon was saying, as Laura twirled the phone cord around her fingers.

Laura resentfully wished Simon would realise she was busy. She didn't have time to have a long chat with him about Mary. 'Oh, really,' Laura said, looking over her desk for the file she'd prepared for her impending meeting.

'Does she ever talk to you about our grandfather?'

'What? No,' said Laura. 'Listen, Simon –'

'She said something weird today,' Simon said.

'Oh?' Laura was suddenly alert. 'What?'

'Well, she was talking about Guy, how much she loved him, and about Cairo, about their house there, all that.'

'And?' said Laura, unimpressed. Mary was *always* going on about Guy, about how great he was.

'I asked her about our grandfather, about Mum's dad, and what he was like, all that, and she got really cross. Said I was being nosey.'

'Eh?' said Laura. 'Why shouldn't you ask?'

'I don't know,' said Simon. 'It was strange. She wouldn't talk about it. I just wanted to ask her, you know, to find out a bit more about our family.'

Laura suppressed a sigh. Since Simon had returned, he was obsessed with Our Family, where we came from, the roots of the world and how we were all brother and sister – which actually meant Jorgia was his sister too, but it didn't seem to work that way.

'Then she started going on about how terrible it was after Grandfather died. And she didn't know what she'd have done without Guy. How he was so amazing, all of that, when she married him, how she had to look after Annabel too, how odd that was.'

Laura was finally interested, despite herself. 'Why, what did she say?'

'Well, think about it, you know. There's Granny and Mum, and Gran's husband's died, she's on her own with a small child, and then she meets this bloke Guy, falls for him, but she has to bring up his daughter too. Imagine a five-year-old Aunt

Annabel moving in with you. Like having an infant Mrs Thatcher as your flatmate.'

They both chortled. 'Poor Mum,' said Laura. 'So, go on then. What else was she saying?'

Simon paused. 'It was weird, that's all. She was saying something, and then she stopped and she wouldn't talk about it any more.'

'Why? What do you mean?' said Laura. She was intrigued, but she also knew Simon's penchant for cock-and-bull stories that ultimately led nowhere.

'She said she didn't want to talk about it. She was tired. Do you think – does she seem OK to you?'

'What do you mean?' Laura repeated, her tone crosser than she meant it to be. She felt panic rise up in her.

'Nothing. It's just she looks much older these days. Since I've been back. It's probably nothing. She was being a bit odd, that's all.'

'Well, that's Gran,' said Laura. 'She loves a mystery, Simon, you know she does. And she's bored. It was good of you to go and see her, though.'

'I don't know about that,' said Simon. 'I love going to see her. She keeps asking me, though. Keeps saying she wants me to come round and look at more photos. She said she hadn't seen you for ages.'

'I've been busy,' Laura said shortly.

'Oh,' Simon replied. 'What?'

'Work, Simon,' Laura told him, knowing she sounded like a prig. 'I'm in charge of this new project. It's very important.'

'Mum told me about the hiccup,' said Simon. Laura said nothing. 'Haven't seen you properly, sis. We should go out. And what happened to you in Norfolk? Mum was most mysterious about it, I must say. So was Gran, when I asked her. Who have you been getting yourself into trouble with this time?'

'No one,' said Laura. 'Seriously.' She rustled some papers in her in-tray loudly.

'Seriously?'

'God no, they've got the wrong end of the stick. It's nothing, nothing. You know me.'

'Course I do. Why, was it a man situation, then? Who's on the horizon?'

Laura made herself give a little laugh. It didn't sound very natural. 'Blimey. No one. Look, I really can't talk, I have to go.'

'Right,' said Simon. He sounded a little distant. 'Fine. Well, shall we have a drink soon? Be good to catch up with my big sis properly.'

'Come on Saturday, Simon, go on.' Laura tapped her fingers on the receiver. 'Oh go on! We can talk then. Forget about Gran. You were there today, you don't need to go twice in a week. Come on, bro. I miss you! You can even kip on the sofa if you want.'

'OK,' said Simon, relenting. 'OK, of course. I'd love to. Er. Are you cooking?' he asked.

'Paddy's cooking. Well, perhaps we're getting a takeaway. Listen, I have to go, I'll be late.'

She said goodbye, put down the phone and sighed. She looked around the office, tapping her pen impatiently against her mug. Hearing Simon blather on about Mary made her feel guilty. She hadn't seen her and she should. Damn. There was just always something else to do, to do with work, and tidying up the flat, those kinds of things. Sorting things out, being on top of things – now she was the new Laura, it just took up a lot of time, she'd never realised it. Never mind. She'd think about it later. She picked up her bag.

Her latest project, which she was just starting, was Operation Bring Linley Munroe Back into the Fold. She had had a meeting there with Clare Swynford, the co-ordinator for the company, last week, and had prepared a pack of stuff about the programmes they did, the investment opportunities (tax-free) and lots of pictures of smiley happy children, which had won Clare over most convincingly. Today was a different matter, though. She was going back this afternoon to meet Marcus Sussman, the man at the root of all the problems, the one who'd insulted Mrs McGregor and then been outraged at his treatment. He was head of the banking division, and since he'd been the first to volunteer and the first to pull out, Laura was being made to understand very clearly – by Rachel, by Gareth, and by Linley Munroe as well – that he was the cause, but also the solution. He was an important man, and Laura couldn't help feeling he wasn't the kind of person to go gooey-eyed over a cute photo of three children drawing with some crayons.

She wasn't, truth be told, looking forward to it much. She knew what Marcus Sussman would be like. Pleased with himself, too rich, arrogant. The kind of person who ordered a £200 bottle of wine with dinner, not because he really liked it, but because he needed to be seen to have spent that much. But it had to be done, and so Laura slung her bag over her shoulder, picked up her phone and the folder she'd made for Marcus Sussman, and headed out of the office. On her way she passed Rachel.

'Where you off to, then?' said Rachel.

'Linley Munroe,' Laura replied briefly. 'Can't stop, I don't want to be late. The rehabilitation begins.'

'Great!' said Rachel. 'Good luck. Let me know how it goes. You know we –'

Laura knew there was pressure on her; she knew that. In part thanks to her, they were looking at about thirty per cent less funding this year, and it had to come from somewhere. She said, more sharply than she meant, 'I know, Rach. Honestly. I'm going to try my best.'

'Hey – I know.' Rachel patted her arm. 'We're going to the pub tonight if you get back in time, by the way –'

'No thanks,' Laura said. 'I don't know when I'll be back, and I've got a lot of stuff to finish off.'

384

'Just one,' said Rachel. 'Come on. Help me celebrate nine months of being single.'

'I can't, seriously. Count me out. Thanks though. Bye.'

She strode off, leaving Rachel staring after her.

It was a little more than ten minutes' walk to Linley Munroe. Laura prepared her lines in her head. It wasn't a big deal, they had some great new companies who were interested in investing money, she told herself. Linley Munroe wasn't the be all and end all. She knew she'd caused the breach in the first place, indirectly. She had been the co-ordinator, it was her job title, and she'd totally failed to co-ordinate anything at all, because she'd been too busy co-ordinating her next evening with Dan, her emails to Dan and her holiday with Dan. So she knew she had to make it better again, and that's why she was more nervous than she might otherwise have been. It wasn't just that her job was on the line if she didn't pull this off. It was more than that – she felt it was symbolically important, like getting Linley Munroe to give money and plug the financial hole they were in represented the last of the mistakes she had to rectify.

The first signs were not promising. Laura was shown into an office which was a bizarre hybrid of formal leather-bound boardroom chic mixed with glass futuristic Canary Wharf-style modernism. The air-conditioning was turned on full blast. Laura shivered in her thin top and wished she'd brought a sturdy market-trader cable-knit jumper to pop on. She gazed around the office, taking in the black office furniture, the neatness of everything. There was one piece of paper in the in-tray; everything else was filed away. There were no personal effects anywhere, unless an invitation pinned up on the board to what was called an Autumn Black Tie Dinner thrown by some bizarre-sounding organisation with a long, Germanic name could be called a personal effect. Laura thought not.

She waited. And waited. Five minutes turned into ten. The

longer she waited the crosser she grew, but she balanced it with irritation at herself for being too spineless to go out to the scary-looking assistant and say, 'Excuse me, how long is he likely to be?' So she stayed, getting crosser with herself and with Marcus Sussman, and the assistant, whom she thought was laughing at her, feeling inadequate and hopelessly uncorporate.

It was good in one way. It reminded her that she didn't want to work in an office like this, and with good reason. It reminded her how much she loved her job. Perhaps she'd forgotten that lately. Had she? The thought came unwanted into her head that she didn't really *enjoy* it much these days. It was just – she shook her head, trying to work out what it was, and swung herself half around on her wheelie chair. It was the passion for it that she used to have, she realised. Now, she was approaching her job as a mountain to climb, rather than thinking of it as something to embrace, to seize, to throw herself into. Now, since the summer, she thought of it as a challenge, something that she had to accomplish. She just *had* to nail this funding, she knew it.

Oh dear, thought Laura to herself. Have I become one of those people who uses the term 'goal oriented' in normal conversation, and who people don't ask to the pub because all they do is go on about how strong the team is this year? Perhaps, but if she was, what was wrong with that? She wasn't playing any more, she had to keep telling herself that. She smiled again, swung round on her chair, and the door opened.

'Excuse me,' said a voice behind her. 'You must be Laura Foster, yes?'

'Oh my god,' said Laura, clutching the side of the desk and turning herself round on the chair. 'I'm so sorry –'

A tall, beefy man with an eerily familiar face strode forward. 'I'm Marcus Sussman.'

She stood up and held out her hand. 'It's you!' she said.

'You're –' said Marcus Sussman, looking at her with a

momentarily bewildered expression. 'I've seen you before,' he said. His brow lifted. 'Oh my god.'

'Yes,' said Laura.

'You're that girl in the pub a few months back. In Norfolk!' He seemed amazed, although he registered no positive emotion, nor issued a further apology.

'You stole my table, then you spilt your drink over me,' Laura said, in what she hoped was a tone of benevolent amusement.

Marcus Sussman looked at her nonplussed, as if she were talking Swahili. 'Right,' he said.

He was a strange man. She remembered him now. His clothes were beautiful, his shirtsleeves fastened with cufflinks; the tailoring of his suit was perfect, even Laura could see that. The effect on him was odd, though. It was that of harnessing something, hiding something, putting on a costume. He wasn't suave or elegant. He was fleshy, rather large, too tall, his hair was slightly too long, it fell in big bracket shapes on either side of his forehead. And he had egg on his plump silk tie. Or something encrusted – she could see it. Why didn't he flick it off, or notice? Hadn't someone told him?

'Real coincidence, that,' said Marcus Sussman.

Laura wanted to cite her rule applying to Koh Samui and Tuscany – no, not a coincidence at all – but she felt it would be the wrong thing to say, so she merely said, 'Yes, what a small world.'

Again, Marcus Sussman stared at her rather nervously, as if she had just taken off her top and then thrown a brick through his window.

'Will you sit down?' he said eventually. 'Do. Here –' he gestured to the chair from which she had just risen, and Laura, trying not to look confused, sat down again.

He cleared his throat. 'Ah. So – what were you doing there? Holiday?'

'Yes,' said Laura.

'Right,' Marcus replied. 'I've got a friend who lives there, a bunch of us went down for the weekend. Great stuff. Beautiful part of the world, isn't it?'

'Yes,' said Laura. 'It is.'

Marcus coughed into his clenched fist. 'Did you go to Chartley?' he asked politely. Laura decided he was her nemesis, sent to kill her with socially awkward questions.

'Yes,' she said. She looked at her notes.

Marcus said, quasi-nonchalantly, 'Wonderful place, the George. He owns it, old Nick Ranelagh. The marquess, right?' He tapped a pencil on the glass-topped desk, drumming out a rhythm. 'Turned it around, used to be a real dive. Got backing. Investment. Mate of mine sorted it for him. Friend of a really good friend of Nick's, actually. He knows him quite well, you know.'

He nodded at her eagerly, hair flopping wildly. Laura wished he would be quiet, but she knew the rules of the dance, so instead of leaning forward and saying in a lewd old cackly tart's voice, 'Actually, I know him too, *in the worst way*', she said, 'Right. Wow. Fantastic.'

'Yes,' said Marcus more enthusiastically, warming to his theme. 'Great bloke, actually, old Nick. Only met him once or twice before – you know. He took over the house and stuff. Yah. Good bloke.'

'Right,' said Laura again. She dug her palm into the hard plastic ridges of the folder. 'That's fantastic. It's a lovely pub.'

Marcus stood up rather suddenly, and frowned as if she hadn't been given permission to speak. 'OK – it's Laura, isn't it? Let's discuss this, shall we? Look, I'm not going to beat about the bush, I'm pretty fucked off with you guys.'

'I know, you must be,' Laura began, nodding violently so that her neck hurt, to show she agreed. 'And I'm really grateful to you for agreeing to meet me.'

Marcus ignored her and said, 'But we have a commitment to the local community. And I would like to do something about it.

Well, I used to want to – until all this.' His eyes flickered impatiently.

'Right,' said Laura, getting out her folder and taking a deep breath. 'Look – Marcus?' She wasn't really sure if she was allowed to call him by his first name all of a sudden. 'I can completely understand why you feel the programme hasn't really worked for your company.'

'I know why it didn't work for the company,' said Marcus, warming to his theme. 'Because that school's run like something out of *Lord of the Flies*, it's fucking incredible. No monitoring, no one in your office did anything when I rang to complain. I didn't hear from you for weeks, neither did anyone here.' He thumped his fist on the desk, and Laura was suddenly, deeply intrigued about why this – as she'd thought him – slightly twattish man cared one way or the other whether he helped some little kid to read and why he was so bothered about it. In fact, why he was involved in the programme at all.

He said, gathering momentum, 'And – well, seriously. The reaction I got from that stupid woman. McGregor.' He made a hurrumphing noise. 'When I tried to suggest they were doing things wrong – the kids running riot, all that. You know, some little git tried to kill me?'

'Er –' said Laura. 'Volunteers aren't really supposed to suggest changes to teaching policy, Marcus. You're only there to help your designated child with their reading –'

'He got me in a fucking headlock and pulled a knife on me!' Marcus yelled, waving his arms in the air, his attempted air of authority completely vanishing. 'That's why I rang to complain. I kept ringing you and you were never there!'

'Oh god,' said Laura. 'Right. I am sorry.' She put her hand out involuntarily. 'Really sorry. Did you – report it?'

Marcus subsided in his chair, just a little. 'No,' he said. 'I thought about it, but I realised it wasn't ever going to do any good. So I pulled us out of the programme instead. It's a shame. I'm on the board here, you know.'

'Wow,' said Laura, trying to look impressed.

'But that's not the point,' he said, looking cross again. 'The point is, I wanted to put some money into St Catherine's. You know, it's the nearest school to Linley. We have a good reputation for that sort of thing. I thought giving money, investing in the school, might be some way of – you know.' He looked down between his legs at the floor.

Laura didn't know, but she desperately *wanted* to know, was this all a waste of time or not? So she said after a pause, 'No, sorry. Er, some way of – what?'

'Well,' said Marcus. 'You know.' She looked at him encouragingly. He pulled his top lip over his bottom lip, and said quietly, through his teeth, 'Uhm. Well, you know. Doing something, make a difference. That sort of thing.'

She nodded, suddenly enormously touched by him, without understanding why. 'Right,' she said. 'Well, I wanted to be the one to apologise to you personally. It's completely my fault, you know. There's been a – a change in the way we handle the schools and I assure you this will be dealt with in a different way in future. I've put some information together to show you. Can you give me five minutes to go through it with you? So I can change your mind, I hope.'

She smiled at him winningly. He stared blankly at her, then crossed his arms.

'Fine,' he said, after a pause. 'I've got a meeting in fifteen minutes. Let's get on with it.'

'Yes,' said Laura. So she opened the folder and ploughed on.

Ten minutes later, sweat was practically pouring off Laura's brow and she wanted to shake him. It wasn't that Marcus was *rude*, exactly, or intimidating, or even unpleasant. He was none of those things – in fact, there was something almost endearingly odd about him. It was more that he was socially incapable. To Laura, who was used to responding and interacting very much on instinct – often to her cost – he was completely frustrating.

He showed no interest in what she was saying, it seemed, but it wasn't as if he didn't take her seriously. On the contrary. He gave her a mental workout the like of which she hadn't experienced since pretending to be an examiner for Paddy's PGCE exams a few years ago, when Paddy had told her that her knowledge of maths was so bad as to render her educationally subnormal.

She couldn't work out if he was doing it to show her he was top dog, but she thought it was probably just that Marcus was one of those incredibly clever people, and that was all there was to it. His communication skills were zero, but who needed communication skills when you were the kind of person who only had to look at a pound coin for it to multiply itself by ten?

'Here's the last sheet,' said Laura, handing it over almost gloomily, for she could not see any way that Marcus was going to come up trumps and write her a blank cheque. 'This is about motivation, communication performance at schools that have been involved with the mentoring scheme. It shows the positive effect it's had on children's performance. And here –' she pointed on the sheet '– a couple of quotes from people about how much they've enjoyed working with the children. Something you know yourself already, of course –' Too late, she remembered Marcus's kid had pulled a knife on him, damn, so she hurried on, 'er – but for people who want to put something back – that's a really good page of information to be able to show them.'

'If they hate the jobs they're doing and want to do something else you mean? Hurrumphhh,' said Marcus, exhaling loudly.

'Well, no,' said Laura. 'But it's a good way of adding something extra to your life. Someone else's too.'

Marcus said nothing for a moment, but peered at her through his floppy fringe.

'OK.' He flicked his hand out at her dismissively. 'Why do you do the job you do?'

Laura gazed at the egg on his tie again, as he sat there fiddling with his cufflinks, legs sprawled out in a V-shape, awkwardly, almost aggressively.

'Well – er,' said Laura uncertainly. She didn't know how to answer him. She thought of Nick, asking her the same question. How she'd known what to say, felt utterly comfortable talking to him, and the power of that feeling still stung, still hurt more than she realised.

'Erm,' she said, shifting in her seat. 'What do you mean?'

'It's just interesting. Don't you think it's interesting, why people do what they do?'

'Sometimes,' said Laura. 'I think it's interesting when people have jobs you think they're not suited to, but actually they're brilliant at them. Like – my flatmate.'

'Why?' said Marcus.

'He's quite eccentric,' Laura explained. 'Terrible cook, quite insecure, you know.' She didn't know why she was telling him all of this. 'But he's a teacher. And he's brilliant. I've seen him with the children, he's completely in charge, and they worship him. I like that.'

'Surprises you?' said Marcus. He was looking at his fingers. 'Yes, I know what you mean.'

There was a silence.

'I fell into my job,' said Laura, with a wry smile. (She knew, but wasn't going to say, that she had applied for her job three years ago, only because she'd snogged an absolutely gorgeous man at a party the week before who'd told her there was a vacancy there, and even though he worked for a totally different business co-ordination scheme on another council, the old Laura had passionately hoped the two of them would meet regularly and fall in love over literacy initiative brochure meetings. Alas, she never saw him again.) 'But I love it, and I want to be good at it, more than anything.' She realised she was gazing into space, cleared her throat and said, 'How about you?'

'Not sure really,' said Marcus. 'Fell into it too.'

'Do you like it?'

'Not really the kind of job you like or don't like,' he said. 'I just don't think I'd be much good at anything else.' He said it without emotion.

'Oh,' said Laura, not sure what to say, once again. But then Marcus looked at his watch and said shortly, 'I have someone coming in now. The meeting I mentioned. 'Fraid you'll have to go.'

'Of course,' said Laura, springing up like a jack-in-the-box. 'I – er – just let me get my stuff together – er. So,' she stood still and breathed in. 'Marcus, will you talk to Clare? Consider allowing Linley Munroe to rejoin the programme again, maybe think about the investment choices I mentioned? I know she's keen –'

'Yes,' said Marcus. He stood at the door and their eyes met, briefly. Laura looked away and busied herself shoving papers into her folder. She realised, as she stuffed the papers back in a slightly haphazard fashion, that she was waiting for him to say, 'Thanks for coming in', or at least give her some acknowledgement, even if he loathed her and the whole thing, but he just wasn't the type – probably hadn't ever said thanks for anything in his life, it just wouldn't occur to him. He even . . .

'. . . with me to the dinner?'

'I see,' Laura said noncommittally, putting the folder under her arm. God, it was cold, she wanted to be back outside again.

'Forget it,' Marcus muttered, half to himself. 'This way then.' He turned away.

'Sorry,' Laura said. 'I really wasn't listening. What did you say?'

Marcus straightened up, cleared his throat and said in his strange, low voice, 'Well. There's a dinner – for our banking division. Our clients are having it – they're Germans. It's in a couple of weeks. Would you like to come with me?'

'Why?' said Laura, in total astonishment.

Marcus's eyes bulged slightly and he said, 'Right, sorry. We

393

have to bring a date. I just thought – well, I'd like to think about what we've discussed today. I think it could work out, you know. Perhaps we could talk about it again. At the dinner. So I – I just thought I'd ask if you'd like to come.'

Was this how it was supposed to be? Marcus was asking her out. Her. The woman who thought no one would ever look at her again. Laura felt weird, disconnected from the situation. She looked at Marcus and felt nothing, no feelings whatsoever other than a strange, misplaced affection, but perhaps that was a *good* thing, rather than rushing in headlong like before. If it had been – no. It wasn't. Get over it.

She crossed the room, then realised it was even more awkward, being right opposite him, and stepped back, cross with herself. 'Oh god. I'm so sorry. I didn't realise – sorry, I just didn't get that you were asking me on a date. You see – right.' She couldn't feel more stupid.

'No problem,' said Marcus abruptly. 'No. Problem.' Then he did something quite remarkable. He almost smiled. The corners of his eyes crinkled and it was gone almost as soon as it was there, but she knew she'd seen it.

'I'd love to come,' said Laura. She added, 'Sorry to be so stupid, I really didn't realise that's what you meant.' She put her hand on his folded arms. 'Anyway. Thanks,' she said again, like a robot, 'I'd love to come.'

'Really?' asked Marcus. He shook his head, as if in disbelief, and grinned at her once more, showing his teeth in a big, boyish smile. 'Wow!'

Then, following on almost instantly, he snapped his gaze down to the floor and fiddled with his cufflinks. 'Yup, great. And the money – I'll think about it.'

Laura smiled. This is amazing, she thought, looking at Marcus. For the first time in months and months a) I'm in danger of actually being good at my job, and b) on a completely unrelated, yet bizarrely linked subject, I've got a date – with someone who actually wants to be seen in public with me. OK, if you had an

Assemble Your Own Date kit he's not what you'd end up making, but – I like his smile. How slightly touching he is, the fact he needs someone to dry-clean his ties for him so they don't have egg on them. And the fact he asked me in the first place. Yes, this is truly amazing.

'Thanks!' she said, her eyes sparkling at him. 'For thinking about it. And – you know.'

Marcus said stiffly, 'No, thank *you*. It will be my pleasure. I'll be in touch. Do I have your number?'

'No,' said Laura. 'I'll write it –'

'Give it to my assistant,' Marcus told her, still fiddling with his cufflinks. 'I'm due to be in a meeting now. I'm glad you came in, thank you. I'll talk to Clare. We'll discuss this again at the dinner? Thanks.' He raised his hand in a gesture of farewell and walked off, and Laura, watching him disappear around a corner, knew she was leaving another little bit of her old, stupid self behind. She hugged the folder, and looked around Marcus's office.

How strange. She felt totally unemotional about it. Her stomach wasn't churning, her heart wasn't thumping in her chest. She hoped it stayed like that, this feeling, that it didn't change. She clung to the cloak of numbness that hung over her. It was her best friend.

CHAPTER FORTY-ONE

Things may have been going well with Paddy and Becky, but that didn't mean Paddy was any more relaxed as a host than he had been before. When Saturday came, he was like a cat on a hot tin roof, leaping nervously about the flat all day, so much so that he ended up hitting his hand on the kitchen doorframe fairly hard whilst trying to explain to Laura the best way to make lasagne. His finger swelled up, and Laura took over the cooking, as she had known all along she would.

She loved cooking, more so than ever. It gave her a feeling of control, a sense of purpose. She was in charge, no one else telling her what to do, and she loved it, mixing, chopping, stirring, crushing flavours together, deciding what to do next. It was funny, she and Paddy used to cook together all the time, but now she preferred to do it alone. Like most things, these days.

As Laura was putting the lasagne into the oven, and checking her watch, Jo and Chris arrived.

'Look who's here!' said Paddy, ushering them slightly manically into the kitchen. 'Look who's here. Great! Say hello to Laura, and then come and get a drink.'

'Is Becky here yet?' asked Jo, looking round eagerly.

'No, no,' said Paddy, glancing over his shoulder just to make sure she hadn't crept in behind the others, without him noticing her. 'Er – no.'

Laura hugged Jo. 'Hello, love! How are you?' she said, squeezing her tightly.

'I'm good,' said Jo. 'Ohhh,' she said. 'Laura, it's so good to see you.'

'You too,' said Laura, surprised at her normally restrained friend. 'Bless you. I can't believe it's been three weeks, it seems like – nothing, though. It's flown by.'

'I know,' said Jo. 'And yet we packed so much in, you just wouldn't believe it.'

'Sounds like it,' said Laura, smiling brightly. 'It sounds amazing.'

Chris leapt on her enthusiasm, and said eagerly, 'We brought the laptop along, in case you want to see the photos. I know they're probably really boring, but we thought you might be interested!'

Laura and Paddy exchanged looks.

'Ooh . . .' said Laura. 'Yes . . . Let's see, after supper, shall we?'

'Hey, Chris, mate,' said Paddy, lowering his voice suddenly, as was his wont when he was talking to men, especially large, rather masculine men like Chris. 'Hey. Here's a beer. Come and have a look at the new game I got yesterday.'

'Cool,' said the ever-laconic Chris, and they went out together, leaving Jo and Laura smiling at each other across the kitchen table.

'Come on,' said Laura, putting her arm round Jo. 'So. I can't believe how long it's been. I missed you!' She squeezed her friend. 'Tell me all about it. Are you jetlagged? And did you get some good Duty Free?'

'Ooh, yes, a great Chanel lipstick thing,' said Jo, and then she stopped suddenly. 'But hey. Why don't I wait till everyone's here? Chris and I can tell you all about it then.'

397

'Cool,' said Laura, going to the fridge. 'So, what was the best –'

Jo interrupted. 'But first, I want to talk to you.' She stared at Laura penetratingly.

'OK,' said Laura, rather taken aback. 'Here, have a drink.'

'Ta,' said Jo. She patted the laptop, which was very small and neat, much like its owner, sitting on the kitchen table, and ran her hand along the checked oilcloth on the table. It was an instinctive Jo gesture, as if she were checking for dust. Laura watched her fondly.

'Hum,' said Jo. 'So. How are you?'

'Fine,' said Laura, turning back to the sauce she was stirring for the cheesecake. 'Really fine.'

'Not working too hard?'

'Yes, but it's OK,' Laura replied, wondering what she was going to say. Jo was still silent, so she said, 'And it's nothing compared to how hard you work, Jo.'

She knew Jo wasn't really listening. 'You look a bit different,' Jo said after a while. 'It's funny.'

'Like how?' asked Laura, intrigued, but she didn't turn round.

'Thinner. More – I don't know, more grown-up.'

'What do you mean? I look older?'

'No . . .' said Jo, which Laura instantly took to mean Yes. 'No . . . you don't . . . it's just you . . . I don't know, Laura. It's weird. But it suits you. You look great.'

'Thanks,' said Laura, not knowing whether to feel flattered or not.

'But you're OK?' asked Jo. She took a deep breath. 'Anyone, anything you want to tell me about?'

Laura put down her spoon and turned around again. 'Jo. Not this again,' she said, keeping her voice deliberately light. 'What's going on?'

Jo was a terrible liar. 'Nothing,' she said, flushing bright red.

'What do you want to know, then?' Laura asked, crossing her arms.

'Nothing!' Jo cried, her eyes huge in her little heart-shaped face. She slapped her hands down on either side of her. 'Nothing, I just – are you sure you're OK?'

Laura stared at her. 'I have no idea what you're talking about, Jo. Has Paddy been complaining about me?'

'No, of course not,' said Jo. She shook her head. 'I promise. I haven't been talking to him about you. I just – I heard something about you, and –'

'You heard something?' said Laura, slightly louder. Jo shrugged her shoulders. 'What do you mean, you *heard* something?' Still nothing. 'You've been on the other side of the world for three weeks,' said Laura curiously. 'Where did you *hear* something?'

'It's not important,' Jo insisted, backing down. She shook her head. 'Forget it, love.'

Laura didn't want to push it, especially when she hadn't seen Jo for so long, so she just nodded and sucked her lips into her mouth, confused.

'Tell me about Becky,' said Jo, after a moment.

'Well, you'll see in a minute.' Laura turned on the oven, forcing herself not to ask again. 'She's nice. Very sweet. Quite quiet. And – aha!' she said, as Paddy came back into the kitchen. 'Ha! More drinks?'

'Hello,' said Paddy, checking his watch. 'Simon just texted. He's on his way.' He looked anxiously out to the hallway. 'But Becky's not here yet. I might go and get her.'

'Go to her flat and march her up here? No,' said Laura, getting the wine out of the fridge. 'Calm down.'

'I am calm.' Paddy hopped around the kitchen.

Jo watched him. 'You like her, don't you?'

'Yes,' said Paddy. 'I do.' He gazed out of the window. 'Oh no. It's raining.'

'She's coming from the floor below, Paddy,' Laura told him. 'She's not going to get wet.'

'Hm, hm. I know, you're right.' Paddy nodded, as if she'd

made a really extraordinarily perceptive point. 'But it just means the view out of the window at supper's a bit depressing.'

Laura glanced at him witheringly.

'I think it's sweet,' said Jo. 'Look at him, all nervous.'

'No, look at him acting like a four-year-old,' said Laura. 'Calm down, Paddy. She's a girl you like, she's not the Messiah. Now get some perspective, and can you put some crisps into that bowl there please.'

There was silence, broken only by a tentative knock on the door.

'Well, off you go then,' said Laura, as Paddy cast her an anguished look. 'Answer it!'

An hour later they sat down to eat. Simon had talked of little else but Jorgia since his arrival – Jo and Becky each clasped their hands together, said it was wildly romantic and sweet, and hung on Simon's every word on the subject, whilst Laura stared suspiciously at Jo, wondering what on earth she was talking about. Simon then got out a photo of Jorgia to show everyone. He put it on the table, propped it up against the mustard, and Laura couldn't help feeling even more like Bridget Jones at the Smug Marrieds' dinner party, even if one of the couples was half-represented by photo only.

'Jorgia sends her love,' said Simon, at one end of the table, to Laura, at the other end. Jo and Paddy and their respective partners were on either side of them. Becky smiled at Laura and made an 'Ahh' sound. She had brought Laura some flowers, which Laura could tell made Jo think Becky was the nicest person in the whole world. Laura could also tell Jo was gearing up to invite Becky and Paddy round to dinner with her and Chris, so they could talk about mini-breaks together and Jo could show Becky their wedding photos. She could feel it, it was coming, and she knew she wouldn't be invited. Hah, like she wanted to be. She realised Simon was smiling expectantly at her, so she sat up in her chair, and looked at her brother politely.

'That's so nice of her,' she said.

'So, mate. When's she coming over?' Chris asked, handing Jo the salad. 'When are you going to see her?'

A cloud passed over Simon's face. 'I don't know, actually,' he said. He looked rather glum. 'I hoped she'd come as soon as possible, but she still hasn't got the money. She says.' He paused. 'I'm going to go back in about a month's time, though. I haven't spoken to her for a while, that's all.' He sighed. 'I miss her. You know.'

'Yeah, mate,' said Chris. 'I know. When Jo was away for the weekend when we started going out, I missed her!' He looked lovingly at Jo. Next to Jo, Paddy looked fondly at Becky, who smiled shyly up at him. Laura held her hand out for the salad, but Jo bypassed her and gave it straight to Paddy, as if she, Laura, were invisible.

Jo patted Simon's arm. 'It's tough, hon. But good for you. She sounds great.'

'She *is* great,' Simon said eagerly. 'Thanks, Jo. She's – so good, and kind, and beautiful. So lovely!'

'Oh god,' said Laura under her breath. Paddy gave her a sharp look, but Laura was glad he'd noticed, that he was cross with her. She felt destructive, suddenly.

'Some of my special mashed cauliflower, Jo?' Paddy asked, proffering a bowl.

'Er, no thanks,' said Jo. 'Thanks, though, Paddy. So, Simon, what else are you doing at the moment?'

'Nothing really,' Simon answered ruefully. 'I've got to sort it out, really. I've been back for three weeks and I haven't done anything.' He scratched his chin. 'And Mum and Dad are being great, but – well.'

'Well?' echoed Becky.

'Well, I need to get a job, all that kind of stuff.' Simon looked around at each of them. 'But until Jorgia and I work out what's going on I can't, really. I don't want to start applying for jobs till I know if I'm going to be here or not.'

'You really think you might move to Peru?' asked Paddy.

Simon turned to him. 'Yeah, you know, I really might. It's a big step and everything, but – it just feels right. I can't explain it.'

Laura said nothing. She chewed on some gristly meat.

'That's amazing, Simon,' Jo said, smiling happily at him. 'But – wow, that's a big step.'

'I know,' said Simon. 'It is, but it doesn't feel like it, somehow. I can't explain it. I can really see myself moving there.'

'Oh, come on,' Laura cut in suddenly.

Paddy looked down at his plate as Simon stared at her. 'What?' he said.

Laura said patiently, 'Look, Si. It's really great you've met Jorgia and everything. And you love her and all that. But – come on.' She stretched out her hands towards him, in a placating gesture. 'You have to wise up, slightly. You know? You're not going to move there. You might think you are at the moment, but long term – seriously, no way.'

Paddy was still looking down at his plate. Laura tried to meet Jo's eye for support, but she was staring at Simon. She carried blindly on. 'I mean – who is she? This girl? You barely know her. You're completely different! You've got nothing in common! It's never, ever going to –'

'OK, OK,' Simon said suddenly. He rolled his lips into his mouth, pushed his knife and fork together politely, and sat back in his chair. Then he said, 'You think it's not going to work, don't you?'

'Yes,' said Laura, relieved he'd stopped her from going too far, and relieved he seemed to be listening to her. 'Yes, that's it. I'm sorry, Simon, but I just –'

'And what the hell do you know about it?' Simon's expression was ugly. He pointed his finger at her, his voice shaking. 'You're amazing, Laura. What business is it of yours in the first place? Eh?'

'It's not that – it's –' Laura said, taken aback by the vitriol

402

in his voice. She tried to reason with him. 'Listen, Simon. I'm just saying –'

'No, *you* listen,' Simon said. The others were looking distinctly uncomfortable now. He pointed at his sister again. 'You listen, for once, instead of sitting there in that smug, judgemental way you seem to have acquired since I got back, when you don't know the first fucking thing about it.'

'Simon –' Jo began, a look of anguish on her face, but Laura waved her away.

'Oh really,' she snapped back, a flush of anger rising to her cheeks. 'It's none of my business when my own brother's leeching off Mum and Dad, and – and Gran, and lazing around the house doing jack all just because of some random stranger he thinks he's in love with! Oh, no, none of my business, you're quite right.'

'That's what I mean,' Simon said, his voice dripping cold disdain. 'The hypocrisy of it. You should listen to yourself, Laura. It *is* none of your business, OK? I've been back three weeks and I know I have to get a job. Mum and Dad don't mind. *You're* the one who minds. It's so fucking hypocritical! You make me laugh! *You*, all of a sudden judging *me* because you think I'm in some dodgy relationship, when you – you go from one crappy relationship to another, some loser who you think is the answer to your prayers, and you're too fucking stupid to see they're just leading you on! You practically *lose your job* because of it! And when I fall for someone – I know it's hard, I know it's going to be difficult, but I really *love* her, you can't see that, can you, I *love* her – you don't even say "Great!" or "Can't wait to meet her, brother!" No, you sit there with your sour-milk expression, like you've got it all sorted, like you're perfect.'

He paused and wiped his hand across his mouth, breathing deeply. 'I don't understand what's happened to you. You didn't used to be like this.'

Jo was staring at Laura, her eyes huge, shaking her head.

Laura looked at her, perplexed, and then at Paddy, who was looking down at his plate. She knew what that meant. It meant he agreed with Simon. A pain stabbed in her side.

She and Simon knew the drill of their arguments well enough not to let it fester now they were older. And – Laura bit her lip. He was wrong, he was fucking rude and wrong, and it was never going to work out but – it *was* none of her business. So, as they waited for her response, the silence in the room growing more and more awkward, she took a deep, deep breath, fighting the urge to scream, to burst into tears and slap her little brother.

'Sorry,' she said. 'Fine. I just worry about you. Because you're so different. That's all. But you're right. I don't know what it's like, being with someone like that. It's none of my business.'

Simon nodded and looked apologetic. 'I shouldn't have yelled at you,' he said. 'But you don't know what it's like, you're right.'

Jo looked quickly from Laura to Simon, but said nothing. Chris squeezed her hand, and Paddy gave a big sigh of relief and stood up to collect the plates, and Becky stood up too. Laura sat there, not moving. She felt very far removed from her brother then, from Jo and Chris, and Paddy. They didn't understand, they didn't know the whole truth. But that was her business, not theirs, her secret, she wasn't going to tell them. They'd be gone soon, then she could go to her room and curl up in bed and read. Gone soon.

But then Jo said slowly, 'Well, that's not exactly true, is it, Laura?'

'What?' Laura asked, not really paying attention. She put the mashed cauliflower bowl gingerly on top of Paddy's pile of plates as he staggered into the kitchen, followed closely by a rather shaken-looking Becky.

'It's not exactly true.' Jo was playing with her wine glass, sliding it from one hand to the other. She looked from one Foster sibling to another. 'About you being with someone really different from you. Laura does know about that.'

'Yes, I know,' said Simon, slightly impatiently. 'But – well, Dan was a mistake – it was – she screwed it up. Sorry, Laura, but you did – and anyway, he wasn't *that* different, come off it.'

'I don't mean Dan,' Jo said, leaning forward across the table. 'Simon, Dan's not the reason she's behaving like this.'

'What?' asked Laura, bewildered. 'What are you talking about?' How could Jo know about it?

Jo nodded at her emphatically. She reached out, took her hand. 'Love. We were on the same flight back as Fran. Your cousin. And Ludo. Had a long chat with them. They'd been in –'

'Singapore,' Laura finished for her. Why did she know that? Yes, Annabel had told her. 'So?'

'Fran?' said Simon. 'You poor things. For the whole flight? What a nightmare.'

'I don't understand . . .' said Laura.

'We had a long chat,' Jo continued. 'Fran and I. She told me all about your granny's birthday party.' She looked searchingly at her friend. 'About who was there. About who turned up. You know. Usual stuff.'

Laura went pale. She could actually feel the blood draining from her face, it was the oddest sensation. 'Oh my god. Look,' she said, recovering herself. 'They don't know what happened . . .'

'Well, they couldn't wait to tell us all about it,' said Chris suddenly, next to his wife.

'I'm sorry, darling,' said Jo, her eyes on Laura's. 'So . . . it's true, then? Who you met – up there?'

Laura looked from Jo to Chris. 'Er . . .' she said. 'Well, I'm sure if Fran said it was true, it must be true.'

'That's the one thing that makes me feel glad I wasn't in Norfolk,' Simon piped up from the other end of the table. Laura looked dumbly at him. 'Missing Fran and Lulu. Gah.'

'Laura hasn't said anything to you about Norfolk, has she?'

Jo continued innocently. 'Hasn't gone on about it, hasn't sighed and sat around like it's raining on prom night.'

'No,' said Simon. 'Course not. Laura – well, we always know when she's fallen for someone. She won't shut up about it. Sorry, sis, but you do go on a bit,' he said.

'True,' agreed Laura, trying to be amicable and change the subject, to head Jo off. 'Now –'

'That's where you're wrong,' said Jo. She drained her glass and looked at Laura. 'I'm sorry, darling.' She turned to Simon. 'What if I told you your big sister spent her holiday with your parents having some grand affair with the Marquess of Ranelagh.'

'Who?' asked Simon blankly.

Jo and Laura were sitting by the pile of newspapers that needed to be recycled, and to Laura's immense horror Jo pulled the supplement with the offending article off the top of the pile. Why hadn't she thrown it away? Why the hell couldn't she bring herself to just chuck it in the bin? Laura watched as Jo smoothed the newspaper on the table, and jabbed at it with her finger. 'Third most eligible bachelor in England. His house is over three hundred years old. Look!' She gestured at the picture of Nick standing in front of the house. 'Laura. Is that him? It is, isn't it? He's the one Fran told me you were seeing.'

'What?' said Paddy, standing in the doorway holding the plates for the cheesecake. He shook his head violently. 'Laura? What's going on? *Who*'ve you been seeing?' The spoons on the plate slid onto the floor with a loud clatter.

'Some millionaire marquess,' said Simon, standing behind Jo and peering over the newspaper. 'Laura, seriously? My god.'

'Oh god,' said Laura. She crouched down, picked up the spoons and slammed them on the table.

'Is this true?' Paddy asked, putting the bowls down heavily, sounding like a stern Victorian paterfamilias.

'Er, yes,' said Laura.

'You – shagged – *him*?' Paddy pointed at the paper.

'It wasn't like that,' Laura said.

406

'Him?' Becky said timidly. 'Seriously?'

'Yes, yes,' said Laura. She could feel her ears burning red. 'I was on holiday, in July,' she added, trying to explain it to Becky, who was looking really alarmed. 'I met him – at his house, when we went to look round, you know. Me and Mum and Dad. He asked me out, we had a few drinks. Um. And it was great. But I had to come home.' She smiled at Becky, as if this was completely normal. 'Just a holiday fling.'

She avoided the gaze of Jo, whose small, determined face was watching her, eyes narrow, lips pursed. She turned to Paddy, who was shaking his head at her. He gave her a small smile. 'I knew it,' he said. 'Just knew it. Didn't you?' he turned to Jo.

'Yes,' said Jo. 'Bloody hell, yes. Didn't you?' she looked at Simon.

'Well, Mum mentioned something, and I just forgot about it,' said Simon. 'But I kept wondering what was going on with you,' he added, holding his hands out in a placatory gesture to Laura. 'You've been a right cow since I got home. Hasn't she?' he appealed to Jo.

'Well,' said Jo. 'Not herself. Don't you think?' she said to Paddy.

'Yes,' said Paddy, 'I knew someone else had got to you. Didn't you?' turning to Chris, but Laura, wearying intensely of this Pass the Parcel conversation, said,

'That's rubbish. He didn't "get" to me. It's fine. It was a holiday roll in the hay, and I was sad when it was over, but I'm not sad now. OK?'

'OK,' the assembled company chorused, rather quietly, but Laura was annoyed to realise they obviously didn't mean it.

'A marquess?' Paddy said after a pause, still staring at the paper. 'In his huge, massive house? Did you do it in his house?'

'Do what – oh god, good grief. Is that all you want to know?' Laura said, shaking her head at Paddy in amusement.

'Blimey, Laura,' said Simon. 'You know how to pick them, don't you?'

407

'That's what I thought,' Laura replied lightly.

'A marquess? You must be over the moon,' said Simon slowly, drawing the paper towards him. 'Your very own romantic hero. When are we going to meet him?'

'You're not,' said Laura. 'I'm not seeing him again.' She stood up. 'You didn't bring in the ice cream, Pads.'

'But –' Paddy said. 'Why not?'

'It was a holiday fling, nothing more,' Laura told them again. 'You won't believe me so I can say it till I'm blue in the face, but it's true. He didn't tell me who he was, I thought he was just some ordinary bloke. We were –' She stopped. 'I thought we were friends. Yeah, we slept together. It's a beautiful house. Oh, the idea of it was all very romantic. But it didn't work out.' Under the table, she dug her hand into her thigh. 'He's a bit of a twat, to be honest.'

Paddy stared at her as if he didn't recognise her. 'Really?' he said.

'Yeah,' said Laura, sounding unconcerned. 'Read that – you'll see what I mean. I thought he was quite nice to start with, but actually he's just what you'd expect someone like that to be. Can't really trust him. Bit flash. Posh, you know.' She dropped the last adjective in like a stone, knowing it would drive the point home to these nice, middle-class boys with the inverted snobbery all of them wore as close as a second skin.

'Really?' Paddy said again, nodding sympathetically. 'I must say, he looks it.' He peered down. 'Ooh, look at him here. Yeah, you're right. Does look – a bit, well . . . You know.'

'Actually –' Laura began, then she stopped. She took a deep breath, and turned to her brother, who was staring at her.

He smiled. 'You funny old thing.'

'I know,' said Laura. She took his hand. 'I wasn't being deliberately – horrible. You know. It's just – well, the reason it was never going to work out with me and Nick is, we're so different. Too much difference. It's a fairytale. Fairytales aren't real. And that's why – I worry about you and Jorgia, and I shouldn't. You're right, it's not my business.'

'Ah, sis,' Simon said, putting his arm around her shoulders and giving her a squeeze. Next to him, Paddy put the plates on the table, and Jo and Becky carried on staring at the article. Chris watched them all stoically.

Simon said, under his breath, 'I'm sorry, Loz. I mean it. Let's forget it. But I think you're wrong, you know.' He paused. 'I love Jorgia, that's all I'm sure about. Seriously. You don't fall in love with someone because it's convenient.'

Sadness flooded into Laura's heart, a great wave of it, overtaking her so unexpectedly that she was almost knocked out by it. She felt so alone, all of a sudden, and she couldn't understand why, when here were her two best friends and her brother. What if Nick was here, she thought for a second, and she could put her head on his chest, feel him draw her close into his body, feel safe, as safe as she had in his house, in bed. What if she could tell him all of this, how would it be? She wished . . . No, she reminded herself. Forget it.

'It wasn't just that –' Laura said. She tried to explain, but she knew she couldn't, didn't want to. 'Yeah, I'm sure you're right.'

'I don't understand, though,' said Jo. 'It was just that week, right?'

'Right,' said Laura. She handed out the bowls.

'And you haven't seen him since?'

'No. Wasn't really going to work out. Like I say, we're too different and everything.'

'Fran said he came marching into the house like Mr Darcy,' said Jo. The others looked up, fascinated.

'Fran talks crap,' Laura said.

'And,' Jo said, not listening to Laura, but conveying the story to the rest of the table, who were agog, 'he was obviously mad about her, and then he whisked her off to a ball at his house in the evening. And that he's *gorgeous*.'

Laura laughed, she didn't know how else to react. 'About three per cent of that is true.'

'Which three per cent?' Simon asked.

'He came to the house, and –'

'He met your parents?' Paddy put in.

'Yes!' Laura replied, exasperated. 'Well, for about two seconds. And yes, I went to his house, but it wasn't a ball. It was a family dinner. And I drove myself. And I'd been there before, so –'

'How many times?' said Jo. 'In his *room*?'

'Oh,' said Laura. 'It doesn't matter. Look, it was . . . it was . . .'

'Just for the summer, I know,' said Jo. 'But – did you like him?'

Laura said simply, 'Yes.' She looked up. 'So there we go.'

'Did he like you?' Becky asked.

Laura could see Nick's expression, the way he stared at her as if it was only them in the whole world. She was not in the room any more. She was in the library at Chartley. Nick, staring down at her. Looking at her as if he wanted to drown, like he was the one who needed rescuing as much as her. And when she held him that night, and softly kissed the baby soft hair that curled at his temples as he slept on her, his skin against hers.

She stared blindly at them. 'Yes, he did.'

At the other end of the table, Paddy got up, and ushered Chris towards the Playstation, along with Simon. Left behind, Jo looked at Laura, shock on her face, and Becky said suddenly, 'Um. This is none of my business, but – why aren't you seeing him any more then?' Laura and Jo swivelled round to look at her. 'Sorry,' said Becky. 'It's really nothing to do with me. I just –'

'She's right.' Jo nodded. 'She is, you know.'

'Well,' said Laura, trying to explain. 'It's – you see –' She paused. 'Just because he's perfect on paper doesn't mean it's going to work out. It's not always like that. That's what I used to think . . . and . . .'

410

'Right,' said Becky, looking awkward as Laura trailed off. Her throat felt thick. On the sofa, Paddy was gesturing for the corkscrew, and Becky got up to pass it to him.

Jo said nothing, but looked at Laura, as if she wasn't convinced either. 'He's got a girlfriend, now, anyway,' Laura said.

'So?' said Jo. 'Perhaps it's not serious.'

'Yeah, right. Some rich girl, heiress person. Beautiful. Thin. Loaded. Your basic nightmare.'

'Well,' said Jo. 'So what?'

'I thought maybe it didn't matter, all of that –' Laura tapped the paper on the table lightly. 'And then – you know. Stuff like this, this article, reminds me it does matter. Reminds me I'm still not quite there yet. Need to stop being so hopeless, head in the clouds, you know.'

'Are you sure it wouldn't work?' Jo said urgently, in a quiet voice. 'Are you sure you don't want to see him again?'

Laura wanted to laugh. They were two totally separate things, weren't they? Of course she was sure it wouldn't work. And of course she wanted to see him again. Her eyes filled with tears. Mistake, mistake. She could not let Jo see her cry, could not let them see it meant anything to her. She looked up, across the room. Paddy had one arm around Becky's waist, and was kissing her on the neck, trying to get the corkscrew off her. She was yelping with pleasure, smiling wildly as Simon and Chris watched indulgently, checking out the Playstation games with one eye.

'Oh darling,' said Jo softly. 'You're not very happy at the moment, are you?'

'I am,' said Laura. 'Jo, please don't.'

'You're not happy,' said Jo. She looked at Paddy and Becky. Laura wiped her nose on her arm, breathing raggedly.

'I've got a date next week,' she said weakly, as a diversion tactic.

'Well, that's good!' Jo replied encouragingly. 'Do you like him?'

411

'Oh yes,' said Laura. 'He's – yeah. He's great. Met him through work. He's a financial analyst something. Er – seems really nice.'

'What's he called?'

'Marcus,' said Laura reluctantly, and the image of Marcus fiddling with his cufflinks loomed large in her mind's eye.

'Look, there you go then!' said Jo, trying to seem inordinately pleased. She said breezily, 'No more marquesses, eh? A nice, normal date with a nice, normal bloke, just what you need.'

'Er –' said Laura, not sure how to respond. 'Well – I suppose so.'

CHAPTER FORTY-TWO

'When do you have to meet this man, darling?'

'Not till seven thirty, don't worry.'

'Here, one more glass? And I'll just go and get the necklace.'

'Absolutely, thanks, Gran. This is really kind of you.'

'Well, it's lovely to see you, my darling girl.'

Laura drained her glass and her grandmother poured some more champagne into it. 'There you go,' she said, and she padded back into the kitchen to put the bottle in the fridge. 'I'll just get the necklace.' She disappeared down the corridor.

Laura gazed around the flat, and looked out of the window. It was a still, light autumn evening, with just a hint of cold in the air. She was meeting Marcus at a champagne bar near the Royal Courts of Justice where the dinner was taking place, and since Marcus had rung her up the previous morning to confirm, and mentioned casually that it was very formal black tie and could she please be dressed appropriately ('Classic,' Jo had said when Laura told her this. 'He obviously thinks you dress like a hooker'), Laura was demure in a black velvet dress falling just below the knee, tied with a pale silver Regency-style ribbon high on the waist, but she needed something else to not feel cheap, and so she had rung up her grandmother and, killing two birds with one stone, asked if she could a) come to see her that evening to b) borrow her diamond necklace, which had been Mary's own grandmother's.

From the window in Mary's sitting room one could see across the rooftops of central London, down south to her beloved Selfridges, towards Mayfair and Hyde Park. The sitting room was light, filled firmly with old, odd pieces of furniture from Mary and Guy's travels. An old Moroccan rug, woven with gold, hung on the wall. A mahogany bureau, stuffed with letters and housekeeping files, all written in Mary's huge, looping scrawl. There on the wall was the picture of Guy that Laura loved so much. He was standing in the garden at Seavale, the sea in the distance, leaning on a spade and smiling at something past the camera. A rough cloth sunhat was jammed on his head. And there, staring up at him with frank adoration, was a very small (Laura thought four, perhaps) Simon, naked except for a pair of towelling shorts, gazing with his mouth open. Laura smiled as she looked at the picture again, crammed in there next to a hopelessly young-looking Mum and Dad on their wedding day and a very stiff Annabel and Robert standing in a formal-looking portico. It was funny how much Simon resembled his step-grandfather. He was slow to anger, quick to laugh, just like Guy had been.

After what Simon had said to her the previous Saturday, so cold and harsh, after Laura had seen the open disdain in his eyes, she had taken a long, hard look at herself. Was she different now? She knew she wasn't the wide-eyed romantic she'd been a year ago. But had she, in trying to turn over a new leaf, to protect herself, gone too far the other way? She thought of Jo's comforting hand on her arm as she tried not to cry, thought how nice it would be simply to burst into tears, tell her all about it, how much she missed Nick, how she thought Mary might have been right all along, but she had the feeling it was too late.

It wasn't too late for her, though, she knew that now. She wasn't going to change again. She was just going to stop being this way or that way and simply be herself again. Stop hiding. Stop dressing things up in fairytale costumes or dressing them down, packing them away and keeping them hidden. Just be herself. Go on dates, work hard, have a laugh. Enjoy herself.

She looked at her watch. 'You OK, Gran?' she called.

She could hear her grandmother in her bedroom, clinking various boxes open and shut, and remembered what Simon kept saying about Mary. She was being a bit odd, he thought. She was going over the past too much, not her sunny self, getting confused about things. Laura thought it was probably that Simon was surprised to find his grandmother was older than he remembered. She wasn't seventy any more, she was eighty-five, she didn't seem it but she was. Perhaps it was time for her to start slowing down. Laura smiled wryly as she thought of her grandmother's reaction if she tried to tell her she ought to be taking things easy.

'Here it is,' Mary appeared, shaking her fist in the air. 'It wasn't where I thought it was, I couldn't find it. Silly of me.'

She opened her hand. Against the wrinkled, soft palm lay an old link chain and at the centre a cluster of stars, with hairy, twirling tails, intricately and beautifully made. One stone caught the light outside and twinkled quickly.

'Let me put it on you,' Mary said, and she shuffled past the armchair, and slid the necklace around Laura's neck. 'Look at yourself,' she said.

Laura patted her collarbone, loving the feeling of the scratchy, cold metal on her skin, and stood up to look in the small looking-glass by the balcony door.

'It's lovely,' she said. 'Just lovely.' She was glad her hair was up, twisted loosely into a chignon, so that the necklace could be seen. It was beautiful. Laura took Mary's hand.

'Thank you so much for letting me wear it tonight. I'll take good care of it, I promise.'

'Of course you will, darling,' said Mary, staring at the

necklace. 'You'd be wise to, anyway,' she said, turning away. 'It'll be yours one day, when I'm dead. Then you can wear it all you like.'

'Well,' Laura said, slightly briskly. 'We don't know that, do we? It should be Annabel's, and anyway, I'm not having this conversation with you, Gran!'

'Not Annabel's,' Mary said stubbornly. She picked up her drink, still standing in the middle of the room, and said rather gothically, 'You're my blood daughter, not her.'

'Mum is, you mean,' said Laura, feeling rather uncomfortable. 'Who?'

'My mum. Angela. She is.' Laura pointed to the wedding photo of her mother on the wall.

'Yes, yes,' said Mary impatiently. She blinked, and said accusingly, 'Stupid, stupid, we shouldn't be talking about this, you know.'

You were the one who started going on about bloodlines, like we're descendants of Edward of York during the Wars of the Roses, Laura wanted to say, but she didn't, she patted the necklace again and said, 'Well, thank you so much. I'm so excited.'

'More excited about the necklace than this date, am I right?' said Mary, and she gave Laura an appraising stare. Her eyes danced, and Laura laughed, partly with relief.

'Er,' she said, picking her glass up again and twisting it round in her hand, 'Well, I don't know about that. Marcus – he's –'

Marcus had an invitation for the dinner sent to her, 'Miss Laura Foster', in thick cream card with gold around the edge, and today she had received flowers at work, a huge bouquet with a message that said, 'I look forward to tonight. Yours, Marcus', which made Shana and Nasrin almost apoplectic with mirth, but which Tim and Rachel had said solemnly was Very Nice of him, only Laura had heard them out in the stairwell laughing about something five minutes later and she suspected it was that.

She thought it was nice, very, very nice. How many people actually did that, and wasn't it awful that girls spent their whole time complaining about boys and saying they were crap – and then when a boy did something totally lovely and thoughtful, they laughed at him, like it was pathetic and needy and a bit strange? So what if she wasn't madly in love with Marcus; she'd only met him once, properly, he'd asked her on a date, and he seemed nice if a trifle – well, odd. Nothing ventured, nothing gained. The new Laura. She smiled at Mary.

'Yes?' said Mary, encouragingly.

'Ahm,' said Laura, not sure how to start. She caught her grandmother watching her, with her bright, clever eyes that missed nothing, and thought, Actually, it's pointless to try and spin this for you.

'Heard from that nice young man lately?' said Mary.

'What? Him? No. No,' said Laura, giving her grandmother a quelling stare. She took a sip of her drink.

'Nothing?' said Mary.

'Nothing,' said Laura, then realised it sounded as if she was expecting to hear something. Of course she wasn't. 'No, nothing. You sound like Aunt Annabel.'

'What do you mean?'

'She rang me –' Laura began, then noticed the look on Mary's face, the one which brooked no criticism of Aunt Annabel. Laura knew she wouldn't be able to explain it to her grandmother, so she just said, 'Oh, nothing.'

'She's excited about it,' said Mary unexpectedly.

'Oh good grief,' said Laura. 'There's nothing to be excited *about*. She's never called me before, why's she suddenly so interested?'

'Perhaps she was glad to have something to call you about,' Mary pointed out.

'I doubt that, highly,' Laura muttered. 'When was the last time she called Mum up, just for a chat?'

'Oh, darling,' said Mary firmly. 'Your aunt and your mother –

they're very different. But they're more alike than you think. You all are. Annabel – she does love you, you know.'

'We're not alike,' said Laura, thinking of her and Simon, her mum and dad and their normal, easy life, and the Sandersons, so grand, so snobbish, so riddled with strange and foreign customs, ideas about life, and at the head of them Aunt Annabel herself.

'That's just not true,' said Mary softly. 'You have far more in common than you realise. Far more.' She ran her nail around the edge of the glass, picking up the sheen of perspiration that clung to it. 'Why do you want the world to be black and white? It's not.'

Laura looked down at the rather cheap velvet material of her dress. 'I don't,' she said, wondering whether they were still talking about Annabel or not.

Her grandmother was silent, and then she cleared her throat. 'Do you mind if I say something?' she said suddenly.

'No . . .' answered Laura uncertainly, thinking that if yet another person was about to have a go at her she might just throw her hands up and scream, especially if it was Mary, whose good opinion mattered to her so much.

'I think you have too many people telling you what to do and telling you what you're like,' said Mary flatly. 'Don't you?'

'Yes,' said Laura, nodding fervently, thinking of Jo, Simon, everyone at work, even Nick telling her she was weak, pathetic.

'I'm not going to tell you how I think you should live your life, or what I think you should do,' said Mary. 'Now's not the time. But I will say this. Don't try and paper over things that matter, Laura. The cracks will appear. Maybe not immediately, but they will.'

'What do you mean?' Laura said quietly, not wanting to know but feeling she had to ask.

Her grandmother said firmly, 'Just what I say. Don't paper over cracks, over things you think you can't cope with.'

Mary's melodious voice grated on her nerves, and Laura

stood up; she had to get out of there, suddenly the flat was not warm and cosy and full of memories, but crowded and claustrophobic, closing in on her. 'I have to go, you know. I'm going to be late.' She gathered up her bag and little evening cape. 'Sorry.'

Mary was unperturbed. 'Fine. You look beautiful, Laura,' she said, standing up slowly and smiling at her. 'I'm – I am proud of you, darling, you do know that.'

'Oh,' Laura said. 'Thank you, Gran.' She kissed her. 'Thank you.' She went to the front door, Mary behind her. 'I'll call you soon,' she said. 'Thanks again, Gran. Lovely to see you. Sorry it's been – so long.'

'Don't worry,' said her grandmother. 'It will always have been too long, darling.' And she closed the door.

Laura walked slowly down the stairs, wondering if she should go back up, shake Mary out of her strange mood, and then reminded herself nothing would be accomplished by it. Paper over cracks? What was she talking about? Everything was fine, she was going on a date, with no expectations in mind other than a nice evening, and with the hope that she might get some money out of Marcus for the programme too. She was on the way, it was a fresh start! She wasn't papering over anything, and it was silly to say she was.

Pah. Laura shrugged her shoulders as she reached the bottom of the stairs. The hunter moon was rising as the sun disappeared. It was huge, golden, so low in the sky and so close she felt as if she could reach out and snatch it. Laura stared at it through the glass-panelled front door of the mansion block, as it hung above the wide boulevard down towards Oxford Street, then she stepped onto the pavement and hailed a cab, following the moon east towards the City.

CHAPTER FORTY-THREE

'It's very kind of you to invite me,' said Laura, when she was settled at a table with Marcus twenty minutes later, a glass of champagne in her hand.

Marcus gave her an unsmiling smile, and looked round the crowded bar, which, on a Friday night in the City, was pretty much wall-to-wall bankers, lawyers, and accountants, male and female, dressed in suits or black ties, throwing money around like it was going out of fashion. He said stiffly, 'My pleasure. Why not.'

'And – Marcus, thank you so much for the flowers, it was incredibly sweet – er, kind of you. Again. Thank you!' Laura said, feeling completely embarrassed at this, though she couldn't work out why.

'Really, it was my pleasure, as I've said,' Marcus said repressively, as if her mentioning the flowers was disgusting. Laura sighed inwardly and ran her hand lightly along the back of her neck. She was here, it was fine, and she was going to enjoy herself. And she was going to get Marcus to commit to the sponsorship programme. She smiled across at her date, willing herself not to burst into tears, and Marcus met her gaze, looking rather surprised. He straightened up a little, fiddled with his tie and said,

'Laura. I'm not being very expansive, I fear. I very much enjoyed meeting you. And it is my pleasure that you've agreed to accompany me this evening. I'm honoured.'

'Er,' said Laura, not sure how to respond. 'Well, thank you there. It – it's great.'

'I've looked over the material you sent me and Clare,' said Marcus. 'I *think* –' he touched her arm, lightly '– there may be a way we can join your programme, give you some money.'

'Really?!' said Laura, her face lighting up. 'That's wonderful, thank you!'

'Let's see, let's see,' Marcus admonished. 'Let's talk about it at dinner. We need to discuss it a little further, but – well, all being well – ah.' He raised his eyebrows at her.

'Well, thank you for thinking about it, anyway,' said Laura. 'Wow.'

No one from work knew Laura was here tonight, but she'd dropped enough hints about Linley Munroe that they were all super-curious about what she was going to pull off. She imagined the scene on Monday, her casually sauntering into the office, Rachel and Nasrin going over some figures, wondering how they were going to explain to Gareth that the investment still hadn't come through, as Laura nonchalantly said, 'Oh, the money? Yeah – I've sorted it. No sweat.' Then high-fives all round, Rachel's face lighting up with a smile the way it used to, before horrible Boyd from Nottingham dumped her and Laura started screwing things up . . . She luxuriated in the image, and then came back down to earth with a bump, to find Marcus staring at her, and realised she had to get through the evening first, before this was in the bag.

Silence descended again, unwelcome, unasked for, but thankfully Marcus took the conversational plunge. He took a deep, shuddering breath, adjusted his tie and said, 'So. Let's talk about it later, eh? Tell me. Where do your parents live?'

Laura smiled at the obviousness of the social questioning. 'Harrow,' she said.

'Ah,' said Marcus. 'Chap in the office next to mine went to Harrow.'

'Not that bit, I bet,' Laura said patiently. 'My mum and dad live in deepest suburbia. About ten minutes off the main road. You have to drive for miles to find a shop selling milk, it's all mock-Tudor semis and cul-de-sacs. But it's nice. How about you?'

'What?' said Marcus.

'Are you from London?'

'Yes, yes,' said Marcus.

'Where?'

'Near Camden,' said Marcus vaguely, and Laura didn't push the subject further, knowing from experience that when people seem noncommittal about something they are doing it deliberately.

'But yeah. I live in Vauxhall now. You know those apartments? Over the Thames?'

'Wow,' said Laura. 'How great.'

'Yep. It really is. Pretty expensive, but worth it, I can tell you. Very good investment for the future, you know.' Marcus stuck his lips out and nodded, his eyes half-closed. 'Not sure if I'll stay there forever, but it'll definitely work as a rental. Some guy like me in a few years' time.'

His eyes boggled at her, and Laura nodded, pretending to look interested. 'I'll move on and up then, you know.'

'Mm,' Laura said.

Marcus leant back in his chair and gave a mock yawn. He stretched his arms. 'Yep. Probably to Balham, you can buy a good-sized family home there, although it's pretty damn expensive. Still, it'll be very handy for me. For the City.'

'Yes,' said Laura. 'I like Balham.'

'Plus,' Marcus nodded at her, looking pleased, 'it's a nice area for kids on the weekends.'

'Right,' said Laura, then realised she didn't understand. 'Why?'

422

'Well, there's shops and cafés, and the park nearby, and of course you can drive to Richmond –'

'No,' Laura interrupted. 'Why do you need a family home?'

'For the family,' Marcus said, looking irritated again.

'You're – not –' Laura instinctively grabbed her bag in case she needed to make a hasty exit. 'You're not *married*, are you?'

Marcus looked amazed, and for a split second Laura thought, Oh god! How could I have got this so wrong? Again? But Marcus said abruptly,

'Of course I'm not. Do you think I'd ask you out if I were married? What kind of man – no, of course I'm not.'

'Good, good,' said Laura, surreptitiously putting her things back down on the seat again. 'Sorry. It's just I thought – you were talking about family homes and everything, the cafés and stuff. I assumed you might – er.'

'I'm merely expressing – trying to say that – it's of no importance,' Marcus said.

'Sorry,' Laura murmured quietly, looking at the table. She felt sad again. 'I didn't get it.'

'I was just thinking aloud,' said Marcus after a pause. 'You know. If one were married. Where would one live. Have to think about that kind of thing these days.'

'Even if you're not going out with someone?' Laura interjected, then regretted it.

But her companion said, after another pause, 'Well, yes.' He smiled, for the first time that evening. 'Bit tragic, isn't it?'

'What?'

'Planning where I'd live if I was married. With children.' He cleared his throat with a long, drawn-out sound like a firing range. Laura looked at him, smiling self-consciously. She saw his large fingers, mechanically clutching his cufflinks; his large, normally expressionless face now wearing a rather anxious mask. His beautifully pressed dinner jacket, the studs of his shirt perfectly done up except for one, missing, just visible if you

423

looked, hidden by the jacket. Her heart contracted with sadness as she looked at him. He needed a wife, he needed someone to love him and look after him, a nice girl to move to Balham or wherever with him, who would think he was absolutely marvellous. In his way, he was a hopeless romantic too.

She looked at him. 'You look beautiful tonight,' Marcus said, as if he were talking about the weather. He leant forward and kissed her on the lips, rather heavily and clumsily, almost defiantly, and sat back again. 'Thank you,' he said formally.

'Hey! Ah,' said Laura, rather flustered, feeling she should thank him too, or write him a formal letter:

Re: Your kiss on the eve of September _th, 7.55 p.m.
Thank you for your attention in this matter. I have several queries which I would like to draw your attention to.

(i) My client, Miss Laura Foster, would like to make you aware that in respect of this she will happily go to the dance with you but there will be no horizontal action between yourself and my client.

(ii) Your kissing action is not bad, but you are hereby notified that the object of the exercise is not to try and suck my client's lips into your mouth in a sea anemone-like motion, it is rather off-putting and makes it hard for my client to breathe.

(iii) My client has now had four glasses of champagne thanks to you and her grandmother, Mrs Mary Fielding, and is on the way to having had too much to drink, so you should be aware also that Baileys makes her throw up. Do not give her any.

Now that he had staked his claim, as it were, Marcus seemed to relax visibly. He stood up, and offered Laura his arm. 'We should be on our way, if that's OK,' he said, and picked up her cape and put it round her shoulders.

'What kind of people are going to be there?' asked Laura, as he opened the door for her.

He took her arm. 'Oh, all sorts,' he said, smiling rather indulgently at her as if she'd asked an adorable question.

They were opposite the Royal Courts, and Laura could see black ties and evening dresses trickling in through the elaborate stone gates, up the steps. They stopped at a zebra crossing. Laura said, 'No, I mean – tell me a bit about it. So, are these your clients?'

'Sure. They're a big German bank. They have investors of their own there too. They have a lot of very rich private clients, so it's a formal affair and there are often some pretty important people there. But yeah, they're all good guys. Should be fun.'

He took her arm as they crossed the road. 'Right,' said Laura, thinking that sounded like anything *but* fun, and already so confused by the progress of the date so far, her role therein and the evening ahead of her that any action on her part would be pointless. She squeezed his arm. 'God, Marcus – who's that?'

A tall, blond man, maybe in his late fifties, had got out of a car that had pulled up in front of the building. He was opening the other passenger door, from which emerged a woman so overly made up, so wholly encrusted with jewellery and sparkle that she looked like a mannequin. Her dress was slathered in multicoloured sequins, it fell against her body like a sheath. Her hair was rigid and yellow on top of her head, and her face was compartmentalised into a series of smooth, bright colours: huge red lips, pink, slanting cheeks, hooded eyes painted blue, a smooth brown forehead. She took her companion's arm and looked impassively around, disdain writ large on whatever part of her face still held expression.

'My god,' said Marcus, grinding to a halt.

'I know,' said Laura. 'She looks ridiculous.'

'No,' said Marcus. 'I didn't think they'd come. That's – Lars Thorson.'

'Who?' said Laura.

'Lars Thorson. Don't you know who he is? He's – well, he's the richest man in Sweden. Invested in tech stock when it was still geek territory. That's his wife, Tania. Right old slapper,' said Marcus with relish, pulling away from Laura to get a better look. Thorson. Laura looked at Marcus in panic, trying to reassure the inner voice of warning in her head. 'Good god, look at her,' Marcus continued, his eyes lighting up. He stared openly at the couple in front of them, as Tania Thorson rearranged her shawl. He turned to Laura. 'God, can't believe it. Tania Thorson. She used to be a bit of all right. Look at her. She looks like a –'

'Right, right,' Laura said, steering him towards the circular doors. 'Right. And,' she said, not wanting to ask the question, but knowing she was going to, 'Don't they have a daughter?'

'Yep, they do. Cecilia. Very fit. Used to come to presentations with her daddio. Funny that,' said Marcus, squeezing in the door behind her and practically propelling her round, his hand on her back. 'Just remembered.'

'What?' said Laura as they emerged on the other side, feeling slightly dizzy.

'She's going out with Nick now – also known as the Marquess of Ranelagh. Yeah. She's called Cecilia. Mate told me he was giving her one these days. Hope she doesn't take after her moth— Hey! Hey! There he is!'

'There who?' Laura said, her brain spinning, as the doors behind them kept revolving, spilling out people who pushed past her, swarmed around her. She couldn't see Marcus, he had vanished, she could hear his voice but where was he?

'Nick! I say!'

The sea of people cleared, the way parted, and there was a newly invigorated Marcus patting someone on the back, someone who turned around to face her as Marcus was saying, 'Good one! Good one! Let me introduce you, old chap, this is my gorgeous date for this evening, Laura. Hey, Laura. This is the Marquess of Ranelagh, my dear. You've visited his place, you know. You told me.'

426

'Yes,' said Laura, mechanically holding out her hand, looking up into Nick's face. 'Hello.'

'Hello,' said Nick, meeting her gaze. His short dark hair was combed and neat, his evening dress immaculate, his expression remote. His other hand was in his pocket and he squeezed her hand, then dropped it, looked from one to the other of them. Laura's arm fell by her side, a dead weight, as she watched him, not knowing what to say.

'Nice to see you, Laura. Marcus – would be great to catch up. Maybe later. Excuse me. I should say hello to the Thorsons, they've just arrived.'

'Course you should, mate!' Marcus winked at him, hugely gratified at being present for this. He put his arm proprietorially around Laura, as if to say, We're all in the same boat, aren't we?

Laura rocked against him, feeling like a dead weight, realising that, for Marcus, this was shaping up to be a great evening; whereas for her it was up there with her grandmother Deidre's funeral and the time Simon was sick over her brand-new Levi 501s just before her first date with Sean Phillips when she was fifteen.

'See you later,' Nick said politely. He smiled briefly at both of them. 'Have a good evening. Good to see you both.'

He walked off, towards Tania Thorson, who was walking stiffly along the hall, and Laura watched him put his arm round her fondly, kiss her, make some joke. He hugged Lars and shook hands with a couple of other people who'd arrived, all serious, slick, wealthy-looking. Marcus gazed at them, almost hungrily. Laura stared at his companions, then back at Nick. Her hand stole up to the necklace, and she stroked it gently.

CHAPTER FORTY-FOUR

The next two hours were the loneliest of Laura's life. The rain began soon after they arrived, and all evening it thudded on the roof, throughout the drinks at the front of the hall, where she stood mutely by Marcus's side as he roared with laughter and slapped backs with a succession of identical-looking, identically dressed men. He was happiest, she soon realised, in the company of other men. The blokes, the guys, the chaps he worked with, who moved vast amounts of money from A to B and then made it into C.

She hung back as he networked, tried to do her bit as The Date, tried not to scan the crowd, a polite smile plastered to her face, until they were ushered further back along the huge, echoing, vaulted hall for supper. The moment they were seated and had each been presented with a laminated cardboard folder about the achievements of the German bank over the last year and Going Forward, Marcus turned away from her to the man on his right, with whom he proceeded to have a similarly raucous conversation. He would turn to her occasionally and ask her if she was OK, and then almost immediately turn back with enthusiasm to a long discussion about the rise of the hedge fund.

'Sure you're OK?' he said to her on his third swivel round.

'I'm absolutely fine,' Laura replied, lying through her teeth. Marcus smiled at her.

'Marcus,' Laura began, determinedly. 'I wondered, by the way – about the donation we discussed –'

'What's that?' said Marcus.

'The sponsorship programme,' Laura reminded him, putting one finger on his arm.

'Oh, absolutely,' said Marcus. 'Absolutely.'

'Can we – should we talk about it at some point? Firm up the details?'

Suddenly, Marcus's hand shot out, and clamped itself around her leg. Laura immediately felt like a prostitute touting for business, or some kind of dodgy honeytrap, as Marcus's fingers clumsily patted her skin and he turned towards her, gulping his wine greedily.

'Have you –' she faltered, and looked down at his hand, high up on her thigh. He squeezed her leg, and smiled at her amicably.

'Great,' said Marcus. 'Remind me about it later. Just got to ask this chap –' and he turned away again. Laura sank back in her chair, dispirited. Apart from the hand on her leg, she might as well have been invisible, she thought wretchedly, and outside the wind whistled along the glass, rattling it as the rain beat down.

Periodically Marcus would squeeze her thigh, and it reminded Laura of when she and Simon were small, on the sofa in the lounge at Heathcote Road, watching TV after school, and Simon would suddenly poke her viciously in the ribs. She would poke him back. They would sit there, in huge tension, not knowing who would dare to poke next, and when it came each would scream with the recognised shock of it. So Laura felt as she gazed around her table, around the room, trying not to look bored, waiting for Marcus's next rather hard, crab-like squeeze on her thigh. It did not make for a particularly relaxed dining experience.

The man on her left was a kind, polite German banker, who tried his best to engage her in conversation, but his English was not great, Laura's German was non-existent, the rest of the table was fairly loud, and the noise in the hall grew ever louder, with guffaws and shouts echoing out, a bit like the last day of term at a particularly muscular boarding-school. The first two courses inched by in what seemed to be an eternity of time, during which the hands on the huge iron clock high up in the vaulted ceiling barely seemed to move, the noise seemed to grow louder, and the food – especially the watercress mousse – felt like slimy slabs of sponge in her mouth.

Was it that Nick was there, over there, past the next table, just visible if she tilted her head very slightly? Was it true that she could really look over and see him any time she liked, after two months of separation, remember all those things about him that she'd forgotten, the cast of his jaw, his shoulders, his expression when he smiled? Or was it that she had finally realised she didn't know him, would never know him, that this was the world he lived in, not the one he had pretended to show her over the summer.

She stared at him through the sea of black-jacketed shoulders, and just once allowed herself to wallow a little. To remember dreamily how unreal and fantastical that time at Chartley had been. Like a favourite film or a childhood holiday that takes on the golden-hued appearance of a fairytale, every day long and sunny, every event magical. Here he was again, and she could see him out of the corner of her eye, whenever she wanted. She realised now the past two months she had got so used to *thinking* she saw him everywhere – on the street, in the pub, on the tube – that she was always turning her head to see if that tall, dark man in the corner was, in fact, Nick, come to find her. And now, that tall, dark man in the corner was, in fact, Nick. But he was with someone else and she –

As Lars Thorson leant forward to say something quietly to

Nick, and he looked blankly into space as he listened, nodding, Laura remembered with a stabbing agony the last time she'd seen him, how the holiday had come to an end. She took a deep breath. Could Nick really be enjoying this evening? Was he really the person who could get satisfaction from smarming up to some rich industrialist and his wife? And their thin, bloodless, humourless daughter?

For Cecilia Thorson was there, very much there, sitting up straight next to him, and that was really the only interesting thing about this evening. Laura wished she could stop staring at the two of them, so poised, so glamorous, so – *grown-up* looking. They reminded her of effigies from medieval tombs she had seen on a school trip to France years ago – side by side, her straight hair, straight nose, long, thin face, elegant pursed lips; him taller, prouder, statesmanlike. Not someone she knew or remembered at all. Laura shook her head.

'OK there?' said Marcus's voice suddenly, close to her ear. His rather large nose brushed unexpectedly across Laura's neck. She jumped, realising she was staring at Nick, and she saw him turn instinctively, his gaze meeting hers across the room. She swivelled round to Marcus, who was making a kind of guzzling, gurgling sound in her ear, which surprised her, until he said, with an effort,

'You do look – gorgeous, you know, L-Laura.'

'Thanks,' said Laura, who was never sure how to respond to compliments like that. *Yes, I know. No, I don't, what are you talking about?*

'I – I just want to . . . grrr.' Marcus shook his head, and made a sound like a small bear.

Oh dear, thought Laura. Please let this be an upset stomach rather than a prelude to sex. Because Marcus, if you seriously think you're getting some tonight you are Wrong Wrong Wrong.

'Having a good time?' his voice murmured heavily in her ear, sounding rather like an unskilled Barry White impersonator. Laura had to fight back the urge to reply in kind: 'I sure am, baby, how you doin'?' She bit her lip, and Marcus, taking this for an encouraging sign, squeezed her thigh again.

'Oh Marcus –' said Laura feebly. 'Don't – don't do that. It's . . . you know.'

'Oh,' said Marcus, sitting back in his chair suddenly. 'Sorry.' He looked mortified, his hair flopping sadly on each side of his head like a bunny's lop-ears.

Laura felt mean. 'Sorry,' she said. 'It's just – anyway. Are you having a good time?'

'Yep, absolutely,' said Marcus. 'Really interesting bloke next to me, used to run the Singapore arm of this start-up we invested in a couple of years ago.'

'Oh. Hey. That's so . . . cool. Cool!' said Laura, unsure of the correct response. She was even more aware of the conversational gap between them. 'So you –'

'Anyway, how about you?' said Marcus enthusiastically. Laura realised he was a little drunk. His mouth was slacker, his eyes duller. 'You having a good time?' He leant forward again. 'Sorry, haven't had time to talk,' he said. 'Very glad you came. But must talk to people. You sit there.' He patted her thigh again, as if she were a tiny leprechaun who might hop off her seat and run wildly amongst the guests throwing gravy around and causing havoc.

'Right,' said Laura, picking up her fork to push an uneaten pile of chocolate mousse across her plate. She wanted to hate Marcus, be furiously cross with him, blame him for Nick being there, for how crap a time she was having. Paddy had gone for a drink with Hilary tonight after work in Shepherd's Market; she could be there too, dressed normally, sitting there having a laugh, instead of here, feeling this awful, and she wanted to blame him for it, but she couldn't. No, she had to go through with it.

This was a watershed evening for her, she realised. Perhaps the presence of Nick was a sign from the gods, a symbol of how strong she had to be, what she had to pull off. She was on a date, and she was going to get Marcus to give the school-sponsorship programme a big donation, or die trying. She could still do it. She had to. Wasn't this what she'd been in work early trying to sort out during the endless weeks since she came back from Norfolk? Building up contacts again, putting together information, cajoling, flattering, skirting around the issue like the dancing of a gavotte – and nothing, nothing from any of the other companies so far, and Rachel was depending on her. More than that – she *had* to pull it off, or else her job was in jeopardy again. And even more than that, perhaps, she had to do it for herself. Laura girded her loins again, set her face in a stern expression and said firmly,

'Marcus. Can I get you a coffee? And then can we talk about the sponsorship programme, before we have too much to drink and forget?'

'George! Hi! Good to see you, mate. Listen, about the liability claim,' said Marcus suddenly, turning his back on her to address a man standing behind him. His left hand shot out and clamped down on her leg again. Laura snarled crossly to herself, and realised she had to calm down. Time to while away five minutes in the loo, she told herself. She took her bag and made to stand up, but just as she gingerly put her hand on Marcus's to move it, she noticed Cecilia Thorson standing up with her bag, heading across the room. Laura shrank back in her seat. No thanks, she thought. I don't want to be loo buddies with her. She watched as Cecilia sailed gracefully past, her expression proud, unruffled. Laura watched her from under her eyelashes, her hand clutching Marcus's in a frenzied grip. Damn it.

She looked up at the clock on the wall and then around the room. It was nearly ten o'clock, she'd been there for two hours. The rain was still pounding relentlessly on the glass roof. The tables were breaking up; pudding was being served but people were moving around, men and women nonchalantly leaning against chairs chatting to each other. The polite German man next to her had disappeared. It was getting late. She had to rescue this situation, but how? Perhaps she should just go, she thought hopelessly. Face Rachel's hopeful expression on Monday and admit failure.

As if answering her thoughts, she turned to find Marcus's hazy stare fixed on her. He half-licked his lips, a tiny unconscious movement. Laura realised he had passed from being a bit intoxicated to properly drunk.

'Laura,' he said. 'Witchu. Wouldchu like – what are we doing later?'

'Er –' said Laura uncertainly. 'It's not over yet, is it? Oh, no. What a great evening. Perhaps . . .'

'Come back to mine,' Marcus urged, hedging his bets with the optimism of the drunk. 'Go on! You'd like it.' He patted her arm, his hand sliding heavily down her skin. 'Please.'

'Well, thanks,' said Laura, feeling a bit like she was wrestling with an octopus, only a drunk octopus in a dinner jacket who was head of some important league under the sea. She removed his other hand, which was making its way between her knees. 'Look, Marcus, I think I'd better head off. We can talk on Monday,' she said flatly.

Marcus sat up and said, 'Come on, Laura. You really shouldn't go, you know. Really should stay.'

'Why?' said Laura, not looking at him. She began to put her cape on.

'You should . . . be being more nice,' said Marcus, lolling softly forward so that he was propped up by the table. 'Be nice. I've taken you out and everything. Wanted to discuss the – the, erm, the thing – the thing with the schools. Them. And now you're not even being very nice. Are you?'

'Oh my god,' said Laura, freezing, with one arm in her cape and one arm out of it. This is what it must have been like to be Michael J. Fox's mum in *Back to the Future*, being forced to make out with the boorish villain in his car at the prom.

Everyone else had left their tables, and the majority of the crowd was moving back into the Great Hall. Marcus looked up at her resentfully. 'God, Laura. Don't you like me? Am I . . . ugh.'

'I'm sorry, Marcus,' said Laura, not sure how much of this was drunk Marcus talking and how much was potential date-rape Marcus talking, and not willing to hang around to find out.

'Who the hell do you think you are?' Marcus's voice was slurred. She couldn't see his face, he was staring at the tablecloth. His hand was still on her arm; it slid off onto the table. 'You can whistle for it. The money. Bloody sorry I ever asked you.'

'Fine,' said Laura. 'Look – I'm sorry,' she repeated, and suddenly it made her furious she was saying sorry, and a sense of impotent anger at her own failures – all of them, all alive and present and jogging into each other in this bloody huge room – made her stand up. She pulled her arm through the cape in one almighty wrench, feeling the lining tear slightly. 'I'll –' She looked down at Marcus, who was gazing up at her, with the vacant, uncertain look in his eyes that she remembered from before, but it wasn't enough to stop her. She turned on her heel – she'd always wanted to know exactly what that was, and now she knew – then strode towards the door without looking back, not knowing whom she despised more at that moment. Herself, for getting all excited about the evening, stupid girl. Herself, for trying to mix business with – pleasure, if that's what this was. Or bloody Marcus, for – well, being a fruitloop. Hopefully just a drunk fruitloop. As she reached the first set of doors, a voice behind her said,

'Hello, Laura, how are you?'

Laura spun round, her heart in her mouth, but standing there was Charles. Lovely, dependable Charles. She looked up at him, and he smiled at her with his kindly smile and said,

'You have a face like thunder. Is everything OK?'

'Yes,' said Laura, nearly laughing. 'Charles. It's so nice to see you! How are you? You're here – with –'

She trailed off, not sure what to say next.

435

'Nick's just saying goodbye to Cecilia,' said Charles, looking at her carefully. 'I'm sure he'd love to know you're here, though, Laura. I should –' He looked around.

'No! No,' cried Laura insanely. 'I've seen him already, we've said Hi! Don't worry.'

'Oh,' said Charles, and an expression of – what it was, Laura didn't know – crossed his face. He shifted a little. 'So, who was he? The chap you were with tonight?' Laura bit her lip. 'The one I saw you shaking off? I was about to come over, actually, see if you were OK, but just as I was going to you were up and away.'

'Ha,' said Laura, feeling exhausted all of a sudden. 'Just – oh, some bloke.'

'Are you leaving?' Charles asked, gesturing towards the main doors. Laura nodded. 'Some bloke, eh?' he said, falling into step beside her.

'Yep,' said Laura. 'It's a work thing. Oh,' she said rather brokenly. 'Never mind.'

'Oh, go on,' said Charles, his voice warm. 'I've spent the evening in between some bloke moaning about his interior decorator in Chamonix, and a really attractive girl from the bank who asked me if I was gay. Can't get worse than that, can it? What's up? Tell me.'

They were in a human traffic jam, as people clogged up the doors, uncertain what to do as the rain lashed the pavements. Laura laughed softly and looked at him, remembering how easy he was to talk to.

'Well,' she said, and briefly outlined the reasons for her presence there. As she finished with, 'And now I don't know what to do, I said I'd get the money, I promised I'd be better at my job,' she realised she was sounding like a five-year-old who isn't allowed a pet rabbit, but she couldn't help it – she felt stupid, standing there, all dressed up, having danced out of Mary's flat thinking she had the chance to make things right at work. Why, oh why. But there was something hugely comforting about Charles, and

436

as they inched forward in the queue for the exit, she said, 'I'm sorry. God, I keep saying that tonight. But I am.'

'For what?'

'For being so boring. It's so stupid,' said Laura. She shook her head. 'Forget about it.'

'So, what are you going to do? About the money, I mean?' Charles asked.

'I have ways and means,' said Laura, smiling with a confidence she didn't feel.

'Good for you,' said Charles. 'I bet you do,' and he patted her shoulder reassuringly.

That was almost too much for Laura. She gulped, and said in a wavering tone, 'Thanks, Charles. Thanks a lot,' and he gave her a quick, slight grin, as they stood together in silence.

'Where are you going now?' Charles asked as they got to the lobby. He looked out through the doors onto the Strand, staring thoughtfully at the rain as it splashed into puddles.

'Well,' said Laura, looking at her watch. 'God, it's still early-ish, isn't it? I think I'm going to head into Soho.' She took a deep breath, and said, 'Actually, I want to go home. I'm really tired and I need to – to think it all through.' She looked up at him. 'I think I'm going to get a – Oh.'

In slow motion, Laura saw Nick arriving as if in a dream, patting Charles's shoulder, saw him as he saw her, raised his chin, faced her. She saw all of this as if they were under water, moving slowly, as if it wasn't her, someone else instead, as if she had no control over what she said or did, didn't know what to think, what to say.

Charles said, 'I'll go and see where the car is.' He nodded politely at Laura, and stepped aside.

'Laura,' said Nick. His expression held no emotion whatsoever. 'Nice to see you.'

He looked at his fingers, flicked something imaginary from one of his nails, and smiled at her. His expression was cold and his dark eyes rested just above her head. It was strange, she remembered his eyes were normally so full of warmth, emotion, flashing with anger or amusement, and to see him like this was – it was almost like seeing a corpse, a waxwork of him. This wasn't the Nick she knew.

This is who you are, isn't it, Laura thought with a flash of clarity. You really are this person most of the time. She looked at him, and didn't know what to say. The events of the evening were catching up with her, in gradual motion.

'I have to go,' she said, starting away.

'Of course,' Nick answered, his voice slightly raised. 'Well. Goodbye, then.'

Laura looked back at him. 'Say goodbye to Charles for me, will you? Tell him I couldn't stay.'

She headed for the door, and felt a hand on her arm. 'It's raining,' said Nick's voice in her ear. 'Look, Laura, why don't we give you a lift to wherever you're going?'

'No thanks,' said Laura desperately. 'I'll get a cab.'

She turned to look at the steady column of men and women in evening dress, fluttering and cooing on the pavement outside, as the rain came down more heavily and steaming cabs filled with passengers passed by.

'It's pouring with rain, everyone's leaving, you're wearing virtually nothing. You'll never get a taxi. Come with us and I'll drop you off.'

'I –' Laura said, shaking his hand off her arm, very tired. 'Oh, please just let me go . . .'

'Come on, Laura,' said Nick. 'Let us give you a lift. Please.' His jaw was set. He said, not looking at her, 'Charles is with me, he can keep the peace.'

'Honestly, don't worry,' Laura told him, her mother's fear of socially awkward situations settling over her like a cloud. 'I live in North London, it's miles away.'

'Well, that's perfect,' said Nick. 'We're going that way anyway.' He unwrapped his scarf. 'Great. There's Charles.' He hailed his friend. 'What news?'

'Car's outside, Nick,' said Charles.

'We're giving Laura a lift back to North London,' Nick told him. 'Because it's on our way.'

Charles's expression didn't flicker. 'Great,' he said. 'Let's go.'

He opened the door for Laura, and she felt something light drop onto her shoulders over her thin evening cape. She looked down. It was a scarf.

'Keep the rain off,' Nick said.

Out on the pavement, a smartly dressed man was rushing forward with an umbrella. Nick put his arm under hers; she felt the slight pressure of his hand guiding her. Her eyelids were heavy; she felt dizzy all of a sudden. She climbed into the car and straightened her skirt, pulling it over her thighs. Nick stood looking down at her for a moment, and shut the door with a bang. She heard him throw the umbrella into the back and have a brief conversation with the driver, as Charles slid into the front seat, and then Nick got in next to her. The car smelt of leather, and was luxurious, oddly stifling.

'Thanks, Paul.' Nick nodded at the driver, and they moved away without noise.

CHAPTER FORTY-FIVE

She may have been feeling totally drained, and wanting to bang her head on the window, but Laura was a trooper. No matter that the evening had begun badly and ended disastrously – she briefly considered whether there was any chance the Marcus she had left semi-conscious at the dinner table could still be the Marcus who would ring up on Monday with a donation to the sponsorship programme for £20,000, and then realised the answer was no – she wasn't going to behave like a five-year-old. No matter that it was pouring with rain. No matter that her date had been drunk and a bit weird, and Nick had been there with a beautiful blonde millionaire's daughter. She could still make civilised conversation, be polite.

'Thank you for this,' Laura said, shifting on the leather. 'It's really kind of you.'

'Not at all. My pleasure.'

Laura fell silent, aware it was just the two of them talking whilst Paul the driver and Charles in the front pretended not to be listening. Nick seemed to be completely at ease with it, of course. She looked at him, sitting comfortably next to her, his beautiful grey wool coat glistening with raindrops, one arm flung across the back of the seat, one strong brown hand resting lightly on the leather, just a little way away from her head.

She wasn't really sure what to do or say next. All the cheerful, socially adept questions she could possibly ask him – Have you had a nice evening? Who was on your table? How's the estate? Ha ha, well, isn't it strange, bumping into you like this? – sounded too loaded to her, and the ones she really wanted to ask – What's going on with Cecilia? Have you missed me, because I've missed you? Can I lick your face, or would that be weird in the back of the car? – were obviously not suitable. So she pulled his scarf around her a little more, and sank down further into her seat.

'So . . .' said Nick. He tapped his fingers on the head-rest behind Laura, and she jumped. 'Sorry,' he said. He touched her shoulder lightly. 'Sorry, Laura. I'm – this is weird.' He looked at her frankly, and Laura turned to him.

'It is, isn't it?' she agreed, remembering again with a rush of – what? – something, how nice he was, how easy and straightforward, and wondering how she could ever have thought he was remote or hard to understand.

'Good evening, wasn't it?' Nick said. 'Lovely atmosphere. Very relaxing. German bankers are my favourite bankers.'

'Good?' said Laura, laughing. 'Ooof. What a night. I thought it was never going to end. How can you do it?'

'I don't, that often,' said Nick. 'But I was in town, and Lars . . .' He trailed off.

Laura was determined now to be chipper, upbeat, polite. He had made the effort, it was up to her to repay him. 'Is that Cecilia's dad?' she asked, in a tone of polite interest.

'Yes,' said Nick. 'Nice bloke. He's really helped me out over the past couple of years, and he invited me. I thought it would be rude not to go.'

'Absolutely,' said Laura airily. 'Yes, these things can go on a bit, can't they?'

Nick gave her a strange look. 'Go to them a lot, do you?'

'Oh. Well, you know, here and there,' said Laura, trying to sound like she knew what she was talking about.

'Go with Marcus, do you?' Nick asked.

'Er,' said Laura. 'Well, tonight I did.'

Nick flicked a piece of dust off his coat. 'Surprised to see you with him.'

Laura thought of Marcus, not the Marcus she'd run away from, the one lying drunk and semi-comatose on the table, but the one who had kissed her rather determinedly at the bar, holding her hand. His old-fashioned courtesy, how he just wanted to meet someone nice. She said defensively, 'He's all right. OK?'

'I'm sure he is.' Nick's face was in darkness, she couldn't really see it. 'Sure he is.'

The car drove steadily along the Strand, its wide pavements glossy and black in the rain. Charles turned to Paul, and asked him about directions in a quiet voice. They were alone in the back.

'How's work?' Nick asked suddenly.

Laura knitted her hands in her lap. 'Um. OK.'

'What does that mean?'

'It means . . .' Laura cast around in her mind for the right response. 'Oh,' she said wearily. 'I'm not sure.'

'You've got your job back, though?' he queried, and there was concern and interest in his voice.

'Yes, but –' She put her palms flat on her lap, not knowing how much to say, wanting to tell him everything, knowing she should keep it all back. Laura turned to him, but she still couldn't see his face, and so she just said, rather weakly, 'Yes. I did.'

'So why –' Nick began, but Laura found herself putting her hand up.

'Do you mind if we don't?' she said. 'Talk about it? Bit stressed about it at the moment. I think I've cocked up. I don't want to think about it, not tonight.'

'Anything I can do?' Nick asked. Laura gave a hollow sigh, under her breath, and he said immediately, 'Sorry. That's probably the least helpful thing someone can say.'

442

'No,' said Laura quietly. 'Thank you, though.'

'I'm serious,' he said, his voice close by. 'If there is anything, Laura – Ever.'

She nodded. There was a ball of air in her throat, pushing down into her chest, making it hard for her to speak. He watched her as Laura shrugged her shoulders, trying to look unconcerned, and she felt she merely succeeded in looking a bit stupid.

'And how are you?' she asked, pulling herself together. 'How is everything at Chartley?' She stopped, realising she sounded rather like Aunt Annabel.

His voice soft with amusement, Nick replied, 'Great, thank you. It's a little quieter since the summer, of course. Since you were there.'

'Yes, I can imagine,' Laura said, her head on one side, trying to pretend he was just a tourist guide, and she was a tourist. 'Um. What are you up to at the moment, then?'

'Well, the crops are all in, and that's gone well and the weather held out which made it easier, so that was good.'

'Ah,' said Laura, trying to sound informed. 'The harvest.'

'Yes,' Nick said gravely, but his mouth twitched. 'The harvest. And we've just started a major project, cataloguing all the paintings, sculptures and so on, in the house. Going to take a few years, but it's important, needs to be done.'

Laura always loved hearing him talk about the estate, what he was doing with it. 'Really? For insurance, or . . .?'

'Insurance, yes, and so we have an idea of what's there.'

'Like what?'

Nick moved slightly closer towards her, half an inch, almost imperceptibly. He paused, before saying, 'Well, when my father died everything was a total mess. When I went through his study for the first time I found two paintings, little watercolours. Didn't think anything more of them. Turns out they're sketches by this Victorian artist, worth about ten thousand each. Dad had just shoved them in a cupboard, years ago.'

'Blimey,' said Laura. 'He must have had no idea.'

'He did,' said Nick, his voice flat. 'He bought them for my mother, as a wedding present. We found the paperwork. They were framed. He'd obviously taken them out of their frames, and rolled them up, put them out of sight.'

'Oh,' said Laura. She looked down. Their knees were turned towards each other, almost touching. She said quietly, 'That must have been a bit weird. For you.'

Nick ran a hand through his short hair, distracted, and glanced out of the window. 'Bit weird, yes,' he said, turning back and smiling slightly at her. 'It's funny.'

'What's funny?' asked Laura, watching him.

'I haven't said this to anyone. But I keep thinking about her, lately.'

'Who? Your mother?'

'Yes,' he said. 'I don't know why. I spent so long training myself not to miss her when I was younger. So sometimes months go by and I don't really – wonder about her. What she's up to, how she is. And then sometimes,' he looked at her. 'Like lately. Since you left. I keep thinking about how she is.'

'Really?'

'Yes. I want to see her again. You know.'

'Nick, she's your mother,' said Laura simply. 'Of course you want to see her again.'

'Yes, of course,' he said, with a trace of the old impatience. 'But you don't understand.'

'I know I don't,' Laura said, shaking her head.

'Sorry, that's wrong,' he amended. 'You do understand. About some things.' His eyes were on hers, with an expression half-sad, half-smiling, that she found terribly painful. They said nothing, but looked at each other in the darkness.

'You should get in touch with her,' Laura told him firmly.

Nick shook his head. 'Thank you. No, I don't think that would be a very good idea.'

His arm was still behind her, on the back of the seat; he flung it next to his thigh, and drummed his fingers on the leather.

444

'Perhaps you're right,' he said eventually.

'But you're the only one who can make that move,' said Laura. She wanted to bridge the distance between them, make it all all right for him, but she couldn't. 'Trust me. I know.'

'And how do you know that?' Nick asked, amused.

'Well, I don't know,' said Laura frankly. 'I know what I think you should do.'

'As ever,' he said, his voice low. 'That's Laura. Rushing in, speaking before she thinks. Bossing people around, setting fire to things. Being hugely rude. And . . . running away, when I don't want her to leave.'

His eyes flicked up to the front seat, where Paul and Charles were still engaged in low, desultory conversation, and he looked back at her and down again. She followed his gaze. His hand was inches away from hers, as they both rested on the seat. She remembered his touch, how warm and strong he was. She closed her eyes, briefly, overwhelmed with wanting to hold his hand just once more, to lean against him. Both of them looked down at their hands, neither of them saying anything, though Laura desperately wanted to say something, the right thing, wanted to move her fingers towards his. And then Nick lifted his hand and scratched his cheek, and it was as if the spell was broken.

'You didn't reply to my text,' he said eventually, in a low voice.

She shook her head, not trusting herself to speak.

He smiled, and said, 'So, here we are. I made up my mind I wasn't going to speak to you when I got into the car.'

'That's nice of you,' said Laura, recovering herself.

'I mean it.'

'Really?'

'Yes, Laura. The way you left . . .'

'I know,' said Laura. The car reached the end of the Strand, they were at Trafalgar Square, and light flooded across Nick's face as they drove through the Square and under Admiralty Arch.

'Do you understand why I had to leave?' she asked, hardly breathing, wanting him to give her the answer she didn't dare to hope for.

'I didn't, no,' he said. 'Absolutely not.'

'Really?' said Laura, her heart pounding.

'Not at first, no,' said Nick. He nodded to himself. 'But now I do.'

'Oh,' said Laura. 'Right.'

She knew exactly the reasons why she'd left, why she'd given up on them, but she couldn't, at that exact moment, remember what those reasons were. 'It's just – not meant to be, is it, I suppose,' she said, scanning his face, but his expression was formal, closed again, and she couldn't read him any more.

'I don't think it is,' he said. 'If that's what you think too.'

Laura rubbed her eyes and looked out on the Mall as they drove sedately along the wide, tree-lined boulevard. The rain had stopped. She looked at him, suddenly, and caught him staring at her with that old, familiar look, his eyes searching her face, drinking her in. His lower lip was caught between his teeth. He winced, as if he was biting down too hard, and wiped his hand across his mouth, smiling at her.

'Is that what you think?' she said, looking intently at him. 'Really?'

'Yes,' said Nick. He gave a half-smile, his hand on her leg. He patted it. 'Funny, isn't it.' She felt the warmth of his skin on hers.

'Nick –' Laura whispered. 'I think –'

A beeping mobile phone buzzed angrily in the background. Nick pulled his phone out of his pocket, as Laura sank back into her seat again.

'Hello. Good. Thank you. And you. Thank you.'

His tone was expressionless. Hearing the break in conversation, Charles turned around in his seat and peered at her. 'Oh, hello, Laura!' he said, as if he was surprised to see her there.

446

'Hello, Charles!' Laura said. 'What a shock, how long have you been there?'

'Oh. Ha ha ha,' said Charles, looking confused. 'I'm sorry to disturb you, Laura. I just wondered –'

'No. It's a friend. She was at the party.' Nick's voice was quiet, he turned to the window, but Laura could hear every word. 'I'm giving her a lift home. No. Cecilia, I've told you –'

Charles started talking over him. 'Where in North London do you want us to take you? I just wondered.'

They were at Buckingham Palace, turning up towards Hyde Park Corner. Laura pressed her hands to her cheeks, the events of the evening crowding in on her rewinding noisily like a tape. Marcus kissing her, in the bar. His hand on her thigh. The feel of Mary's necklace on her skin. Nick's hand, next to hers, but so far apart. She looked down at her lap, saw her bag with the list of points about the investment programme she was going to give Marcus sticking out of it, and anger and sadness and frustration at her own failure washed over her, this time with such force that it nearly knocked her back against the seat. What was she doing, in this car, with a man who clearly wasn't ever going to be hers? How had she managed to get herself into such a stupid situation again? How was she going to make it right with Rachel, who had put her faith in Laura, only to be disappointed again? She dug her nails into her palms. She had to get out, she had to get out.

'Actually, Charles – I'm meeting some friends just off Piccadilly. Can you drop me at Hyde Park Corner?'

'Really?' Charles asked, as they swooped past Green Park. 'I thought we were –'

'No, it's fine,' said Laura, panic in her voice, as Nick put the phone down, frowning, and shoved it into his pocket, almost viciously. 'I'll just hop out here. It's only quarter past ten, you know. Still time to meet them.' She tapped the handle. 'Can I get out?'

'You're going?' asked Nick. 'What?'

'Yes,' Laura gabbled, trying to stay calm. 'My flatmate's in a pub just round the corner from here. With some friends. I'm going to meet them.' She clutched her bag. 'Thank you, Paul,' she said, as they drew up on Piccadilly. 'I'll just hop out here.'

'Why on earth do you want to get out here?' said Nick. 'We can give you a lift home.'

'I want to meet my friends.' Laura knew she was sounding slightly shrill. 'Please. It's been a – weird evening, what with one thing and another, you know – and I have to explain it at work, about Marcus . . .'

'What do you mean?' Nick interrupted. 'What's Marcus got to do with work?'

'Oh god, nothing, nothing,' said Laura, pressing her hands to her cheeks, which were burning red. 'Just – just please let me out.'

'Laura.' Nick took her hand then, curling her fingers up, wrapping his hand around hers. 'What's up? Are you OK?'

She couldn't look at him, couldn't bear to let him be kind to her, that was worst of all. She cleared her throat. 'I'm fine,' she said. 'Just – need to get out. Please, Nick. Honestly.'

'Don't go, Laura,' Charles said in a low voice. 'Please.'

'I think she wants to go,' Nick murmured. She turned to him, but he flashed her half a grin, almost a grimace. 'Well – Laura –'

'Yes,' said Laura, opening the door.

'Take care,' he said, and tapped her on the shoulder.

'Nick –' said Charles, looking at his friend. 'Don't you want to –'

'Laura has to go,' said Nick. 'Don't you, Laura?'

'Yes,' said Laura, knowing she must win in the 'Who is the Most Nonchalant' stakes. 'Thanks for the scarf, Nick. Bye. Great to see you again!'

Charles turned away, and sighed.

She squeezed Charles's shoulder and got out of the car, and

as she did she felt Nick clutch her wrist, only for a fleeting, tiny second, and then it was gone. She looked into the dark interior, wanting to see his face once more, but the engine roared up again and they were off.

Laura breathed in deeply, watching them go, and walked up the quiet street, not looking, not caring, and when she opened the door into the steaming pub, full of wet drinkers, happy drinkers, drunk drinkers, she leant against it for a second, desperately wanting to turn around to see if he was there, in case he'd got the car to come back and find her. But she knew he wasn't going to do that. She looked across the tiny pub, and caught sight of Paddy and Hilary sitting in the corner. Her feet hurt. She made her way over to them.

'So,' Hilary said, taking a drag of her cigarette. 'Paddy tells me you've been sleeping with a duke, or something. *And* you had a date tonight. How the hell was it?'

CHAPTER FORTY-SIX

By the end of Friday night, curled up against Paddy on the last tube home after a few more glasses of wine, Laura was in two minds about what had happened that evening. She kept trying to think it all through, and then her brain hurt, and she fell asleep until Paddy had to wake her up by yanking her hair.

But on Saturday, Laura woke up convinced Marcus would still give them the money, that her job was OK, and, more importantly, that Nick still felt something for her – she knew it. It was there. It was hard for them both, but there was just something there. She bounded around the house all day, feeling chipper, made a cake, cheered Simon up when he rang to complain about how he and Jorgia had had a row, bought some odd-looking crocus bulbs from the corner shop and planted them in her window boxes, then went to Shana from work's birthday party in Dulwich and had a great time.

On Sunday, however, she woke up absolutely certain that Marcus would wash his hands of the programme forthwith, that Rachel would be forced to sack her, and ultimately that Nick had been, very kindly, giving her the brush-off, telling her they couldn't be together, that Cecilia Thorson was his bride-to-be – and hey, fine, whatever, you know. And she couldn't get rid of that feeling of creeping, enervating, horrible Sunday certainty, coupled with despair at herself once more for mucking it all up, *again*. She couldn't have a proper conversation with Nick – she was emotionally stunted and pathetic. She'd basically led Marcus up the garden path – how totally unprofessional could you get? And she'd led Rachel and Nasrin and the others up the garden path too – making them think the bad times were over, that she, super-girl Laura, could sort it all out for them. Hah. What a joke.

It ruined her mood. She ate the cake, she shuffled around the flat, she sat on the sofa in her duvet watching *Countryfile* and the *Coronation Street* omnibus, and ate a whole packet of Ginger Nuts dipped in tea. When one of the Ginger Nuts fell into the tea, almost whole, she cried. Paddy and Becky retreated downstairs to her flat, leaving Laura alone in her self-inflicted misery. If he was bad, she was worse. She felt like she was in a boxing ring, being bounced from side to side by a much tougher opponent. Bounce. Bounce. She couldn't decide, couldn't decide if she was going mad or if the answer was obvious? Bounce, bounce.

Thankfully, someone else made the decision for her.

When Laura got into work on Monday morning, she was later than usual – which, since her time of the New Leaf, was virtually unheard of – and Rachel and Nasrin were both there, poring over an Excel spreadsheet, which Laura knew very well had all the figures for the year on it – because they spent most days poring over a version of it, totting things up, taking other things away, desperately trying to save their programme, pull more money from a hat like the proverbial rabbit. Her heart sank even further, from somewhere around her stomach right into her pumps. This was it. She squared her shoulders.

'Hey! Laura! I hear Shana's party was good,' said Rachel.

'What?' asked Laura, looking around her, distracted. 'Oh! Yes, yes. Yes. Brill party. Brill. Eee. Ant. Loved it. *Loved it.*'

'I said it was good,' said Nasrin. 'I didn't say it was brilliant.'

'Right,' said Laura. 'You're right. Yes. Hey, Rachel. Lovely top.'

'Oh, thanks,' Rachel replied, looking down at her chest as Laura sat down at her desk with a clatter, and switched on her computer. 'It's really old, actually. Thanks! So, Laura –'

'Did anyone see the golf?' Laura said loudly, desperately.

'The golf?' Nasrin asked. 'Why would I see the golf? Why would you, for that matter?'

'It was brill,' said Laura. 'Brill. Eee. A – oh shut up,' she muttered to herself, under her breath.

Rachel walked over towards her with a smile on her face. 'So –' she said. 'So, Laura . . .' She gestured for Nasrin to join her. Nasrin followed her. 'Hey!' Rachel caught sight of Shana in the doorway, just arriving. 'Come over here, listen to Laura, she's got some good news for us!'

Laura wanted to curl up and die, to quite literally just stop existing.

'Is this about the money?' said Shana. 'I kept meaning to ask you on Saturday, but I hardly saw you. Go on! What is it?'

'Yeah,' said Nasrin. 'Come on, Laura!'

Laura looked up at their hopeful faces. She had never felt more worm-like.

'Um,' she began. 'Look. Rachel. I know I said the money was in the bag . . .'

'What?' said Shana.

'But,' Laura continued, keeping her voice steady. 'Friday was a bit of a disappointment –'

'How so?' said Nasrin.

Tim appeared in the doorway. 'Hi, you lot!' he called. 'Cool! Is this Laura's windfall? Our ticket out of the doghouse?'

'Hi! Hi!' Rachel said, gesturing to him. 'Get over here!'

Laura wanted to shoot her for being so dense, for making this so very, very much harder than it needed to be.

'Oh god,' she said flatly, as Tim stuck his head between

Nasrin and Rachel, putting his arms around them, like they were an England football squad singing the national anthem. 'Look,' she bit her lip. 'It's bad news, I'm afraid.'

'What?' Rachel asked.

'He said we could whistle for it. The money. Marcus did,' Laura said almost incoherently.

'He said what?' Rachel asked.

'The money. He's not giving us anything. He said we could whistle for it.'

'Whistle for it?' Rachel repeated, like she was new to the English language.

'Yes,' Laura replied patiently.

'That's really weird,' said Rachel.

'Why?' Laura asked.

'His assistant rang just before you got in. Said the cheque was on its way.'

'What?' Laura cried in disbelief. 'Are you sure?'

'Absolutely,' said Rachel. 'Actually, it's not a cheque,' she smiled. 'It's a bank transfer, but, you know, it's still cold, hard cash. Thirty thousand pounds! Laura, you're a genius.'

She bent over and kissed Laura on the cheek. 'He's not in this week, your friend Marcus. He's on holiday for two weeks.'

'Oh,' said Laura.

'It was his assistant I spoke to. Marcus rang from the airport to ask them to do it. Isn't that nice of him?'

'Well done, Loz,' said Nasrin, nudging her.

'Yeah,' said Shana, slapping Laura really hard on the back, so that she coughed and spluttered. 'Job well done.'

'I don't get it,' Laura muttered, but she could feel a ray of sunshine stealing over her. She wasn't a screw-up. Marcus didn't hate her. She wished he wasn't away – it was annoying, but she'd just have to make it up to him when he got back. Oh, she'd misjudged him and no mistake. He wasn't a slightly overweight drunken lech. He was a misunderstood philanthropist, and, in her opinion, a great, understanding man.

Who obviously had no memory of what he did when he was drunk.

The office settled down to the Monday routine. Laura could hear Rachel in her office, on the phone to Gareth. 'Yes! It's going straight in, today! I know! Well, it was absolutely Laura's doing, we're so proud of her. I know. Yes, of course. I agree. It's fantastic.'

Laura rang Marcus Sussman's line but it went to voicemail. She opened her emails, whistling.

Laura,

I'm sorry about the way I was on Friday. I understand you had a bad evening for other reasons as well. We still have unfinished business, you and me. Don't you agree? I don't really understand what's happened and I think we're both too proud to admit it. Will you come up to Chartley for the weekend in two weeks' time? We're having a belated Harvest Festival dance, a charity thing. I think you'd enjoy it. And the house is beautiful in autumn, you should see it at its best once more.

Let me know by return of email. Don't call me. My phone isn't working.

Please don't mention this to anyone else, of course.

Nick

PART FOUR

CHAPTER FORTY-SEVEN

'Gran? Granny? Are you there? Can I come in?'

Laura shuffled impatiently in the draughty hallway of Crecy Court and checked her watch: about an hour until the train for King's Lynn left. She knew her grandmother was in; she'd seen Cedric on his way out, he'd told her she was.

'Gran?'

Eventually she heard sounds from inside the flat, creaking on the parquet floor. 'Granny,' she said again. 'It's me, Laura.'

The door opened about a foot. Mary's face appeared round it. 'Oh,' she said. 'It's you.'

'Gran, hi. I just came to give you the necklace back.'

'Come in, come in,' said her grandmother, opening the door a little wider. Laura looked at her curiously as she went in. She was as immaculately dressed as ever, with a large, sparkling paste brooch on her white shirt. But she looked tired, very tired. Her eyes, usually alive and sparkling, were devoid of emotion. She nodded at Laura, motioned her to sit down.

'I'm sorry I've had it so long –' Laura began.

'It's fine, darling,' Mary said. 'Fine.' She walked over to the window and looked out at the sky, darkening in the late afternoon.

The general view amongst the family was that Mary had

457

'gone downhill', as Aunt Annabel so annoyingly put it, in the last couple of weeks. Something was worrying her, and the result was as if her brain were short-circuiting. She worried endlessly, didn't know people sometimes when they came to see her. She didn't want to see people when they arrived, and asked them constantly when they were going. Annabel in particular seemed to invoke her ire more than others. Mary could barely stand the sight of her, and Annabel, along with Lulu and Fran, had recently been ejected from Crecy Court by Mary and Jasper and made to wait outside on the pavement for Robert to come and pick them up. (Laura and Simon couldn't help smirking a little when they heard that.)

But Laura thought her grandmother looked OK. She wasn't acting bewildered or wearing slippers to go to the shops, or shuffling round in her nightie at four thirty in the afternoon. She just looked tired, and not particularly happy, staring out of the window, not really looking at anything.

Laura said, 'I can't stay long, Gran. Sorry. I thought I should let you have it back, though.' She took the necklace out of her pocket, feeling the cold stones clustered in her hand.

'Thank you, darling,' said Mary, turning away from the window, shaking her head as if coming alive again. 'Very kind of you. Where are you off to?'

'Well,' said Laura. 'Actually, I'm off to Norfolk for the night.'

Mary's eyebrows shot up. 'Ye gods and little fishes. Well!' She clapped her hands together. 'Have a drink.'

'I don't have time.'

'Just a quick one. I have some wine open, as it happens.'

'What a surprise,' said Laura cheekily.

'Don't be rude, young lady.' Mary pointed at the cabinet; Laura got two glasses as she fetched the bottle from the kitchen.

'So. You're off to Chartley, are you?'

'Yes,' said Laura, leaning forward and hugging her knees. 'Thanks,' she added, taking the glass.

'Where's your aunt going tonight?' Mary asked suddenly.

'Annabel?' Laura replied. 'Good grief, no idea. Why?'

'Nothing,' said Mary. 'She telephoned me earlier, to tell me some rubbish about some old colleague of Guy's who's been made a CBE – good grief, as if I care, I'd completely forgotten he even existed, haven't seen him for twenty years. Good grief, she is a dreadful social climber,' Mary said blithely. 'Well, anyway, she said she was going to Norfolk tonight. I could have sworn it.'

'Help,' said Laura, laughing.

'Well, exactly,' said Mary. 'Watch out. Dear girl, but she can be so vexing. I'm quite out of patience with her at the moment, you know.'

'Why?' asked Laura, wanting to know.

'Nothing in particular,' said Mary, brushing her hands together. 'So, tell me. Needham. Vivienne's son. What happened, may I ask?'

'I don't know,' Laura replied. 'Actually, I really don't know. I saw him a couple of weeks ago – when I was on that date.'

Mary nodded. 'Hm, yes. The young banker. What was he called?'

'Marcus,' said Laura.

'Yes. What happened to him?'

Laura clapped her hands. 'He got drunk, made a pass at me and then passed out. And now he's gone on holiday, and his company's donated a huge sum to the school-sponsorship scheme. It's very weird, but I don't care. We've got the money.'

'Oh, well done you,' said Mary. 'Darling. They should have had you during the Second World War. You're rather like one of those Russian spies who'd get the chaps awfully drunk and then get what they wanted out of them.'

'I hadn't thought of it like that,' said Laura, rather pleased. 'I thought I made a bit of a tit of myself. And him. Poor bloke.'

'Oh no,' said Mary. 'Marvellous behaviour. You used your powers for good. So you haven't thanked him yet, then?'

'No, he's been away,' said Laura. 'Back on Monday. I will then. I'm really going to thank him, too.'

Laura had had a flash of realisation about Marcus since the ball, and in his absence. He'd be perfect for Rachel. She just knew it, and she was going to set them up when he got back. A few weeks ago organising a set-up would have been anathema to her; now she was excited about it. Rachel hadn't been on a date for ages, and she was so sweet and kind, and just looking for someone who wanted to buy a big house in Balham and fill it with lots of rather stocky, strange children. Enter Marcus. OK, he was a bit weird. OK, he probably liked being tied up and whipped – Laura's imagination was running on overtime in this department, obviously – but there was something about him, something lovable, and Rachel herself had a really filthy streak – and the dirtiest laugh in South London. Laura rubbed her hands together and smiled at the thought of it.

'So tell me,' said Mary, sitting down in her chair. She blinked rather heavily, and took a few shallow breaths.

'Gran? Are you OK?' asked Laura.

'I'm old, Laura,' Mary replied. 'That's all.' She took a sip of wine. 'That's better.'

Laura frowned at the bottle. 'I'm not sure that's medically approved, you know, Gran.'

'Rubbish,' said Mary. 'I'm strong as an ox. Never felt better.'

She fell silent. The clock ticked loudly on the wall, and Laura thought about all the times she had sat in this flat, with her grandmother, talking about things, many things, life, love, relationships, work, family. All the important things. The funny thing about Mary was you could get straight down to it, no meandering around. Laura could talk to her grandmother about anything that was on her mind, and sitting there, taking it all in, she realised then how lucky she'd been.

'What time's your train?' said Mary.

'Just under an hour. I had better go, you know.'

'Of course. Why are you going?'

Laura was flummoxed by the question. 'What?'

'Why are you going, tell me?' Mary stretched out a hand, and looked at her wedding ring.

Laura thought about it for a moment. She looked directly at her grandmother. 'I don't know,' she said. 'I want to see him, I suppose.'

'Darling,' said Mary, and then she stopped.

'What?'

'Nothing,' Mary replied. 'You know your own mind. And so does he. You must trust to that.' She cleared her throat. 'It's a formal dinner, is it?'

'Yes,' said Laura. She looked at her watch, knowing she was a bit late, but desperately wanting someone's advice, approval, for what she was doing. She was nervous, and she didn't want to be; unsure, and she didn't know why. 'Can I show you the dress I bought?' she asked.

Mary said, with real pleasure, 'Of course you can,' as Laura fumbled with the zip of her bag, and pulled the dress from its tissue paper.

She loved the dress. She had bought it rashly, excitedly, in a little shop in Hampstead the previous weekend, biting her nails at the bill, at the indulgence of it. It was claret-coloured, heavy silk, with wide shoulder straps plunging diagonally and twisting over the empire line. It hung just below the knee. She had spent ages choosing it – she wanted to look elegant, sophisticated, but she didn't want to look like, well, a tweedy dowager. She had picked that dress out thinking of Nick, wondering if he would like it, hoping he would, wondering why he'd invited her, looking forward so much to seeing him again, being able to tell him how stupid she'd been, how stupid they'd both been . . . Laura's stomach lurched as she shook it out and held it up to show Mary, who fingered the fabric lovingly.

'Silk, beautiful.' Mary nodded her approval. 'It's perfect. Really. He's a fool if he doesn't think so.' She glanced at her wrist. 'You know, darling –'

461

'I should go.' Laura stood up resolutely, suddenly filled with happy, nervous excitement, like a child before its birthday party. 'Oh, Gran. Thank you. Bless you. I'm so glad –'

Mary made to stand up, and sat back abruptly again. 'Oh,' she said. 'Damn it.'

Alarmed, Laura crouched down beside her. 'Granny?' she said. 'Are you all right?'

A small smile crossed Mary's face. 'Ha! I'm fine. You'll miss the train, come on now. Just a bit of indigestion, I let Jasper and Cedric take me out to that new steak place for lunch today.' She stood up this time, clutching Laura's arm. Laura felt the pressure painfully, but she said nothing. Mary walked to the door. 'Go away. I order you,' she said.

'Granny – I'm going to get Jasper.'

'He's out. I just want a little nap,' said Mary. She smiled brightly at Laura, and suddenly Laura felt stupid. Mary looked full of beans, alive, her eyes sparkling again. 'Don't treat me like a child, Laura, I'm fine!' she said. She caught her arm at the door. 'Darling, have a wonderful time, won't you?'

'I don't know,' said Laura. 'Are you sure you'll be all right?'

'Yes,' said Mary firmly. 'Good grief, the fuss. Now, enjoy yourself.'

'I hope so,' said Laura. 'I'll call you tomorrow, come and see you on Sunday maybe?'

'That', said Mary, 'would be heaven.'

And she kissed her and shut the door gently. Laura turned to watch her grandmother as the door closed and her face disappeared.

She was late for the train and almost missed it. Racing up the platform, Laura flung herself into the first-class carriage, then had to scrabble unhappily, clutching her bags, her knuckles grazing on the plastic seats as she passed through two more first-class carriages, a buffet car, a goods compartment, before she reached the first standard class. It was mercifully thin of fellow passengers.

She pushed her bag into the luggage bay and curled into a seat, tucking her feet up under her. As the train pulled out of North London, into Hertfordshire, she gazed unseeingly out of the window, staring blankly at the gently undulating autumnal landscape, the neat garden cities, the strange, dark sky.

It was autumn now. Late autumn. She had failed to notice it, tucked up in the landscape of the city, but here, out in the countryside, opening up in front of her as the train sped on, she could see the seasonal change. The velvety orange and red of the trees, pulsing across the landscape, the empty, churned fields. The thin, pure sun, its rays weaker and weaker in the late October afternoon.

Charles was meeting her at the station. He had rung her to confirm the time just as she was leaving the office. She wished it had been Nick calling to confirm, but no, trusty Charles, yet again, to the rescue – Laura shuddered when she remembered all the very many ways in which, over the past couple of months, Charles had seen her at her absolute worst.

And now here she was, on her way to Chartley, trying not to get too excited, but also just simply happy that he'd been the one to do something about it, and that she was going to see him again. One part of her said: It's great, he knows you've both made mistakes and he wants to start afresh. The other part, the part she wished didn't keep beating on the door of the first part, said: This is weird. He hasn't spoken to you, he just sends you abrupt emails, he can't even be bothered to come and pick you up at the station. If he does still feel something, why can't he just say so, or invite you down for a normal weekend? Why this dinner-dance thing?

Laura pulled her cardigan closer around her, shivering slightly. She felt uneasy, and she didn't know why. So she picked up her book and tried to read, but she found she couldn't concentrate. The same sentence kept cropping up and she would realise she hadn't read anything at all, had been gazing vaguely at the words, easily distracted down another path.

It was a biography of a family of girls in the eighteenth century who had risen from relative obscurity to marry rich and powerful men. They were all vastly clever and talented, beautiful, and determined to wrong social ills, one by one; their husbands all loved them passionately and supported them, when they weren't dashing off to fight battles, help the king, improve working conditions, invent things, make millions, and so on. There were lots of letters from each of the sisters, to each other and to their respective husbands, all terribly worthy, and they all seemed deeply wonderful in every way; but Laura, who was still very much on a no romance, no Georgette Heyer, no fairytales diet, found herself wishing passionately that she was reading some honest-to-goodness heart-stopping book about a plucky young heroine. A plucky young heroine whose carriage suffers an accident, and who is left stranded on the side of the road wringing her hands in despair, until a handsome but arrogant-looking stranger rides up and offers her the use of his hunting lodge until some more commodious arrangement can be made.

Laura sucked a strand of hair as the train passed through Ely station. She put the book down and looked thoughtfully out of the window. No! The plucky heroine's hostess screams in horror when the heroine finally arrives at her destination. You sought shelter with . . . Lord Ely? The most notorious rake in all England? Oh, Laura, Laura dear, we must not speak of this, or your reputation will be ruined forever! He is a dreadful man, my dear, most dreadful. Now, his cousin, Sir Hugh Letchworth. A most pleasant gentleman, despite his obnoxious connections . . .

No, no, no. Laura shook her head. Why do you complain, when you go and do the same thing all over again? And her mind wandered, thinking how funny it was she was here, and no one apart from Mary knew she was here. She hadn't wanted to explain it to anyone; she'd told Paddy simply that she was going to stay with her parents for the night. What would her mum say if she knew? Or Jo? Jo would worry that Laura hadn't packed the right things, had left something behind. And her mum would say, 'That's nice, dear.'

The truth was she knew she was doing the right thing; that whatever happened this evening she was glad to be going, glad he had asked her to come and see him. She was also glad it was at Chartley; she loved it, but she feared it too, and she had to get over it. Mary's voice echoed in her ear, 'You know your own mind. And so does he,' and Laura smiled to herself, picked up her book again and tried to read, but it was impossible, and so she looked out of the window, towards the setting sun, and sat in silence, mulling it all over and drinking in the motion of the train and the view through the window until it came to the station.

'Laura,' Charles said, bending forward to kiss her. He took her bag. 'It's lovely to have you here. Thank you so much for coming.'

Laura always wanted to feel awkward in Charles's company, until she was with him and realised how easygoing and kind he was. He shut her into her seat, then climbed in next to her and said, 'I'm glad you came.'

She said cautiously, 'Well, it's lovely to be here.'

Charles pulled out onto the open road. His eyes were fixed on the road ahead. In a toneless voice, he said, 'Nick's going to be chuffed, too.'

I should bloody hope so, Laura wanted to say, but she didn't. She sat in silence for a while as they turned down thin roads, banked on each side with hedgerows, and above them the huge Norfolk sky opened out above the flat landscape.

She felt nervous; she let the nerves slide in and around her, enjoying the sensation. It felt as if she had been numb ever since she left Norfolk three months ago, and that little by little over the past couple of weeks that layer was coming away. It wasn't because of Nick, she realised. It was because she'd finally realised she needed a balance, the balance between being hopelessly head-in–the-clouds about everything and being Mrs Danvers for the rest of her life, dour and dressed in black, and frowning on anything enjoyable.

So, as they went along, Laura was torn between the desire to clutch Charles's arm and say, 'Take me back to the train station,' so she could go back to London, spend the evening with Mary, finishing off the wine and talking to her about everything under the sun, and the desire to clutch Charles's arm and say, 'Go faster,' so that she could be there, at Chartley, see Nick waiting on the huge front staircase for the car, watch his face light up as he saw her in the front seat. She was torn between wanting it to be over, wanting to know the outcome, the resolution to this weekend, and wanting this feeling of excitement and anticipation never to end.

'Who else will be there this evening, then?' she asked Charles.

'Let me see . . . various people from Chartley, and from the village. Some cronies of Lady Rose's, on some committee of hers, something to do with pheasants or game or something. And some bods from London, some to do with this ownership scheme we're running for the estate workers; Nick's being given an award for it.'

'What?' said Laura.

'Kind of like a right-to-buy scheme,' said Charles, steering carefully past another car on the road. 'Most of the people who live on the estate and in Chartley village, they don't own. They're Nick's tenants. Have been for generations. Nick's started this scheme to help them buy their houses themselves.'

'Oh,' said Laura. 'Really? Wow. That's amazing.' She looked down at her nails.

'Absolutely,' said Charles with enthusiasm. 'It's been fantastic. Take-up rate is huge. Very popular. Of course, it's not popular with the trustees, and so on. He's had a battle on his hands there.'

'Why?' said Laura.

'Well, think about it,' said Charles. 'He's giving away his property. Bit by bit. Breaking up one of the last great estates in the country. They're furious. So's – well.' He paused.

'Who else?' asked Laura encouragingly.

'Lady Rose. Very cross with him, I'm afraid. Well, she – there you go, anyway,' said Charles, and Laura knew that was all she'd get out of him.

'So, he's getting an award tonight?' said Laura.

'Not really, no,' said Charles. 'They're coming down, the charity committee, to see the effects of it. They want to give him an award, but of course Nick's said no. Hates that kind of thing. Stupid idiot. He doesn't realise – well, once again, there you go.'

'That's amazing,' said Laura. 'I didn't realise he – he could do that.'

'Of course he can,' said Charles. They reached a T-junction. He stopped the car and looked at her. 'Laura, I don't mean to pry, but can I ask one thing?'

'Yes,' said Laura, not knowing what the question would be and so slightly nervous.

'I don't understand something. About you and – and Nick. Please – he doesn't know I'm asking you this.'

'Yes,' said Laura. 'Go on, what?'

Charles put the car into gear, but he carried on looking at her. 'Did you honestly not realise who he was?'

'When?' said Laura, stupidly.

'This summer, Laura. When you met him. And you thought I was Lord Ranelagh, not him. Did you – seriously, did you not think it was him?'

'No!' said Laura. 'He told me you were. Why would I think any different?'

'He didn't,' said Charles. 'You assumed. He never actually lied, did he?'

'Well, no,' Laura concurred, conceding this was the truth. 'But why do you find it so weird? I just didn't realise.'

'That's what I find so strange,' said Charles, pulling out again. He was silent for a moment, then he said, 'I just – I always think of him as – as this Person.'

'What person?'

'A – a lord, a grand personage. You know. We're friends, have been for most of our lives. I see the real Nick more than most people. But part of me always sees him as – the Marquess of Ranelagh. Can't help it, just do. Owner of this beautiful estate,' he waved an arm, encompassing the fields around him. 'Descended from generations of Danvers and Needhams. The lord of all he surveys. He's an incredibly important person, not just because he's famous or whatever. But because he's in charge of hundreds of lives, looks after millions of pounds' worth of wealth. It's funny. I can't ever forget that.'

'Well,' said Laura. She thought of the Nick she'd known that summer, the Nick she still knew, who missed his mother, who snored in his sleep. 'He wasn't when I met him, was he?'

'No,' said Charles, and his smile was sad. 'That's why you're special.'

Charles grew more nervous as they approached the house, Laura could tell, though she didn't know why. Afterwards, it made complete sense of course, but as they drove through the Chartley lands and then onto the estate, turned into the driveway, saw the sign Laura had seen those months ago with her parents, she had no idea what lay ahead.

'Right, right, we're nearly there,' said Charles. The car crawled slowly up the driveway. The autumn sunset had begun, and the light filtered through the trees. The view was carpeted with trees of all different colours, pink, red, gold, orange, green. A light mist sat in the valley sloping away to the left; the park itself was ablaze with colour. As they sat in the car, Laura craned her neck eagerly for that first sight of the house, to see what it would look like in this light, this time of year.

Gradually, the hall slid into view; section by monumental section, as the drive curved towards it. Laura had forgotten how huge it was, just how imposing. She looked up to the East Wing, to make out Nick's room. It gave her a context, a sense of familiarity in this bewildering, vast landscape that she knew and yet felt so alien in.

'Look,' said Charles, as they reached the house. He turned off the engine. 'I'll go in. I may be a minute or two. Stay here, OK?'

'In the car?' said Laura.

'Yes,' said Charles. 'I have to – to check something. And I'll – I'll find Nick. Don't want you wandering around the house getting lost, and all that.'

'Er,' said Laura, confused. 'OK, of course.'

'Great,' said Charles. He opened his door, and got out. He looked in at her from outside. 'I really won't be long, honestly. I just have to find Nick, and explain something to him, and find out – er, what your room is, yes, that's it, what your –'

'Charles?' came a voice from behind him, and Charles spun around. Appearing through the fast-falling dusk was an unmistakable figure.

'Nick!' Charles said, his voice rather high. 'My god, hello.'

Laura sat still in her seat, not knowing what to do. Something wasn't right, she couldn't make it out.

'Hello,' said Nick. 'Where have you been? I've been looking for you. You've been ages. You said you were – hello. Is that someone in there? Have you got someone in the car, Charles? Well, I never. Hello?'

He bent down, his arm on the roof of the car, and looked in. His expression froze.

'Laura?' he said, his voice soft, hoarse almost.

'Hello,' said Laura, suddenly shy. She clambered out of the car, and stood across the bonnet from him and Charles.

Nick stared blankly at her. 'Sorry. What on earth are you doing here?'

'Er –' Laura said, not sure if he was joking or not. 'Am I early?'

'Nick,' said Charles, putting his hand on Nick's shoulder.

'Laura – here.' Nick turned to Charles. 'You're here,' he said, turning back to her. He looked at her, almost desperately. 'Why have you come back? Now?'

'You invited me!' said Laura, half-laughing, trying to keep her voice light. 'You can't change your mind.'

'Nick, listen,' said Charles, more loudly.

'What?' Nick asked. 'What's going on?'

A kaleidoscope of images and words started rushing through Laura's mind. The email. The broken phone. Charles's nerves. Nick's expression.

'Oh god,' said Laura. She looked at Charles. 'Charles –?'

'I invited her,' said Charles, standing straight and looking at Nick. 'I invited her down. Pretended to be you. I thought you should see her again. I thought you two should – sort it out. There are things you need to tell her, Nick.'

'You did *what*?' Nick said, advancing towards him.

'Oh shit,' said Laura. 'Oh no. No, no. You sent that email, didn't you?'

'Yes,' said Charles. His expression was defiant, aggressive, as with those who know they are wrong but feel they have just cause to be. Across the bonnet, Laura and Nick stared at him, as he stood between them. 'I'm sorry,' he said. 'Well, I'm not sorry. She's here now, Nick. She can't go back till tomorrow. I know you both hate me, but – but I did the right thing.'

Laura swallowed, and shifted on both feet. She didn't know what to say. The gravel crunched under her shoes. She wished she was anywhere. Anywhere but here.

'The right thing –' Nick swore under his breath. He took a step towards Charles. 'Charles, you – oh god. What have you done?' He grabbed the shoulder of his friend's jacket.

Charles stared at him impassively. They were still for a few tense seconds, then Nick released him and stepped back.

From behind them, through the vast wooden entrance doors, came a lilting voice. 'Nick! Nick, darling! Come inside! I can't find the drinks. I'm thirsty!'

As if she were a housewife ordering her husband around through the patio doors at a barbecue, there at the stop of the steps was Cecilia Thorson, in a headscarf, wide printed skirt, pretty little pumps. She fluttered, birdlike, halfway down the stairs.

'Nick? Nicky,' she said across the driveway. 'Are you coming?'

'What's she doing here?' said Charles sharply, under his breath.

'Rose invited her,' said Nick. His lips were thin, his voice expressionless. 'She turned up about fifteen minutes ago. Now do you see what I mean?'

He turned towards Cecilia. He didn't even look at Laura, or Charles. He took a deep, ragged breath, and said, 'Yes,' looking up at her. 'I'm coming, Cecilia.'

His back was still turned to Laura. 'Get her a room,' he said in a low voice to Charles. 'She can be your date tonight. I'll talk to you about this tomorrow, Charles.'

And without another word, he strode away towards the steps. He took them three at a time, meeting Cecilia, took the outstretched hand she offered him and led her inside. Laura watched him as if it were a scene from a film, not her life. She put her hands to her throat, trying not to retch. She couldn't breathe.

CHAPTER FORTY-EIGHT

Any additional worry that Laura might have had about being an uninvited guest for whom there was no room was swiftly put aside. Charles, mortified, ushered her in – through the front doors. At least that was something, she thought in a daze – if she'd been swept in by the back door, almost like a call-girl on hire for the evening, she would have *walked* all the way back to London. She was met by Mrs Hillyard, who, with calm professionalism, treated Laura's arrival as if it were entirely part of a plan; as if she were a deeply welcome guest. Within two minutes, Laura had been shown to a pretty little room, decorated in toile de Jouy and replete with flowery porcelain, on the north side of the house, towards the sea.

'Drinks are in the Great Hall at seven p.m.,' she said with a smile. 'Do let me know if there is anything you need, Miss Foster.'

Let's see, thought Laura, as she sat on the edge of her bed. A revolver with three bullets, one for me, one for Nick, and one for bloody Charles? A helicopter out of here? And a memory wipe? Look on the bright side, she told herself, as a tear rolled down her cheek and she sniffed, loudly. At least the slight question I had in my mind about whether this was going to work out or not has gone. At the ridiculousness of that statement she gave a watery chuckle. 'Oh,' she said, turning round and opening her bag, trying not to give in to it all. 'This is completely absurd!'

She opened the case. There, lovingly packed at the top, hastily rewrapped in its paper, was the claret-coloured dress she had bought to wear that evening, and at the sight of it, the memory of buying it, the memory of showing it to Mary a few hours ago, when she had been so full of excitement and anticipation, Laura's resolve crumpled and she cried. She bit her lip hard, walked over to the wardrobe and hung it up. It swayed in its old wooden teak case, in solitary splendour.

The matching bag and shoes that she could also ill-afford she put at the foot of the bed, and then she looked around the room. The old, gun-coloured radiator was on the other side, miles away from the bed. Was it even on? She suspected not. She suspected she would freeze tonight. She took out her underwear and shuddered. Unpacking was becoming like a horror film with lots of flashbacks, each item invoking a new memory of the stupid, pathetic hope with which she had packed it, and a corresponding moan from her of how stupid she had been, how completely embarrassing this all was . . . The jaunty little cardigan and jeans that she'd packed for Saturday, not knowing what they'd be doing, hoping it would be something as wonderful as the summer . . . Ugh. She pulled the cardigan out and put it on, threw the suitcase on the floor and kicked its contents under the bed. The room was still cold, she realised; she went over to shut the window.

Outside, on the terrace below, a man in a long white apron was polishing a series of silverware: candlesticks, plates, platters, trays. The doors to what Laura thought were the kitchen were flung open, and he was chatting away to someone invisible inside. A rather recalcitrant, awkward-looking teenager stood next to him, polishing with a distinct lack of enthusiasm. Around them was a buzz of activity, although always dignified. People kept emerging, shaking various things out, consulting with the polisher. Two gardeners trundled past, each pushing wheelbarrows. They stopped at a respectful distance from the silver-polishing, made a few enquiries, went on. In the distance the pine forest was black against the early evening sky. Around Laura in the great shell of the house lights were coming on, illuminating the façade as she looked out of it.

She had never felt more alone, more out of place, more unwanted. It was an odd sensation, the numbness before the real pain kicked in. She didn't know which was worse.

There was a knock at the door. She opened it, and there was Charles.

'Hello,' said Laura, slightly coldly. She turned away.

'Laura,' said Charles. He bent his head formally, as if supplicating himself before her. 'I came to tell you I'm so sorry for this bloody awful situation. I'm a total idiot. Should never have tried to pull something like this.'

He couldn't meet her eye.

'I know,' said Laura, trying to be understanding, he looked so desolate. 'Never mind.'

'No,' said Charles, flexing his fingers in agitation. 'Listen, Laura. You know I had no idea Cecilia would be here.'

'Obviously you didn't,' said Laura wryly.

'You know Nick didn't either. He's furious with Rose for inviting her.'

'Bully for him,' Laura murmured.

'Laura, there's nothing going on between them, you do realise that?'

'Are you serious?' said Laura. 'Don't be ridiculous.'

Charles hopped from one foot to the other. 'Well, of course there's something going on, but it's not what everyone thinks.'

'Well, I think they've had sex. I think he met her because her parents are incredibly rich and on the lookout for a nice catch for their millionairess daughter, and his sister will do anything to get them married,' Laura said. She was biting her lip, trying not to let him see she'd been crying.

'Right,' said Charles. 'Well, you're right about that – but –

I was only trying to help.' He sank onto the bed and rubbed his eyes. 'And of course it's all messed up. He's furious with me. Never seen him so cross.'

'Well,' said Laura. 'Oh Charles, don't look like that.' She wiped her nose on her forearm, and sat down next to him. 'You were honestly trying to do him a favour. He can't really be that cross with you, can he?' She sniffed loudly. 'He doesn't really care that much, you know.'

Charles stared at her. 'Don't you know why?' he said. 'You really don't know why he's furious that you're here? And she's here?'

'No, why?' said Laura.

'Think about it,' said Charles. He got up and stood there, looking down at her. Laura's face was blank.

'God, the two of you,' he said eventually. 'You're as bad as each other. You're both just too bloody stupid to see it.'

'What do you mean?' Laura asked. She shook her head, staring up at him blankly. Her pupils felt dilated; her limbs were heavy, she was tired with the shock of it.

'Work it out for yourself, Laura,' said Charles. He flicked her cheek with his finger; an oddly touching gesture. Laura smiled. 'I'll pick you up at seven p.m. tonight, then,' he said, heading for the door.

'Do I really have to go tonight? Face all those people?'

'Nobody knows, do they?' Charles pointed out.

'You're right,' said Laura. 'It's hardly like the girls in my sixth form are waiting downstairs to laugh at my shame.'

'Exactly. Get dressed, you'll feel better, smile that lovely smile of yours and you'll be fine. I promise.'

Laura smiled at him gratefully. 'Thank you.'

'See you later.'

It was five thirty. She was suddenly exhausted. She looked at the pretty little bed, covered with old lace cushions, the bedstead she knew was real old cast-iron, not bought on sale from a bed warehouse in Dalston, and lay down on it, closed her eyes, and fell asleep. She thought she heard the door open, but she said, 'Shoo,' and turned over and carried on dozing.

Laura woke up to a loud knocking on her door. Without looking at her watch, she knew instinctively that it was Charles, and that she was late. She jumped out of bed, trying to ignore the head-rush it gave her, and hopped to the door.

'Shit,' said Charles, gazing down at her. He was in a smart suit, his short hair carefully wetted and combed back. Laura followed his gaze, from the creased jacket she hadn't taken off since the train, her rumpled skirt, and her hair, which she could feel was standing up in odd places all over her head. She rubbed her eyes, and put her hands to her hair experimentally. Hm.

'It's seven o'clock,' said Charles desperately. 'Laura, did you –'

'I fell asleep,' Laura replied. 'I was tired. Shit. Sorry.'

'You've got five minutes,' he said helpfully. 'I'll wait outside.'

'No, no,' said Laura. She didn't know Charles well, but she knew him enough to know his idea of hell was tardiness of any kind. She patted his arm. 'Go down, Charles. I'll see you down there. I'll be ten minutes at the very most, and I mean that.'

'Are you sure?' said Charles. 'I can hold the fort. Explain you're on your way.'

'Oh Charles,' said Laura, leaning wearily against the doorframe. 'You are totally perplexing to me. Who's going to care if I'm late or not? No one even cares that I'm there in the first place.'

'I do,' said Charles kindly. He looked her up and down, sucked his lips in and smiled. 'And Nick does, even if he might not show it.'

'Charles –' said Laura gently. 'Please don't.' She coughed. 'Look, it's going to be hard enough to get through this evening as it is. If you keep being jaunty and optimistic I might actually lose what remaining cool I have and belt you. So –' she said, trying to sound mock-scary, when in reality she wasn't angry, simply tired, dead tired, wanting to fall asleep and never wake up again '– we'll go, have some nice food and wine and chats, and tomorrow, first thing, you drive me to the station. OK?'

'Well,' said Charles doubtfully. 'Maybe not first thing. This harvest festival dance – it goes on pretty much all night, you know. You don't want to miss out.'

'God, you really don't get it, do you, Charles?' said Laura, and she made to shut the door. 'See you down there.'

'I'll be waiting for you downstairs, by the door. Hurry up!'

He shut the door. Laura stood up straight. Right, she thought. Right, then. If this is as bad as it gets – bring it on. I'm going to do it. It's going to be OK.

Twenty minutes later (it would never have been ten minutes, never), Laura nervously clutched the huge newel post at the top of the Grinling Gibbons staircase and began her descent. It had taken her a good few minutes to find the Grand Staircase in the first place. She had got lost, gone down and up various corridors and into various alcoves, feeling totally insignificant, like a dormouse. She peered down, into the Great Hall at the bottom, where the guests were all congregated, on their second glass of champagne. Laura descended as quietly as she could, trying not to draw attention to herself. It was a hard staircase to navigate in high heels – the railing had clumps of terribly intricate grapes and apricots and at once stage what looked alarmingly like a real-life rat but she thought must be a squirrel – and she didn't know what to hold on to and what might fall off. Halfway down, she looked across at the wall and saw a normal, everyday railing attached to it. She clicked her tongue, but it was too late to stagger across the wide steps and start using that instead. Typical. So she carried on, negotiating the steps and the carved fruits of the world with the utmost care, taking in the scene below her as she descended, as best she might.

It was as if the stage was set for something – Laura didn't

know what. There was a sense of expectation in the air. A long night was ahead of them, all those present clearly knew that. It wasn't the terrifying set of people Laura had thought it might be – posh, ghastly, noisy, superior – certainly nothing like last time. That was something. There were a few Colonel Mustard types, but there were also lots of quite nice, ordinary-looking people. Everyone was in suits and smart dresses, Laura was relieved to see. She hadn't been sure of the dress code when she bought the dress; she had hoped it would hit the right note and, looking down, she knew she wasn't going to look out of place, sartorially at least.

A little way further down, the vast staircase curved gently and revealed the full mass of guests. There he was. In the corner of the room, by the fireplace, talking quietly to someone, smiling and looking amused, as Cecilia Thorson, decked out in what looked like a peach chiffon tutu, complete with matching bag and shoes and – good god, thought Laura, is that a silk *parasol*? – stood attentively by his side. Laura looked at him, then at the view around her, the old sensation of her last night in Norfolk assailing her again. She thought of what Charles had been saying in the car that afternoon about Nick. All of this was his. This vast, airy hall, its great tapestry hanging along the north wall, the rest of the room lit with paintings and armour. Out across the floodlit, smooth terrace, all the way to the folly at the top of the distant hill, and far beyond that. And these people in this room, most of them owed their living to him. To that one man.

As if she had called his name, Nick turned abruptly and looked up as she came down the stairs. He looked at her briefly, as if to say, 'Are you OK?' and when Laura nodded, he raised his glass, still unsmiling, gave her one more look, a strange, cold look, then turned back. Laura stood still, not knowing how to move. She could see Charles waiting by the stairs for her, and she made her way to him slowly as he pushed through the crowd to greet her. He ran up the last few steps.

478

'Laura,' said Charles. He kissed her hand. 'My dear girl. You look sensational.'

'Pff,' said Laura, articulately.

'Oh,' said Charles. He came up so he was level with her, and they were both standing on the same step. 'One more thing, Laura. I thought you'd want to know. I nearly forgot. There *is* someone else here you know.' He assumed an innocent expression. 'That's nice, isn't it?'

'Me? Who?' said Laura suspiciously, her eyes scanning the crowd.

'Your aunt. Annabel, is it?'

'What?' said Laura blankly.

'Annabel Sanderson. She's your aunt, isn't she?'

'Yes,' said Laura slowly. 'Of course. Oh god.'

Lady Rose's cronies. Charles had said they were coming. Aunt Annabel was one of them, she knew it. They were on some committee together; she'd said so in the summer. Several times . . . Mary had known as much this evening, but she hadn't wanted to spell it out . . . Oh dear, oh dear. This evening was presumably the zenith of her social-climbing aspirations – being invited to a private dinner and dance at Chartley Hall. With the Marquess of Ranelagh – and her own niece, whom Annabel was convinced was his One True Love . . .

Laura looked wildly around her. Aunt Annabel was in the crowd somewhere. She was there. It made complete sense, but why, Laura thought, clenching her fists and casting a baleful look heavenwards. Why?

Charles adjusted his tie. 'Anyway –' he said.

'Good god.' Laura realised she had to say something. 'She's a . . .' She was about to say 'dreadful social climber', in unconscious echo of her grandmother. She smiled to herself. 'Hell. She's quite something. Have you met her?'

'Oh yes,' said Charles politely. 'She's charming. Very pleased you're here. Look – she's waving at you.' He pointed in the direction of the crowd.

Laura didn't look. 'She knows I'm here?' she queried, in some alarm.

'I was introduced to her and she saw me adding your name on the seating plan for the dinner. She was – very excited.' Charles coughed. 'As well she might be. I told her you were my date for the evening, by the way. Just so she knows.'

'Thank you,' said Laura.

'Anyway. Come and say hello.'

He took her by the hand and led her through the heaving crowd to the centre of the room, and there, a determined expression on her face, was her very own Aunt Annabel, wearing what Laura immediately categorised as Posh Lady's Formal Attire # 1 – a black velvet cocktail dress, with a jaunty red silk bolero jacket. There was a lot of corseting going on; Laura could tell from the rather stiff way the usually rather stout Aunt Annabel was standing.

Lady Rose was a little way away, immaculately attired in a beautifully tailored raw silk suit, talking expressively to Lady Lavinia, decked out in a kind of long, flowing teepee of a dress. Next to her stood a nervous-looking youth. Sean, Laura remembered with clarity. Sean from the village. Laura was surprised to feel a strange stab of familial relief to see her aunt, waiting for her alone in a sea of unknown faces, someone wholly familiar.

'Hello, Aunt Annabel,' she said, putting her hand on her aunt's starchy silk shoulder. The whole situation was suddenly too much for her; Laura felt as if she were in the scene she'd been making up in her head on the train, and was overcome with the urge to snort most unedifyingly with laughter. She wished she had a fan she could hide behind and say, 'La! Sir, you are too kind!'

'Laura, well!' said Aunt Annabel, grasping her shoulders and looking at her appraisingly with a fond, almost girlish glint in her eye. She kissed her. 'What a lovely surprise to see you here. Charles was just explaining how kind it was of you to accompany him tonight.' There was a faint but audible tone of surprise in her voice; Laura knew it for what it was, a classic Aunt Annabel manoeuvre. Translation: *What's going on? I thought you were with the marquess, dear? I hope I haven't misrepresented the situation to all and sundry? Well. I say.*

'Well, dear, it's lovely to see you,' Annabel went on. 'We are *so lucky*, aren't we?'

She gave the word 'aren't' about five syllables; Laura gave Charles a look, but he smiled impassively back.

'Lady *Rose*', said Aunt Annabel, practically bowing her head at the name, 'was *delighted* to hear you were coming tonight, Laura dear. I must take you over to say hello to her.'

'No,' said Laura, panic rising within her. 'It's really – it's OK. I've met her.'

'Nonsense,' said Aunt Annabel. She waved over towards Lady Rose, who turned with a fixed smile on her face and saw Annabel and Laura together. Her smile grew cold, and she touched her palm with the pads of her fingers in the most cursory wave, and turned back to her conversation.

'Oh,' said Annabel slowly. 'She must be busy.' Laura almost felt sorry for her aunt, though not quite. Annabel smiled brightly after her. 'Isn't this lovely?' she said.

It was strange, but Laura suddenly found herself thinking that Annabel sounded almost like Laura's own mother, who was constantly trying to smooth things over, make everything socially acceptable. Angela was often flustered, nervous about things. Laura had never seen her aunt behave the same way. It was funny how people were all the same in different contexts. Annabel looked brave, and shrugged her shoulders. Laura said, in an effort to be sociable,

'So, Aunt Annabel – who else is here from your committee?'

'Oh,' said Aunt Annabel, looking around, 'not that many people. She mentioned that we were all invited at the last committee meeting, a few weeks ago. We're on the same pro-hunting lobby-group, you know,' she said to Charles. 'The Backboners, we're called.'

'Ah,' said Charles. 'Right.'

You're a total fraud! You don't go hunting! Laura wanted to yell at her. The nearest you've ever got to tweed is the Austin Reed sample sale! But instead she nodded politely at her aunt, who said blithely,

'Well, yes. But the invitation was all rather vague. Lady Rose is so busy I had to really track her down, call her office a couple of times to be sure of the details. And most couldn't make it. Such a shame. So wonderful, though. To be *here*.'

'Hm,' said Laura.

'Yes,' said Charles politely. 'Well, wonderful that you could be with us, Mrs Sanderson. Ah, here's some more champagne. Would you like a new glass?'

'Thank you,' said Aunt Annabel, smiling at him with what Laura could only assume was an attempt at a coquettish flutter of the eyelashes, which she found most off-putting.

Charles handed her another glass from the tray and, as the waiter had vanished, put the old glass down on a sideboard.

'I do hope it's all right to leave glasses on the side here!' said Aunt Annabel, regaining her composure. 'Can you imagine the havoc a ring mark would cause! Wonderful. Oh, look. There's the marquess.' She flicked a glance at Laura. Laura followed her stare across the room, and saw Nick watching them through the crowd. She stared back at him, not knowing what to say.

'Oh Charles,' said Annabel, who had obviously performed a formal ceremony in her room of throwing caution to the winds and was now being as embarrassing as possible. 'Who's that girl standing next to him?'

Laura watched as Lady Rose appeared beside Cecilia Thorson, took her elbow, and smiled charmingly at her. She said something to Cecilia, who laughed loudly. Nick said nothing. He carried on looking at Laura.

'That's Cecilia Thorson,' said Charles. 'Um. She's a friend of Nick's.'

'Right,' said Aunt Annabel. 'Well.' She looked at Laura,

482

obviously rather confused. Cecilia put her hand on Nick's arm. Laura stared at them, and he stared back at her, his eyes eventually flicking to Annabel and Charles too. Then he smiled across the room, just at her, and she didn't know what to do.

Annabel saw this. She said nothing for a moment, and then she looked at her niece. 'So, Charles,' she persevered, 'you know Laura too, then?'

'Yes,' Charles said, intervening gracefully. 'She knows us both. Very lucky we are.' He patted his stomach. 'Ah, here's a tray of delicious canapés. Mrs Sanderson, may I tempt you?'

'Yes please,' said Annabel, plucking a tiny vegetable roll off a tray. 'So, can you tell me *what* that idiotic young man is doing with *her* then, when he should be over here with my niece?'

'Oh god,' said Laura, trying to hide behind her champagne glass.

'No, I can't tell you that,' said Charles, trying not to smile. 'Can't tell you that at all.'

'Humph,' said Annabel, almost grumpily, and Laura stole a glance at her aunt, trying not to want to . . . like her.

CHAPTER FORTY-NINE

Apart from the twin social demons of her aunt Annabel and
Lady Rose Balmore, and apart from the constant jabbing pain
in the side she got every time she saw Nick with Cecilia
Thorson, Laura had to admit the Harvest Festival looked like
being a good party, if only she'd been able to throw herself
into it. By eight o'clock the Great Hall was rammed with
people, all sorts of people, mostly from the village and those
who worked on the estate; there were children running around,
hiding under tables, playing catch in the entrance hall. Charles
pointed out the housing committee who were so impressed
with Nick's innovative scheme, four or five of them, all huddled
together in black, looking worried, looking nervous and highly
out of place. They clearly felt out of their depth. Laura wished
they wouldn't; even she could see, after a couple of glasses,
that it just wasn't that kind of party. It wasn't, funnily enough,
an Annabel/Rose party. She had thought it would be, rather
stiff and formal and posh. It was nice. Relaxed. When someone
stood on the table, a short fat man with a florid face, and
shouted that everyone should go through, she found herself
smiling and laughing with people, total strangers, as she filed
into the Ballroom, where two hundred people were sitting
down to dinner.

The atmosphere couldn't have been more different from her last dinner at Chartley; even the Ballroom looked different. Suspended high above them, two huge chandeliers sparkled gently, giving out a soft light. The crystals reflected the light from the hundreds of candles on the tables and in alcoves on the walls. The huge polished wooden floor gleamed warmly; at one end of the vast room a great fire leapt in the hearth. There were four long tables, each banked high with sparkling crystal glassware, some of which also caught the light and twinkled. The scent of flowers, lilies and roses filled the room; they were everywhere, on the table, on the windowsills. Laura stood in the doorway and looked up and down the room, giving a small gasp as she took it all in. It was beautiful.

To her pleasure, she was next to Charles on one side. He was opposite Lady Lavinia and Sean – and this seemed to flummox him somewhat. Especially since Sean seemed to be suffering from some kind of physical complaint throughout dinner; he kept jerking unexpectedly, and Lavinia would look up and around her demurely. Laura watched her. She didn't know if Nick's sister was really manipulative, or just in a world of her own. On her other side was a nice man from the village, Rick, who owned the butchers, and had just started using only locally sourced and produced meat. He had supplied the sausages that evening. They were having bangers and mash, piles and piles of it.

The food was delicious. Laura realised she was absolutely starving. The sausages were incredible, properly meaty, seasoned, tasting of real, good things. The potatoes came from the estate, earthy, velvety, creamy. The tables were groaning with food, the waiters never stopped going round with wine. The noise in the Ballroom grew and grew, the sound of people chatting, drinking, laughing – having a good time. Laura couldn't see where Nick was, and after looking for a few minutes she gave up. She turned to Rick.

'Wonder who drew the short straw and had to work

tonight?' Laura said, indicating one of the waiters as they passed. 'Bit unfair that they're on and they have to wait on their colleagues.'

'No,' said Rick, putting a huge dollop of mustard on his plate. 'Waiters are all hired for the evening. No one at Chartley works the night of the Harvest Festival.'

'Really?' said Laura. 'Blimey.'

'Oh yes,' said Rick. 'His lordship's most particular about it, you know. Won't hear of it. He says, if you're having a party for the estate, it's a party for everyone. So everyone comes. But you know, that's the marquess for you. He really is –'

Laura couldn't really bear another long exposition from yet another person about why Nick was just the greatest person in the world, ever. So she said, because she was genuinely interested, apart from anything else, 'Can you tell me something then? What's the difference between a proper sausage and – you know, a horrible one, one that looks like whipped pink cream?'

'Well,' Rick began.

Opposite her, Sean jerked suddenly again, and said urgently, 'Lav— oi, don't *do* that, OK?'

Lavinia looked at him innocently. 'What do you mean?' she said primly. Her eyes danced.

Laura looked at her. She really was beautiful, not at all like her sister. She looked very like the photo of her mother that had been in that newspaper article about them all. Very Sixties, ethereal and pale, with lots of eyeliner and piled-up Titian hair – and the slightly unconvincingly ethnic outfit, which annoyed Laura. She wanted to take it off her and pop her into a nice simple Audrey Hepburn-style gown. Then she realised she was sounding awfully like her mother, and smiled.

As Rick described cuts and prime hunks of pork and seasoning, Laura turned to smile at Charles, to find him staring helplessly at Lavinia. She didn't even need it confirming – the look on poor Charles's face said it all.

Lavinia looked across the table at Charles, a mischievous expression on her face.

'Rick!' Rick ground to a halt. 'Charles, darling. Sean says I'm being naughty. I'm not, am I?'

'Yes, you are, Lavinia,' said Charles, and he sounded rather stern. 'Stop it. It's not right. Leave him alone.'

'Thanks, mate,' said Sean, looking wildly around him, then back to Lavinia, who looked solemn for a second, and then slid her hand into his lap again.

'Lavinia!' Charles said sharply. 'I won't tell you again. You will not behave like this. Not tonight. OK?'

Lavinia looked up at him, rather surprised.

'Charles!' she said. Charles met her gaze impassively. 'Oh, right,' and she leant back in her chair, accepting defeat. She yawned. 'I'm so bored . . .'

Laura found herself wanting to reach across the table and slap her face repeatedly, and also to tell her to wake up and smell the coffee in the shape of lovely, kind Charles, so obviously head-over-heels in love with her. She didn't think Lavinia deserved anyone to point things out to her though. She was too self-centred. She gave her a semi-second glare, and said brightly to Charles,

'It all seems to be going really well, doesn't it?'

Charles was gazing again. She kicked him. 'Charles!'

He turned to her and widened his eyes, as if trying to bring himself back to reality. 'My god,' whispered Laura. 'You really have got it bad, haven't you?'

'I don't know what you mean,' said Charles, clearing his throat and delicately arranging the cutlery. The noise in the Ballroom seemed to grow a little louder.

'Lavinia,' Laura hissed. 'You're in love with her!'

'I am not,' said Charles indignantly.

'Yes you are,' Laura replied firmly. She smiled with pleasure, and clapped her hands softly under the table. 'Oh, this is wonderful! It's like something out of a Victorian novel.'

Charles looked down and cleared his throat again. He said stiffly, 'Do be quiet.'

'No,' said Laura. 'I'm your date for the evening, remember? So you have to put up with me. And my ghastly relations. No, Charles, I know exactly what it's about. You're in love with Lavinia.'

'I'm not enjoying this,' said Charles, looking up briefly across at Lavinia, who was nibbling Sean's ear. His face was puce.

'Sorry,' said Laura, feeling momentarily contrite. 'Golly,' she said. 'You must really regret having asked me tonight.'

'Pretty much, yes,' said Charles frankly. 'Now be quiet.'

Laura stole a glance at him. 'I think you should do something about it,' she said after a pause. 'I'm telling you, she needs someone like you. To bring her into line. And you need to look after someone.'

'I assure you –' Charles said, trying to keep his voice low.

'Sshh,' said Laura, paying no attention. 'You love Lavinia. You have a complex about being in love with your best friend's sister.'

The tips of Charles's ears grew pink and he sank further down his chair.

'You also have an even bigger complex about not being good enough for her, because you're only a simple maiden from the village. And all that.'

'I'm not a maiden, Laura, that's not – well, I suppose –'

'And just when, after years of building up to it, you've finally plucked up the courage to ask her out, cleared it with Nick – she starts screwing some teenager who can't say "Please" and "Hello" without getting confused. Oh, Charles.'

'Look who's talking,' said Charles, sitting up crossly.

'What?'

'You're a fine one to start lecturing me about having a complex about being the simple maiden from the village,' said Charles. 'Do you not *listen* to yourself?'

Laura had been so caught up in the romance of Charles's situation that she wasn't really paying attention. 'Oh,' she said.

'Exactly,' said Charles. 'It's not that simple.' He looked across at Lavinia and Sean, who were whispering to each other, and blinked very slowly. 'Now,' he said, opening his eyes. 'Tell me. The Chartley satellite dish is on the blink. Have you seen the new series of *Curb Your Enthusiasm*?'

The band had started setting up at one end of the room; people were clearing the tables away; guests were starting to move around. The lights were low. In the din of the room and with the softness of Charles's voice Laura had to lean closely towards him to hear what he was saying. She patted him on the shoulder consolingly, and looked up to find the Marquess of Ranelagh crouched down, having a conversation with Lavinia opposite. His eyes flicked over to Laura and Charles, who sprang apart.

'Hello,' said Nick, standing up. 'I was just making sure everything's OK this end. How are you all?'

He addressed the question to the table at large, and nodded easily as some people raised their glasses to him, others carried on eating, others called out thanks or rude jokes.

'Great bangers, Rick,' Nick said, nodding at Rick. His hands were in his pockets; he took one out and shook Rick's. 'Thanks a lot. Remind me to come down tomorrow and we'll settle.'

'Of course, my lord,' said Rick. Laura was watching Nick; she saw a tiny muscle flex in his cheek involuntarily, and she realised how much he hated the title. She smiled at him, in what she hoped was an amicable, grateful way.

'Having a good time?' Nick asked her.

'Yes, thank you,' said Laura. She was, she realised; much better than she'd expected. 'It's wonderful. Charles is –'

But she got no further. He nodded, just like his elder sister, and turned to talk to Charles, leaving her addressing thin air.

Laura sat there for a moment, as Charles shifted around in his seat and asked some technical question about the remote control on the gates so that people could leave through the main entrance no matter how late. Nick replied shortly. Tears she could not control filled Laura's eyes. She murmured to Rick, 'Excuse me,' and pushing her chair back, stumbled towards the Hall. People were standing, sitting, talking, laughing; no one noticed her as she crept out of the huge room and clattered across the Great Hall, suddenly silent and dark, long, moonlit shadows falling across the grey stone floor.

From behind the staircase, deep within the bowels of the house, Laura could hear the clatter of feet growing louder. She looked around wildly – she didn't want anyone to see her. There was another door leading off from the Hall, and she ran through it, and found herself in a gloomy, long room.

CHAPTER FIFTY

As her eyes grew accustomed to the darkness, Laura jumped. She looked around her and realised she was in the Picture Gallery. Sculptures were scattered the length of the room, Cupids, Graces, sleeping fauns and dying centurions, all in bone-coloured marble. The floodlights outside gave the unlit room and the figures within a ghostly, ethereal quality.

Lining the walls were portraits, all in the same ebony frames, rows of Needhams and Danvers, rows of marquesses, all watching her, their eyes following her around the room. Laura shivered and hugged herself, stroking the silk on her shoulder straps. It was eerie – she felt as if she had stumbled into another world. She stared around her in wonder. So, this is what I missed when I left the tour early, she thought, and gave a tiny laugh in the silence of the room. There was a dimmer switch on the wall; how incongruous, she thought. She made to go and turn it on, then thought better of it. She shouldn't really be here, she ought to go back, only –

And suddenly a voice behind her said, 'Laura?'

She turned, and there was Nick, leaning against the open door.

He came into the room, walking towards her, and said, 'What are you doing in here? Catching up on your sightseeing?' His face fell into shadow as he stood beside her.

Laura said, 'I – I wanted some fresh air.'

'It's rather hot in there, isn't it?' he agreed.

'Yes,' Laura replied, although she was actually quite cold. 'Yes, it is.'

'You seem to be enjoying yourself,' he commented pleasantly.

'It's a beautiful room,' said Laura, all at once perfectly calm. 'I hadn't seen it before.'

He began to walk slowly down the length of the room. She fell into step beside him, and they were silent for a moment. He looked sideways at her and cleared his throat. Indicating one of the black-framed portraits, he said in a conversational tone, 'Very beautiful. Yes. Let me give you the guided tour.'

'Don't you have to –' Laura made a helpless gesture with her hands.

'Have to what?'

'Do something? Look after the guests?'

Nick put his hands in his pockets and turned towards her. 'I don't suppose anyone will miss us for a few minutes, Laura.'

She blushed, feeling like a silly schoolgirl, but before she could say anything he pointed to the painting nearest to them. 'So. Have you seen this, here? It's supposed to be a Holbein. Unsigned.'

Laura recovered herself. 'Really? My goodness.'

They walked a little further, and she noticed they were perfectly in step, his tread firm against the light clatter of her heels, almost like a dance.

'One of the jewels of our collection, this painting. Can you see?' He put his hand lightly on her shoulder and turned her slightly away from him.

'Yes,' said Laura, trying not to relax into his touch. 'Who is this?' She noted, almost with detached amusement, that her nails were digging into her palms, like she was nervous, but she didn't feel it – did she?

Nick said, 'Lady Ranelagh, Restoration period. She may have slept with Charles the Second – but then, who didn't.'

'Who didn't,' Laura echoed. She stared at the subject, a

woman with tumbling, golden curls, a confident expression, almost pursing her lips, in love with life. 'It's lovely. She looks nice, doesn't she?'

'I always think she must have been fun to have around,' said Nick. 'Her husband raised the money for Chartley. Got it off Charles the Second, I think, basically for prostituting his wife out. It was her idea.'

'Families!' said Laura. 'My dad's mum used to get me and my brother to wash her neighbour's car and in return he'd mend her garden fence. It's very much the same thing.'

She was joking, but Nick stopped and stared at Lady Ranelagh again. 'You know, it kind of is the same thing, actually.'

Laura laughed. 'No it's not.'

'People are more alike than you think, you know, Laura.' He moved off smartly without saying any more. 'Right. Let's go a little further. Here, Lady Charlotte Needham. She married Lord Hastings. It's by Reynolds.'

'I love that,' said Laura, admiring the girl with black ribbons in her dark hair and a grave, rather serious expression. 'She's sweet. She looks like –' she was going to say, 'your sister, Rose', but didn't think it would be the right thing to say, and yet there was a look of Rose about the girl's dark, candid eyes, her rather purposeful features.

Nick carried on and she fell into step with him, down the long, dappled gallery, where faces caught the moonlight and smiled at her.

'And here is the seventh marquess, after whom I am named,' he said, and Laura looked up to find the real portrait of her old friend, the one who had started it all. The seventh marquess smiled benevolently down at them, and Laura's heart stopped again, remembering how she had felt, that funny, romantic, silly evening as she found the postcard on the bus home.

'He looks . . . just like you,' she said.

Nick bowed slightly. 'I'm honoured,' he said. He started walking again, his face impassive.

'Who's that?' Laura asked, stopping again. She pointed up to a portrait of a woman in a long, black dress. Her face was in three-quarter profile, her hand resting lightly on her breastbone. Beside her lay a photo, and a vase with blossom in it. It was a stark, spare painting, the only decoration the woman herself, and Laura stared, transfixed, because she was so lovely.

Nick said nothing.

'It's your mother, isn't it?' Laura asked, suddenly realising.

'Yes,' said Nick. 'This is when she got married. In 1959. She was only twenty-three. She'd already been acting for about six years by then; she was pretty young.'

'She's beautiful,' Laura told him honestly.

'She was,' said Nick. 'I don't know now, I haven't seen her for years.'

'How long has it been?' Laura asked softly.

'Since I was eleven. 1981.'

'And it's true – you've *never* seen her again?' said Laura.

'No,' Nick replied. His voice was bleak. 'We weren't allowed to.'

'Have you thought about it any more?' Laura gestured writing with a pencil and paper. 'I mean – getting in touch with her?'

'Oh, Laura.' His hand was on his forehead, he was himself suddenly. 'God, I just don't know how to go about it. It's easier to just think you'll do something about it one day, to save yourself actually doing something about it that day. You know?'

'I know,' said Laura. 'I do know. Oh Nick. You have to see her again. You really do. If only for yourself, you have to . . .'

He looked so dreadfully alone, in his black jacket, the hollows of his cheekbones dark in the moonlit room, his eyes unreadable. She stared at him, drinking in the sight of him, her heart clenching as she thought how vulnerable he was, despite everything that he had.

She went over to him. 'Not my business,' she said, and shivered. 'I'm sorry.'

He looked down at her. 'What for, Laura?' he asked, smiling.

494

'What on earth for?' and he took her left hand in his right hand, and put it in his jacket pocket, then did the same with her right hand, his fingers closing around hers, so that she was facing him. He said quietly, 'So. I thought we weren't speaking to each other.'

'You were quite horrible to me the last time I saw you,' said Laura.

'Laura, shame on you.' His hands, in his pockets, tightened around hers. 'You were the last person I was expecting to see there. That was a good day, that day, and you came along and ruined it.'

'Charming!' said Laura.

'I mean,' he said, his mouth close to her ear. 'That was the first day I hadn't thought about you. Constantly. And then there you were. Having a really bad day. And I was trying to make it better, but I didn't know what to do – what to say . . .' he trailed off. 'How's work, by the way?'

'Work?' said Laura, momentarily wrong-footed. 'It's fine. Great, actually. Much better than when I last saw you.'

'Really?' he replied. 'Why?'

'Oh –' Laura looked around her, weighing up whether to go into Marcus's about-turn, and found the eyes of an Elizabethan lady in a ruff on her. She looked down. It wasn't important, not here, she shouldn't bother him with it all, even though she really wanted to. 'Nothing. Don't worry about it. But thanks, though.'

'Really?'

'Absolutely,' she said, wishing she could talk to him, tell him everything, but not feeling able to here, under the collective gaze of his family, alive and dead. 'I'm sorry about that night. It was – weird.'

'You ran off,' said Nick. 'Again.'

'Well,' Laura shifted on her feet. 'I'd had a bad evening. And I felt completely out of place. And then Cecilia phoned you, and – I just thought you were being polite, and trying to get rid of me.'

'She was checking up on me,' said Nick. 'I should have told her to go away. I'm sorry.'

'And yet here she is again,' Laura pointed out.

He sighed. 'I know. Look, I promise you there's nothing going on between me and Cecilia. My sister invited her tonight. Nothing to do with me.'

'Where is she then?' Laura said curiously.

He jerked his head up. 'Actually, she gave up. Told me I was pathetic and went to bed about fifteen minutes ago. Her bed, obviously. She's got her own room. She has, Laura. Believe me.'

'Nick,' said Laura, putting her hands up. 'Really – it's none of my business.'

'Isn't it?' he asked, his voice reverberating in her ear, his lips close to her hair. 'It's nothing to do with you, is it?'

'No,' said Laura, shaking her head and looking up at him, bemused. 'Nick – you're the Marquess of Ranelagh. I'm nothing. Well, not nothing, but – you can do what you want, I don't –'

'You still don't see it, do you?' said Nick. 'Seriously, you still can't see it?'

'What?' Laura asked.

He ran his hands through his hair and, not looking at her, said, 'What if being with you was the first proper conversation I've had with someone for years? That I felt like the person I really was, for once?' He backed away and gripped his tie, loosening it. 'God, Laura. Don't say that, not you, especially not you.'

'What do you mean?'

'You can't see it, even now?' he said tiredly. 'I'm not the Marquess of Ranelagh, that's not me. That's the thing I inherited, just like you inherited your total stupidity from some family member of yours; I don't know who.'

Laura gasped in outrage, and he smiled wickedly at her in the darkness. She shivered.

'I'm sorry. You're cold.' He looked at her appraisingly, then took off his jacket and put it around her shoulders.

'Thank you,' she said.

'My pleasure,' he replied, mock-formally. He took a quick breath, and said, 'We seem to have been going around in circles, haven't we? But let me just say this.' His voice was softer. 'I'm not the Marquess. I am sometimes, of course. But I'm still the person you met this summer, before it all got confusing, bogged down with all that other crap.' Laura made to say something; he held up his hand. 'Listen to me, Laura. I'm Nick. My mum ran off with someone when I was eleven, I haven't seen her for over twenty years and my dad and I didn't get on. He was a bully. I liked geography at school, I hated French. I like *The Sopranos*. I don't like Arsenal. When I was in America for the summer when I was nineteen I slept with a stripper.'

'Really?' said Laura, interested despite herself. 'Where?'

He shook his head, trying not to smile. 'Tell you later. Let me finish. All of that stuff, I could talk to you about. About how much I love the house. About the way to run things, how it all means so much to me. Just like any other job, without all this other crap getting in the way.'

'What crap?'

'You know,' he said impatiently. 'Fawning. Ceremony. Old ladies in car parks. Insane men with tour guides. People bowing, asking the same questions. All the time. It's my responsibility. I have to deal with it, and I don't mind, in fact I'm proud of it, but you – you made me feel like a real person for once. And I – I wanted to do the same for you. I wanted you to feel better about yourself, to realise how completely, totally wonderful you are, Laura.'

He took her hand and kissed her palm gently, his forehead touching hers, and out of the corner of her vision Laura saw the portrait of his beautiful, smiling mother, her dark eyes watching them. She gave a ragged, deep sigh, as Nick pulled her towards him. He bent his head and whispered, 'Oh, Laura . . .'

'No,' Laura heard herself say. She looked up. There, on the

opposite wall, the seventh marquess stared down at her, clutching his book. 'I can't, Nick. Not here.'

She stepped back a little from him.

'What do you mean?' said Nick, his brow furrowed, his face instantly closing up.

'Not here,' Laura said softly, making a tiny gesture with her hand. 'These – all of them. I can't.'

'I don't understand,' he said, releasing her other hand and shaking his head slowly.

'Nick,' said Laura. She had to make him see why it was so important. '*They're* the reason we can't be together. All of these people, here.' She gestured the length of the room. 'You and me – when I'm with you, it doesn't matter. And I can see you in my flat,' she added, rather inarticulately.

'What on earth are you talking about?' said Nick. 'I've never been to your flat.'

She took his hand. 'I mean, I can see you talking to my friends, lying on my sofa.' She squeezed his hand; he had to see what she meant, had to. 'Us, together, normal. That's why I – I thought I was falling in love with you. Not because of any of this stuff. The fairytale romance bit of it, Nick – I don't want that. I just want you, do you understand?'

His jaw was set. 'Laura. But all of this – this *is* me.'

'Oh, I know it is,' said Laura impatiently. 'But you just said yourself, there's a big part of you that's you, just yourself, and *that's* the bit you need someone to share with you.' His eyes searched her face; she looked at him, imploring him to understand. 'And here – this room, all these people. *They're* the bit that complicates everything. They're the reason we can't be together.'

She lapsed into silence, still holding his hand, not knowing what to say next.

Nick laughed suddenly, in the gloom of the room, a warm, comforting laugh. 'Laura, oh Laura.' He stroked her collarbone, and she shivered at his touch.

498

'What?' she said.

'You're right, you know, but I think you're taking it too seriously.'

'I –'

'Look,' said Nick, with the air of one trying to be reasonable. 'I want to talk to you. Properly, about all of this. But I want to kiss you first. You're right, this room's a bit daunting. So, let's go somewhere else.'

'Just like that?' Laura asked. 'It's as simple as that, is it?'

'Absolutely,' he replied. 'The trouble with you is you over-think everything. I like you, you like me. Let's go and sit on the steps and talk. Without Great Grandmothers A, B and C watching us.'

He bent his head and kissed her, quickly, hard on the lips, and then said, 'OK?'

'OK,' said Laura. 'OK.'

'Come on,' he said, holding her hand again, and they walked back along the length of the room, and stood in the doorway. Laura could see Charles circling in the background of the Great Hall. She was sure he was looking for Nick and she didn't want him to come, didn't want them to have to separate. She wanted to stay like this forever.

'Well, I'm glad I've seen this room anyway,' she said. 'I don't want you to think I didn't like it. It's – er, it's lovely.'

'What a polite guest. My pleasure,' said Nick. 'All mine.'

'All yours,' she said, laughing at the absurdity of it all. 'I'm glad you found me here.'

'I was looking for you, Laura,' he said. 'And now let's go.'

The doors were flung open. Charles strode into the room, his phone in his hand. 'There you are.'

'Hey,' said Nick, but Charles wasn't looking at him, he was walking towards Laura.

'Laura, my dear,' he said, with the same kind face he always had. Laura smiled at him, but her blood froze as she looked into his eyes, saw their expression. 'Your aunt's looking for you. You're going to have to go. It's – it's your grandmother, Laura. She's had a massive heart attack. She's in hospital. It's not good. She's asking for you, Laura. Your mother needs you to go back to London. Tonight.'

CHAPTER FIFTY-ONE

As long as Laura lived she would never forget that journey. Bizarre details. The mints Aunt Annabel had in her car. The travel atlas; half the cover was torn off, so unlike the Sandersons. The way Annabel drove, wildly, hunched over the steering wheel, her face pale in the darkness, her make-up like a mask. Those things that Laura had unpacked so carefully, painfully a few short hours ago now flung randomly into the suitcase. They should have just left, should have asked the others to send things on, Laura realised afterwards as the journey went on, going deeper into night, as Annabel drove in silence and they both had time to think.

Yes, Laura had time to think; hours of time. It was over three hours from Chartley Hall to the hospital in town, but what could she think about? Nothing. Her mind couldn't concentrate, couldn't think of what she might find there, what might not be there. And what had just happened, in the Picture Gallery. She didn't understand, couldn't process it all. When she tried to think about it, it was as if her brain short-circuited. Nick had offered to drive. Annabel had practically pushed him away, racing to the car, roaring away from the house in a frenzy that Laura had never seen before.

They tried to talk, at the beginning of the journey, but both of them were so overwrought and worried that their conversation was in bursts, short and sharp.

'Where are they?' Annabel asked, as Laura put down the phone to her mother. They had been driving for over half an hour. Laura glanced at a sign; they were still in Norfolk. Oh hurry, hurry, she thought, please hurry.

'Still at the hospital. They're all there.'

'Who?'

'Mum, Dad, Simon. Cedric and Jasper. And Fran and Robert.'

'Where's Lulu?' said Annabel instantly.

'I don't know,' Laura trailed off. 'I didn't ask.'

'Why isn't she there?' Annabel said.

Since she had no way of knowing or finding out, Laura said nothing.

'What did they say?'

'They said she's unconscious now. But she has been talking. I think –' Laura's voice faltered; she wasn't used to saying things like this, didn't know the language. It was too easy to default to clichés from hospital television shows, or books. 'I think she's worse.'

'What's she been saying?' said Annabel sharply.

'I don't know,' said Laura. 'Mum didn't say. Except – she was – except she was asking for me. And Simon. She recognised him.'

'Just Simon?' Annabel hunched over the steering wheel even higher, peering at the road ahead as if willing the car to take flight and fly, soar across the countryside, take them back to Mary.

'I don't know,' Laura said again, feeling helpless. 'I don't know.'

'Well, you're her grandchildren, not Fran, I suppose.' Annabel cleared her throat. 'And if Lulu's not there – perhaps she's waiting for her to get there.'

'I'm not sure,' said Laura. 'Aunt Annabel – I don't think she knows what's going on.'

There was a dull stabbing pain behind her eyes, like something crawling, scratching them. This was all wrong. Mary wasn't someone in a hospital, dying! She was the most alive person Laura knew. Her place in the world was so sure. She knew what she knew, so certain of everyone and everything, which was why she was the most reassuring grandmother one could possibly have.

'Come on, come on,' Annabel muttered. She bit her lip. Laura looked at her. She looked awful; it was as if she had aged about twenty years, but there was something more than that. Her composure was the first thing that struck you about Annabel; it was her most noticeable quality, more than her glossy brown hair, her perfect make-up, her glamorous, determined air, her rather braying voice. It was the quiet certainty that her world was right, that she was right. That having Delia Smith's cookbooks in the kitchen was . . . strange, to say the least. ('Looks very *useful*, Angela, dear.') That going on holiday to Spain was . . . bound to be full of horrifically lower-class people. ('Isn't Majorca rather *hot* at this time of year?') That Harrow was an extraordinary place to voluntarily locate and bring up children. ('Do you have friends there, dear? Really?') Now, Laura felt she was seeing a tiny bit of the other Annabel her aunt might be for the first time, and it was a strange experience.

They were on a main road, finally, thankfully, and the electric strip-lighting overhead bathed their faces in a ghostly green light. It was one of those endless, featureless roads, its only characteristics of interest blue signs, chevrons, cones. Nothing else was visible from the road. They could have been anywhere in the country. Laura blinked, trying to remember where she'd been, but already the memory of Chartley, of Nick and what he had said, what it had all meant – it was racing far from her mind, already framed and deposited in a memory bank, a lovely pure snapshot of something in the past. She couldn't connect it with this.

Laura shunted down in her seat, wrapping her slightly-too-big-for-her jacket around her for warmth. Jacket? She looked down. She was still wearing Nick's jacket, the one he had put around her in the Picture Gallery – that was the same evening, wasn't it? Her mind scrabbled to remember, and the creatures pinching behind her eyes grew more frantic.

'Are you cold, Laura, dear?' said Annabel, her voice quiet and hoarse. 'Perhaps we should stop here and get some coffee.'

'No, no,' said Laura, pleading, feeling a wave of panic at the suggestion. 'No, please, Aunt Annabel, please – just keep driving.'

'Of course,' said Annabel. She flicked a look at her niece, very briefly. 'Darling. You mustn't get too upset, you know.'

Don't say it, thought Laura to herself. I'll be fine if you don't say it.

'. . . She's eighty-five, you know. She's had a good life. A very good life.'

'Shut up,' said Laura quietly, ferociously. 'Don't, Aunt Annabel. I mean it, don't.'

'Laura!' said Aunt Annabel, but her voice was still soft. 'Listen to me. It's not a cliché with your grandmother, you know. She has had a good life. One of the best. Wonderful times she had with – with Guy, and everyone. She's been everywhere. She knows everyone. She hasn't had a moment's illness.'

'That's not the point!' Laura cried. 'She wasn't ready! It's not her time, it's not. Why couldn't she –'

'Laura, Laura,' said Annabel. She reached across blindly for Laura's hand with her own, took it and squeezed it. 'Do you really think that's true? That she isn't ready to go? Because I don't.'

'How can you –' Laura began, and her voice trailed away as she remembered Mary only yesterday, wincing with pain, and then her face clearing, as if she wasn't in pain any more.

'I love your grandmother very much,' said Annabel. 'She's like my mother. I don't remember my mother at all. So Mary brought me up when she married my father.' She spoke as if

504

she were talking to herself. 'She was so in love with Guy. Always. He was the love of her life. When he died she wasn't the same. Of course, she's been fine these last few years. But she misses him. And lately – oh, I don't know –' She shook her head, arched her back, as if trying to stretch herself, shake herself out in the confined space. 'I think lately, the last couple of months, she's – changed. Well, we know she has. She's wanted to go. I think she knew it was time.'

'Time?' said Laura, not believing her. 'How can she have known it was time? How can she have given herself a heart attack, Aunt Annabel? It's not possible.'

'It is, if you just give up,' said Annabel. 'And darling – I think it's time you called me Annabel, you know. You're not fourteen any more.'

Not knowing what to say to the twin points of this last sentence, Laura lapsed into silence, counting the miles again, willing the journey away. And then she remembered saying goodbye to Mary, was it only yesterday, in the hallway of her flat, and she knew that her grandmother had known it was the last time, and the blood in her veins froze.

It was around four in the morning when they reached the hospital. Neither of them said anything, but they jumped out of the car, walking, almost running with haste, trying to find their family, looking for the signs amongst the Seventies glass-and-concrete building. The wards were deserted. Laura and Annabel raced in step, following the directions they'd been given. As they approached the ward Laura saw a sad, defeated-looking man, sitting on his own on a bench, just staring into space, and she felt totally alien to him. What was she doing here? And then she remembered. Of course, she thought inconsequentially, of course, he's no different from me. We're the same. None of us wants to be here. He's not here as much as we aren't, not really.

They turned the corner. 'Here,' said Annabel, clutching

Laura's arm in a vice-like grip. 'It's this one. They said, down this one. At the end.'

There was Angela, walking down the corridor towards them. Laura could see her, was nearly there, she could see her mother's face, the tears running down it, she was holding something in her hand, and she was shaking her head, shaking her head and crying out loud.

'Laura, oh Laura,' she said, as Laura reached her and enfolded her in her arms, surprised to find that her mother was smaller than her, shocked at how vulnerable she felt.

'Is she –' Laura said, not able to finish the question.

'Yes,' said Angela, sobbing into her shoulder. 'She's down there. Just a while ago. Too late, you're too late.'

She buried her head even deeper into her daughter's neck, and made a sound almost like a howl, whilst Laura stroked her hair, not knowing what to do. Suddenly, holding her mother tight, Laura felt closer to her than she ever had done, and she couldn't explain why at that moment, except it was as powerful a feeling as anything she'd ever known. There was a brief moment's calm, and Laura breathed out, not knowing what to say, as her mother blinked into Laura's jacket and stepped back. She wasn't looking at Laura, though. She was looking past her. At Annabel, standing behind them.

'You knew, didn't you?' Angela said.

'What?' said Annabel.

'You knew she was ready to go.'

'Yes,' said Annabel briefly. 'Angela. I'm so sorry, darling.'

Laura had never heard them talk to each other like this. Like they were sisters, rather than polite acquaintances in the same book group, which was how they usually addressed each other. She looked down the corridor, all the way down. She could just see some figures standing there; they were men. Simon was one, she was sure. Dad and Uncle Robert. They were facing them, watching. She couldn't see their expressions. Annabel stood there, turning her car keys over and over in her hand. Again, Laura didn't recognise her. She looked like a little girl. She reached out and patted her stepsister's hand, awkwardly.

The figures were advancing towards them, Laura could see. Simon was first, his hair standing on end, his face hollow. As he approached, he opened his eyes wide, as if he didn't know what to do. He hugged Laura, and George, behind him, threw his arms around them both.

'Hello love,' he said, and kissed his daughter's ear. 'Glad you're here. Glad you're here.' He went up to his wife and put his arm around her, as Laura turned to Simon.

'When?' she asked him.

'About an hour ago.' Simon spoke quietly. He pressed his thumb and forefinger to the bridge of his nose and breathed in, a hissing sound. 'Yeah. It was another heart attack, Laura. After it happened she wouldn't have felt anything. She just – slipped away.'

'Did you see her? Did you – talk to her?'

'No,' said Simon, and his lip curled in on itself, like he was trying not to cry. 'We didn't. When Cedric found her, she was . . . pretty much gone anyway.' He wiped his face on his sleeve, and pulled Laura towards him.

'Let's go home,' said Laura. She touched Robert's arm briefly; he was on the outskirts, mutely watching the scene before him. 'Robert, I think you should take Annabel home,' she said. 'She's been driving for hours, she must be exhausted.'

Annabel, who had been looking quietly at Angela, turned at this. 'Fine,' she said blankly. 'Fine. Where's Fran?'

'On the phone to Lulu, outside. Come on,' said Simon, taking his cue. 'Mum – Dad? We're going home.'

'We can't just – leave her,' Angela said.

'Yes we can,' said Simon. 'The doctor said so herself. You can come back tomorrow to arrange everything then. Cedric and Jasper are still here, they're going to stay.'

He looked at Laura. 'Do you want to see her?'

'Yes,' said Laura quietly. 'Just a minute, Mum. Annabel – you coming too?'

She walked to the end of the corridor. Jasper and Cedric were sitting there, even more incongruous in this setting than any of the rest of them. They stood up, rather creakily, as Laura and Annabel approached.

'Dear girl,' Cedric whispered. He kissed her. 'She's just in there. Wouldn't have felt a thing. Smile on her face when I found her, you know.'

Laura only half-heard him. She was opening the door to the tiny room, not at all afraid of what she might see. She knew it was her grandmother, she knew she had been ready to go, and Laura knew she had to see her again, that death was not frightening when it looked like this. Mary was lying under the sheets, one ringed hand resting on her chest. Her eyes, so full of life, were closed. Without its usual animation, her face was solemn in repose. She was not there any more.

Laura kissed her forehead. Mary's skin was cool and smooth, sweet-smelling as always, that old-fashioned powder she used, and Laura turned away, feeling as if her heart was breaking. A tear dropped onto the sheet, onto Mary's hand. This was the last time she would see her. But she was not there any more, she had to keep remembering that.

Her parents were waiting for her in the doorway. George put his arm around his daughter. 'Let's go home, love,' he said. 'Time for bed.'

CHAPTER FIFTY-TWO

'Of course I'm coming tomorrow,' said Paddy.

'But Paddy – it's a Thursday. How will you get the time off?'

'I've cleared it with my head of department,' Paddy explained, standing up rather straight. 'I explained it to them. Said I had to go to a funeral. They're going to have my classes covered. It's only the afternoon, isn't it? No problem.'

They were in their kitchen. It was Wednesday, the day before Mary's funeral. Laura had just got off the phone to her mum, and was drying plates in a rather desultory way, staring out of the window. Paddy put his arm round her and squeezed her. 'Want to be there, to make sure you and Simon are OK,' he said rather stiffly.

Laura buried her head in his armpit gratefully, trying not to let him see how very touched she was. She and Paddy didn't do excessive displays of emotion. 'Right,' she said. 'Oh Pads. Thanks a lot.'

'Not at all,' said Paddy. 'Jo's coming too, she's got the afternoon off as well. She's coming here, she'll drive us.'

'Wow,' said Laura. 'I didn't know that.'

You know times are serious when your friends are making arrangements about you without telling you about it, Laura thought. She put down the tea towel and turned around.

'Thanks,' she said, taking the glass Paddy proffered.

'How's your mum?' Paddy asked.

'She's fine,' said Laura.

'Really?'

'Yes,' Laura replied. 'You know, she really is. We all are.'

That evening, Laura went to her parents' for supper. When she arrived, her mother was on the phone to Annabel in the hallway. She raised her eyes at Laura and blew her a kiss.

'How're you?' Laura said to her brother, as they were making drinks in the kitchen.

'I'm OK.' Simon was slicing a lemon, he didn't look up. 'How about you?'

'I'm OK.' Laura flicked through the Stately Homes calendar on the kitchen counter, and looked round the kitchen, cosy and warm in the chill October evening.

'Wish tomorrow was over,' said Simon. 'I hate funerals.'

'No, really?' said Laura. 'Actually, though, you know, I'm almost looking forward to it.'

'Really?' Simon handed her a drink. 'Why?'

'You know, it's Gran.'

'True,' said Simon. 'Still . . .' He looked sadly at the photo of Mary sitting in her deckchair at Seavale. 'Wish she was here instead.'

Laura shook her head, her eyes filling with tears, because of course that was what she wished too, more than anything else, but she felt this very strong feeling of calm about her grandmother, and kept remembering what Annabel had said.

'Burr,' she said, sniffing. 'Stupid.'

Simon hugged her. 'Ah, sis. Don't cry.'

'M'not.' Laura wiped her eyes. 'How are you, tell me. How's Jorgia?'

Simon said casually, 'I've got a job, you know.'

'What?' said Laura, peering down the corridor to where Mum was nodding silently, still on the phone to Annabel. 'What can they still be talking about? What? You've got a *job*? Doing what?'

Simon shrugged. 'Working in a garden centre.'

'What?' said Laura, not quite able to process the information her brother was giving her. She stared. 'A garden centre? Why?'

'I love gardening,' said Simon. 'I want to be a gardener.'

'No you don't,' said Laura, bewildered. 'Who are you? What are you talking about? What about Jorgia, about going back to Peru?'

'I do want to be a gardener,' said Simon, slightly stubbornly. 'I love gardening, you know I do.'

It was true, Simon did love gardening, always had done.

'Where?' said Laura, trying to get a foothold on it all.

'Out towards Windsor, quite near here actually. It's that house. Myddleton Manor. You remember, Mum and Dad used to take us when we were little. It's got the boating lake, and the ponies. Just off the M4.'

'Oh my god, yes!' said Laura.

Simon said, 'You should come up one day. Gran was going to come, next week,' he said, remembering suddenly. 'You should come instead. There's a café!'

'Well, I do love a café,' said Laura.

'And a stately home,' said Simon. 'You love those too, always have done. Can I eat those crisps, do you think?'

'Hm,' said Laura.

'So – what happened then?' Simon shovelled the crisps into his mouth. 'You went back up to that bloke's house, didn't you?'

Laura shook her head. 'Yes. Well. No. Yes, I did, I – actually? Let's forget it.'

'No, tell me,' said Simon. 'What's going on? You like him, I mean you really like him. I can tell.' He ate some more crisps, but looked at her sideways.

'You know what?' said Laura frankly. 'I actually have no idea what's going on. But I think he needs to sort himself out a bit. And so do I.'

511

'Right.'

'And till then, let's forget it. Come on, tell me what's going on with you and Jorgia. How is she?'

Simon said, 'Me and Jorgia. It's over.'

'What?' said Laura, looking at him in distress. His face was impassive. 'Why? Oh, I'm sorry.'

Simon said, 'We were too different, Laura. She – well. It's not going to happen. We had a big argument last week. And we talked yesterday – we both kind of agreed. You know? So. Yeah.' He shrugged, a completely boyish gesture. It said, I'm not fussed. It meant, I'm really upset, but I'm a man, so no chance I'm going to talk about it.

'Oh Simon.' Laura looked at her brother.

Simon gazed up at her. 'It's weird,' he said. 'I really thought we'd make it work, you know?'

'I know,' said Laura. 'I'm so sorry.'

Simon coughed. 'I'm OK, honestly. Well, kind of. It's weird, though. I was talking to Jo the other day, and we were saying how different our lives are, all of that. And I looked at her and thought, yes, but I still know you. I *know* you. Who you are and all of that. What kind of person you are. I don't really know that with Jorgia. I loved her. She's beautiful. I loved her family, their lifestyle. But I didn't really know her.'

'But you would have done, with time,' said Laura, feeling panicked all of a sudden. 'It's not important, that stuff. You'd have worked it all out. Don't you think?'

'No,' said Simon impatiently. 'You don't understand. I don't mean all of that. Of course I would have done, I'd have got to know her better. I just mean, I *know* Jo. I know who she is, really well. And that's not because she's been our friend for years and years. I mean that, it's comfortable, she's from our group, she does the same things we do, she thinks the same way. Jorgia and me –' He made a helpless gesture with his hands. 'I don't really know her. Does that make sense?'

512

Laura looked at him. After a minute she said, 'It makes a lot of sense. A lot of sense. But . . .'

'I know I was harsh to you, that night at supper,' Simon said. He handed her the crisps. 'I'm really sorry. I've felt really bad about it –'

'Simon, don't, seriously,' said Laura. 'I'm the one who should feel bad about it. I was too judgemental, too hard on you. I just – I thought I knew it all. I was wrong, I'm sorry.'

'Maybe you were a bit,' said Simon. 'But actually – the point you were making – you were right, you know.'

'What do you mean?'

Simon shifted in his seat so he was facing her. 'You jumped down my throat but you were right. We're too different, Jorgia and I, and there was no way to overcome those differences. Two different worlds.'

She said, 'But you said, Simon, you said that people don't fall in love with each other because it's convenient. They fall in love because they fall in love, and that's it.'

'Well, yeah. I suppose that's still right. You don't choose who you fall in love with. But that doesn't mean it can work out. That doesn't mean it can last. Seriously, Laura. You and the marquess, I mean. You knew what you were talking about. It'd never work, you're from two completely different worlds, and, like you said –' He shook his head.

'But Simon –' Laura put her hand out and patted his arm. 'Si, I think I've been completely wrong about it. I think you can make it work. Differences don't matter. Honestly.'

Simon just wasn't really listening. He said glumly, 'It's like me and Jorgia, man. I've been so convinced that it was going to work. I really thought she was the one. I still think she is.' Simon rubbed his chest, like he was in pain. 'I think I wanted it to self-destruct, so – hey! Why are you laughing?'

Laura caught his hand. 'Oh, I don't know,' she said, leaning forward and helping herself to the crisps too. 'We're as bad as each other, you know. Terrible.'

Angela came into the kitchen, then. 'Sorry about that, darlings,' she said, rubbing her hands. 'Your aunt's convinced herself she's organising a state funeral. She keeps telling me about all these wonderfully glamorous people who've rung and said they're going to be there.' She picked up a lid from a pan on the stove. 'I've no idea who any of them are, but they sound terrifying.' George appeared from the conservatory, holding a hammer. 'Put that away, dear. Right. Let's have supper.'

All four Fosters ate quietly together, with no one saying much, but nothing really needing to be said, and after Simon and George had cleared away and gone off to do some man-style thing in the conservatory, Angela and Laura were left sitting next to each other on the sofa.

Angela said, 'Do you mind if Simon stays in Mum's flat for a while? Just a while?'

'Course not,' said Laura. 'What a great idea.'

'Well,' said Angela. 'It needs someone there whilst we decide what to do with it. I was there today, and there's such a lot of stuff. What will we do with it all?'

'I don't know,' said Laura, tentatively patting her mother's hand. She looked at her. Her eyes were bright with unshed tears, but she was composed.

'No, I don't either,' said Angela. She took the neat little cloth that had been part of the tea-tray, now back in the kitchen. It was embroidered, a pretty floral thing. She smoothed it out on her lap, and looked at her daughter.

'I don't know what she'd want me to do with it, either,' she said. 'Whatever I do, I'm sure I'll get it wrong, you know. Ha.' She smiled. 'Which reminds me.' She reached into her handbag, which was by her feet. 'I found these. In her bureau drawer.'

She handed Laura a letter, in Mary's writing, addressed to her. It was clunky, heavy.

'What is it?' said Laura.

'No idea,' said Angela. 'I got one too, so did Simon.'

'But,' said Laura, slightly alarmed. 'What does it mean?'

'I think it means she knew she wanted to write to you,' said Angela.

Laura clutched the letter in her hand; she wanted to open it, and at the same time she didn't want to know.

'Don't you wish you could have one conversation with her about it instead?' she asked. 'With Granny, here?'

'Of course,' said Angela firmly, folding the cloth neatly into quarters. She pressed it down with her hand. 'But it's funny. It makes me realise, all these years –'

She trailed off and stared into space.

'What, Mum?' said Laura gently.

'Well, it makes me see. I was in the flat today, looking around, thinking is there anything we need to take now, and your aunt was being so dreadfully bossy and instead of being cross and saying nothing, it made me feel –' she looked up to the ceiling '– so happy. And it's funny. I look back, down the years. And I realise how happy I've been. How lucky we all are. What a lucky family we are, to have each other. To have this house. Oh, I know, it's not an interesting life, it's not full of glamour and drama, but it's the life I wanted. I've never wanted anything more, you see.'

George was coming through from the kitchen. There was a scuffle as the tray of drinks hit something. 'Oh, dear,' they heard him say, and there was a bit of muttering. Laura looked back at her mother.

'Honestly, darling. Never wanted more than your father. It's strange, isn't it? I thought I'd miss the life I had, the travelling, the rather posh girls and boys I met, the excitement of it. I never did, not once. Since the day I married him, and we settled down – I honestly don't think I would have changed a thing.'

A tear dropped from her cheek onto the folded cloth; Angela brushed her eyes.

'I've been happy. I never really thought about it like that, before Mum died. I've been happy.'

The door opened. George came in, holding a whisky bottle and four glasses.

'I thought a little toast was in order, ahead of tomorrow's events,' he said.

'Oh, George,' said Angela, putting her head on one side.

Simon followed his father in. He took the tray from George, and gave one glass each to his mother and sister, and then handed one to his father. George poured them each a tot, then cleared his throat, still standing, and said,

'Well. A toast. Stand please.' Laura and Angela stood. He raised his glass, met his wife's eyes. 'To Mary,' he said. 'In loving memory.'

'To Mary,' they said in unison. Laura looked around the room at her family. Granny would be glad, she thought. Yes.

Simon dropped her home, and Laura climbed the stairs up to the flat, tired and confused, the letter still clutched in her hand. She had to remind herself it was Wednesday, and normal life was carrying on. It was strange to have been at work this week, to speak to people on the phone, to do normal things. She wanted to say, my grandmother died on Saturday. I'm very upset. So's my mum. But actually we're fine. A grandmother dying – it wasn't a big deal. It was sad of course, people were kind to you. Rachel had bought her some tulips, had been lovely, because she knew how close they were. But it wasn't a life-changing thing. Yes, they said, you'll be sad, oh, when's the funeral, right. Oh, that'll be nice. Lovely. It was the kind of grief people are able to talk about, console each other on. Whereas Laura knew it was something different; it was really strange. She felt like a new person, that her life had undergone a seismic shift one way. She knew who she was, whether she was at home with her parents, or back at her own flat, or sitting at work. She knew who she was.

She saw herself for once without pretence, not as a girl from some book, in crinoline, dipping low in a curtsey at a ball, or as an evangelical new person who was going to sort her life out, who brooked no argument, who let no one into her life, who did not suffer weakness or fools. She was just – herself. She looked at the letter, there in her hand, and carefully tore it open. A velvet pouch slid out, and two sheets of paper.

CHAPTER FIFTY-THREE

Darling Laura,

I am writing this letter to you in the full expectation that you may not read it for a few years, although I suspect and hope it may be sooner than that. It is a beautiful September day as I sit here at my bureau. Cedric is upstairs, on his balcony; he is singing something rather jolly, Puccini, I think. He is watering his plants. I can see the very tips of the trees in Hyde Park. It is sunny and dusty. The leaves are rather crispy. Summer is over; everyone is waiting for autumn. I love this time of year. The summer fatigue. I am alone in loving it, I think. But it reminds me of Cairo.

I want to tell you something, Laura. I have always tried to hold back from telling you what to do, because I have always felt you had enough people around you directing you, and perhaps you needed someone with whom you could just talk. But now I think it may be time, time for me to be honest with you. As honest as I can be. I do this because I want you to be happy. More than anything, I want you to be happy, for you have great happiness and love within you, Laura darling.

You will find enclosed the necklace I lent you, which

you have always loved. I would like you to have it, please. It gives me great pleasure to know that after I am gone, you will be the one to wear it. It is valuable; more valuable than you realise, for Guy gave it to me, bought it for me in Cairo, when we first met.

We were both married to other people, you knew that. That was when we met. When we fell in love. You did not know that. My first husband, James Dearden, was the man I married when I was eighteen, and it was because of him that I moved out there. I was so young; I had never left England before. To be in Cairo – oh Laura, the heat, dusty, pervasive heat. When you have lived through endless British winters with no such thing as central heating, no money for fires, the constant heat was like a drug to me. I was so happy. At first.

But James was not a good husband. I tried, Laura, but I was too young, too selfish. He and I – we should never have married. He was not a bad man, but I believe he became one. He could be vicious, boorish, unpleasant, dull – and stupid. I could forgive him most things, but not that. He hated Egypt, the people, the life. He only liked the club. And drinking. I look back and try to remember, and I don't know that we were ever happy. When I had your mother, it got worse. He didn't care, wasn't interested. He wanted a son. Your mother was a beautiful baby, so good, contented. She was perfect, and he didn't care. He couldn't see it, and I hated him for that.

When the war came, people were evacuated, mostly to South Africa. But I stayed there. I was still only twenty-four when I met Guy. He had just arrived in Cairo; I felt as if I had been there for decades, in a living tomb. James and I were barely speaking. There was danger everywhere, nothing was certain. Guy knew no one. He was entirely alone, he was working for the army, a translator, a sort of traveller, someone to smooth relations out with the

Egyptians. He had been everywhere, travelled to so many places already. He made me laugh. I understood him, even though we were very different. He was my age. James was forty, darling, to me he was an old man; he was drinking more and more. He beat me. The first time he beat me, I ran to the club, and Guy was there. We began an affair, I suppose you would call it, but that sounds so tawdry, so implicitly temporary. This – it was true love, I knew it from the start. Do you remember that story I used to tell you, about the trip to the desert, to the pyramids, to see the sun rise? Darling, it was true, I promise, but that was when it all began, when I was still married. But I simply knew, so well that I did not stop to analyse it. He was the love of my life. Still is.

Guy had been married, darling. Lucy, his wife, had died in England, and they had had a little girl. That was Annabel. And after the war was over, she came out to join him. I always remember the first time I saw her, at a party at the club. In the garden it was, shaded and green. One of the few green places there. I remember how I smiled, and said hello to her. She was a pretty little thing. I watched Guy with her, this funny little toddler clutching his leg, and I hated myself with all my heart and soul, every part of me, because I was glad his wife was dead, glad I had never known her, and I wished my husband was dead, wished we could be together. Yes, I did. I remember going to the English church and taking communion the next day. I remember how I felt, how much pleasure it gave me to kneel at the altar with a heart full of black things, full of adultery and jealousy and murderous rage and spite. Daring God to throw anything more at me that he could. Knowing I was untouchable, that nothing could hurt me any more. I remember the feeling; I remember so much of it all.

To not be with the one you love, Laura, the one person

you should be spending your life with. It's like a kind of living death. To wake up every morning and know you are still here. To have that brief, sweet moment of blankness, before your mind reminds you who you are, and why you are unhappy. It was like hell. A living hell of the heart's own making.

You know that James died. He had a heart attack, brought on by years of drinking, years of unhappiness. Almost six months later. I could barely believe it. And I hated myself for it, too. Guy and I were married a year later, everyone said how lucky we were to have found each other, and no one ever knew, no one knew I had lied, that I had prayed for this to happen. Not even Guy. We had forty-five years together, Laura. We brought the girls up together, we travelled the world. We were never apart. And no one could have been happier than us, except for one small thing: we lied. And oh, it doesn't matter! It doesn't matter!

I have always thought Annabel knew there was something between her father and me, before James died. I think she would remember . . . seeing things. Perhaps not, but I have always felt she knew. And I have always felt guilty about Annabel ever since. We both did. She never mentioned it, all those years. She has never seemed to mind. But I do, and I don't know why. Lately I do.

My mind is wandering. It is hot, out here on the balcony. I have the photo of Guy in my locket; I am looking at it now, as I write these words to you, Laura. I am very tired these days. Very tired, and cross. I worry, I feel myself starting to worry. I am old, Laura, and my life has been wonderful. This is what I wanted to say to you: you think of me as so resolute, and so proud, and so confident, always have been. And what terrifies me is that forty-five years ago I nearly made a dreadful mistake. I would have stayed with James, I know, because I was

521

afraid to leave. Afraid to leave a man I didn't love, who beat me, who was a drunk, who didn't want me or our daughter in his life. That is what terrifies me, in the night, that if James hadn't died, I wouldn't have had the courage to seize happiness for myself, for Angela, for Annabel. For Guy and I. I took the coward's way out, and did nothing.

Don't be the same, Laura. When I think about what you might be missing, it terrifies me on your behalf. I think you might have missed the right person, your true love, because you have spent your life looking too hard for him. You have a great capacity to love, Laura. Don't run away from it. Use it. Stop wasting it. Throw yourself into it, and don't be scared. I promise you with all my heart that you will never live a day where you regret it.

Don't be afraid, my darling. I am so proud of you. Remember, I love you. That will never go away.

Granny

A postscript: Did I ever tell you about the summer Guy and I lived in the South of France, in the early Eighties? I know I did. Most interesting. We lived next door to a fascinating couple. Frederick Needham and his wife Vivienne. I think you know who they are. She left her husband – his own brother – and her three children, and the greatest house in the country, to be with him. Oh, you would have thought they were a golden pair, in their lovely house. Flowers everywhere, a riot of bougainvillea; a simply beautiful view of the sea. They could sit there together and look out at it all day, every day.

But they weren't happy. They were miserable. She ran away rather than face her unhappiness, and she was paying for it. Their love wasn't strong enough to withstand it. She missed that lovely boy of hers; we often talked of him. She should never have let him go. Vivienne followed her heart without thinking of the consequences. I think you used to be rather like her, Laura. Not any more. Now I worry that you think too much about the consequences of things. They are not important, as she had discovered. A society scandal – what is that, compared to a mother's love for her son? She lost far more than she gained, simply by caring too much about the proprieties, for listening to the outside world's chatter and clamour. So she never went back to see her children. Never. She decided to be unhappy instead. That was the penance Vivienne has decided to pay.

She was so proud of him. I liked her very much. I think she would like you.

Goodbye, my darling.

CHAPTER FIFTY-FOUR

On Thursday lunchtime, Jo arrived to pick Laura and Paddy up, to take them to the church. They were going to meet the rest of the family there. It was a grey day, the sky a uniform blanket of cloud, and Laura was in her room, hunting for her scarf.

'She's in the car, outside,' Paddy called through the door. 'I'll go down – see you in a minute?'

'Sure,' Laura yelled. 'I won't be long, sorry.'

The scarf usually hung at the end of her shelf. It had fallen on the floor. As she bent down to pick it up, she noticed, hanging on the back of the door, Nick's dinner jacket, the one he had put around her shoulders – was it only six days ago? She had put it on a hanger; she didn't quite know what to do with it. She stroked the fabric softly. Holding the scarf, she stood up and realised Mary's letter had fallen out of the bag on her shoulder. She scooped it up and stared at it, at the sloping, scratchy writing, the black ink on the cream paper. She patted the necklace around her neck. Jo's horn beeped tentatively outside, and Laura realised she had been standing there for a minute or so in front of the bookshelf, looking at this letter in her hand. Something clicked inside her and she pulled out one of her old cloth hardbacks and put the paper inside the pages.

Shutting the book, Laura put her bag over her shoulder and left the room, closing the door behind her. She never read it again.

Angela had said quite firmly that they should meet at the church, which was around the corner from Crecy Court. It was as if they were merely meeting at Mary's flat, she said. She didn't want them turning up in a grave, solemn column. Laura agreed to her request, rather surprised, but she was glad of it, glad to have Jo and Paddy to walk down the aisle with, through the light, airy church crammed full with people. Mary had many friends, and it seemed they had all turned out – of course. Laura scanned the crowds.

'I don't know who half these people are,' she hissed to Jo, as they made their way down the aisle.

'Well, they obviously wanted to come, didn't they?' Jo patted her arm. 'They loved her. I think that's really nice.'

Jo and Paddy escorted her to her seat at the front of the church, and found one themselves, further back. She sat down, next to Simon, and leant over to kiss her parents. George patted her knee. Across the aisle sat the Sandersons. Annabel was rigid, dressed entirely in black, wearing a small black hat with –

'Is that a *veil* Annabel's wearing?' Laura whispered to Simon.

'Yes,' said Simon. 'She's got gloves on, too – look.'

Sure enough, Annabel was decked out in white kid-leather gloves, completing the impression that she was, in fact, a school mistress from the Thirties. Or, Laura thought to herself with a smile, a living, breathing version of Mrs Danvers. She sat there, expressionless, and then, as if aware of Laura's eyes on her, turned slowly and gave her niece a smile of great sweetness. Laura looked at her, and thought how like her own mother she was, and an idea took root in her head, a small idea, but one which, when she thought about it, made perfect sense. And then they stood up, because the coffin was arriving.

*   *   *

The service was short, only two hymns and one reading. Jasper gave the address. He said, looking down at Mary's extended family, that she had been all things to all people, and so he didn't have much to say, because they should not be sad, they should be happy. 'That is why we do this today – to celebrate someone's life. In Mary's case, it truly is a celebration. We will not be sad –' he said, rather theatrically wiping a tear away from his cheek. 'Rather, we will celebrate, and imagine her welcoming us at her flat, or at Seavale, or, before that, for those many of you who knew her when Guy was alive. The way she would say hello, with that sparkling look in her eyes that we all knew so well. The way you knew when she was enjoying herself or, alas, when she was terribly bored by what you were saying.' The congregation laughed. 'I shall miss her,' he said simply. 'That's why I'm sad. But I think she's happy, now she's with Guy.'

Cedric, magnificently attired in a purple floral cravat, did the reading. Laura was amused to note, even through her distress, that his appearance caused a frisson of excitement in the church. This was exactly his crowd, she thought. If, at my funeral in fifty years' time, Jude Law got up and gave a reading, there'd be the same reaction. Half the congregation going, 'Oh my goodness! Is that Cedric Forsythe? My lord! My dear, isn't he handsome?' and the other half going, 'Who's that bloke?'

He read John Donne's *Valediction: Forbidding Mourning*, and he wasn't theatrical – for once. He was quiet and dignified, and as his voice rang through the church, the thick cloud outside seemed to lighten, just a little, and it was bright inside, and as Laura looked up and down at her family, all of them, she thought about things that had gone before, things that were happening now, and about her grandmother's letter, how life was for the taking.

It was not sad; she knew it wasn't, and yet she kept crying throughout. But it didn't matter. She knew she was crying for the right reasons. Looking at her mother, and her brother, she knew they were thinking the same. She wished she could see Mary one more time, just once, to tell her all the things she wanted to, to ask her so many more things. But she couldn't. Mary had known it was her time to go. She wanted to be with Guy, not with them, and now she was.

As they filed out of the church, towards the cold, white London light, Annabel took her niece's arm.

'How are you, Laura dear?' she said.

'I'm OK,' Laura replied. 'How are you, Annabel? That was a beautiful service, thank you.'

'Well, I think we did her proud,' said Annabel. 'I know your mother was worried it'd be like a Russian Orthodox Easter service – about five hours long. But, in the end, I thought about what your grandmother would have wanted. I think she would have wanted that.'

'You're right,' said Laura, smiling at her.

'Very hard woman to really know that well,' said Annabel. 'And I knew her almost as long as your mother.' She frowned, and they stopped at the porch of the church as the coffin was loaded into the hearse. Angela and George were the only ones going on to the crematorium; the rest of the party were gathering back at Crecy Court for refreshments. Angela stepped back a little and stood next to her stepsister, and Laura saw them look at each other and smile, so very alike.

'Everyone can walk to Mum's flat whilst we're at the crematorium, that's OK, isn't it, Annabel?' said Angela, appealing to her to organise things.

Annabel seized the mantle of team leader. 'Cedric and Jasper will lead you all to Mary's flat, where there are refreshments,' she boomed in a loud voice. Laura turned around, only to find Fran and Lulu cringing behind her. She smiled at them, recognising their embarrassment.

'Walk with us,' said Fran solemnly.

527

'Yes, of course,' said Laura. 'I wanted to ask you, anyway –'

She was just casting about in her mind for something else to ask Lulu and Fran, something easy and conversational, when Cedric appeared beside her. 'Hello, old girl,' he said, squeezing her waist. He shot Lulu and Fran a blank look; they shrank back, darted out of the way, and hurried on.

The other mourners followed them, led by Jasper and Annabel, and Laura took one last look inside the church as the doors were closing.

'Walk you back to your grandmother's, eh?' said Cedric, and they set off, Laura's arm through his, bringing up the rear.

'You read beautifully, Cedric,' Laura said. She leant against him.

'What? Oh, thank you. Thank you,' said Cedric, batting his eyelashes. 'Well, you know. I loved her, your grandmother.'

'I know,' said Laura.

'Asked her to marry me about four times,' said Cedric conversationally. He looked up at the sky, around at the narrow townhouses lining the road down to Baker Street.

'Really?' Laura wasn't that surprised, she knew Cedric worshipped Mary.

'Yes, but she always turned me down flat. Said she would never marry anyone after Guy, and I should go away and find someone else. Quite rude sometimes, actually.' He ruffled his own hair. 'Women.'

'I can imagine,' Laura smiled. 'She was quite . . . scary sometimes, wasn't she?'

'Oho yes,' said Cedric. 'Very much so. Did I ever tell you about the time . . .'

Jasper appeared. 'Come on, old boy. You've got the keys. Stop messing around and hurry up.'

'Well,' said Cedric crossly. 'I . . . Excuse me, Laura,' and he strode off, leaving Laura smiling after him, watching the procession disappear down the road.

'Excuse me?' came a tentative voice behind them.

She turned round. There, on the pavement, was a woman in a headscarf, an ancient Burberry tightly belted around her tiny waist, holding a long, black umbrella in her tiny gloved hands. She looked about seventy, possibly younger. She looked at Laura expectantly, her huge dark eyes full of concern.

'Have I missed Mary Fielding's funeral?' she asked. 'I only flew in this morning, and then my train was late, I –'

Laura gazed at her, and then at the others disappearing down the road. Suddenly she recognised her, and she knew who she was talking to.

'I'm afraid so,' she said. 'I'm so sorry.'

'Oh dear,' said the woman. She caught Laura's hand impulsively. 'I did want to say goodbye. She was so wonderful, you know, so wonderful. I haven't seen her for – golly, it must be twenty years.'

Laura couldn't stop looking at her, fascinated, and not just by her extreme beauty.

'You're – Vivienne Lash, aren't you?' she said.

'Yes, yes,' said the woman, a lovely smile breaking out over her face. 'How did you know that? Most of the people who recognise me these days are extremely decrepit.'

'I just do,' said Laura, smiling at her.

Vivienne Lash glanced at her, then up and down the road. 'Oh, I'm so cross with myself for being late. I wanted to say goodbye to her.' Her eyes were sparkling with tears, but she blinked rapidly, looked around. 'Goodness,' she said, her eyes flitting ahead of her. 'Isn't that Cedric Forsythe, ahead of us?'

Cedric had stopped to marshal his flock across a zebra crossing, his walking stick waving in the air. Laura said, 'Yes, it is.'

'What a small world, how funny. He was so kind to me. I should go and –' She dug her hands into her pockets, a curiously familiar gesture, and then shook her head. 'No,' she said, after a minute. 'I'll let you all get on, darling.' She looked at her curiously. 'Were you her granddaughter? Are you . . . Laura?'

'Yes,' said Laura, amazed.

'She used to talk about you all so fondly. Ah, and here you are.'

'Come and have a drink with us,' said Laura. 'Come and say hello to my parents, and . . . the others. I'm sure they'd love to meet you.'

'No, no,' said Vivienne Lash, still smiling, but backing away. 'I won't intrude. I wanted to come to the funeral, that was all. No fuss. Now I must get going, darling. Oh, it's so nice to have met you at last.' She kissed her on the cheek and darted away, ballerina-like.

'Can I get you a cab?' Laura called. 'Are you sure you don't want to come back?'

'No, darling.' Vivienne Lash stopped still in the middle of the road, and turned around. 'I'll go straight to the station, thank you. Thank you!' She waved her hand.

'Where are you going?' said Laura.

'I'm going to Norfolk,' said Vivienne Lash. A huge smile curled around her face, and she caught her hands together. 'I'm going to see Nick, my son.'

Laura nodded numbly, and Vivienne Lash said in a low voice, 'Yes. My son.'

Her voice broke, and one little hand flew to her mouth. She cleared her throat, breathing in rapidly through her nostrils.

'I'm sorry,' she said, looking back up at Laura, with an expression so like Nick's, yet which was so poignantly maternal, that Laura was overwhelmed by the force of it. 'It's rather important to me,' she said simply. 'I haven't seen him for – for a long time.'

'Yes,' said Laura.

'I've been very stupid. For far too long.' She tightened the belt around her waist. 'Far too long. Waste of time. All that time.'

Laura watched her shyly, not sure what to say.

'So, then,' said Vivienne Lash. 'I really must go.'

She took Laura's hand in hers again for a second, tripped nimbly down the street, and turned a corner. Laura stood still and watched her, and then suddenly she called out, 'Mrs Needham?'

Vivienne Lash turned around. 'Yes, darling?' she said.

A car drove past; she was on the other side of the street. Laura crossed hurriedly, fearing she might have vanished by the time she reached her.

'Can you do me a favour?' she said.

'Of course,' said Vivienne Lash. 'What is it?'

'It's a long story,' said Laura. 'But I know your son.' She put her hand on some railings; she felt suddenly light-headed, the shock of the day's various events catching up with her.

'Do you?' Vivienne's face lit up. 'How wonderful. Nick? How do you know him?'

Laura said, smiling, 'It really is a very long story. Can you just tell him something from me? Can you tell him – tell him –'

She paused, not knowing what to say, and Vivienne Lash watched her expectantly.

'Tell him', Laura said eventually, 'that you saw Laura. And that she still has his dinner jacket, and she thinks he ought to come to her flat and collect it, since he wears it such an awful lot.'

Vivienne Lash mouthed the words to herself. She nodded, and looked at Laura thoughtfully.

'Mary's granddaughter,' she said quietly. 'Well, well.'

'Is that all right?' Laura asked.

'Of course, darling. I'm an actress, I can remember any lines, you know.' She kissed Laura again. 'I am very glad to have met you, my dear. I'll see you soon, I think. Now,' she threw her umbrella lightly from one hand to the next, 'I must go,' and she flew down the street, one hand on her hair, looking about fourteen.

Laura leant against the railings, lost in a world of her own.

After a few moments she realised Cedric was calling her name, and she ran towards him, towards the others, turning to see if Vivienne was still there, but she had vanished like a puff of smoke.

CHAPTER FIFTY-FIVE

Autumn had come and gone in a flash, and now winter was here. It whistled through the bare branches outside Laura's window, clacking on the glass in the night and causing her to wake up with a start. It crept in under the gap in the front door, through the sash windows of their sitting room. It glittered and sparkled on the frost on the cars in the morning. It coughed and wheezed on the tube, randomly spreading seasonal malaise. Suddenly it was dark, all the time. Through the streets, on her way to the tube station each morning, Laura stomped her feet in her boots, hugging herself and shivering in the bitter cold. Paddy had bought a ridiculous, loudly patterned tweed coat, which he said made him look like Sherlock Holmes, but which Laura felt privately made him look like Compo from *Last of the Summer Wine*. They would walk together, swooshing the leaves out of the way, chatting about the day ahead of them.

One day, when winter had fully set in, Paddy and Laura were walking down the road together, and Laura was trying to look interested whilst Paddy agonised about what he should buy Becky for a Christmas present.

It was nearly December, a month after Mary's funeral. Laura's parents were, astonishingly, on a really rather adventurous holiday. George had booked a trip to the Galapagos Islands for them both, asserting his role of head of the family so boldly that Laura and Simon had spontaneously broken into a round of applause when their parents announced it to them. Annabel, of course, was a little sniffy, calling it a ridiculous waste of money. It was a sign that perhaps things were starting to settle down that Annabel felt able to start being a disagreeable old cow again – as Simon had put it to his sister afterwards.

Simon was living in Mary's flat for the time being; sorting out things, but keeping the place occupied. He was going to see Jorgia in the New Year. Laura didn't know what would come of it, but she was glad he wasn't giving up just yet. His job at the upmarket garden centre was going really well; he obviously had a flair for it. Laura suspected he rather liked being the young man in amongst a lot of rather older men (with trim moustaches and creased slacks) and women (wearing those sweatshirts that said things like LONDON * PARIS * WINDSOR!). She also worried that he was turning into an old man, since he seemed to spend most of his evenings with Cedric and Jasper at Crecy Court, smoking panatellas and drinking whisky, listening to Jasper's tales of love and betrayal amongst the artistic community in post-Second World War Cornwall and Cedric's increasingly fantastical ramblings amongst the film sets, theatres, dressing rooms and premieres of the British film industry during its Fifties peak.

In her own way, Laura missed her grandmother much more than she had realised. She knew why, she knew it would pass, but as the weeks went by and she carried on in her own life, she realised she had so many questions she'd never asked Mary that she wished she had. About her life, about how much she had loved Guy, about all of that. She felt as if a light had gone out of her life, someone who understood her had gone, and she felt that she had never really tried to talk to her own grandmother, otherwise she would have found all this out. Now it was too late.

A month had passed since Mary's funeral, and she had heard

nothing from Nick. What had happened when his mother arrived? How had they been together? Was it awful for him, or wonderful? Was he glad? She wanted to know if he'd got her message, but she realised that was a slender thread to hang a relationship on. The two of them were better off apart, perhaps, and as her life settled back to normal it grew easier to persuade herself of that.

Laura hugged herself as she walked next to Paddy, and, realising her thoughts had drifted, as they did more than she would like these days, she nodded intelligently and tried to pretend she had been listening all along.

'Anyway. So, Becky says she doesn't want an expensive handbag, but does that mean that's actually what she *does* want?'

'I don't know,' said Laura, trying to concentrate again. 'I think, knowing Becky, that means she doesn't want one.'

'Do you think?'

'Absolutely. She's a sensible girl, you know. She's not like . . . like –' she was going to say Amy, but realised that might not be apposite.

'Were you going to say Amy?' said Paddy, smiling at her.

'Well, yes,' Laura replied. 'God.'

'They're getting married, you know,' Paddy said suddenly.

'Seriously?' Laura asked. 'When?'

'After the baby's born. Chris told me. I didn't know if you'd want to know or not.'

'Oh Pads,' said Laura. She patted his Sherlock Holmes-like sleeve. 'Bless you. I think that's great. Good for them.'

'Well, I hope so,' said Paddy. 'You OK?'

'Honestly, I am,' said Laura. 'I can't believe it was a year ago, you know. Almost exactly a year since that all started up. Gosh, I was stupid.'

'He was stupid too,' Paddy said loyally, but as Laura made to protest he said, 'Yes, but you were pretty dim about it all.'

'Hah,' said Laura. 'Oh well.'

There was a pause; they both kept on walking.

'Laura,' said Paddy after a while. 'I've been – wanting to ask you something.'

'What?' said Laura.

'Well . . .' Paddy appeared to be in the early stage of a nervous tic. His face was twitching, solemnly. They stood by the kerb. 'Look. The thing is . . . I want to ask Becky to move in with me.'

'Oh,' said Laura, and nearly walked out in front of a car.

Paddy pushed her out of the way. 'I'm sorry to spring it on you like this. I haven't asked her yet, you know. Wanted to see what you thought.'

'Hm,' said Laura, nodding.

'I know it's a bit soon,' said Paddy. 'It's only five months. But, you know something? I know it's right.'

Laura nodded again. Paddy stood up straight.

'I keep thinking, all these years I've been mooning around after girls, hoping to get them to notice me, and Becky's been downstairs for the past two years, right under my nose, and I almost didn't do anything about it. And that's ridiculous. I'm sorry, it's awful to be kicking your best friend out into the street, but – can you see what I mean?'

'It's a bit of a shocker,' she said eventually. 'But that's great! Just great.' She hugged Paddy. 'I'm really pleased for you, man.'

'It's not going to be for a couple of months,' Paddy said. 'She could say no, too – so don't pack your bags just yet . . .'

'I won't,' said Laura. 'But I'm pretty sure she's not going to say no, Pads.'

He kissed her on the cheek. 'You're the best, Laura. Thank you. I'm sorry, this is a bit of a crap time to spring this on you, but . . .' His face brightened suddenly. 'Hey! Simon's going to Peru in February, isn't he?' Laura nodded. 'Couldn't you stay in your grandmother's flat for a bit?'

'I could,' said Laura. They crossed the road. 'But you know,

I think it's time I moved on somewhere else. Grew up a bit. Bought a place of my own, maybe.'

'Well,' said Paddy.

'Or I could just move into Becky's flat,' said Laura, half-joking, but Paddy thought it was a great idea, the simplest solution to the question, and Laura spent the rest of the walk to the station persuading him that if she needed a change, moving downstairs wasn't necessarily it.

When they got to the tube station, they went their separate ways. 'Thanks, Loz, again,' said Paddy, patting her arm. 'Just for being pleased for me, even if you're not.'

'I am pleased for you,' Laura said honestly. 'I really am.' She took her book out of her bag. 'Right. You'd better go, isn't that your train?'

'What's this?' said Paddy, holding up her copy of *Regency Buck*. 'Back on the Georgette Heyers again, Laura? Oh no . . .' His face paled, and Laura snatched the book back.

'I know what I'm doing this time,' she said, nodding wisely. 'Seriously! Everything in moderation.'

Paddy nodded, unconvinced.

'I'm reading *Trainspotting* next, for a bit of balance,' said Laura, pushing him away. 'Now go! You'll be late!'

She watched him run down the tunnel, and smiled as she walked to her own platform, shivering in the cold. She thought of Dan and Amy, engaged; Dan, on this platform, waiting for her, and it could have been another person. It was, really. She was older. Not necessarily wiser, not necessarily fundamentally different. But . . . she'd changed, she knew that. Whether for the better or not, she wasn't sure. She wasn't necessarily happier than she had been, she thought, as she sat down on the bench she and Dan used to share. Then she thought about it again. Yes, she *was* happier, she realised. Happy by herself, happy not to depend on the heady rush of a new crush to buoy her up. She laughed a little to herself – how boring that sounded for a girl who'd loved and lost one of the most eligible men in the country – and picked up *Regency Buck*. Sometimes fantasy was better than reality. As long as you didn't let it take over. In moderation, as she'd assured Paddy. Obviously.

It was a Friday. All through the day, as Laura fielded calls and tapped away at her desk, she kept thinking about Paddy, about leaving the flat. It made her feel sad, but at the same time she knew it was a chance to move on, for both of them. To think, a year ago, that twelve months on Paddy would be about to ask a girl to move in with him – and she might say yes. Laura couldn't wait to discuss it with Jo. It was wonderful – but weird, at the same time.

Laura left work on the dot of five thirty. She poked her head into Rachel's office on the way out.

'I'm off,' she said, waving. 'Have a lovely weekend. I emailed you next year's term dates.'

Rachel looked up from her desk, where she was applying some lipstick. 'Are you going already?' she asked, astonished.

Laura came further into the office. 'Yes –' she began. 'I'm sorry – I hope that's OK?'

'Of course it is!' Rachel said, pleased. She smacked her lips together, and smoothed down her dark mulberry-coloured shirt. 'Laura, you haven't left before seven for weeks. This is great!'

'Oh,' said Laura. 'Phew.' She eyed her boss curiously. 'What are you – oh my god. You've got a date, haven't you?'

'Yes . . .' Rachel said, blushing rosily. 'Maybe . . . Not sure.'

'It's with Marcus!' said Laura. 'It is! Oh my god! Is it tonight? Second date?'

Rachel and Marcus had been on a date the week before, finally set up by Laura. Laura had not had particularly high hopes because of her previous experience with him, but she'd been determined to do it just in case. She clapped her hands in excitement. 'Oh my god. Wow! You never said, you just said it went OK and you weren't sure!'

'Well,' said Rachel crossly. 'It was OK. It was really nice, actually. I just didn't want to go around yelling about it. Now shush, stop getting over-excited.'

'No!' yelled Laura again. She collected herself. 'Sorry. Wow. Where are you going?'

'Some corporate thing at the Opera House,' said Rachel uncertainly. 'It's through work, some German bank. We're meeting for a glass of something beforehand.'

Laura's heart sank, recognising the signs. 'Oh,' she said.

'Yes,' said Rachel. She looked solemn. 'I can't believe he's asked me. Lucky me.'

'Lucky you,' echoed Laura, smiling, and she felt her throat constrict with emotion, though she didn't really understand why. 'Well, we – er, we love Marcus. I'm – sorry, by the way,' she said. 'Can you tell him I'm sorry I haven't been in touch? Since he got back? You know, Granny's funeral and everything. I hope he got my letter, saying thank you for the money.'

'I don't know,' said Rachel. 'That's the funny thing. I mentioned the donation last time. Didn't want to go on about it – it's a date after all. You know what he said?'

'No?'

'He said he didn't know anything about it.'

'What?' Laura said 'But . . .'

'Yeah.' Rachel brushed some bronzer onto her cheek. 'I keep meaning to ask someone about it, actually. Haven't done. I mean, the money's there, it's all fine. So I just never thought –'

'That's weird,' said Laura.

'It is weird, isn't it?' Rachel agreed, her face clouding momentarily. 'But I think Clare must have sorted it out off her own bat. Not Marcus. Which means –'

Which means my date with him was actually a total waste of time, thought Laura, smiling to herself. It seemed like a long time ago now. Funny.

'Have a lovely weekend,' Rachel called as she left.

Laura walked out onto the street, into the cold December air, and caught a bus, which she didn't usually, but she wanted

539

to see the Christmas lights across town. Paddy was staying the night with Becky, and she was having Jo and Hilary over for supper.

Marcus Sussman and Rachel. Becky moving in with Paddy. Well, well, well. She sat on the bus as it bumped slowly up Tottenham Court Road, and looked out of the window, drinking in the bustling, energetic, aggravating sea of humanity below her, people on their way home, people on their way out. She was happy just to gaze, and plan through the menu for tonight in her head, happy to let the week's events, the day at work, wash over her.

When she got back to her dark, cold flat, Laura turned all the lights on, unpacked the food, put a CD on, and started cooking. Soon the kitchen was filled with a warm, spicy fug, as Laura absorbed herself in what she was doing, chopped and fried and sautéed and mixed in complete happiness. She was just finishing off, and thinking she should start to set the table, when she dropped a spoon into the casseroled sauce of the lamb shanks by mistake. It splashed everywhere, and Laura cursed, feeling some of it hit her on the face.

'Ouch,' she said, licking her cheek experimentally, and grabbing a tea towel. 'Bollocks,' she added, as she looked at the clock and realised it was seven thirty and they'd be here soon. Jo was always, always bang on time. The doorbell rang. 'Shit!' she said, dabbing her face with the towel and walking towards the speaker phone.

'Hello,' she said, licking her lips as she spoke into the phone.

There was a crackle, then silence, then a low, familiar voice said, 'Laura. It's Nick. Can I come up?'

CHAPTER FIFTY-SIX

'What?' Laura asked, her hand flying to her cheek. 'Who?'

'It's me, Nick. I'm coming up.'

'You –'

'Oh, thanks,' came Nick's voice more indistinctly, and she heard someone in the background say, 'You want come in, boy? Come in.'

'Mr Kenzo,' Laura said loudly into the speaker. She dropped the phone so it hung off the wall, and opened the door. She stood there for what seemed like hours, but of course it was only a few seconds, hearing voices growing louder as they approached, and eventually Mr Kenzo and Nick appeared together on Laura's landing.

'Hello, Laura!' said Mr Kenzo happily. 'Your friend, he was outside, I've let him in! Good evening, sir.'

'Good evening,' said Nick. 'Thank you for the recommendation.'

'What?' said Laura, standing aside to usher him into the flat, as Mr Kenzo unlocked his door.

'I want to go to Marmaris, and your neighbour was kindly explaining when the best time to go is,' said Nick imperturbably.

'You want to go to . . .?' Laura said helplessly. 'Get in.'

'Bye,' said Mr Kenzo loudly as she shut the door. 'Goodbye!'

'Hello,' said Nick, as Laura shut the door and leant against it, staring at him.

'You're in my flat,' said Laura, not knowing what else to say.

'Well-spotted,' said Nick. 'Is this the sitting room?'

'No,' said Laura. 'Oh. I – yes. I mean yes.'

'It's really nice,' said Nick.

'I'm moving out, actually,' said Laura. 'I'm being kicked out.'

'Well, it's not that nice, then,' he said. 'Right. Aren't you going to offer me a drink or anything?'

Laura said nothing, just carried on looking at him there, leaning against the door.

'What are you doing here?' she said, after a while.

'You told me to come and collect my dinner jacket, Laura.'

'That was over a month ago,' said Laura. 'And I didn't tell you. I told your mother to tell you.'

'Well, I had to discuss it with her. Think about it for a while.' His eyes were warm, full of laughter. 'Can I have a drink? Just of water, if you don't have anything else? It's a long drive.'

She didn't know what to say, was unable to process the request. She said stupidly, 'Why are you here?'

'And – well, this isn't quite the way I wanted to say it, but – I wanted to talk to you.' He was looking at her, determined.

'About what?' said Laura, and then she remembered the lamb shanks bubbling on the stove. 'Argh,' she cried, and ran into the kitchen. 'Oh dear. Open the door again, would you?'

The meat was caramelising somewhat, a little crusty and fried around the edges. A moment later and it would have burnt. Laura turned it off, and sat down at the kitchen table. Nick was in the doorway.

'You're here,' she said again, helplessly.

'Oh god, Laura,' said Nick, slightly impatiently. 'If you're going to act like someone with learning difficulties, I'm going to wait outside.'

'OK, OK,' said Laura. 'Tell me, then. Tell me why you're here.'

There was a pile of tea towels on the table. Paddy had taken them out of the washing machine and dumped them there. She started smoothing them out, folding them over and over.

Nick watched her and said nothing for a moment, then he walked towards her and leant against the counter, still standing. He cleared his throat.

'I'm here to tell you I'm in love with you,' he said, matter-of-factly.

'What?' Laura replied.

'Yep,' Nick said. He nodded. 'I wish I wasn't, most of the time. But I am.'

'You –'

'Yes,' said Nick, matter-of-factly. 'It's a real pain.' He pulled her to her feet and wrapped his arms around her. 'You are a thorn in my side, Laura.' He bent his head and kissed her. After a few seconds he lifted his head, still holding her tightly. 'A beautiful, annoying thorn in my side. And I can't seem to get rid of you, of feeling like this. So that's why I'm here. I'm in love with you, and I know whatever you say I always will be.'

He kissed her again. 'I thought you should know,' he said, his voice a little hoarse.

'My god,' said Laura. 'We're in the kitchen.'

Nick laughed, and held her tighter. He looked down at her, and kissed her gently. 'Oh, Laura.'

She lolled against him, pressing her body against his, feeling as if she was coming alive as she touched him. Nick, here, in front of her, holding her.

'Laura, I know you think us together is going to be hard. I know you think we're too different, that it's all too odd. But it's not. It's something my mother said to me when I saw her. If you find someone you love, you have to do something about it.' He took a deep breath, and ran his fingers through her hair, gently. 'I tried to do something about it before, you know. To help you, to make things better for you. But it wasn't the right thing to do. I should have just come down here straight after you left me, told you that I love you, that I wasn't going to let you go.'

'What did you do instead?' said Laura, intrigued.

'It doesn't matter.' Nick kissed her again. 'Does not matter at all.'

Recognition struck her; she pressed her hands on his chest and stepped back. 'You,' she said, nodding. 'You gave the money. Didn't you? You gave the money to the programme at work!'

'No,' said Nick.

'Yes, you did,' said Laura, staring up at him. He grimaced, and then inclined his head slightly, looking uncomfortable. 'Oh Nick. I knew it wasn't Marcus! It was you! Why did you do it?'

'I wanted . . .' he said, shaking his head. 'Laura, you were so upset, that night in the car. I just wanted everything to be better for you. I thought I couldn't have you, that we were never going to work out, and it really got to me, seeing you like that. You were so mysterious about work – and everything – and then when you left Charles explained what had happened with Marcus. So,' he bent his head, 'I thought, well, if we can't be together, I can still do something to make your life better. And other people's, too,' he said disingenuously. 'But you most of all.

'This is what my mother said to me,' he went on. 'She said I was a fool if I let you get away. She told me to stop making odd gestures like bailing you out at work, anonymously. She told me to get down here and tell you I love you. Myself. In person. Because if you love someone, you have to be brave and tell them. Don't let them go.'

'That's what someone said to me,' Laura told him, thinking of Mary and her letter. 'And I didn't listen.'

'Well, you should have. And if you say no, I'm going to spend the rest of my life trying to convince you I'm right. I promise. I won't leave you alone. Because it's not about who's what or where or anything. We should be together. The other stuff doesn't matter. That's all.'

'We should,' Laura echoed. She was feeling faint. She never felt faint. Her head was spinning, she felt light-headed, weightless

544

in Nick's arms. She leant against him again, tingling with happiness. 'Yes,' she said. 'We should. Who cares about the other stuff?'

'You mean it?' he asked.

'I do,' Laura said, looking up into his face. 'You know something?'

'What?'

'When I think about us I've always seen us at Chartley. Not here. I tried to picture it, but I always thought this –' she gestured around the kitchen '– might be weird, having you here.'

'And?'

'And it's not,' said Laura, smiling up at him. 'It makes perfect sense. I like your house better, though.'

'Shall I take you up there tomorrow?' he asked. 'For the weekend? Would you like that?'

'I can't think of anything I'd like more,' she said. 'Is – there anyone there?'

'No,' he replied. 'Mum left last week, but she's coming back for Christmas. No sisters, either. Just you, me, and Chartley.'

'And all the ghosts of relatives past,' said Laura.

'Yes,' said Nick. 'But they don't matter, do they?'

'No, they don't,' said Laura. 'They just don't. You and me. That's what matters.'

Then he kissed her again, her head in his hands, just the two of them, wrapped around each other, clinging desperately to each other, and Laura gave herself up to the sheer enjoyment of it for several minutes, or it could have been hours, days, she had no idea, for once it was just the two of them, alone in time and space, nothing else to bother them, no geological layers of mistrust and anger and exes and stupid things like class and money . . .

'Er . . . Laura?'

Laura and Nick sprang apart, and looked into the hallway. There, in the corridor, looking completely shell-shocked, were

Jo and Hilary, each clutching their handbags and a bottle of wine. They each said,

'The front door was open . . .'

'The entry phone was off the hook . . .' then trailed off into silence, as Laura looked at them, not sure what to say.

Nick coughed, and stood up straight. 'Er, hello,' he said.

'Hi,' said Jo and Hilary in unison. Hilary raised her hand, weakly. Jo's mouth was wide open.

Laura looked at them, then back to Nick. She smiled at him, a small, definite smile. He looked down at her and smiled back, his eyes full of understanding and warmth, and the amusement she knew they shared, which was why she loved him and knew him better than anyone else. Why he was hers and she was his. She stepped forward, holding his hand.

'Jo, Hilary,' she said. 'I'd like you to meet Nick. The Marquess of Ranelagh. Er . . . he's staying for supper. Aren't you?'

'Yes, if that's all right with you two?' Nick asked.

Hilary and Jo nodded mutely, and Nick looked around the kitchen.

'Right,' he said, taking off his jacket. 'Why don't I set the table?'

ACKNOWLEDGEMENTS

There are so many people I'd like to thank, especially all my friends and family for everything over the past year or so. But in particular I want to thank Mum and Dad, Caloo (hiya) and Brendan (hurrah! You can run but you can't hide! The ring is on her finger!), and the following people for their encouragement and support: Hannah Cleaton-Roberts, Thomas Wilson, Clare Betteridge, Jo Roberts-Miller and Jo Michaelides, as well as Pippa, Rebecca and Sophie for the same, plus the fantastic day trips to stately homes (Reb and Pip) and to the Harrow Mark One (Soph). And to my aunt Judy for the horticultural advice!

Thanks again to all my lovely colleagues at Headline for being so fabbity fab fab fab. I am very fortunate to work with you, my liver less so.

A huge thanks to everyone at HarperCollins. My arms are all bruised from pinching myself so often, I can't believe how lucky I am. Thanks to Amanda Ridout, Katie Fulford, Alice Russell, Sara Foster, Sylvia May, Karen-Maree Griffiths, Kate Elliot, Clive Kintoff, Wendy Neale and the rest of the sales team. Massive thanks again to brilliant Lee for the stunning cover. Helen, thanks a million, I hope you know how grateful I am.

Never use your considerable powers for evil. Special thanks too to Max, you supremely clever and talented lady, for everything but especially your fantastic notes and grace under pressure. I'll miss you! And Mama Lynne Drew, my endless gratitude. I love eating cakes in the shape of shoes with you.

Also thanks to Alice Saunders, Petra Lewis and everyone at LAW, as well as Raj Patel for keeping me on the straight and narrow.

Finally, sincerest thanks and love to Agent of the Year Mark Lucas, who is never happy, demands the best – but gives it too, and who is a deeply kind and great man, much as he pretends otherwise . . . Thank you.

Going Home

Harriet Evans

Some families warm your heart. Lizzy's makes her head spin.

Home. For most it's a place of calm and safety. For Lizzy Walter, things are a bit more complicated. Keeper House – the family home deep in the countryside – has always been where Lizzy can escape her London life and ease her heart and mind. But trouble is on the horizon.

For a start, her entire family are hiding something. Then the Love of Her Life makes an unexpected reappearance – just when she thought she was starting to get over him. And now Keeper House itself is in peril. By the time the Walters gather for a summer wedding, the stakes have never been higher – for Lizzy, for her family and for love…

The most refreshing read of the summer – a sparkling cocktail of comedy and romance.

'A joy from start to finish – sharp, funny and modern as well as warm, cosy and nostalgic.'   FIONA WALKER

'A lovely, funny heartwarmer… Evans' comic style and loveable characters make it effortlessly readable.'   *Marie Claire*

'Enchanting.'   JILLY COOPER, *Sunday Telegraph*

ISBN 0 00 719844 2

Enjoy a FREE romantic weekend away*

How to book:

Send this page with your till receipt and a self-addressed envelope to:

TLC Marketing plc
PO Box 468
Swansea, SA1 3WY

You will be sent a **FREE romantic weekend break** voucher, valid in over 200 UK hotels.